Angel of Chaos

By

Debra Dunbar

Anessa Books, Bethesda, Maryland

ISBN:150256937x
ISBN-13:9781502569370

To Dr. Hadley Tremaine (1939–2001), Chairman of the Department of English, Hood College, Frederick, Maryland, who taught me that there is great treasure to be found in what others consign to Hell.

~1~

"A ny offspring judged to be Nephilim shall be terminated. Reinstatement of the sire into the angelic ranks is pending, blah, blah, blah."

Okay, so Gabriel didn't really say the "blah, blah, blah" part, but he might as well have. I'd much rather have gouged my brains out my ear with a dull knife than sat through this Ruling Council meeting, but it was part of my duties as the Iblis — the leader of the demons. You'd think Satan would be able to shirk this sort of thing, but the big angel beside me ensured I sat through every boring second. There was no hiding from him. I'd tried last month and he'd found me in a Dutch brothel, dragging me naked down the very hard wooden stairs before gating me to the meeting. Yes, I'd remained naked for the whole interminable thing, since I haven't figured out yet how to create clothing. Not that any of the angels cared. They were far more interested in the other, much newer, additions to my anatomy.

I swept a wing back and forth, the tip tracing a gentle figure eight across the beige carpet. Like steel to a giant black–feathered magnet, every angelic eye in the place watched. They were cats, riveted by the red light of a laser pointer. I expected them to pounce at any moment.

One did. Power radiated from the angel beside me, almost painful against my skin. He reached out with his spirit–self, caressing along my non–corporeal self.

Stop. You're driving us all crazy. Poor Rafi is on the verge of a heart attack.

He wasn't the only one. The new guy hadn't taken his eyes off my wings since I'd arrived, and Sleepy, or was it Sneezy, looked ready to shoot a load into his pants.

Two angels had gone missing from the Council while I was away in Hel. New Guy had taken one spot, and an empty chair held Uriel's place. Gregory refused to discuss their whereabouts or the circumstances of their absence, claiming it was an internal matter.

I glanced over at him, lifting a finger to run along the ridge of one of his primary wings. The guy had six of the things. Even hidden from sight, I could "see" his and the other angels' wings. They appeared as wispy tracings of golden light here in this physical plane, visible only to angelic eyes until they were revealed in corporeal form in their feathered glory. I'd learned to hide my own too, but every so often my control slipped and a pair of huge black wings burst into being, knocking all sorts of shit over. I didn't even try to hide them at the Ruling Council meetings — it was too much fun watching the angels drool over them.

Cockroach. Stop. Now.

Uncharacteristically, I heeded the warning note in my beloved's voice and relaxed my wings, holding them still. One by one, the angels around me focused their attention back to the stacks of papers before them.

"On to the kill report." All the angels turned their stacks of paper to the appropriate page as Gabriel continued. "We have several items of old business to review before we move on to recent occurrences."

I doodled on my documents, wishing I had a Danish nearby, or at least a donut. This meeting really needed a food fight to liven things up a bit.

"... long overdue. All in favor?"

Did sloths have tails? No, no they didn't. I was going to draw one anyway.

"All against?"

I raised my hand. No matter what it was, I was pretty sure I was going to be against it.

"Oddly unanimous. Shall her punishment begin immediately following the meeting?"

Wait — what the fuck? "Whose punishment? Not mine. I haven't done anything wrong."

Well, beyond killing an angel and exploding an entire island.

Gabriel lifted his fists up, only to bring them down hard upon the table. "The four–nine–five report for Joseph Barakel?"

I frowned. "Who the fuck is Joseph Barakel?"

Raphael put a restraining hand on his brother, who had turned an interesting shade of red. "The human in Northern Virginia who you claim died of natural causes in your presence? The one with a seventeen golf handicap and elastic–waist pants?"

Oh yeah. I'd thought he was the human sent over to guard Amber by her elven mother, but it turns out he was just a socially inept pedophile and murderer.

"It *was* natural causes. Why is this still coming up in meetings? The guy had a heart attack. Happens to humans all the time."

"It's not the death itself that we're judging at this point, but your tardiness in delivering the revised report."

New Guy. Pretty balsy of him to bust my chops when he'd only been on the Ruling Council for a few months. I glared at him, and he squirmed, dropping his eyes and fiddling with the papers in front of him.

"Fine. But there are extenuating circumstances to my so–called tardiness. An *angel* tried to kill me, and I was recuperating in Hel. I think we need to vote on whether I get an extension or not."

There was a rumble noise from Gregory, and I realized he was trying to hold back a laugh. Unsuccessfully. "Darling Cockroach, we *did* vote. And you yourself voted against an extension."

Shit. I needed to start paying more attention at these meetings. If only they weren't so fucking boring.

"Are we to assume you don't have the report for Tyrone Cochran completed either?" Gabriel had a little smirk on his face. Asshole.

"No. I was excused for a special project on behalf of the angelic host—"

"Extended," Gregory interrupted. "Not excused, just given additional time."

I glared at him. "Yes, but then I was *banished*. At the very least, I should be given another forty–eight hours."

"You were in Hel for months. The report should be complete," Gabriel interjected.

"There's no internet in Hel." I looked around the table, searching for something to throw at the angel. All I could see were reams and reams of paper. "I didn't have a copy of the form, and it's not like I've memorized all two–hundred pages of it. Or that I had *hands* most of my banishment to complete the fucking thing."

"Oh, give her an extension." Raphael grinned at me. With Uriel gone, he was the only one I could halfway count on to vote in my favor. "She's already got three rotation cycles naked and restrained for the other report."

Three? Fuck.

"She does not take her duties seriously. I vote 'no'." It was that other guy — Sleepy or Sneezy. I couldn't tell which. One was gone, so I was going to call this one Sleazy as a compromise.

"Do you really want her in Aaru for six rotation cycles?" Rafi let that uncomfortable idea hang in the air a moment. "Do you really even want her there for three?"

There was a long, awkward silence. "Okay," Gabriel grudgingly announced. "I vote for one rotation cycle, and forty–eight hours to complete both reports."

"Forty–eight hours doesn't begin until after my punishment ends." I'd learned to clarify these things, otherwise I'd leave Aaru and only have twelve hours to do two reports — two two–hundred–plus–page reports.

"All in favor of one rotation cycle punishment, to begin at sunrise tomorrow, and forty–eight hours following the end of punishment for the submission of both reports?"

Everyone raised their hands, myself included. Phew. Bullet dodged.

Hours dragged on while the angels discussed stupid shit and I struggled to pay attention. Finally the meeting was adjourned, and, one by one, the angels gated back to Aaru. I held back, wondering if it would be wiser to take a bus. My teleportation skills were pretty bad, and it was likely to take me half the day to actually make it back to my house. I looked at Gregory with what I hoped was a pitiful expression. He might love me, but he was just as likely to leave me stranded in a Marriott conference room as offer me a lift home.

"Okay. Come here, Cockroach." He sighed, but looked oddly pleased at the prospect of escorting me back from the meeting.

I folded my midnight–black wings tight against my back, concentrating to hide them like he'd taught me. The angel's lips twitched into a smile as his eyes traced the outlines that were still visible to him. I felt myself warm under his gaze as I walked into his arms.

"Home, James," I teased, rubbing my face against the soft cotton of his navy polo shirt.

Enfolded, crushed against the angel's chest, I relaxed, resting my weight against him. This was home — being in his arms like this. My spirit–self reached out to his, merging into a line of translucent white where we joined. No matter what happened, I had this. I felt him let out a breath and rest his cheek against the top of my head. We held, frozen in time. Then we moved in a disorienting jolt through a fold in space. I arrived in my kitchen, dizzy and lightheaded but still safe in his arms.

"Coffee?"

I nodded against his chest, not wanting to let go, just breathing in his odd scent and rubbing the non–corporeal parts of myself against him. We hadn't kissed since that time so long ago in Alaska. I knew better than to push him, but I desperately wanted more than his arms around me.

Slowly he pulled away and began the routine of preparing coffee, measuring the grounds exactly and carefully adding the water. He pulled two cups from the cabinet, taking the cream from the fridge and a bowl of sugar from the counter.

"Should I meet you in Aaru tomorrow morning, or will you come get me?" My punishment was on my mind, for more than one reason. Yeah, I hated being in the sensory vacuum of Aaru, but I relished having him all to myself for the entirety of my sentence.

"I'll come get you." He sighed dramatically. "Sunrise, Cockroach. Please be ready."

Nope. I'd be in bed. Naked. Hopefully he'd get ideas that would result in us being very late getting to Aaru. The coffee maker beeped, and Gregory poured me a cup. Then he proceeded to dump an obscene amount of sugar in the other cup, add a splash of cream and a slightly larger splash of coffee.

"Would you like a knife and fork to go with your coffee?"

It was hardly liquid at this point, with all the sugar he'd put in it. Gregory still didn't sit down for pizza and beer with me, but he'd developed a rather sinful addiction to coffee and snack foods — especially potato chips. I took it as a good sign.

The angel took a sip of his drink, eyeing me over the rim of the cup. "So ... how are things in Hel?"

It wasn't like him to make small talk. There had to be something behind his question. He'd have to come right out and say it. I wasn't very good at subtle hints.

"Hot."

"I would assume so." He set his cup down on my counter and folded his arms across his chest. "Can you elaborate further? Is there anything notable occurring with the residents?"

I shrugged. If he wanted elaboration, then I'd give it to him. "The demons are the usual bunch of psychotic assholes — nothing new there. The elves are still squabbling between themselves and trying to wiggle out of their agreement concerning the humans. I've heard a rumor that some trolls have disappeared from the Pteras Mountains. No big loss. Those things are huge smelly rocks that eat everything in sight. Blech."

"Speaking of elves...."

Ah, here we go. Finally.

"One of my gate guardians claims to have seen one cross the gates in the accompaniment of an incubus."

I smirked. Leethu's household were really skilled at elf–impersonation. How awesome that they were popping around, messing with the angels' heads this way.

"Was the incubus one of my household?" I totally owed Leethu for this one. How funny.

"No. He was unaffiliated."

Hmm. That meant he had his own household and hadn't folded it under another demon's mark. Either he was high up in the hierarchy, or as stubborn and independent as I was.

"The elf was female. Her clothing was what the humans are currently wearing, and it was torn and bloody."

Bloody in human clothing *definitely* didn't sound like an elf. "It was probably a demon skilled in form creation. Good prank, though."

He nodded, picking up the mug to take another swig of coffee. "That's what I had thought. The guardian insisted that it wasn't a demon — that she could tell. She chased after them but lost them in the parking lot when they stole a car and took off."

I laughed, choking on my coffee. "They stole a car? Think about this a moment: an elf crosses the gates, which none have done in over two–million years, and she chooses to do it wearing nasty human clothing, and with a sex demon. Then they both do a mad dash through a shopping mall and steal a car — neither of which an elf has seen or experienced before. An elf in a car — that's just hysterical."

"I'll admit it seems improbable, but then another angel claims to have seen an elf in the southern part of this continent, repairing natural habitat that the humans had damaged."

That seemed more in keeping with what I knew about elves, but still the whole scenario was as believable as alien–abduction stories. Invasion of the Elves. It would make an awesome B movie.

"Okay. Let's say they're right — why would one or two elves decide to cross *now*, after so long? And what do they do when they cross? Sneak around hugging trees and committing grand theft auto with a demon?"

He waved a dismissive hand and placed his empty coffee cup back on the counter. "Just keep your ears open for anything that might confirm this on your side. Let me know if you find anything out — even if it seems inconsequential."

Bossy. Although after billions of years bossing his siblings and the other angels around, it was probably a difficult habit to break. I glared at him. "Yeah. I'll do that. Sure. Uh–huh."

Gregory caught the sarcastic tone in my voice, and his face relaxed in an unexpected smile. I couldn't help but respond in kind. I'd do just about anything for him when he smiled at me like that. I didn't resist as he took the coffee cup from my hand and placed it beside his own then once again pulled me into his arms.

Our spirit–selves joined at the edges, tantalizingly close to ecstasy, and oh–so intimate. I rubbed my physical body against him, running my hand down his arm. Tanned flesh followed in my wake, warm and sensitive. The angel shuddered, and I was unsure whether he was enjoying the physical sensation he'd always found so painful before.

"Show me your wings." The command was weakened by the huskiness of his voice.

What was it with the damned wings? It's not like they all didn't have the same things attached to their backs, although in different colors. The whole fascination reminded me of human males' constant imploring for women to 'show me your tits'.

"I should at least get some cheap plastic beads out of the deal, or dinner at a fancy restaurant. I think you need to give me something in exchange."

"Maybe I will."

He lifted my chin with a finger and bent his lips to mine. It was almost too much — the feel of his spirit easing into me as his tongue scorched my mouth with the sharpness of a thousand needles. Pleasure and pain, physical and beyond. I burrowed my hands under the edge of his shirt, scratching the sensitive sides of his torso with my nails. I felt him bite down with piranha teeth into my lower lip, and I did the same to him, tasting him, merging as our spirit–beings were — as I hoped our bodies would.

I broke our kiss, needing the air that he never seemed to need. I felt his arousal against me, and I reached up a hand to touch his face; a perfect replica of tanned flesh. There was a pulse that beat strong in the hollow of his throat, and his muscles shivered as I explored them with my fingers. He was so close, his vibration level nearly on par with mine. I looked into his black eyes, feeling drunk as I swayed against him.

"I want you."

He leaned his forehead against mine. "And I want you."

Then why were we not naked and grinding away on the kitchen floor?

"But I need to get back to Aaru."

Fuck. Or rather not–fuck. Damn it all; this angel was the worst tease. He might have the patience of Job, but I sure as hell didn't.

"You're killing me, you know. Killing me."

He laughed then kissed me again. I felt like I was falling into him, one half of a whole. It had been far too long since we'd been together. I wasn't sure how much longer I could wait.

"Tomorrow morning," Gregory said, stepping back. I caught my breath, thinking for a moment he meant that we'd be angel fucking at sunrise. Then I realized he was talking about my punishment in Aaru. "Be ready."

I was ready now — for other stuff having nothing to do with my punishment. Gregory caught my pouty look and pulled me toward him, tempting me again with the caress of his spirit–self.

"Perhaps tomorrow will hold more than just punishment." His voice was deep and silky smooth. I closed my eyes, falling into that voice, into him. "You'll be naked and restrained. How could I resist my very own imp in such a compromising situation? Surely I'll be forced to take advantage of you while you're so vulnerable."

The panic I usually felt at the thought of being non–corporeal in Aaru faded. He'd be there, with me. And it sounded like that one rotation cycle could be a lot more fun than the others had been. I leaned against him for a few more precious minutes, savoring our connection and wishing life and duty didn't have to constantly tear us apart.

The angel rubbed his cheek against the top of my head and stepped back. His reluctance was palatable, and his hands lingered as they slid down my arms.

"Be ready," he reminded me.

He gated away, and I ground my teeth in frustration. I *was* ready, right now. But not for a rotation cycle in Aaru. If I didn't get it on soon with this angel — like tomorrow, I was going to explode. Or jump him. Duct tape clearly wasn't an option, but I'd picked up a few things in Hel that might be as useful on angels as they were on demons. Lust raced through me as I envisioned having Gregory bound and helpless at my mercy. Or me bound and helpless at his mercy. Yeah — a much better scenario.

Arrrgh! I slammed the coffee cups in the sink and rinsed them, frustrated beyond words. A cold shower was in order, then perhaps a trip to the gym after lunch. A good five miles on the treadmill might do something to drive this terrible need from my body. If not, there was always Leethu's sex toys still upstairs in the guest room.

~2~

I was freshly showered and eating lunch when I heard the knock. My friends just walked on in, and Gregory seldom used the physical entrances to my home. I went to answer it, hoping it was one of the local missionaries — the day begged for some comic relief.

An angel stood at my front door. A few years ago I would have crapped my pants, but now I just took a bite of my sandwich and looked him over. This one was less androgynous than the others, although still the typical fair–skinned blond. Clearly masculine, he was dressed in jeans and a navy polo shirt. I noted that he didn't look nearly as good in the signature clothing as Gregory did.

"Yeah? What do you want?" I took another bite of sandwich.

"I'm requesting asylum."

Well, that was a new one. I knew things had pretty much blown up in Aaru while I'd been banished, but I hadn't realized the situation was bad enough that an angel would choose Hel over his homeland.

"The demons will kill you in two seconds flat."

"The asylum isn't for me. It's for her."

He motioned, and a woman came from the shadows of my porch. A human woman. She was in her early thirties with the tanned skin, black hair and angular features that hinted at Native American or mixed Spanish heritage. She was also hiding what I assumed was a curvy figure under a very unflattering, extra–large blouse. And she was very carefully not meeting my eyes. I crammed the rest of the ham and cheese into my mouth.

"She'll probably last more than two seconds, especially if she's a screamer."

My words were muffled by the food, but the woman clearly understood. She paled and took a step backwards. The angel laid a firm, restraining hand on her shoulder. She snarled, dislodging his hand with a jerk of her arm. Interesting.

"Not in Hel. I'm asking for her to have asylum here."

I choked a bit trying to swallow. "Here, as in this plane of existence? Dude, I don't have any authority here. Per our contract, this is part of your holdings. I'm just a guest with special privileges. Talk to the big guy."

The angel was beginning to look irritated. Or maybe he was nervous. Either way, the constant looking around or the glare coming my way weren't adding to the peaceful calm of the fall morning.

"Your house. Asylum for this human woman and all she carries into your house."

I looked over at the large purse draped across the woman's shoulder. Asylum for her and her purse. I wondered if the request included the rocking Steve Madden boots she had on.

"How long?" I already had Nyalla living with me and often served as a hotel–for–demons when members of my household came over. I didn't relish having another human, one I didn't know, living here, no matter how awesome her footwear.

"For the remainder of her natural life."

Fuck. Humans didn't live very long, but that didn't mean I wanted one shacked up in my house for life. I quickly calculated the likely term and swore. Damn, that would really put a cramp in my lifestyle. I opened my mouth to say "no" then looked at her boots once more. They were distressed brown leather, with a hint of a biker look about them. Brass studs decorated the toe and the back of the heel. She'd laced them halfway up then wrapped the excess lacing around her ankle to tie at the back. The tops flopped open with the sort of casual defiance I admired. Her blouse might look like a giant sack, but she had great taste in boots.

"Do I get to keep her stuff after she croaks?"

The angel didn't hesitate. "Yes. All she carries will be your responsibility, now and after her death."

The woman didn't seem too happy about any of this, but she kept silent. I looked down at the Steve Maddens. I could be responsible for a pair of boots. It's not like they were going to run around causing trouble — at least off of my feet.

"This is a significant favor you are requesting of me." With angels, demons — it didn't matter which — everything boiled down to favors.

He nodded, trying to hide a wince and not succeeding. "What can I do to repay you for this, Iblis?"

That was the fastest capitulation I'd ever witnessed. Either this angel was the worst negotiator in Aaru, or the woman had done something particularly heinous. What could a human possibly have done that she'd require demonic protection? Did she piss off an entire continent of werewolves? Kill a family of vampires? I eyed her with sudden respect and actually began to get excited about what her presence might bring to my door. I had enough to do with the continued elven shit storm in Hel, my onerous Ruling Council obligations, and my dwindling financial empire, but the prospect of pissed off vampires storming my house lightened my spirits considerably.

"Three favors. No restrictions. No time limit."

"Done."

What the fuck? Well, I'd just bought myself a human and all her baggage, which, thankfully, included a sweet set of boots. I stood aside, and the angel put a hand on her shoulder to urge her forward through the doorway.

"Get off me." The woman yanked her arm away. She glared at the angel a few seconds before crossing the threshold. I noticed he remained on the other side.

"Which choir are you in, and how should I contact you?" I knew better than to ask his name. Angels were worse than we were when it came to that sort of thing. I doubted I'd even get any info on his choir out of him, but it was worth a shot.

"You don't need to know my choir."

Yeah, just what I'd thought.

"I'll contact you," the angel continued.

Like hell he would. "That's unacceptable. If I've got a troll chewing off my legs, I want to be able to call in my favor right then — not two months later when you happen to show up."

His eyes darted past me to the woman. "I'll be back in a few months to visit. We can work out the details then."

"I don't know who you think you'll be visiting, but it won't be me," the woman snapped. "Or anything I'm 'carrying' either."

Wow. Pretty hostile when an angel had just granted three favors in return for her asylum. I wondered again what the woman had done, and why she was so pissed off at her benefactor.

"That's fine, but I still want a way to contact you in the meantime. There's a good chance I'll get into some kind of trouble before you come back to visit. I've got a premonition I'll need to cash in at least one of those favors in the next few weeks."

"I can't do that."

"Then take this bitch and go on home."

The angel looked around the bushes, as if the bad guys were ready to spring on him at any moment.

"Come on, dude. Ain't got all day here. Things to do, and all that."

Instead of responding, he handed me a glass bead and vanished. Okay, that was a level of paranoia I hadn't seen before. I examined the glass bead, noting the flecks of gold that swirled through the green before sticking it in my pocket and shutting the door.

"What's your name?" The woman was standing by my dining table, rigid as a fence post. Her hands were white fists by her side. I got the distinct feeling she desperately wanted to stick a knife in something. Maybe me, maybe that angel.

"Harper."

Her voice was strong and unwavering, but she remained tense, her eyes averted. I sighed. "Okay, Harper. You can call me Sam. Take the first room at the top of the stairs for your own. Will your angel friend be sending over luggage? Clothing? Personal items?"

"No. I left rather unexpectedly and have nothing but the few things in my tote and what I'm standing in."

As interested as I was in acquiring what she was standing in, the hostility in her voice drew my attention away from her shoes. I could practically hear her teeth grinding from across the room.

"No big deal. Make me a list, and we'll go online later and order stuff."

Nyalla had wreaked havoc on my cash flow with her altruistic gestures and ghoul–related repairs. Now I had another mouth to feed.

"Can I have your shoes?" I might as well get something out of this deal right now.

She removed them and extended the boots toward me. "Everything I carry is yours to guard and protect."

I hesitated, wondering why the hell I was supposed to protect a pair of Steve Madden boots. Her expression was resigned, but her voice still held a note of fear ... and a whole lot of anger.

Screw it. I snatched the boots. Then I shooed her upstairs, taking note of her size so I could get her the bare essentials on my way back home.

"Who was that?"

I spun around, putting the boots behind me. Shit. I hope Wyatt didn't just see me take a woman's shoes literally right off her feet.

"A house guest." Damn, I'd put the woman in Leethu's old room. Hopefully she liked all the sex toys and magazines.

"Sam's hotel, huh?" He walked across the room and kissed me on the forehead. Wyatt smelled of sunshine and hay — so human.

"What's this?" He pulled away and ran a finger over my bottom lip.

"Bit my lip." I didn't say *who* bit it. Gregory and Wyatt had come to an odd sort of friendship during my banishment in Hel. Wyatt seemed to be accepting of my relationship with the angel, but I didn't want to rub his face in it.

"Ouch. Are you heading to the gym? I won't keep you. Just wanted to stop by before I go up to Baltimore."

Wyatt had suddenly become motivated. He had all sorts of contracts now with different gaming companies, and a few dealing with network security stuff. I was glad he was busy and not moping around while I raced off here and there with my crazy Iblis duties.

"I'm back in the angel jail tomorrow morning."

He grimaced. "I kinda figured that was going to happen. How long this time?"

"Just the one rotation cycle, thanks to Raphael. I've got forty–eight hours to do two four–nine–five reports, though."

I looked up and met Wyatt's eyes, trying for a pleading, helpless expression. He sighed.

"Okay. Give me their names and what you know about them and I'll get started on the reports."

Wyatt was the best. It was like having a smart kid do your homework for you. I gave him all the information I knew about Joseph Barakel and Tyrone Cochran.

"On it. But you owe me for this one." Wyatt grinned good–naturedly.

"Hot wings?"

"Charity work."

Fuck, I hated when Wyatt made me do charity work. "The nursing home again?"

He frowned. "Not after Boomer bit that guy."

"It wasn't his fault," I protested. "They're always giving him doggie biscuits; he thought the staff had provided a special treat. Honestly, the guy looked dead to me, too."

"The soup kitchen is no longer an option either."

I'd put hallucinogenic drugs into the soup. A good time was had by all — at least until the cops arrived.

"Can't I just buy you some hot wings?"

Wyatt looked stern. I could see him thinking through all the charitable activities on his list and weighing his desire to reform me against what sort of havoc I would cause.

"Steak and lobster." The guy wasn't cheap. Still, it was better than picking up trash alongside the road, or cleaning dog kennels at the animal shelter.

"Deal."

"Go to the gym. And call me when you get out of jail. I'm already dreaming of a juicy prime rib."

I grabbed my bag, tossing him a smile over my shoulder. "Make reservations. I'll throw on the little black dress and we'll celebrate my bail with food."

~3~

When I returned home, I pulled the Suburban around to the barn and unloaded the various sacks of feed and mineral blocks. Grabbing the shopping bags off the rear seat, I kicked the barn door closed behind me and headed toward the huge French doors that flanked the rear of my house. There, slouched in a lounge chair by the pool, was an angel. This one I recognized.

Raphael looked hardly angelic in his snug khaki shorts and silky, black t–shirt. His ebony hair shone deep purple in the sun, his wings a tracing of gold light extending beyond the sides of the chaise. He lowered his mirrored sunglasses as he saw me and wiggled his eyebrows.

"What's cooking, good–looking?"

That had to have been the worst pick–up line I'd ever heard, although for an angel it was pretty hip. Slang wasn't exactly a strength for them.

"Dinner. And I'd like to eat it, so tell me what the fuck this visit is about and take a hike."

I liked Rafi. I should have been a bit nicer to him, especially since I needed to count on his vote in Ruling Council matters, but I just couldn't summon the teasing, friendly Sam Martin. I was sexually frustrated, burdened with stupid work shit, and I'd spent most of the day shopping for my new houseguest. The thought of Harper sent my eyes scanning the nearby bushes for humans — particularly female humans. If Rafi was going to try to stick me with another angry, hostile woman seeking asylum, I'd run his wings through the chipper–shredder.

The angel swept the sunglasses off his face, and they vanished from his hand. "Aaru is falling apart. Some groups want to resume contact with the demons, others want to subject demons to a forced breeding program, and others feel we should be able to breed with the humans. We can't keep up with all the violations of our laws. Even the Ruling Council is divided on what our future should look like and how we should achieve it."

The transformation from playful, lighthearted Rafi to this serious one was disconcerting. Not as disconcerting as his words, though. I knew there had been an uprising, but had thought the rebels had been taken out, or at least scattered and rendered ineffective. No wonder Gregory was distracted. No wonder he'd had to run back to Aaru this morning. This was interesting information, but I wasn't sure what Rafi expected me to do with it.

"So?" I shrugged. "Why should I care about what happens in Aaru? I've got Hel. Heaven is your problem, not mine."

Raphael shot me a perceptive look and sat up, leaning his arms on his knees. "Maybe because the angel you love cares about Aaru? With Uri out of the picture indefinitely, I'm the only progressive on the Council. It's you and me, babe."

Gregory was progressive — sometimes. Sometimes not. Two against four wasn't a majority. Even if Gregory did vote our way, it would just deadlock the issue. I still didn't see what I was supposed to do about any of this. Or why I should care. Yeah, I wanted Gregory to have his beloved homeland, but he surely didn't need an imp's help on that front.

"Don't you want demons and angels to be able to form partnerships, to join, perhaps even to breed? You have a voice on the Council — don't you want to have an equal say in matters here with the humans, and in Aaru?"

I didn't give a shit about matters in Aaru, or here with the humans. Or did I? Dropping the shopping bags on the flagstone patio, I plopped into the lounge chair next to Rafi. It drove me nuts how the angels hovered over the humans, watching for any slip in their collective vibration level, any backsliding in their evolution. I hated their constant obsession with Nephilim, their heavy–handed treatment of the werewolves. I did want a say in those things, even with my already–overloaded schedule. And demons joining with angels? A thrill ran through me remembering the sensations I felt just being next to Gregory. Leethu had begged for an angel of her own — how many others would want the same?

Plus I saw us with clear eyes now. The rigid stagnation of Aaru, the devolving and brutal state of Hel — this would be good for all of us. But in spite of being the Iblis, I was still only an imp. And two, possibly three, on the Ruling Council weren't enough to enact the kind of dramatic change Rafi was proposing — even if some factions wanted it.

Raphael got to his feet, sunglasses appearing in his hand with a snap. "Think about what I've said. Let me know if you have any ideas. I may be an Angel of Order, but I'm eager for some chaos in Aaru."

With a flourish, he put on the mirrored shades and vanished, leaving me sitting on a slightly damp lounge chair with an armful of shopping bags beside me. Ideas? Like the dating game for demons and angels? I had a vision of that television show The Bachelor, only for beings of spirit. Who would Gabriel present the rose to? Leethu? Dar? One of the Low in my household? I laughed just thinking about that staid angel wooing a demon and scooped up my bags to head inside.

Harper was in the kitchen, chatting away with Nyalla as they cut vegetables. The smell coming from the stove was amazing, and I sniffed appreciatively. Nyalla's cooking skills tended toward re–heated leftovers and microwaved eggs. Clearly, Harper was feeling more at home and less the angry psycho she'd seemed when she first walked through my door. Or not. As I walked in, the woman fell immediately silent and tensed, her grip on the knife alarmingly firm.

"Oh, did you pick up some things for Harper?" Nyalla put her knife down and took the plastic bags from my hand. "I'll run these up to her room."

"No. I will."

Either my new guest didn't want Nyalla in her room, or she was unwilling to be in the kitchen alone with me. I was betting on the latter. Harper took the bags from Nyalla with a tense smile, knife clutched tight in her other hand. I edged out of her way and watched her walk up the steps, thinking that the knife was probably going to stay in her room, under the pillow. This woman was dangerous. I had no idea whether she planned on sticking me with that piece of cutlery, or was preparing for the angel's return visit. I hoped it was the angel.

"You are so sweet to take her in like this." Nyalla beamed at me. I looked guiltily down at my new boots. I was probably going to have to give them back. The loss of an awesome pair of Steve Maddens versus a disappointed Nyalla ... yeah, I'd have to return them. Eventually.

"She's really angry right now and worried about the future, but she'll settle in. I know how overwhelming life changes can be. Can we use the other bedroom as the nursery? I know that will leave you without a guest bedroom for Dar and other demons, so maybe we should just put an addition on the house instead."

If there was one thing Nyalla was good at, it was spending my money. I couldn't seem to be mad at her though, even with my Corvette broken beyond repair and my safe half empty. It *was* a good idea. My household had reached astronomical proportions, and I needed to have more space to put people up. It would probably be wise to have a guesthouse to separate my demon family from the others.

Nursery?

My heart lodged somewhere in my esophagus, and my eyes locked on Nyalla's thin waist and flat stomach. Holy shit on a stick, what had the girl gotten herself into?

"I'll fucking kill him," I snarled. Nyalla stared at me in surprise, far more composed in the face of my temper tantrum than she would have been this past summer. "Who knocked you up? That cop? The guy at the beach? Who got you pregnant?" If she refused to answer me, I'd kill both men just to be thorough. Nobody messed with mine. Nobody.

"Me?" she squeaked, her eyes round. "I'm not pregnant. I use the condoms that Candy bought for me. It's Harper who's pregnant. Didn't you know? Isn't that why you gave her asylum?"

Although I wanted to explore the notion that my prudish werewolf friend was supplying Nyalla with birth–control devices, my mind locked onto the other of the revelations.

"Harper? Pregnant?"

"Uh, yeah." I heard the implied 'duh' in Nyalla's voice. "She's *showing*, Sam. How could you not notice? The woman looks ready to give birth any month now."

It wouldn't be the first time I'd been blind to something right in front of my face. Gregory often told me I needed to pay more attention to details, to examine the obvious first before chasing improbable scenarios. Not that I intended on taking an angel's advice on that one, even if it was an angel I loved and admired.

"Pregnant? I thought she just had really bad taste in clothing. I mean, her boots aside. That top is hideous. You could hide two linebackers in that thing. How the heck was I supposed to see a baby bump under twenty yards of gathered paisley fabric?"

Nyalla sighed and turned back to chopping bok choy, muttering under her breath about obtuse demons.

Harper, pregnant. I could think of only one reason an angel would have been so eager to gain asylum for a pregnant human that he would agree to my outlandish demand for three favors. No wonder he hadn't wanted to tell me his choir or name. Blondie in the blue jeans had been a bad, bad boy. And I was so keeping these boots.

"Yes, she's pregnant. She's not too happy with the father right now either."

Neither was I. My mind whirled, and I plopped down on one of the kitchen stools to think. Harper hadn't looked pregnant to me, and I wasn't sure how accurate Nyalla's estimation of the woman's due date was. Hopefully she was terribly wrong and the baby wouldn't be arriving for another six months or so. What the fuck was I going to do with a human baby in my house? From what I'd seen, they seemed to require a whole lot of specialized crap, and they ate and pooped all the time. And screamed a lot. I couldn't kill it, not after I'd sworn to protect the damned thing for its entire life.

"He just ditched her here, never to see her again?" I asked, half to Nyalla and half to myself. "Got her pregnant then dumped her off at Satan's Home for Unwed Mothers?"

Nyalla stifled a giggle. "That's funny, Sam. I don't really know the details, just that she feels betrayed by him and is angry with herself for thinking she loved him. She's confused."

She's confused? I didn't know how to take care of a baby, let alone a Nephilim baby. Did I need to hire a couple of dwarves to foster the child? Bring them over from Hel? Would the kid be like the half–demon humans I'd seen over the centuries, or sort of angel–light? Shit.

"I guess we better start a nursery," I said slowly, a little worried when I saw Nyalla's radiant expression. "Do you know exactly when she's due, or are you just guessing?"

"I don't know exactly. I think maybe a few months, unless she's having twins or something."

Twins? My breathing went into overdrive, and I felt a panic attack close in on me. Paper bag. I needed a paper bag to breathe into before I fucking passed out. Two infants? There better not be two babies in that woman or I was going to lose it. Baby Daddy was in for a serious hurting the next time I saw him.

"Ooh, I can introduce her to Shelly and baby Jack, and Candy and Michelle. We can have a baby shower for her. Isn't that a funny term? Like we're going to drop babies down from the ceiling."

Nyalla's voice faded into the background, and I nodded, sure I was agreeing to all sorts of things I'd regret later. An angel had fucked around with a human and left me holding the bag. That pissed me off just as much as Gabriel's unbending stance on those stupid reports. Angels. Only one of them wasn't on my shit list right now — although Gregory tended to bounce back and forth between lists. And I guess Raphael was okay at the moment. The rest of them could go to hell.

I so wanted to rat this guy out to his higher–ups, rub it in their smug faces that they were screwing up the humans so much more than we demons had ever done. But I'd promised to protect Harper and all she carried across my threshold. If I told, I'd have an army at my door demanding I give up the woman and her unborn child.

Stupid vow. These shoes were so not worth it.

~4~

I woke up significantly after dawn, realizing that Gregory was perched behind me, sitting on the bed. I rolled over and met his eyes.

"That's creepy, you know. It's got to be nine o'clock in the morning. Why didn't you wake me? Or better yet, crawl under the covers naked and get busy?"

My smile faded when he continued to stare at me, his black eyes serious. "There is a human woman in your house."

My blood felt like it turned to liquid hydrogen. Harper. How had he known the woman was here? Damned angels.

"I have several women in my house. Nyalla likes to have friends stay over sometimes."

I really sucked at lying, and growing a big–ass set of feathered wings didn't seem to enhance that particular skill.

"One of Nyalla's friends is pregnant."

Shit. Shit, shit. "Yeah, humans do that breeding thing with frightening regularity. She's got another friend that's a widow with a baby. I can't begin to tell you what a pain in the ass it is when *she* comes over. That thing smells like powder and laundry soap and makes these horrific cooing noises. Makes my skin crawl."

"This one has lain with an angel."

Shit. "It was me." I forced a bland, hopefully truthful, expression onto my face. "Couldn't help myself. She's totally hot, and you know how fond I am of that particular sin."

Gregory's expression turned dark, black irises spreading outward to engulf his eyes. "I'm not an idiot, Cockroach. I know the difference between demon and angel–marked humans; I know the difference in their offspring. I've killed too many Nephilim not to know the difference."

I tensed. The only thing that kept me from going on the offensive and yanking out my sword was the note of sorrow in his voice. "Why kill *them* and leave the demon hybrids to live?"

He sighed and leaned back against the pillows, running a hand through his chestnut–colored curls. I relaxed slightly in response to his posture. He hardly looked like he was going to leap out of bed and skewer Harper with his sword.

"Demon/human hybrids are usually powerless, and I'm reluctant to punish humans for our inability to keep demons on the other side of the border. Angel hybrids are dangerous and powerful. They can do great damage among the humans if left to live."

"I'm calling bullshit on that." I sat up, unconcerned at my nudity. Demons weren't exactly modest, and I had a faint hope that Gregory might take notice of all the naked flesh and decide to do something about it. It didn't work. His eyes remained north of my bustline, brows raised at my words. "Why aren't you reluctant to punish humans for your own inability to keep your cocks in your pants? Just monitor the Nephilim, and if they fuck up, kill them. Don't do some preemptive genocide and make up lame excuses to salve your conscience."

His jaw tightened. Fists clenched my comforter, digging in hard. Gregory had always struggled with anger. Too bad. I was an imp. I lived to push everyone's buttons.

With a deep breath, he relaxed his death grip on my bedding. "Demons can breed amongst themselves, so demon/human hybrids are a relatively rare occurrence. We can't. If we don't take a hard line on this, the Nephilim will outnumber the humans in a generation."

"So kill the offending angels, not their innocent offspring."

I actually felt a wave of sadness from him. Even without our physical bond, we still shared this connection. "Death is not nearly the deterrent you think it is, Cockroach. The loss of one you love, especially one of your creation, is far worse."

I thought of his brother, how they'd fought against each other in the wars, how he'd probably died long ago, and I reached out to lay my hand on his arm. My spirit–self caressed comfortingly against his.

"I'm sorry."

I still didn't agree with the policy, which sounded far more demonic that something the angels should be capable of, but I hated to see that look on his face, to feel his pain of loss.

"That's why Uri is gone." His voice was low, and as he turned to look at me, I felt as though I could see right down into his soul. "She lost her life–mate and her only offspring in the war, as well as our brother. The guilt of turning her back on them has been too much for her, and she's set aside her halo to walk in pilgrimage."

I had no idea what the fuck that meant, but I rubbed along his arm in sympathy. "How long will she be gone?"

He shrugged. "Until she forgives herself. That might be an eternity."

In the meantime her seat would remain empty, a placeholder as mine had been for millions of years. Gregory hadn't given up on his brother, and he'd not give up on Uriel either. I sighed and rested my cheek against his arm, feeling the cool, smooth, inhuman surface against my skin.

"The question though, Cockroach, is what do you intend to do with this pregnant human and her offspring?"

I had no idea. "Flay the flesh from their bones and eat them?" More like 'defend them with my life', but that hardly seemed an action worthy of the Iblis.

Gregory turned his head to look down at me, his dark eyes solemn. "That's what I'm afraid of."

I wasn't sure if he meant what I'd said, or my unspoken response.

"How ... how did you know she was here?" I suddenly thought of Raphael's visit last evening. Had he also sensed Harper, realized the baby she carried was half–angel?"

"The energy signature of the baby. It's faint, but even in utero, Nephilim show signs of their power. Some of it affects their mothers, making them resistant to magic and enthrallment, giving them strength. Once the child is born, the mother will be as she was before, and the Nephilim's energy signature will spike."

"And that's how you track them?" Worry knotted my guts. "How far away would an angel have to be to detect the energy signature of the fetus?"

His eyes searched mine, and he reached out a hand to caress a lock of my hair. "I didn't sense the Nephilim until I was actually inside your house. Even then I wasn't sure until she got up late last night and walked near your bedroom door."

Phew.

"Of course, Hunters have greater skills when it comes to sensing Nephilim energy signatures."

Not so phew. "So am I to expect a bunch of these Hunters at my door? How great are their skills?"

He smiled. "Don't concern yourself. Unless a Hunter happens to wander down your street, they're unlikely to sense the Nephilim. Once it's born — that's when they'll be knocking down your door to enact justice."

Justice hardly seemed the correct word in this instance. Hopefully I'd have a few months to figure this all out. Hopefully longer. I frowned, trying to envision Harper's round form under the voluminous shirt and calculate her due date. It was no use. I'd just have to ask the woman once I got back from my little stint in Aaru.

"Ready, Cockroach? We can't be late to your punishment. Everyone is waiting."

I should have realized by his words that something would be different, but I was too busy fretting over what to do with this stupid baby of Harper's. Our trip through Aaru wasn't the typical routine I'd grown accustomed to. This time we attracted a procession before we reached my punishment spot. I could feel the angels all around me, crowding as close as they dared with Gregory by my side. There was the usual fascination with my wings — which had burst into full view as soon as I'd arrived. I felt the angels' curiosity, but also hatred. Their desire to do me harm scraped against me like a dulled knife. It was like a gallows walk, only I wasn't heading for my death, and no one was throwing tomatoes at me.

I glanced at the big angel by my side, wishing I could edge closer to him. It wouldn't look good for me to show any weakness. My sword would command respect, but I was also afraid it would seem like a challenge — or a prop to hide my fear.

"Wow, I'm not exactly feeling the love here. What's going to happen when I take up permanent residence?"

Gregory gave me a stern look, but I saw him clamp his lips to keep from smiling. The angels around me sent up a buzz of rapid mind–speech.

"I hear there's some nice real estate in the sixth circle. Or I might just lease Uriel's, since she'll be gone for a bit. No reason to keep the place empty when she could be turning a tidy profit."

As we walked, I continued to discuss my pending relocation, decorative touches I'd implement, who I'd have visit me from Hel. Finally we arrived at a spot I recognized. Aaru was a wasteland of sensory deprivation, all white nothingness, but still a part of me felt the subtle changes as we moved from section to section. This was familiar. And so was the angel whose non–corporeal form approached.

"Gabriel will be overseeing your punishment this time." Gregory's voice was full of regret, and I felt a surge of irritation. This was supposed to be our time — illicit angel sex while incarcerated. My fantasies were all being shot to Hel.

I felt Gabriel's smug satisfaction. *I will ensure her vibration level improves with the experience. As she is so eager to take up residence, it is my responsibility to help her better fit in.*

What? No! In spite of my comments about moving in, I hated Aaru with a passion. Being stripped of my physical form, deprived of my energy usage was terrifying. The only thing that made the experience tolerable was Gregory next to me, holding me and comforting me through the entire thirty–six hours. Gabriel hated me, and the feeling was mutual. I didn't want him to see me panicking, didn't want to hear him mocking me for my fear. How could the angel who professed to love me abandon me to this ... jerk?

I felt his touch, reassuring along my spirit–self.

There is a crisis, Cockroach. Aaru is still experiencing rebellion.

I felt a twinge of remorse, remembering what Raphael had told me of their troubles. Again this stupid situation in Aaru was interfering with my life — with my *love* life. Rafi was right. I was going to have to insert myself into yet another ball of shit if I ever wanted my life to be the indolent fuck–fest I'd been dreaming of.

I understand. I did understand, but I still didn't like it one bit.

I trust Gabe, and although you and he are like oil and water, you can trust him too.

He was gone before I could reply. Not that I knew what I would have said, anyway. I didn't want to be *that* girl — the needy demon, pulling her archangel away from a crisis so he could hold her hand while she sat in jail. Instead, I turned to Gabriel and nodded.

"I'm ready."

Suddenly it did feel like an execution. We moved forward, and I felt Gabriel's touch. We'd fought physically many times before, but never had our spirit–selves gotten this close. I flinched instinctively. It wasn't Gabe; it was all the nightmares of Ahriman that came flooding back to me. Gregory's touch was far more intimate, and with him I felt none of this knee–jerk panic, but with another angel … it was just too close to everything I'd been through in Hel.

Gabe held very still, giving me space to compose myself. I talked myself down from the ledge, breathing deep. This might have been a solitary punishment in the past, but I had no doubt that thousands of angels watched me this time.

Dissolve.

My physical being vanished, and I metaphorically held my breath, trying to keep the panic at bay. This was Aaru. I wouldn't die. I wouldn't rip and tear, or come apart as I'd nearly done when I'd blown myself up on Oak Island. So many triggers, but like with my walk of shame, I needed to power through it and hide my weaknesses.

Only you angels could make being 'naked' so boring, I told Gabriel loud enough that the others could hear. *And I've just had a Brazilian wax job, too. Completely wasted if I don't have a body to show it off on.*

Restrained.

I felt a silicone–like coating cover my store of raw energy. I was defenseless, unable to form a physical body or anything else. Surprisingly, that was far less frightening then Gabriel's touch had been.

Pfft. Where are the handcuffs? Silk ties? Restrained, my ass. Give me two hours and a roll of duct tape, and I'll show you restrained.

I expected to be left alone, but Gabriel hovered. I hoped he wouldn't be here the whole time. As much as I dreaded being left vulnerable and alone, I really didn't want him around to see me weak and afraid.

You are to remain here in contemplation for one rotation cycle, naked and restrained. Do not call upon the Sword of the Iblis or it will be considered an attack upon Aaru.

With that he vanished, and I felt the emptiness. Not even the hate–filled angels were nearby. It was as if I were in the middle of space, all alone. His last words had held unexpected comfort, though. In spite of the surface threat, he'd told me that my most powerful defense was still available to me in an emergency. If I truly needed it, I could turn to my sword. It would be an act of war, and I had no idea how I was supposed to wield a sword with no physical body, but still it was comforting to know I had an option.

It seemed like years had gone by. My initial panic faded into a sort of numbness. I held as still as possible, trying to appear stoic and resigned. Meditation, contemplation was absolutely beyond my abilities in any circumstance, but especially here in Aaru. I nearly wept when I felt him, warm and reassuring against me.

Very poised, little Cockroach. You appear quite noble and centered here in your solitude.

I wasn't. Good to know I was a better actress than I was a liar.

Can the others see us? Hear us?

It had been at the edge of my mind, and the reason I'd tried so hard to present a strong front: just because I couldn't sense any angels nearby, didn't mean they weren't there.

If they come near, yes. Gabriel chased them all away. An audience isn't in keeping with the purpose of this exercise. Adequate vibration levels and a centered spirit are best achieved in solitude.

A whole lot of meaningless words, but at least I got the part where no one was around. I wondered for a brief second how my vibration levels were. I didn't really care, but I was curious if Aaru had any sort of effect on me beyond the panic and strange itchy feeling.

Of course, there is no improvement in your vibration level, no matter how your emotional state might appear.

Ah well. I rested against him, in a non–body form of snuggling. This is where I felt centered. It wasn't that his presence strengthened me, made me feel powerful. With him by my side, I felt at peace, as though I'd finally come home. He balanced me, as if we were at opposite sides of a fulcrum, even though we were folding into each other, resting together with our spirit–selves merging along the edges.

I rejoice in your misdeeds, Cockroach, just so I can have these perfect moments with you in Aaru. I hate that our internal squabbles here have stolen some of that time from me.

From us. I rubbed against him in a long caress, regretting my feelings of hurt and suspicion when he'd left me with Gabriel.

So … are you sure there aren't any others around? Because I've always been a bit of an exhibitionist. And you did leave me yesterday with some very tantalizing promises.

I surrounded him, taking him into my center, merging together. Then I quickly withdrew — teasing, to see how he'd respond. Angel fucking was one of the highlights of my existence, but I'd yet to do it in Aaru, where we could completely join without the need to retain a link to the physical. Just our spirit–selves, without fear we'd lose control and wind up dead. The idea was freeing. And beyond erotic. Sinning in heaven — it was totally on my bucket list.

Bad imp. It is completely disreputable for someone of my level to join here in Aaru. I took heart that he sounded as if he had every intention of being disreputable. *I don't know if I can besmirch my reputation by even considering such a thing. Joining in Aaru — how terribly sinful.*

I would have rolled my eyes, if I'd had any. *Oh, but it's fine for you to do it out of Aaru? What happened before the war? Did angels sneak elsewhere to join, like human teenagers?*

No, before the war we joined where we liked. Things are changing, Cockroach, but we must allow for the reluctance many angels have to alter attitudes they've held for nearly three–million years.

I thought briefly of Raphael's comments, but there were more important things to do than mull over the politics in Aaru. I continued to stroke him, to merge sections of myself with him, only to pull back. Angels might want committees, studies, a million years to change, but I wasn't about to wait that long. *Fine. But I want you now, without the need to hold back. All of you joined with all of me, the way angels are supposed to be.*

If he'd been in physical form, he would have caught his breath. There was a second of hesitation, and then I felt the intensity of him against me, hotter than a volcano erupting.

I opened up and fell into him. We remained individual beings, but our new position increased all the places where we touched and joined. Together then apart. We built a rhythm composed of moments of attachment and moments of separation. It was like a dance, a symphony, a duet where emotion and intensity increased with each movement.

Even mind–speech was beyond me at this point. All I could do was feel — which was odd given the sensory deprivation of Aaru. We swirled together, the moments of separation lessening until we'd reached a point of no return. Faster, closer we moved until we came together in a translucent beam of opalescent light. One. Inseparable. Unlike before, there was no easing back, no return to our physical bodies. We just remained as if we were one being, each in absolute harmony with the other.

This is how we would be if you came to Aaru with me, Cockroach. We could spend an eternity as this and let the world pass us by.

It was a seductive idea, worming its way into my heart and mind. I could leave it all behind — the stupid Iblis responsibilities, the elves, the humans, that damned pregnant woman and her half–angel fetus, werewolves. I could retreat with Gregory and spend the rest of time with him.

He knew as well as I did that it couldn't be. Slowly we separated, returning to individual existence, but always keeping a slight connection with each other. I wanted to lie to myself, to promise that someday we'd be able to leave the world behind. But I was a terrible liar.

It's time to return to your home, Cockroach.

Punishment flew by when he was with me, but there were reports to complete, a pregnant woman in my home, and my earthly household to take care of. Thankfully Dar and Leethu had been handling the Hel end of my business interests the last few months, because I had no time left for them.

Ready.

I created my human form as we arrived in my kitchen, enjoying the feel of my naked skin against Gregory's usual jeans and navy polo.

"Coffee?" he asked after holding me a few moments longer than necessary.

I nodded. There was comfort in our routine — coffee and conversation. Even if the occasional physical foreplay left me unsatisfied, I always hoped sex — angel or otherwise, would happen.

"What's going on in Aaru?" I asked as I watched him spoon grounds into the filter. "Can you tell me, or is that top–secret stuff?"

It was my turn to grill him for details. Hopefully I'd glean something I could use. Hopefully something he said would spur that great 'idea' to form that Raphael so desperately wanted.

Gregory frowned in concentration at the dark specks, removing a few before putting them into the maker. "There is great unrest. Angels are falling at a rate not seen since the tenth choir. Some feel that breeding with the humans should be allowed and regulated. Others feel that programs should be in place to allow breeding with the demons."

I'd come close to being on the receiving end of one of those breeding programs. That wasn't something I wanted to see become an official Aaru–sanctioned event. The Bachelor for Heaven and Hell seemed far more appealing. Or maybe an online dating service — Infernal Mates dot com. I could manage to insert that option into the mix.

As for humans and angels — well I didn't have anything against Harper, but angels swarming around snatching up all the human females didn't seem like a good plan.

The angel punched the brew button on the coffee machine. "No one agrees on what these programs should be, and another group strongly resists any change." The angel rubbed the back of his neck. It was such a human gesture that I couldn't help but smile.

"What do *you* want? In an ideal scenario?"

He smiled, his eyes warm as they met mine. "Like it was. Angels find partners and agree to breed based on mutual attraction and desires."

I grinned. Yeah! Another vote for Infernal Mates dot com.

He pulled two mugs out of the cabinet. "Of course, you're the only Angel of Chaos, so demons would need to continue to live in Hel away from their partners. I don't know how well it will work, either. Not all demons are quite as accommodating as you, Cockroach."

I'd never considered myself particularly accommodating, so his words were a bit of a shock. I'd need to remedy that. Try harder to be a pain in the ass.

"Demons would love to put angel fucking on their resume, but I don't see much advantage to the angels. Do you think the joining would be that much of an incentive? And then there's the issue of offspring — offspring that could just as likely wind up a demon as an angel."

"An Angel of Chaos," he corrected as he poured our coffee. "New creation would correct the devolution that inbreeding has caused among the demons. It would be a step toward remedying the mistakes made in the war and the treaty."

When an angel older than the sun admits to a mistake — one he's held firm to for two–and–a–half–million years, you take notice. My head spun with the significance of it.

"So do it. You're the big guy, the eldest of the brothers of the Ruling Council. Make it so. I'll vote your way, and I'm pretty sure Raphael would too."

He handed me a mug of coffee, his lips twisted in irony. "If only it were that easy, Cockroach. Too many are afraid of change. And my own behavior rubs their noses in it. I won't give you up, can't give you up, but right now, I'm part of the problem. One of the others on the Council needs to lead on this one."

I sipped my coffee and thought of the Ruling Council. Uriel was off on sabbatical, or whatever. Gabriel had a stick up his ass. Sleazy was pretty forgettable, as was New Guy. Raphael was in favor — did he have enough power to enact change without his elder brother leading the way?

"I don't see why you can't just lay down the law. You're more powerful than any angel I've ever seen, and I've seen a lot over the last few months. Push the change through."

Gregory shook his head, looking upward. "Such a demon still. Change without adequate buy–in doesn't stick, and policies that are forced down everyone's throat only breed further rebellion. Once we get everyone to center and put aside their emotions, we'll begin with exploration — focus groups and studies for a few–thousand years, then maybe some modeling."

Angels moved with the rapidity of cold molasses. Not that the faster speed of change in Hel was yielding stellar results. The small colony of humans established at the edge of the Cyelle forest were constantly subjected to attacks by curious demons and resentful elves. Raphael was right — I needed to assist however I could with healing wounds that had festered for nearly three–million years, but, judging by the last few days, it seemed this was going to happen at the expense of quality time with my angel.

"Guess this means you can't hang out and watch NCIS reruns today."

"No." Gregory kissed the top of my head and put his half–full coffee cup in the sink. "I've stayed too long as it is. I'll see you in a few days, Cockroach."

"Promise?"

"I promise. We can do what the humans call 'date night'. We'll watch movies. I might even risk my enlightenment to try some of these 'hot wings' you and Wyatt keep talking about."

"How about you risk your enlightenment even further? Hot wings can lead to all sorts of life–changing, naughty behavior, you know."

He smiled. "We'll just have to see how things go, won't we? Perhaps it will be a night for sin."

I felt empty the moment he was gone. Even the knowledge that he'd be back in forty–eight hours to pick up my reports wasn't enough to cheer me on. Moping, I walked with my coffee cup through the French doors and around the sun–lit pool toward the barn.

I had taken to letting the horses graze for short periods of time instead of all day long. The lush, green grass plus my limited free time to ride meant all three were getting fat. It wasn't quite evening, but I figured I might as well let them out of their stables for an early dinner.

A strange thumping noise came from the barn, accompanied by a soft voice. I peered around the edge of the door and saw Harper rubbing Vegas' neck as she fed him bits of cookie with the other hand. Gone was the fury she wore like a cloak around her, and in its place was an aura of peace. The woman cooed to the Quarter horse then moved on to give Piper the same loving attention. Diablo strained across the stall divider, begging with an outstretched head until it was his turn. Done petting the horses, Harper turned to survey the barn, a tiny smile on her face. Rubbing a hand along an oak support post, she looked up and leapt to grab the edge of a steel beam.

The rounded bump of her belly pushed against her shirt, a stark contrast to the lean muscles in her arms and legs. She swung like a monkey from the beam, reaching up to hook her other hand on a wooden cross piece. Face red with exertion, she pulled up and planted one foot against the upright post. Walking her feet toward the ceiling, she released her hold on the beam and stretched her hand toward a second cross piece. And fell.

I caught my breath as she landed hard on her ass, dust rising in clouds from the floor. Before I could come forward to ask if she was okay, the woman's anger returned like a tidal wave. Jumping to her feet, she snatched up a shovel and began hitting the oak post with all her might. It was a tough wood, but the woman still managed to put a few dents in the upright before throwing the shovel aside and collapsing on the floor in a flood of tears.

"I hate him. I hate what he did to me. He should have just let me die."

The other horses cowered in the rear of their stalls, but Diablo snorted in sympathy, unalarmed by her shovel violence. I frowned, wondering what she was talking about besides her obvious resentment toward the angel that had knocked her up.

"Why me?" She asked the demon horse. "Why not one of the others? He should have let me die. I hate the zombie I became. I hate the person he turned me into."

Anger I could handle, but this torrent of despair was beyond an imp's ability to cope with. I snuck back toward the house, feeling as guilty as I did helpless for leaving her there with only Diablo to comfort her.

~5~

H ere you go." Wyatt plopped two large stacks of paper on our table. They didn't exactly add to the ambiance of fine dining, but I was more thrilled over their appearance than the broiled lobster.

"You are the best boyfriend ever."

I paged through them as Wyatt sipped his wine, a smug smile on his face. He'd been thorough. Very thorough. Every detail of the two humans' lives that could be discovered over the internet was in these four–nine–five reports. My head was swimming about five pages in, so I pushed them aside and returned my attention to the dead crustacean on my plate. I trusted that Wyatt had done the reports with more detail than even the most anal of angels. Time enough to read them tomorrow. I had expensive food to eat.

"How was that thing in Baltimore?" I asked, swishing a chunk of lobster meat in butter.

"Kind of a good news/ bad news thing." Wyatt refilled his wine glass. "They've had a huge security breach, but it's weird. It's the same profile as the hacker that nailed Chromium Medical last month. They're thinking of installing Genus Micro's system, but want me to go to Chicago and check it out first. Genus charges a fortune and they want to make sure it's worth it."

I had no idea what he was talking about, but I smiled and nodded enthusiastically. "So this Micro guy is in Chicago?"

"Genus Micro is a company. They're based in Silicon Valley, but all the big IT firms will be at the expo in Chicago."

"Sounds fun." It didn't, but I'd learned that comments like this were what humans wanted to hear in conversation regarding their activities.

"The expo is next month, but I'm going to head out early and talk with a few other companies, see what their experience with Genus has been."

"This wine is really good. Have some more." I filled Wyatt's glass to the brim, hoping more alcohol would facilitate a change in subject to something less boring.

"I'll head out tomorrow to Philly, then on to Detroit then Chicago."

Tomorrow? It seemed like we hardly saw each other anymore, like our lives were drifting in opposite directions.

"I'll miss you." It was true, although I missed what we used to have more. When it came to humans, more than their existence was fleeting. They seemed to change right before my eyes, every last one of them.

Wyatt grinned, drinking a significant amount of wine from his glass. "I'll miss you too, Sam. Let me know if you need anything else for your reports."

Sheesh. I hoped the angels didn't want anything additional. These things in my bag must have weighed twenty pounds each.

"Nyalla tells me you've taken another human under your wing. A pregnant woman?"

Ah, that's why Wyatt was so accommodating about the reports. He was rewarding what he thought to be a kinder, gentler Sam. I glanced down at my boots with a stab of guilt.

"Harper. Some angel knocked her up and dumped her at my doorstep. I've got to take care of her and the baby until they die a natural death."

To my relief, Wyatt didn't focus on why I had to do these things, but instead began to express outrage over the angelic sperm donor, demanding to know why Gregory didn't do something about such an abuse of power.

"It's complicated. Gregory is trying to do something about this, but the long–term solution isn't one that the angels are going to adopt overnight. In the meantime, she's got a death sentence over her head, or maybe just the baby's head. I haven't read those particular articles or sections, or whatever, yet."

"They'd kill her?" Wyatt thundered. "One of their own broke the rules. Why don't they kill him instead?"

I finished my lobster and drank the remaining butter right from the little round ceramic ramekin. "My sentiments exactly. But in the meantime, I'm not really sure what to do with this woman, or the baby once it arrives. I've got no idea how to take care of human infants, let alone a half–angel one."

"I'm sure the mother will do the majority of the caretaking." Wyatt hesitated, wine glass halfway to his lips. "Wait. How did you get in the middle of this mess? I can't imagine what would have caused an angel to think that you'd be a suitable protector for a pregnant woman."

I should have been insulted, but Wyatt was right. "I kinda got tricked into it. And I don't think the angel knew where else to turn."

Wyatt frowned thoughtfully. "Where do the other angels hide their Nephilim? I mean, it's not like this has been the only one, and from what you've told me, the angels haven't been able to catch them all. Where are these half–angels? And who is hiding them?"

He had a point. I'd been too busy with my punishment and the pissed–off pregnant woman living in my house to give much thought to the bigger picture. "I'm assuming some group of angels hides them. Maybe they turned him down? He's a bit of an asshole, and the mother of his child has some rather violent tendencies."

"Could be. Still, I think you should try and find out how the other Nephilim are escaping notice. No offense, Sam, but this woman and her baby are bound to be safer there than in your house with demons running around all over the place."

And Hunter angels on my doorstep the moment the thing popped out of its mother. Trust Wyatt to point me in the right direction, even if he didn't always approve of my methods. We finished dinner and headed home as I dreamed of one last night in Wyatt's arms before he headed off for a month or more. I wasn't completely surprised when he stopped in front of my door and kissed my forehead, giving me a brief hug.

"Got an early flight tomorrow," he said apologetically. "Call me and let me know how things are going?"

An early flight had never kept him from my bed before. I tried to keep my smile bright as I reached up to kiss his cheek. "Text me and let me know you've landed safely, okay?"

"Okay."

Wyatt jogged off toward his house, the fading light glinting off his blond hair. I watched him go, knowing that the sun wasn't the only thing setting right now.

~6~

Nyalla was sitting at my dining room table with my laptop open before her.

"I hope I'm not cramping your style," she said with a sheepish smile. "You and Wyatt never seem to have time together anymore. I can take this upstairs if you all want to watch TV or ... something."

I looked down at Wyatt's sister and stroked her dark blond hair. "Nah. You stay here. Your brother headed back to his house for the night."

I tried to keep my voice casual, but Nyalla wasn't fooled. "I'm sorry, Sam."

"Don't be." There were more types of love than stars in the sky. I'd always love Wyatt, but our feelings had shifted and morphed with time. So different then the feelings I had for Gregory — the kind that bound two people together for eternity, even beyond death.

Nyalla tilted her head and looked up at me with a little smile. "I like that angel of yours. He's scary, but I like him."

"Me too." I thought about Gregory, and something deep inside me warmed. I more than liked him.

The girl looked up from the computer screen again, her expression turning wistful.

"I wish I could find someone I felt that way about."

She was only twenty–one. I was glad things hadn't worked out with the cop or that guy at the beach. Nyalla was far too young to be diving headfirst into that crazy marriage–and–kids thing humans seemed so eager to do.

"Patience, Nyalla," I told her, sounding ridiculously like Gregory. Wincing at the uncomfortable similarity, I looked over her shoulder. "What are you doing? Looking for another vacation destination?"

"Dating site."

I leaned closer. Maybe I could get some ideas for Infernal Mates. Couldn't be that different — matching up demons and angels based on mutual interests. Although finding mutual interests might be more difficult than it sounded.

Nyalla clicked a few buttons and an array of photos popped up on the screen. Attractive young men in a startling state of undress scrolled across the page. "I'm not having the best of luck."

"Hmmm." Michelle had filled me in on the trials of attempting to find a life–mate over the internet. From her hair–raising stories, it seems humans were far better liars than I was. "How about this one? He looks cute."

He did. Washboard abs, and the boxers slipping low off his hips were a nice touch. I'd do him.

"I know! We emailed a few times and exchanged some pictures, but now he won't talk to me. He's blocked me."

She said the last with a hurt voice. Asshole. How dare he do that to Nyalla? What was there not to like about my precious human girl?

"See? He sent me this picture of his genitals, claiming that he was hung like a horse."

I looked at the picture. Not the most flattering lighting in the world, but selfies weren't exactly easy on the eye. From what I could see, the dude had a good–looking cock, in my opinion.

"As well–endowed as he appears to be, clearly he's never seen a horse before. I mean, there's no comparison there. So I sent him this picture in return."

I choked back a laugh. There was a picture of a horse's lower region, the animal's member fully extended and erect. Nyalla had captioned it with some precise measurements.

"How in the world did you get Diablo to do that for a picture?" Yes, I recognized my horse, although I'd never been up close and personal with his dick.

"I asked him. He's a very nice horse. And the internet had all sorts of information regarding size and girth of animal reproductive organs."

I was just glad she hadn't taken a measuring tape to Diablo. "So, I'm guessing this sexy, young man felt intimidated by what he perceived was some equine competition?"

Nyalla's shoulders slumped. "He called me a freak. Then he blocked me."

I bent down and gave her a hug. "Pretty harsh coming from a guy whose second email to you included a cock shot."

She turned to me, her blue eyes clouded with worry. "I am a freak. I'm trying, but I just don't fit in here with the rest of the humans."

"Look at who you're talking to." I tugged a lock of her long hair and grinned. "A demon pretending to be a human. Then there's Candy — a werewolf who hides who she is from the humans, and your stepsister, Amber. Heck, even humans have secrets they only tell the few they truly trust. You'll find someone, Nyalla. In the meantime, have fun. Surf. Scuba dive. Have sex with lots of boys — but don't get pregnant." I added the last with a note of panic in my voice. Damned humans reproduced like rabbits.

She smiled. "That reminds me. I don't think Harper is doing too well."

What now? That crazy human would be the death of me. Had she fallen from the barn rafters and landed on her head? Gotten kicked by one of the horses? Injured herself in another violent tantrum with the shovel? Now I was even more panicked. I still sucked at healing anyone but demons. Did human doctors make house calls anymore? Was it safe for her to leave the premises and go to prenatal appointments? What the fuck was I supposed to do?

"No, no," Nyalla reassured me. "The baby's fine. Her physical health is fine. She's just so angry."

"Tell me about it." The woman had been angry since the first moment I'd laid eyes on her. I doubted that situation was going to change any time in the near future.

"She feels abandoned, and friendless. She's been deceived and doesn't know who to trust anymore."

Well, that wasn't my fault. I wasn't the one who fucked an angel — no, wait; I did fuck an angel, although we hadn't gotten around to the physical kind of fucking yet. Damn it all.

"Should I go talk to her? Do you think it would help?" I hoped not. I hoped she'd just stay in her room, or that she and the baby would somehow magically disappear.

"Please?" Nyalla's face radiated happiness. How could I say 'no' to that face? "I told her that you had an angel you were in love with, and that they weren't all jerks like hers had been. I told her that you were really nice for a demon. I think she'd be a lot less worried about her future if she knew she could trust you, that you'd truly protect her."

How did I become the 'nice demon' that people could trust to protect them? I needed to do something about this — clearly my reputation was in danger of becoming squeaky clean. Maybe I could head out after midnight and key some cars, or spray–paint lewd drawings on the side of police cruisers.

I climbed the stairs, dread in every step, then knocked on Harper's door. There was no response, so I peeked in to see her sitting against the headboard of her bed, clutching a knife in one hand as she stabbed a pillow. At this rate, I wouldn't have a single home furnishing intact by the time the baby was born.

I figured the answer to a request to come in would be 'no', so I stepped over the thick line of salt and sat as far from her as I could on the edge of the bed.

"Everything okay? Do you need anything weird, like pickle–flavored ice cream? Deep–fried Spam? Chocolate–covered crickets?"

What the heck was I supposed to say to a pregnant woman who was brandishing a knife and had lined her room in twenty pounds of my expensive sea salt?

"No. I'm fine."

"That doesn't look like fine." I gestured toward the pillow. "Look, I know you're pissed off at that piece–of–shit baby–daddy, but try not to take it out on me or my pillows. I haven't done anything but take you into my home, provide you sanctuary, and buy you toiletries."

And take her shoes, but that was beside the point.

"You were tricked into it. I've been told about demons. I know what you'd do to me if you hadn't vowed to protect me."

I sighed, thinking she was the only one who considered me anything besides a 'nice' demon. "Yeah, well I *have* vowed to protect you. Something I'm regretting right now as I watch you stab my bedding."

Harper looked at the pillow, and something like shame flitted across her face. "You're right. I'm sorry. I've no right to take this out on you. Or your pillow."

"Do you want to talk? I'm not human, and I've never created offspring, but I've spent a lot of time with angels in the past few years. We could get drunk and have a bitch session if you want to."

Harper sat silent, looking first at me, then at the thick line of salt around her room. The knuckles of her knife–holding hand were white, and I noted her nails on the other hand had been chewed to the nub, cuticles raw and bleeding. A twinge of sympathy went through me, but there was nothing I could do for a woman who clearly wanted me, and everyone else, as far away from her as possible.

I sighed and stood to leave.

"Do you really have wings?"

I turned to look at her. She lowered the knife and nibbled on the edge of her finger.

"I mean real wings, not demons wings. Nyalla said you had wings."

I revealed my massive wings. They began as a tracing of gold light before bursting into form, taking up the entire width of the room even though I had them folded partially closed. The whole time, I kept a close eye on Harper, making sure she didn't freak out and lunge at me with the knife. I might be able to quickly fix a stab wound, but that didn't mean I'd enjoy being sliced up.

"He ... I only got to see his wings once, and that was by accident. I never got to see anything of him that he didn't want me to see. I don't think I ever really knew him. And now I know it didn't matter to him at all. *I* didn't matter to him at all. I was just a means to an end. A brood mare."

I winced, contrasting her angel with Gregory. My angel knew who I was inside, loved all the ways we were different.

"There are assholes in every species. Don't let your anger for him consume the rest of your life."

I twitched my wings, anger of my own blooming as I thought about the asshole who had betrayed her trust. Harper's eyes drifted to the black feathers, and her gaze softened.

"Can I touch them?"

"As long as you put the knife down." I understood now why angels didn't run around with their wings exposed. Shit, these things were sensitive.

The woman set the knife on the table and approached the far edge of my wing. Stretching her arm out, she gently ran the tips of her fingers over the feathers.

"How did this happen to you? I was told that demons had no wings beyond the foul ones their low vibration level allowed."

I was really getting pissed at this angel baby–daddy. What a racist douche–bag.

"It's a long story. An angel bound me, but it was sort of fucked up, and this was the end result. We were once all like this, you know. We weren't always demons."

She backed up, toward the bed, reaching behind her to grab the knife off the bedside table. "But you're demons now. Some say even with the wings, you're still a demon."

"I think I'm something in between. Not demon enough for my brethren in Hel, and not angel enough for those in Aaru. Whatever. I can't waste time worrying about it."

Silence stretched on between us. I wasn't sure what to do. Should I leave?

Harper sat on the edge of the bed then seemed to come to some sort of decision. With a slow movement, she opened the drawer on the bedside table and slid the knife into it. "Nyalla says you are in love with an angel. That he loves you back."

"Yes." There was no hesitation in my voice.

She closed the drawer and raised her hand to gnaw at her thumb. "I thought I was. I thought he loved me back."

The words were a whisper, and her pain shone out of her dark brown eyes. I hid my wings and walked over to sit on the bed, keeping a few feet between us.

"How did you meet him?"

Harper looked down at her lap. "I grew up in Colorado. The wilderness was right outside; it was my backyard. I'd skied, backpacked, and climbed since I was able to walk.

Those sort of activities are like riding a bike for the kids out there. By the time I was in college, I was doing big climbs with a group of friends. Mostly day or weekend trips, but after college we'd all save like crazy to do one big excursion each year."

I sat with uncharacteristic patience as the woman plucked stray bits from the bedspread. Maybe I needed to get her some Xanax. Between her stabbing habit and this one, my bed covers were going to wind up looking like her fingernails.

"Last year my friends and I had saved enough to go on a sweet ice climb in Alaska. We did a couple of day climbs around Anchorage then hiked to Spencer Glacier for our big climb. It was an amazing trip — we took sea kayaks from basecamp to the ice edge, and then we headed up the ice walls. The glacier is fairly stable, but even so, there are crevasses, moulins, ice caves, and a mountain of snow above. Conditions change as the glacier moves, so even experienced climbers and guides need to be aware."

She took a couple of deep breaths then clutched her hands tight in her lap. "Anyway, there was an avalanche. We didn't just fall off the mountain; we fell with about five–hundred pounds of snow and ice. I don't remember much — just waking up surrounded by blue and white, breathing in a tiny space that surrounded my head. I kept hoping my friends were okay and that they'd find me, that help would arrive soon. The snow — it weighed so much, and I knew my legs were broken, maybe even my back. The space around me was so small that the oxygen wouldn't have lasted more than a few hours. I lay there, knowing I was as good as dead, and that only a miracle would save me."

"Shit." I might be a near immortal, but I could imagine her pain, and the fear and resignation that an inevitable death must have brought her.

"I was in and out for a while — no idea how long — then I saw a bright light. It took a while for my eyes to adjust, for me to realize that I was on top of the snow and ice. An angel stood over me. I don't know how I knew he was an angel — I just did. I thought I'd died."

I made a sympathetic noise. "When I first saw my angel, I thought I was going to die."

Harper gave me a smile that transformed her face. I suddenly saw the lively, outdoorsy woman she'd been back then.

"Well, I wasn't afraid. I was accepting. I hadn't exactly led a blameless life up until then. I mean, I was pretty solid on the Ten Commandments, other than the occasional coveting of the neighbor's BMW and the like. Still, I figured all that was the past, and I'd just need to accept whatever judgment came my way."

None of that made any sense to me whatsoever. If some angel showed up and tried to judge me, I'd smack him upside the head with my sword. Or a Danish. Or maybe a plate of hot wings. Fucking prudes.

"He bent down and kissed me, and all the pain went away. I could feel my legs and back straighten. They tingled, felt warm. And then he was gone. I heard shouting, and a rescue crew airlifted me out. Everyone said it was a miracle because I had no injuries. My friends hadn't been saved, though. Days later, their bodies were recovered, buried under twenty feet of snow and ice."

"You were lucky." I wondered why the angel had been there at exactly the right time, why he'd chosen her. The whole thing stank like a dead groundhog in the August sun.

The laugh that came from Harper was short and sharp, full of bitterness. "At first I agreed, but now I know better. My friends were lucky. I should have died with them. A part of me *did* die that day. The only thing left when they airlifted me off that mountain was a shell of a woman."

"But you saw him again." It couldn't have been a coincidence. This angel picked her, saved her then went on to have a very forbidden relationship with her. There was a part

Debra Dunbar

of me that wondered if he'd fallen in love with the girl he'd saved, if it was all innocent, but the demon in me knew better. We weren't that different — angels and demons. There was a good chance he'd just taken advantage of the situation — or even caused it in some way.

Harper shook her head and continued. "I chalked the whole thing up to a hallucination, but at the hospital I saw him, as well as the week after I'd been released. Every day I'd catch sight of him walking past me on the street, getting a cup of coffee while I sat and drank mine, or eating at a nearby table."

She paused in her shredding of the comforter and held her hands outward with a shrug. "I figured it was some kind of sign from my unconscious self, that he was truly my soul mate. We began talking, then dating. I never knew he was an angel, a *real* angel, until after we'd been together for a few months."

I reached out and caught one of her restless hands in mine. "I'm sorry. Sorry he kept who he was from you, that he got you pregnant and dumped you off here. I'm sworn to take care of you and all you carry, but my primary concern is with you. What do you want? If you had the power to right the world, what would you envision your future to be?"

Harper clenched my hand tight, giving me a wobbly smile. "You're not much of a demon, are you?"

Damn. Nyalla thinks I'm a 'nice demon', and this woman thinks I'm a lousy one. I seriously needed to step up my game.

"If I could go back in time, my friends would be alive. We'd plan other trips, laugh over memories. Then one day, maybe while skiing in Tahoe or rafting down the canyon, I'd meet a man. My heart would beat faster. The moon and stars would freeze as our eyes met, and we'd begin a future together."

My own heart ached for her. "I can't resurrect your friends, but there's no reason why you can't have the rest. Your life is far from over."

The woman smiled, and this time her lips didn't wobble. "Maybe. But for now, I want to have this baby. I want to be able to walk in the sunshine, buy maternity clothes and take pre–natal classes. I want to hold my son in my arms, to watch him grow, to see his first steps, his first day of Kindergarten, to hold him tight when he cries and soothe his fears. I want to watch him walk down the aisle for graduation, for his wedding. I want to spoil his children rotten. Somehow I think that fantasy is just as farfetched as the resurrection of my friends."

This woman might be a lot of things but she wasn't blind to the danger she and her child were in. "And what about the father? What place does he have in this future?"

Harper's face twisted in fury. "Do you know what he wanted me to do? Do you know what he asked ... no, *commanded* of me?"

I felt chilled. Angels considered babies and children free of sin, the highest in their vibration patterns. In spite of that, they still sentenced Nephilim to death. Had the father wanted her to abort the baby? I looked at Harper and shook my head. "What did he command of you?"

"To hide away, and when the baby was born to give it over to monsters to raise. Then I was to come back to him and resume our relationship. How could I do that? How could I ever love him again, knowing that he'd ripped our baby from my arms? How could he ever expect me to feel the same about him after that?"

She'd become increasingly agitated as she spoke, picking at the covers then tearing at her cuticles with her stubby nails. I reached out and captured both her hands in mind, scooting closer.

"How did you get pregnant? I mean... ." How the fuck was I supposed to ask this? I had no idea about angel reproduction. With demons, insemination was always intentional. With angels, I had no stinking clue.

Harper made a short choking noise. Tears welled up in her eyes. "I don't know. I was on the pill, and I'm very careful. No other medicine to interact, nothing. Maybe I'm just that zero, zero, zero, one percent."

Or maybe this angel had his own agenda, which selfishly violated Harper's trust.

"What did he do when he found out you were pregnant? Was he angry? Upset?"

She shook her head. "No, he seemed as if he knew already. He was kind of excited, but worried too. Right away, he said the baby needed to be safe, and that if I wanted it to live, I needed to give it away. Is that true? Was he lying to me?"

Shit. How to break this one to her? "It's true. The angelic host takes a dim view on Nephilim — the offspring of angels and humans. They are condemned to death, and the angels involved in their breeding suffer punishment."

Harper yanked her hands from mine and covered her mouth. Her body shook. "My son is as good as dead, isn't he?" Her words were muffled.

"I'm sorry. He was a total shit — the angel that did this to you. I'll do the best I can to protect you and your baby, but I don't know if I can give you the future you want. Heck, I don't know if I can promise your baby any future at all."

She began crying in earnest, sobbing into her hands.

"Give me his name. Tell me who the father is, and I'll make sure he suffers. I'm the Iblis, the Ha–Satan. I'm on the Ruling Council. I'll see him punished for this, try to get him banished to Hel. Do you know what the demons would do to him there? It would be a fitting end for the shithead that did this to you."

Harper shook her head violently and gasped, trying to get herself under control. "Ben Jackson. That's the only name I knew him by, and somehow I doubt it was his angel name. I hate him. I hate what he's done to me. I'd kill him with my own hands if I knew I could, but I'm not sure I can condemn the father of my child to Hel."

Humans. Sometimes I just didn't get them at all. "Okay. I'll see what I can do to protect your son. In the meantime, pretend you're on vacation. Relax by the pool; check out all the baby stuff online. Do you ride horses? Piper is really sweet. You could safely ride him. Or I could install some climbing handholds on the side of the barn."

I felt so helpless. Nothing I could do would make this right. Nothing would guarantee her baby's safety. All my suggestions were just a desperate attempt to distract her from the grim future ahead.

"Thanks." Harper gave me a watery smile. "You're not so bad — for a demon, that is. Nyalla is nice, too. She offered to have her friend come over with her baby, to make me feel more like this was all normal."

Ugh. More baby smell. I'd hoped to put that off for at least another few months.

"That's a great idea." I forced a smile. "Nyalla has already been decorating the other room for the nursery. She's a very good friend to have."

~7~

Date night wasn't quite what I'd expected. Gregory sat beside me, thumbing through my reports — not exactly the most romantic of activities, but given our other company, it was probably the most I could expect for tonight. Hot wings had been a bit of a bust, and I was suspecting my angel might have vegetarian tendencies. We'd returned to the safety of food groups I knew he was more inclined to enjoy.

Harper sat as far away from the angel as possible, trying to look relaxed as she shot him sideways glances. Her expression fluctuated between anxious and fascinated. Nyalla was on the other couch, as equally entertained by the Three's Company rerun as she was Gregory's strange obsession with snack foods.

"How about Skittles? Have you tried them yet? Or are you more of a chocolate kind of person ... um, angel?"

"I have not had Skittles, or chocolate, but I have discovered that I enjoy Jolly Rancher candies. The watermelon flavor in particular."

Harper pursed her lips. "Cherry. And green apple. I'm a Jolly Rancher kinda gal myself."

I smiled to see her making an effort to join the conversation. "The best thing about Jolly Ranchers is the way they cement your teeth together. Just chomp down hard, and you won't be able to open your mouth without a crowbar. If you've got fillings in your teeth, expect them to come out."

"I have not tried that particular technique, Cockroach." Gregory's voice drawled. His eyes sparkled with humor as he paged through my report. "I will have to try that with the cherry and green apple. And try this *chocolate*, too."

I made a mental note and vowed to pull together a selection of chocolates for an angelic taste test. This was fun, introducing Gregory to food and drink. I hoped it led to all sorts of other sins.

"Why does the Roper woman persist in sexual overtures toward her husband when he is clearly not interested?" He frowned down at one of my reports. I was amazed he even knew what was happening on the show since he hadn't looked up more than once in the last fifteen minutes.

I nodded. "I know. She needs to ditch him and fuck Jack instead. Or get a really good vibrator. Stanley is an ass anyway."

Harper snorted. "Jack? Yuck. I'd pick the vibrator over him any day."

Nyalla shook her head. "Although I suspect Mrs. Roper would welcome sexual relations with either Jack or a battery–powered device; she *does* want her husband. She's trying to connect with him. Even though their relationship is flawed, she offers sex as a way to prove that, deep down, they still love each other. He acts as if he dislikes it, but Mr. Roper still grants her requests for sex. He, too, needs that connection."

Great. My girl was turning into some kind of Dr. Phil. "Nah. He's too fugly to get anyone else in the sack. His wife is the only option available besides jerking off in the shower or paying a prostitute. Mr. Roper is too cheap to shell out for sex."

"He'd have to pay big," Harper commented. "I'd rather sleep with an angel. No offense." She grinned at Gregory.

"None taken."

I was beginning to like this girl. She had mad pillow–slaughtering knife skills and didn't seem to have any problems with vibrators. I wondered if she was putting Leethu's stash of toys to good use.

"The pair of them would be better off remaining abstinent. Jack, and those two young women, too." Gregory turned another page and frowned. "Who completed these reports, Cockroach? The attachments are very odd, and I don't understand much of the terminology."

"Oh, I did them," I lied. "Do you think your brothers and the other ass–wipes will finally get off my back, or am I going to have to go back to jail again?"

Gregory took a deep breath and tossed the heavy stack of papers onto my lap. "Redo the impact analysis. It's weak. The rest will have to do. Just pray that the events in Aaru take enough attention that no one really reads this thing."

***

They did read the thing. Out loud.

"Joseph Barakel seems to have had a lengthy medical history of cardiac weakness." Raphael stabbed a finger at the relevant page. "I appreciate that you've included chemical formulas for his prescriptive medicines."

I had no idea how Wyatt had managed to get copies of the guy's medical records, including doctors' notes, but I owed him far more than steak and lobster for this one.

"Quite the list of homeowners' association violations too. Lawn above prescribed height, unauthorized tree removal, fence the incorrect style for neighborhood aesthetics — oh my."

I nodded at New Guy, sending yet another silent thanks to Wyatt.

"Yes. That plays into the impact analysis. The neighbors were quite relieved at his passing and are happy with the new townhouse owner." I'd come to realize that with angels, the more obscure, detailed shit you gave them, the better. Of course, I'd made up the whole impact analysis, but hopefully, with Wyatt's three–hundred pages of computer printouts, no one would notice.

"I vote we accept the report, in spite of the tardiness of its presentation, and conclude that this human's death was not due to the purely coincidental presence of the Iblis." Raphael gave me a quick wink as he finished. Hmmm. Little brother was a bit of a flirt. Nice to know the angels weren't all such prudes.

"All in favor?"

Even Gabriel raised his hand. I was shocked speechless. Wyatt needed to do my homework more often.

"And now onto Tyrone Cochran." Gabriel motioned, and everyone shuffled papers around to the appropriate stack. I also paged through them, wondering what Wyatt had found out about the drug dealer who'd attacked me in a back alley.

There were some murmurs of conversation amid the flurry of mind–speech. I couldn't follow any of it. Finally they all looked up at me. I held my breath.

"What is this FICO number? It seems to be quite relevant to this particular report."

I stared blankly at Gabriel, my brain frantically trying to assemble an explanation that would make sense to a bunch of angels. "Umm, it's used by a large number of human financial institutions to evaluate an individual's credit worthiness and risk."

The angels stared blankly at me.

"Does this have any relation to the Burrito Scale of Immense Magnitude?" Raphael shook his head, clearly befuddled by the concept of human monetary lending.

"No. Humans work as a giant community. They borrow, and groups who have superior resources lend. Those who lend need to have a system to determine who is worthy. There is a company that has put together a mathematical analysis of a human's status as a borrower. This FICO number represents that."

"Their worth?" A glimmer of recognition lit Gabriel's eyes. "So this number is a symbol of their vibration level? Humans strive for a higher number, a more worthy state of being?"

"Yeah."

Close enough. Besides, I had a bad feeling if I began discussing interest rates and foreclosures, at least one of these angels was going to start overturning the tables of the money changers and the benches of those who sold doves.

Sleazy just about wet himself with excitement. "I had no idea the humans had advanced so far as to evaluate each other by vibration level."

New Guy tapped his paperwork. "Tyrone Cochran's FICO number is 480. What vibration level does that equate to?"

I had no fucking idea. "Bottom of the barrel. Think: cane toad."

Raphael's eyebrows practically hit the roof. "Isn't that the animal that tries to mate with their dead females and the corpses of other species?"

"Yeah, although I have no proof that Tyrone Cochran was practicing necrophilia. I meant that simply as a comparison of vibration level."

The angels gave a collective shudder and paged further through the report.

"And what does 'judgment of default' mean?" Raphael held a sheet of paper up, squinting at it.

Again, I thought it best to keep the notion of money and lending out of the conversation. "He made a promise to someone and refused to uphold it."

New Guy looked aghast. "He broke a *vow*? Even demons do not do such things."

This whole meeting was totally looking up. "Yep. Deplorable behavior. And as you can see, his impact analysis didn't reveal anything significant."

That's where the burrito scale came in. It was all bullshit, but, thankfully, the angels were too busy with rapid mind—speech over the debt judgment and FICO score to notice.

"All in favor?" Gabriel announced as everyone, including my own angel, raised their hand.

"Wait. What are we voting on? All in favor of what?"

Gregory stepped firmly on my foot, and I bit my tongue. Whatever the hell was going on, I trusted him. Kind of. He might be dipping his toes in the waters of sin, but I doubted he would dive under unless I was in mortal danger.

"Then it's unanimous," Gabriel said with a smug smile.

"How the fuck can anything be unanimous when I didn't vote? And what were we voting on anyway?"

"The humans clearly are striving for higher vibration levels. You, as the most knowledgeable among us on human practices, are in an excellent position to ensure their salvation. So you are now responsible for any human with a FICO score of less than five hundred and eighty. The goal will be to raise the overall average score to seven hundred within the next century."

What. The. Fuck. "No problem. I'll just kill everyone with a score of less than seven hundred, and we'll achieve our goal in record time. I might need to bring over a—few—hundred demons to assist me, but we'll get it done before the weekend."

"That's a lot of four—nine—five reports, little Cockroach." Gregory had a smirk on his face that I wasn't trusting one bit.

"I'm not the right person to head up this committee, or project, or whatever the fuck it is. I don't give a damn about vibration levels. Look at me — I'm an imp. My vibration level is in the shitter. I think anything over a six–hundred FICO score is a waste of time."

A few of the angels seemed to seriously consider my statement. The rapid–paced mind–speech returned, and I struggled to keep up.

Imp.

Iblis.

Angel.

Erratic and unreliable.

Limited resources.

Time consuming issues in Aaru.

I finally gave up, assuming they'd communicate whatever their thoughts were once they were finished discussing. It took a while — long enough for me to refill my coffee and poke at the over–ripe strawberries and cantaloupe the hotel staff had set out for us.

"We've discussed and decided that you make a valid point." Gregory's mouth twitched at the edges as he said this. I totally needed to get him alone after the meeting and find out what had really gone on. "Still, you are clearly the most knowledgeable when it comes to humans. We've temporarily assigned you to rehabilitate the humans and raise their vibration levels. You're also assigned the Fallen ones — the lost causes that we have no hope of turning around. That assignment is a permanent one."

Temporary wasn't that bad. All I had to do was really suck at the job and they'd jump to relieve me. I was more worried about these fallen ones — what the fuck was that about? "And what exactly am I expected to do with these lost causes that I'm permanently assigned to?"

Gregory shrugged. "Whatever you like. If you feel they are worthy of reform, then you can attempt it. If you wish to do otherwise, that is your choice. Punishment is sometimes a great deterrent to others who may be wavering on the edge of a bad decision. How you handle these individuals is up to you."

I shot him a quick glance, wondering about his transgressions and whether he considered himself wavering on the edge of a bad decision. I hoped not. I wanted to meet Gregory halfway. I couldn't deny what I was, but I was willing to compromise a bit to make this thing with him work. I hoped he would do the same. Chips and coffee were all well and good, but I needed a bit more sin from him to feel like we were truly the lovers I wanted us to be.

"How do I know who these fallen are? Which are considered mine, and which are still under the Ruling Council's wings?"

Gabriel sniffed, tilting his head to look down at me. "Where vibration level is a consideration, other factors will also apply. You'll need to consult with us and we'll come to a collective agreement."

What a bunch of bullshit. I now had the responsibility for these fallen dudes, and temporary assignment of humans who had poor credit? With seven–billion humans on the planet, they expected me to check everyone's FICO score and vet each one individually? Yeah. Right.

"Sure. No problem." I wanted to get past this Tyrone Cochran thing so I could go home and go about my business. I had statuary to spray paint, and water towers to toilet paper.

"I feel that this individual's death doesn't warrant any kind of censure," Raphael spoke up, his violet eyes meeting mine for a brief second. "All in favor?"

Once again I wished Uriel was here. With her gone, Rafi was the only one I could really count on to vote on my side. Even Gregory sometimes opposed me.

This time my angel raised his hand in support, along with Raphael, New Guy, and Sleazy. Only Gabriel remained opposed. Asshole. I swear I'd find some way to stick it to him eventually. That guy was a total pain in the ass.

The rest of the meeting was boring, as usual. When I could see the faint orange of the sunrise outside the conference–room windows, the angels adjourned, and Gregory took me home. This time I refused coffee and yawned in his arms.

"Sleep with me?" I wanted nothing more than to feel him next to me while I slept through the morning.

"I don't sleep." His voice conveyed amusement, and his hands caressed my back. I leaned against him, feeling the rough cotton of his polo shirt against my face.

"I don't care. I just want you near me while *I* do."

His breath hitched, and I felt the heat of his energy against me. My spirit–self reached outward and connected in a thin band of connection.

"I may need to leave. I can't remain away from Aaru for long."

"I understand." And I did. As selfish as I was, we both had burdens to carry — him more so than I. Someday, maybe, we could have the luxury of uninterrupted time together, but this was not it.

"Then I'll join you in your bed for as long as I can."

He bent down and kissed my forehead, rubbing a lock of hair between his fingers in a caress I'd grown to love. But it was his words that stirred me. I knew joining me in my bed probably wouldn't include physical intercourse, but it was an emotional intimacy that meant everything to me. My angel, curled up against me while I dreamed. The only thing better would be to actually wake up in his arms.

~8~

He was gone when I woke. I went through the motions of my morning routine, helping Nyalla make pancakes while Harper fried bacon. In spite of yesterday's breakthrough, Harper had again retreated into simmering anger. Her knuckles were white as she scooted the bites of pancake around the syrup on her plate, and she was tense as she sat on her chair. She looked like she'd start stabbing pillows at the slightest provocation.

She nearly did when my doorbell rang.

I got up, waving at the girls to remain seated. Candy was coming over to deliver some comps on potential real–estate investments. My friends usually walked right on in, but Harper had taken to locking the doors. All of them. Even during the day. I swore lightly under my breath as I threw the three dead bolts Nyalla had installed after the ghoul incident and flung open the door. Instead of Candy, an angel stood on my doorstep.

"Yeah?" This was getting tiresome. If this guy had a pregnant woman hiding in the bushes, I was going to remove his wings one feather at a time. With my teeth.

He shifted from foot to foot, eyes darting as if he were trying to see past me and didn't want me to notice. A prickle of something electric slid up my spine, and I closed the door against my body, leaning casually against the jam. I could hear Nyalla talking cheerfully in the background and tried to send her a mental message. I had no idea what extrasensory perception Gregory had gifted her with, but I was hoping hard it was telepathy.

She kept talking. I heard Harper respond.

"I ain't got all day. Tell me what the fuck you want, or fly on back to Aaru."

His eyes met mine, and I was reminded of why I hate angels. Well, all of them except for one. Cold. Condemning. Judgmental. They bore into me, sweeping from my head to toes and back up, clearly finding me lacking. His upper lip curled, and I felt a wave of power against me. It was cold and electric, like lightning in an ice storm.

"You've got something I need to collect."

Could the guy be any more fucking vague?

I'd either been spending too much time with elves and angels, or my intuition was kicking in, because I had a bad feeling I knew exactly what he was here to collect. He was a Hunter. Had one truly just wandered down my lane and happened to sense Harper? I doubted it, but I didn't want to think too closely about the alternative right at this moment.

My instincts immediately urged me to summon my Iblis sword, but Gregory had warned me the price I'd pay for killing an angel. I'd gotten away with it once in self–defense, but I doubted I could claim that this time. I'd need to find some other, less lethal, way of disabling this guy.

"Well, shit! Of course I do. Come right on in, buddy!"

I flung the door wide open, ushering him in with a dramatic flourish. He hesitated, his eyes confused for a brief second. Then he walked in, scanning the room. I heard the sounds of dishes clanking in the kitchen, water running, young women chatting. The angel took a few steps forward, leaving his back open to me. Yep, that's what he thought of me. Iblis or not, I clearly wasn't even enough of a threat to warrant a defensive side stance. Idiot.

His eyes tracked Nyalla as she appeared from the kitchen at the far end of the room. She pivoted, calling something over her shoulder to Harper, and then turned to walk out one of the huge sets of French doors that lined the rear of my home. Her gaze passed right over the angel without any change of expression. I would have thought he had some glamor in place to shield himself from her eyes, except she didn't even acknowledge my presence. *Enemy angel at the door. Stay in the kitchen. Stay in the kitchen*, I silently chanted to Harper as I eyed the golf club Nyalla had placed beside the closet door.

Clearly Harper had the gift of telepathy, even if Nyalla did not. She walked out of the kitchen and promptly launched a carving knife at the angel.

The woman either had previous experience in a circus, or all that practice stabbing pillows had produced some amazing skills. The knife flipped through the air and sank hilt–deep into the angel's chest. I was as shocked as he was at this turn of events, but I had a faster recovery time — no doubt because I didn't have a knife sticking from between my ribs. Taking my cue from Harper, I hit the angel across the back of his head with the nine iron.

When Wyatt had shot Gregory, he'd barely reacted, but this guy was no ancient. He did a lovely face–plant onto the floor, landing with a satisfying thump. One of the things I learned early, as an imp growing up in Hel, was that if you wanted something to stay down, you needed to go far beyond what would normally suffice in terms of force. So I jumped forward and began whaling away at the angel with my golf club, which was starting to form an acute angle halfway down the shaft.

"Run!" If Harper didn't get her butt in gear, she was going to find herself in big trouble. I had no illusions that this angel was going to be subdued for any more than a few moments by human sporting equipment and a carving knife. He'd be up and running once the shock wore off, and if he got his hands on Harper, he'd teleport her away before I had a chance to intervene.

My assault on the angel didn't break the pregnant woman from her determined stance, but my one word did. She bolted for the rear of the house, holding several more items of sharp cutlery in her hand.

She'd barely gotten to the rear door before my prostrate angel recovered, rolling over to snatch the golf club and hurl it across the room. It just missed one of my windows — one of the windows newly replaced from The Ghoul Incident. But instead of dashing, or teleporting, after Harper as I expected, my uninvited guest turned on me.

"You *dare* to strike me?"

I dared so much that I did it again, this time with an umbrella from the stand next to the front door. It went the way of the nine iron. Then the angel hit me. Angels aren't much for using their corporeal forms in fighting, so instead of striking me with a fist, he blasted me with that damned white stuff that burned its way through flesh like a hot knife through butter. It tore through my chest, turning my heart into a smoking hole of nothingness. I'd gotten particularly good at surviving as a corpse, but not so good at the dead animation thing. I tried to give the angel my most menacing, Iblis–like glare, but I'm sure the effect was ruined by my body's downward crumple.

Snap out of it. I didn't have much time before he was off after Harper. No time to lie around on the floor, staring at the ceiling and trying in vain to move my limbs. I shook off the numbness and recreated my entire body with a noisy explosion that I hoped would slow the angel. Then I called my sword to hand. I didn't care what the other angels did to me; he'd attacked me with intent to kill. And I had a bad feeling about what he intended to do to Harper — and her unborn child — if he got his hands on her.

I suck at sword fighting, but I didn't have time to be creative, and this was the artifact's preferred form. So there I was, leaping to my feet and racing across my maple floor, stark naked, chasing an angel while awkwardly holding a two–foot sword. Normally I'd have no chance in catching an angel, but I'd gained a significant amount of speed when I got my wings. By the time he'd passed the stables and headed into the open field, I was within striking distance. Good thing, too, as I saw Harper ahead, running much slower with her awkward rolling gait.

As usual, I had no time. Swinging a sword at an opponent while running full speed doesn't allow for much accuracy, but the blade still sliced through his shirt and scored the flesh under it in a neat, diagonal line. The golf club assault had surprised but not hurt him. This had far more impact. The angel arched his spine, throwing his head backward and shrieking as the cut bled iridescent fluid down his back. He'd slowed abruptly with the strike, but my forward momentum wouldn't allow me to do the same. I slammed into his back, tackling him from behind. We rolled along the grass and rocks for several yards. When we finally stopped, I was underneath him, my sword arm pinned against my chest by his weight.

"They'll dust you for this," he hissed, keeping his full weight against my arm while trying to free his hands from under my shoulders. I launched my weight upward, tangling his legs in mine.

"Not if they never find your body." With a twist of my hips I shifted him slightly to the side — enough to free one of his hands, but not enough to free my sword arm.

I bucked as he tried to get his hand around my neck, and he sacrificed the attempt to brace himself with it, still using the force of his weight to pin my sword arm against me. That stupid slippery angel stuff was coating my raw energy, rendering me incapable of anything but a physical attack. Not that I seemed to be capable of a physical attack with him crushing the breath out of me. I continued to jerk and kick, hoping to dislodge him.

There was a flash off to my side, and the angel flew off me, launched several yards through the air by a flying pair of horse's hooves. Diablo. Who promptly disappeared like he always did. Not that I didn't appreciate his intervention. A blur raced past me, and a two–headed dog launched himself at the angel that had just dropped with a bounce to the ground. I scrambled to my feet, using the sword to pull myself upright. As much as I wanted to see Boomer take this angel apart, I didn't want him blamed. And, more importantly, I didn't want him to be hurt.

"Get back," I ordered. Boomer complied with a leap, but not before the angel recovered enough to launch a stream of white. What should have sliced my hellhound in half, burned along one side, removing flesh down to the bone from his head to hip.

Fucker had hurt my dog. No one hurts my dog. With a scream, I ran toward the angel, swinging my sword. He managed to leap to his feet before I reached him. Although my wild swings kept him dodging and ducking, they didn't seem to land any hits. We danced — me forward and the angel backward until his ass hit the wall of my barn. I swung, and he ducked, but that particular sword strike hadn't been meant for him; it had been aimed at a rope to his side.

The blade ripped through the nylon as if it was air, and with a whoosh, a sparkling net scooped the angel and hoisted him up. I smiled, thinking of how lucky I was to have a good relationship with a sorcerer for once, and grateful that I'd been paranoid enough after my banishment to install some special security measures around my earthly home.

I held still, sword at the ready and eyes on the bagged angel, just in case. These nets were meant to hold demons, and I wasn't sure how effective they'd be against an angel. I heard Boomer whine in the background and desperately wanted to go and repair his wounds, but he would have to wait.

The moving bulges in the net stilled, although it still swayed.

"You'll die for this," my captive said.

"Probably." I shrugged, even though he couldn't see it. "You won't be around for my execution, though. Which is of great comfort to me."

The bag jerked. "Do you know who I am?"

"The guy who assaulted me? The guy who intended to drag off a guest in my home to her death?"

I heard an exasperated snort. "*You* assaulted *me*! And I would not have killed the human female. She is not to blame for her situation."

Okay. Maybe I overreacted a bit. "And the baby she carries?"

"Nephilim are condemned to death. Article one nine two three eight, section forty–five, subsection twenty, item two ninety three."

Nope. Didn't overreact at all. I thought about arguing that the baby wasn't to blame for his or her situation either, that the only one to punish for this whole mess was a randy angel who couldn't keep his dick in his pants. Or keep from manifesting one at all. I knew there was little chance of winning that argument, so I spun around and headed for my dog.

Boomer was sprawled across the blood–red grass, his head in Nyalla's lap. The girl made soothing noises, stroking the parts of his face that hadn't been removed by the angel's blast. My fury returned, fanned even hotter when I saw Nyalla's tear–stained face.

"Will he … is he?"

"I'll fix him," I reassured her. "I've done it a million times before. He's a tough hellhound. He's survived worse."

"Can you heal him instead?"

I had no idea how she'd learned the difference. Healing was an angel–skill — one I'd recently acquired. I wasn't completely proficient at it, but it was more thorough and less painful than my demon repair abilities. There was one thing holding me back, though.

"I'm not kissing my dog."

Nyalla raised big blue pleading eyes to mine.

"Seriously. You know what he eats, and dogs don't floss, brush, or rinse with an ADA approved mouthwash. I saw him with a human limb last night. That thing had to have been rotting for at least two months. No way I'm putting my lips anywhere near his mouth."

The girl's eyes grew moist. A tear welled and rolled down her cheek to hover at the edge of her lip.

"Oh for fuck sake!" I grumbled as I stomped over to Boomer.

I was a demon. It wasn't like I hadn't had all sorts of nasty shit in my mouth before. Kissing Boomer probably wouldn't be any worse than that time I gave Grexil head. Blech.

It was worse than blowing a plague demon. Way worse. After I'd finished, Boomer jumped to his feet, tail wagging, while I was retching and spitting on the blood–soaked grass. It was worth it to see Nyalla's joy as she hugged the hellhound.

"What are you going to do with him?" Nyalla waved a hand toward the barn.

Glancing again at the bagged angel swinging around like an oversized piñata, I shrugged. "Leave him there? It's probably safer than cutting him down and trying to duct tape him in my basement."

The girl nodded. "I guess if anyone asks, you can just say you're disciplining a member of your household."

It was so nice to be living with a human who truly understood demons.

"Any idea where Harper may have gone?" For all I knew, the woman could be halfway to Idaho. It would solve a lot of problems if she kept on running and never came back, but I'd vowed to protect her and the baby. I might be just as likely as humans to default on my loans, but I couldn't renege on a vow.

"She was headed toward the Calloway's farm." Nyalla pointed toward the fence line where our neighbors lived, just out of sight. "How do you think the angel found out about her and tracked her here?"

There were only two angels who knew about Harper's condition, and I couldn't believe the baby's father would have risked his offspring, as well as his own life, by spilling the beans. That left only one angel, and my heart twisted to think of that possibility. Gregory loved me, but that didn't stop him from fulfilling his duty as part of the Ruling Council. I couldn't exactly interrogate him without letting it slip that I had a Hunter angel I was holding captive, so I'd have to play my cards close to my chest and watch him carefully. And hope with all my heart that what I was suspecting wasn't true.

~9~

"You're not safe here." I paced while Harper and Nyalla sat at my dining room table, watching me closely. The pregnant woman was pale, her mouth tight. She kept drifting a hand across her abdomen, pausing low as if to reassure herself that the baby was still there.

"She's not safe anywhere." Nyalla voiced the words none of us wanted to say. "They'll send someone else, and although that angel didn't want to enter your house uninvited, he would have if you'd refused him entry."

Harper's fingers curled against her stomach. "At least you have some way to fight them off. I'm useless against them. Most everyone is useless against them."

I eyed her speculatively. "There has to be some safe place, some way of hiding from them. Angels fall with hypocritical regularity. I can't believe every one of their offspring is aborted."

"I don't know." Harper frowned, staring down at her knuckles. "All I know is that he wanted to take my baby from me as soon as it was born and give it to some monsters to raise. I'd never have seen my son again."

What monsters? Her words made me think that there must be Nephilim somewhere, and at least some of the angels knew where. "What did Baby–Daddy plan to do with you during your pregnancy?"

She shook her head. "He didn't seem too worried about it until this past week. I'd argued with him before and told him

I wasn't going to give up the baby, ran away even, but he didn't say anything about me being in danger until he brought me over here."

I blew out a pent–up breath I hadn't realized I'd been holding. Maybe Gregory hadn't betrayed me. Maybe the secret had leaked before Harper had even shown up at my door.

"Will more angels come?" Nyalla gnawed her bottom lip. "I saw you fighting that one. If you hadn't had an elven net, I'm not sure you would have won."

She was right. Even with the Iblis sword, I sucked in this sort of combat. Mentally I calculated how many elven nets I'd need to order then began to laugh somewhat hysterically as I envisioned angels strung up from trees all over my property. Harper and Nyalla both looked at me, confusion in their eyes.

"Sorry. I'm sure this is just the beginning, which brings us back to finding a safe place for Harper. Maybe these monsters would take you in. If they can manage to hide Nephilim, they should be able to hide a pregnant woman."

"I won't. I won't." Harper's voice rose, shrill with panic and anger. Nyalla reached out to capture her restless hand.

So much for that idea. "Or I could send you to Hel. Totally safe from angels. All you'd have to worry about there is demons dismembering you, or elves enslaving you."

The woman didn't look any more enthusiastic about that idea.

Neither did Nyalla. "She's *not* going to Hel. I'd never condemn another human to that, even if it's just for the last few months of her pregnancy."

I frowned. It wouldn't be just the last few months of her pregnancy; it would be for her whole life. The baby's too. If Harper wanted to keep this child, Hel was the safest place to do it. And the irony of Hel being the safest alternative wasn't lost on me.

"There are a group of humans that chose to remain there, free in their own lands, Nyalla. She could learn Elvish, raise her baby there."

"And do what?" she argued. "Harper would be in the same position I'm in, not speaking a word of their language, not possessing any skills of value. Plus, what about the baby? What are Nephilim like? Do they have the same volatile nature as demon newborn? What demon would you trust to guide it and teach it control? Or would you foster the child out to dwarves like the rest of your race? Once someone realized the baby was half–angel, there would be a price on the child's head."

She was right. Every demon would want the status of having a half–angel in their household. Damn.

"I'm not going to Hel." Harper's eyes glittered with determination, and although she spoke as if she meant Hel the place, I got the feeling she also meant hell the metaphysical concept.

"Then what do you propose?" I was frustrated. As much as I loved the idea of beating the shit out of angels, I doubted I could hold them off for long. And if the Ruling Council got involved... .

"I want to stay here." Harper glanced over at me, and I couldn't' miss the tentative trust in her eyes. "You didn't turn me over to that angel. You told me to run. You risked yourself and your hellhound to defend me. And at the end of it all, the angel who came to kill my child is hanging from your barn. I want to stay here. With you."

Well, I guess I better hone up on my angel smack–down skills. "I've vowed to take care of you and the baby. And your boots. But there are limits to my abilities. I can't guarantee that eventually some angel isn't going to get past me and grab you."

She clenched her jaw and lifted her chin. "I'll take my chances."

I took a deep breath, thinking that her chances were slim. "Okay. Now, we need to consider who leaked the information of Harper's pregnancy to the angels, and how widespread the knowledge of it may be." There wasn't a scheduled Ruling Council meeting for another two decades, but shit kept coming up that prompted unexpected ones. I didn't want to be blindsided by an impromptu meeting where I was accused of harboring someone in violation of one nine four whatever.

Harper stared at me with dark, thoughtful eyes, raising one of her hands to gnaw at a stump of fingernail. "I don't know. Ben began to be worried about my safety this past week, so maybe someone followed him to my house, or noticed him slipping out of Aaru."

"Would he have told anyone?" I was grasping at straws. "He wanted you to give the child up. What better way than having an angel show up with abortion on his mind to convince you that the baby needed to be elsewhere for its safety?"

She shook her head. "I can't see that. He wouldn't risk the child to scare me into compliance. And I doubt he'd trust any angel with his secret."

So that left some mysterious angel that followed him, suspected him. Or Gregory.

"There's always the possibility that someone saw Harper and told." Nyalla wrinkled her nose in thought. "I don't think any of my friends who've seen Harper, or the delivery guys, would have connections in Aaru. Were there any demon or angel messengers that have been by in the last week? Would they perhaps have sensed Harper's pregnancy somehow?"

I shook my head. There hadn't been a demon over from Hel since before Harper arrived, and the only angelic visitors I'd had were Gregory and Raphael. Rafi hadn't even entered the house. There's no way he could have sensed Harper.

"We'll just need to be on guard. I don't know if our captive angel told anyone else about Harper's location. I don't know who he works for. I don't even know which choir he's with."

"Are we going to interrogate him?" Nyalla looked uneasy at the prospect.

"*I'm* going to interrogate him. You're both going to stay here in the house with Boomer by your side."

As stinky as my hellhound was, I knew he'd defend both girls to the death — especially Nyalla. There were going to be times when I would need to be away, and I hated leaving them vulnerable. I'd need to make some sort of arrangements for their protection for those occasions when I was locked up in Aaru, or in a Ruling Council meeting, or at the gym.

I made one quick detour to call Dar before heading out to chat with the suspended angel. The elven net with its contents still swung side–to–side, with more movement than the slight breeze would warrant.

"I'm back," I announced.

"Oh, my heart sings with joy."

Dude had a sense of humor. I stared up at him, wondering what to do. I couldn't risk cutting him down and releasing him from the net, but up there I couldn't see his expression or his reactions to my questions.

"I'm a bit insulted you came alone. I'd always assumed if angels were going to attack the Iblis, they'd raise an army. Instead they send one of you? Shit, I need to step up my game a bit."

He didn't rise to the bait. "Why won't you just hand her over? Let me down and give me the human. I assure you, no harm will come to her. She won't even remember any of this. It's the kindest thing to do — to leave no trace, no memory of our interference in her life."

Kind? He was appealing to my kindness? "No way, Jack. I'm hanging onto her until she has this baby. A half–angel in my household? Totally rocking. Plus I can blackmail the father, and rub the noses of all those Ruling Council assholes in it every meeting. I may just take to hauling the kid around with me to piss them off."

I heard him sigh. "Right. You're seriously going to raise a baby. It'll be dead in two days with you as a foster parent."

He had a point. I had no fucking idea how to raise a child — human or otherwise.

"If it's blackmail and proof of hypocrisy you want, you've got it. Let me down. Let me do my job, and I'll give you the Nephilim's body. It would be far easier to carry around a corpse, and you could still shock everyone at the next Ruling Council meeting."

"Nah. A live baby would create so much more of a ruckus than a dead one. And you look very nice hanging outside my barn door."

The bag jerked and danced. I eyed the rope, wondering if I should reinforce it.

"I'm not the only Hunter," he thundered. "There will be another on the trail soon, and once it's discovered you're harboring the Nephilim, there *will* be an army at your door."

Ah, just what I wanted to know. I'd be facing one at a time. Now if only I could find out how they knew about the baby and where Harper was, I could nip this whole thing in the bud.

"Who do you report to?"

Dead silence. I wasn't surprised, but figured I'd go ahead and ask more questions he'd refuse to answer.

"What choir are you in? How did you know there was a Nephilim, and that the woman carrying the baby was here?"

Nothing.

"Do you know who the father is? Did he put you up to this in order to scare Harper into giving the baby up?"

"Seriously? I'm tasked with killing Nephilim, not scaring innocent human women into sinful compliance. If the sire wanted to do that, he wouldn't be working with me."

At least that got a response. This Ben angel wasn't off the hook, though. I hadn't liked his attitude from the moment I saw him at my door, and Harper's story just lowered him further in my estimation. No, angel–boy wasn't about to let some demon raise his child. He was up to something. But in the meantime, I needed to know more about this angel swinging from the side of my barn, and what I might be facing in the next few months.

I watched sunlight glint off the bag, sending spots of color onto the side of the barn. It might remind me of a disco ball right now, but my original impression had been piñata, and that's what I was going with.

The wooden handle of the pitchfork hit the net with a solid thump. The angel grunted as he swung wildly around. I kept up my rhythm, demanding answers to my questions in time with each blow. No candy came out, but a drop of iridescent liquid formed and fell to the ground. I hesitated, eyeing it with surprise. He was bleeding. He wasn't healing. I knew these nets kept us from using our raw energy to repair wounds, but I'd never imagined they'd keep angels from healing themselves.

"Sad way for an angel to die." I poked the bag a few times to make my point. "Beaten to death by a demon while hanging in a sack."

"You'll be signing your death warrant if you kill me," he snapped.

"Hmm. An angel body is found bruised and bloodied, with no sign of demon attack. What makes you think they'd suspect me? Your death would be a great mystery, pondered for millennia, the subject of all sorts of academic papers and conspiracy theories up in Aaru."

His silence dragged on. "Fourth choir. I report through the Grigori chain of command."

I felt suddenly chilled. He didn't just report to Gregory, he was part of his choir. Had my own angel betrayed me? No, I wouldn't believe that. If he wanted Harper, he would have just taken her the other night as I'd slept. It couldn't be Gregory, but having one of his angels hanging from my barn wasn't going to make him a happy angel.

~10~

"Tell me about Ben."

Harper and Nyalla were sitting on my couch, each facing a different direction to better watch the entrances to my house. I noticed the pregnant woman was once again clutching a knife, several others jammed through her belt. Boomer, the most effective of their weapons, snoozed on the floor, his body half under the coffee table.

The dark–haired woman pursed her lips. "I really don't know much about him. I originally thought he worked at the hospital in Alaska, but after I went back to Colorado, he was there. Strange — in any other circumstance, I would have thought he was some creepy stalker, but I was always so happy when he was around. It was a fuzzy kind of happy, like when you've had a few too many glasses of wine."

Angels. No doubt Ben had worked his mojo on the woman. I'd seen Gregory entrance humans to get his way in airports and shopping malls. If Baby–Daddy had even one–tenth of his power, it was no wonder Harper had fallen in line with whatever he wanted.

"I went back to work, but I felt like I was going through the motions. I didn't climb, didn't hike, didn't want to do anything but be with him." Harper's eyes narrowed. "Now I look back and wonder who that was. It seems like I was watching someone else living my life. It wasn't me."

"What did you do together?" Nyalla asked. "Besides have sex, obviously."

Harper didn't seem disturbed by the girl's bluntness. "I ... I don't know. I remember going out to eat, although, now that I think about it, he never ate or drank anything. He just watched me."

Creepy. Yeah, Gregory watched me sleep sometimes, but I always called him out on it. "How did you find out your boyfriend was an angel?"

"When I got pregnant." Harper bit her lip and turned her head, hiding her eyes from me. "As soon as I saw those two purple lines on the test, it was like I'd received a shot of sanity — like I woke up from whatever groggy state I was in. I wasn't ready for a baby, and we'd never discussed marriage or anything long–term, so when I told him the news, I proposed getting an abortion."

Nyalla caught her breath and held Harper's hand with a reassuring squeeze.

The woman smiled at her and continued. "Ben went crazy. These huge wings exploded from his back in a swirl of gold light, and he glowed. For the first time since I'd met him, I was afraid. He told me there would be no abortion, and if I ever even thought of such a thing again, he'd take away my freedom and lock me up somewhere."

"Asshole," I snarled. "I hope you hit him in the face."

"Nah. I stabbed one of his wings with a butcher knife."

I liked this woman. I liked her a lot.

"He screamed and batted his wings around. There was pinkish–white blood flying everywhere. It burned holes in my carpet and drywall where it splattered. Then he disappeared. I packed a bag and was gone within five minutes."

"How long did it take him to find you?" She was carrying his baby, and I was pretty sure he'd marked her somehow. Baby–Daddy was probably on her before she reached the city limits.

"Five months."

"Five months?" I sputtered. This angel sucked.

"I know! He always seemed to know where I was before — which coffee shop I went to, stores I shopped in. Even if I did something completely impromptu, Ben always knew where I was and when. By the time he caught up with me in Boston, he looked like he'd been put through a wringer. I almost felt sorry for him."

"Five months?" What the hell? I glanced down at the woman's rounded stomach and wondered if her pregnancy somehow negated the ownership mark, or if the unborn child was instinctively protecting his mother. Gregory said she would benefit from the Nephilim's power until it was born. No doubt that was Harper's feeling of 'waking up', why Ben couldn't locate her.

"He was contrite, affectionate, and ecstatic that I was obviously still pregnant. We'd be together always, he told me, but something had changed inside me. I could see beyond his beauty and loving words. I didn't trust him."

"When did he start insisting you give the baby away?" Nyalla asked, still holding Harper's hand.

"This past week. Like I mentioned, he started getting nervous that I needed to go somewhere, and that's when he 'informed' me I would be giving the baby up." Harper's mouth set in a firm line.

So he could no longer track Harper — at least not as easily as he'd once done, and he couldn't influence her. Somehow I doubted Ben was giving up that easily. I planned on poking this angel a bit, just to see what was inside him, but I had one last question to ask Harper.

"What made you decide that shacking up with a demon was better than these 'monsters'?"

She shrugged, a smile at the edge of her lips. "If an angel could be this much of a jerk, I doubted a demon could be much worse."

Fair enough. "You both stay here with Boomer. I'll be back in an hour, tops."

"Are you going to interrogate the angel again?" Nyalla asked.

"Yep." I was, only not the angel hanging outside in a bag.

I saddled up Diablo, giving my angel piñata another poke as we headed out the barn and across the fields. Once I felt I was far enough away, I dismounted and took the little green glass ball from my pocket.

"Okay, Baby–Daddy, time to answer some questions." I crushed it in my hand, pulverizing it with the aid of a small bit of energy. Gold swirled out from between my clenched fingers, rising up past the treetops before vanishing.

Nothing. But it's not like I expected an instant summoning, or anything. I sat down with my back against a boulder and watched cat videos on my cell phone while Diablo grazed by my side. I was beginning to wonder if I would need to call Nyalla and extend my hour to several when an angel appeared in a flash of light.

"Bout damned time." I stood and stretched, sliding my phone into the back pocket of my jeans. "Three favors don't mean shit if it takes you forty minutes to respond when I call."

The angel folded his arms in front of him with a show of arrogance. "Favor. I'll show up when I can, but I'm not going to come racing to your side every time you call. Now, what do you want?"

"A Hunter showed up this morning and attacked us. Harper is gone."

He blanched, which was an impressive feat given his customary pallor. "What? Gone where? Is the baby safe?"

Baby. Not 'is Harper safe'. Asshole. "I was hoping you'd be able to track her. She is carrying your baby, after all."

"I can't!" Ben struggled to control himself. "As soon as I impregnated her ... the baby must be imparting some of his skills to her."

Just as I'd thought. "I managed to catch the Hunter, but I can't safeguard Harper per my vow if I can't find her."

The angel relaxed. "You killed the Hunter? There won't be another for a few days at the most. She can't have gone far. She doesn't know anyone in this area and has no money. I'll track her down."

"Maybe she'll come back." I watched the angel closely.

He shook his head, a smug smile on his face. "Maybe not. She knows you can't protect her. She must be terribly afraid. If the Iblis can't protect her, she won't have any other option."

No option but to do what this angel wanted of her — give up her baby into his safekeeping.

"But I did protect her. I can take care of any other Hunter that shows up. It's no big deal for me to take them out one at a time. She's safe."

I practically heard him grind his teeth. "How long can you keep this up, though? No, she's not safe here." Ben took a few steps back and looked around him, as if he expected to see Harper running across the field. "I'll track her down, but her safety is on your head, demon. If you fail to protect her, there will be no favors."

He vanished, and I watched Diablo graze. This time the smug smile was on my face. The trap was set. Now I had only to wait. And keep Harper safe from harm.

~11~

Dar!" I grabbed my foster brother in a tight hug. He bit me on the shoulder hard enough to draw blood — a more demonic greeting than the one I was using.

"I got the goods." He waved what looked like a shopping bag at me. "Relayed your problem to Gareth, and he sent you cool shit."

I knew the sorcerer would come through for me. Grabbing the bag, I started removing items. Three elven nets, a velvet sack holding black crystal marbles, a wand, an elf button, and a silver collar. I shivered as I touched the collar, remembering the feel of having one around my own neck. As much as I hated to see the thing, I couldn't exactly keep that angel in a bag forever. Besides, I needed the extra nets in case more of them showed up.

"You're lucky he had one." Dar nodded toward the collar. "No one knows how to make them anymore, and all the others were destroyed in an unexpected explosion."

Unexpected for the elves. Not so unexpected for Dar and his buddies.

"Awesome. Help me get this guy down, will you?"

Dar trailed after me as we skirted the pool and headed for the barn. Once there, he smiled appreciatively at my handiwork.

"Is he filled with candy?"

It was amazing how much we thought alike. "Nah. I hit him a bunch of times and all he did was bleed. Grab the end of that rope and—."

I watched the angel plummet to the ground, shrieking the whole way. Dar was holding the end of a singed rope in one hand.

"Oops."

"Here." I extended my hand and Dar took the collar from me.

I had this vague idea that I'd restrain the angel — physically as well as with my newfound angel skills, while Dar removed the net and secured him with the collar. My captive was a whole lot older than me, but I hoped my position on the Ruling Council as the Iblis would give me some kind of hierarchy edge over him. I nodded to Dar, mouthing the words *one, two, three.*

Jumping on top of the angel, I wrapped my hands around what I hoped was his neck and held him down. Dar pulled open the top of the net and we both saw a pair of feet.

"Damn it, Mal, you're sitting on his head."

I had my hands wrapped around his ankles, too. I scooted forward a bit, wiggling around as Dar shifted the net to get to the angel's head. As soon as the guy's face was free, he lunged up and bit me on the ass.

"Hurry the fuck up!" Tears came to my eyes as the angel bit down harder and worked a foot loose to kick me in the face.

"Got him!"

I was hoping the collar had the same effect on angels as it did demons. After all, the net worked. Wrangling his legs into a better position, I twisted my ass free and felt Dar remove the net from the angel.

All hell broke loose. Free of the elven net, he launched into a frenzied physical attack. I was surprised — angels, in my experience, didn't tend to have any sort of pugilist or martial–arts skills. This one did. The right hook to my kidney doubled me over, and an amazingly strong abdominal move launched me forward to smash my nose into his sharp, bony knee. I saw stars, and in a frenzy of motion, he'd dumped me off of him.

"Whoa! We've got a lively one here!"

Dar sounded cheerful. As I rolled over and jumped to my feet, I saw why. The collar worked. The angel wasn't teleporting, wasn't launching white stuff at us, wasn't doing anything but dance around like a junkie high on smack, yanking futilely at the band of silver around his neck.

We circled, jumping forward to try and get a good hold on him. In spite of his distress over the collar, he still managed to fight us off, landing some admirable blows. Fuck this. It was time to bring out the big guns. I reached behind me and grabbed two poles, tossing one to Dar.

They were cable slip snares mounted on poles, commonly used to catch gators. Not that we had gators in Maryland, but any state with a sizable hunting population carried supplies for any sport.

"Wish we had a snatch hook," Dar grumbled.

Me too. Or a bang stick. I didn't want to risk injuring the angel further, though — especially when he'd be unable to heal himself. Eventually I'd have to kill him, but as long as he was alive, I might be able to use him as a bargaining chip. And keep from signing my own execution warrant.

With alligators, the best position to snare is past the head, where the front legs can be pinned to the body. When they thrash and roll, there's leverage and no crack–the–whip effect like there would be if the snare was around their jaws. I'd planned to do the same with the angel, and since he didn't have a tail, I hoped Dar could loop his legs once I got him down.

The angel might know how to swing his fists, but he had no fucking idea what we were going to do with our poles. He kept attempting defensive maneuvers, as if we were going to bust out a shaolin move on him from a kung fu movie. Dar noticed it too, and with a dramatic swing of his stick that would have done Jackie Chan proud, he distracted the angel. I looped him and tightened the noose around his shoulders. Instead of dropping and rolling like a gator, he charged me. I ran backwards, trying to keep my line tight so it wouldn't slip down. With his attention on me, Dar managed to run up and trip the angel, giving him the perfect opening to loop his legs.

We had him. Silver collar around his neck, my snare holding his shoulders, and Dar's holding his legs around the knees. We dragged him with some difficulty back toward the barn, and I jammed the end of my stick into a flag holder. Dar held his end taught, drawing the angel out full length between the two poles. I jumped over our prey to run into the barn and grab two silver rolls off a bench before dashing back out.

"Hurry the fuck up." Dar's arm muscles bulged as he held the angel in place. When had he gotten so buff? Normally my brother liked to sport a nice layer of fat to reinforce his rich–and–lazy status, but in the past few months it had all disappeared to be replaced with sinewy muscle.

I blinked, regaining my focus, and straddled the angel. Then I began to duct tape his arms to his torso, and his legs together. By the time I was done, he resembled a shiny, gray mummy. For good measure, I even slapped a piece over his mouth. I'd need him to talk later, but ripping it off his face would be so much fun.

We both stood back, panting as we admired our hog–tied (or rather hog–taped) angel.

"Where do you want him?"

I was tempted to reply that I wanted him mounted over my fireplace, but over the last few years I'd managed to acquire a small measure of self–preservation.

"Basement."

Dar grunted, and we both grabbed our respective poles, dragging the duct–taped angel across the flagstone, in through the French doors, and down the stairs to my cellar. There we left him, snares and all, and ventured back upstairs for a cold beer. Hey, we deserved it.

We sat in companionable silence on the sectional sofa, sipping our beers and catching our breath. Now that Dar was part of my household, I saw him more than I used to. It was a perk, in my opinion. He might get me into hot water with every breath he took, but I loved him. Life was more fun with Dar around.

"Dude, thanks for bringing my crap over from Gareth. And thanks for helping with that angel."

He raised his glass in a toast. "Anytime you want me to beat the shit out of an angel, just call. I'm always up for that sort of action."

I hid a smile behind my bottle of Bud Light. "How are things back home?"

Home. Hel. Which was only one of the places I seemed to be considering home lately. There was my place here, and that weird spot in the fourth circle of Aaru that I unintentionally transported myself to every time I tried to gate somewhere. Was it normal to have three homes? And since when did I give a shit about what was normal?

Dar took a long pull on his beer, draining half the bottle in one gulp. "Mal, you need to get your ass back to Hel and deal with all the shit you stirred up. There's only so much Leethu and I can do in your absence. Li is putting all sorts of ridiculous conditions on freeing their humans; there was an assassination attempt on Taullian, and Kllee refuses to close their traps, saying they're exempt since they allow humans to return home if they wish."

Stupid elves. Pointy–eared motherfuckers would be the death of me.

"I can't. Most of the stuff Gareth sent over is to protect a human I've vowed to defend. The Ruling Council bullshit has increased tenfold, and I can't leave her with only a wand and Boomer while I'm in Hel for weeks."

Dar shook his head. "Well, everything is going to Aaru in a handbasket."

I winced. Shit. Shit. I just couldn't manage everything I'd taken on. Too many irons in the fire, bitten off more than I could chew, and all those other clichés.

"How is the human settlement working out?"

"Okay so far. Even with Ahriman dead, Gareth and the other magicians have developed a solid trade with the other demons. They've got protection under your name and that of a few high–level demons, which extends to the humans living in the settlement."

At least that was going well. Hopefully all the trouble with the elves could wait until Harper gave birth. Not that I expected the shit storm to end when the baby was born.

"Do you remember Dregvant?" Dar's eyes sparkled, which let me know he'd moved on to a particularly juicy piece of gossip. My brother loved to stir the pot and especially loved showing off how he knew everyone else's business. "He's been running around bragging that he has a breeding contract with an angel."

My eyes about left my head. This cut a bit close to home given what Raphael and I had discussed. Not that I should be surprised it was coming up in conversation. Rumors of my and Gregory's relationship were all over Hel, and the angels were certainly buzzing about it in Aaru too. It was just a matter of time before this sort of thing would be attempted. If it weren't someone stretching the truth, that is. Demons lied, but that seemed to be way too creative for Dregvant.

"Who? When? Where?"

Dar's grin was smug. He prided himself on knowing all the good stuff. "A minor angel named Eirnilius."

I'd never heard of him. "Are you sure?"

Some of the angels had gotten together and decided to end the long infertility spell in heaven by capturing demons and parting them out for breeding purposes. That I could see. What I couldn't see was one of them deciding to do the nasty and breed the more traditional way. Gregory aside, most angels agreed with the separations imposed by the treaty we'd both signed two–and–a–half–million years ago. Rumors, yeah. Some demon trying to make himself look important by lying, yeah. An actual breeding contract? No.

"He's got some knowledge and baubles that I can't see him getting any other way." Dar grinned, slouching back into the sofa cushions.

"Eirnilius." I finished off my beer and sat it with a clink on the coffee table. "You wouldn't happen to know anything else about this angel, would you?"

If I could manage to get some dirt on the angels, then maybe I could leverage it for Harper's protection. Or my protection for harboring her and the Nephilim. Or just rub their smug hypocritical faces in it. I'd been jumping through their four–nine–five hoops, trotting back and forth to their angel prison for the last two years. Time for some paybacks.

"Well, he's from the first choir."

My breath lodged in my throat, and my heart raced like a Formula One car. The first choir belonged to Gabriel. Pious, sanctimonious piece–of–shit Gabriel. What I wouldn't give to hold this one over his head. If only I was sure it was true. Oh, by the fates, let it be true.

"How would they have met? Is this Eirnilus one of Gregory's staff? Or a gate guardian? They're the only angels I know of that would have enough contact with demons to negotiate this sort of thing."

Dar lifted a shoulder and drained the rest of his beer. "I don't know, although I was thinking the same. Bet you'd like to catch him, huh? An angel violating the treaty — it would definitely ruffle feathers on the Ruling Council."

I recognized the tone in Dar's voice and nodded, trying for an air of mild interest. "Well, yeah. But I'd need proof. Can't exactly put my ass on the line with a bunch of rumors, now, can I?"

"I've got proof, but it will cost you."

This was the Dar I knew and loved. "Cost me *what*, exactly?"

My brother waved his empty beer bottle at me. "I'll get to that later. Do we have a deal?"

I sighed and gave him my vow, with the standard disclaimers, terms, and conditions.

"They're to meet tomorrow at this address."

I took the offered slip of skin parchment, noting the location with amusement. Gabriel was going to shit a brick if this was true. The thought filled me with unholy glee. But as much as I wanted to rub this in that smug bastard's face, I didn't want to have this whole thing backfire on me.

"So? An angel and a demon meet. This Eirnilius could always claim it was an accidental meeting, and that he was going to kill Dregvant, or report him or something. This isn't worth much to me."

"Dregvant claims to have a proposed breeding contract signed with Eirnilius' sigil."

Now *that* was something. Even if it turned out to not be true, it was worth my time to check into it and see what I could find.

"Did I mention how much I love you, Dar? You're my most favorite brother ever?"

He squirmed and glared at me. Those were fighting words among demons, but Dar knew I was just being my usual, irritating self.

"Yeah, well you're going to have to live without the services of my glorious self for a few months. I need a vacation. Like right now. That's my payment for this information."

"What about the elven kingdoms you're overseeing? You're my main demon in Hel, Dar. Can't this wait?"

He snarled, and I saw weariness beneath the show of ferocity. "Damn it all, Mal. Get someone else to do your shit. Persilium, or one of Ahriman's former household — they're eager to prove themselves to you. We had a deal. You gave me your vow."

He'd busted ass for me the last year, which more than made up for all the hot water he'd gotten me into with Haagenti. It was sort of his fault I was saddled with this stupid sword and Iblis title, but he'd been more loyal than any demon I'd ever known. And he really did need a vacation.

"Okay, okay. Don't get your tail in a knot. Vacation it is. I have no idea where I'm going to put you, though. I've got a house full of humans right now. Do you mind sleeping in the baby nursery? Or maybe you can crash on the sofa?"

Dar wrinkled his nose. "You're fucking kidding me, Mal. I don't want to vacation at your house. You'll be knee deep in some shit by breakfast tomorrow and dragging me into it with you. I'll be in Chicago. If you need me, call Leethu. Or Radl. Or anyone but me."

Chicago. I gave him a suspicious glance. "Why Chicago?"

He stared meaningfully at the empty bottle. I opened a full beer and passed it to him. "There are a couple of politicians I need to meet with, and a building on the west side that is in sorry need of redecorating."

Corruption and blowing up a high rise. Standard stuff for Dar, but I had to be sure. "There's also a big security conference going on."

Dar snorted. "Yeah. Right. Not my thing at all. Your human is more likely to be crashing computers and embezzling funds than I am." He gave me a sharp, perceptive look. "Ah, so the lovely Wyatt will be in Chicago. Hmm. I wonder if he'd like to play."

My voice dropped several octaves. "Dar, if you lay one furry paw on him, if you even speak to him, I'll rip you to shreds. Understood?"

Dar grinned. "Okay, okay. Don't get *your* tail in a knot. He's your toy. I'll respect your ownership. Besides, I'll have my hands full with my own activities. I'm not about to waste my time at some stupid security conference."

Fair enough. I slugged him in the shoulder, just to emphasize my point. He slugged me back then picked up the television remote to surf the channels. Looking down at the slip of paper in my hand, I chuckled, thinking of Garbiel's face if this whole wild tale was true. Either way, Dregvant wasn't going to be the only demon at this meeting.

I walked Dar out to his rental car and watched him head down the road. By the time I'd made it back inside, Nyalla and Harper were already downstairs, pawing through the goodies on the table like it was Christmas morning and Santa had filled their stockings with candy.

"What does this one do?"

They were practically dancing with excitement over the magical toys. I held my breath as Nyalla snatched up the wand and waved it around like she was Harry Potter.

"No, don't!" I grabbed it and put it reverently back on the table. "For fuck sake, you could have frozen me in this form. That wand doesn't require an incantation, only blood."

"Blood?" She squealed, her eyes wide. "So I slice up my thumb and freeze people in a block of ice?"

"No." I moved the bag of black marbles further from Harper, trying to encourage her to play with one of the nets instead. They were safer. "Slice up your thumb, or bite a hang–nail, and I'll be stuck in this form without access to my demon powers for a week. It only works on demons, although I'm hoping it may work on angels too."

"And those?" Harper reached for the marbles, and I again moved them out of her reach.

"Throw them and they explode on impact."

The woman's eyes grew large. I got the feeling she'd found something she might like better than the kitchen knives stashed in her belt.

"It's not really the explosion that damages us, although that hurts like fuck. The marbles release a spell that acts as a hallucinogenic. It's disorienting, distracting, but, other than that, the results are unpredictable. I might see maggots crawling all over my body, or feel like I've been weighted down and can't move."

Nyalla pursed her lips, touching one of the marbles with a gentle finger. "Illusion?"

"Yeah, but it's not strictly visual. We feel it, smell it — it affects all of our senses, even our perception of energy. Again, I'm not sure it will have the same effect, or even work, on angels."

"Worth a shot." Harper put her hands on her hips and eyed the items with satisfaction. "The net worked. From what I saw of you dragging that Hunter angel into the cellar, the collar–thingie works."

"I hope so." I put a hand on Nyalla's shoulder and smiled down at her. "There will be times when I won't be around, and I want you all to feel free to use these on any angels that show up at the house. Except my angel."

I knew it was a bit of a sweeping statement to lump every visiting angel into the 'threat' category, but I'd rather these girls be safe than dead. The dude in the basement swore he wasn't going to hurt Harper, but who's to say another angel might not feel differently. For a second, I imagined Nyalla using the wand on Raphael while Harper stabbed him full of holes. Yeah, that would be a tough one to explain. It would suck if I ever had to fill out one of *those* reports.

~12~

Dregvant was easy to spot. Of all the men in the place, he was the only one wearing mismatched, garishly colored Ed Hardy shirt, pants, and jacket. Every inch of tanned flesh was covered with more bling than a trophy wife. It hurt my eyes to look at him. And if that didn't clue me in that he was a demon, the fact that he was snorting a line of coke in the middle of a Chuck E Cheese did.

I made my way through the crowds of sugar and adrenaline–fueled children to the table where he sat, just a few chairs down from little Dallas, who was celebrating his fifth birthday.

"Go away, kid," he muttered, not even looking up to see that the human appearance I wore was considerably older than the children squealing three feet away.

I waved a hand, more for drama than any need for magical gesture, and the cocaine vanished. That got his attention. The demon snarled, but his glare changed into shock when he met my eyes and realized who I was. Then he tried to bolt, knocking his chair backwards as he rose.

"Whoa there, buddy." I clamped a hand on his shoulder, and he dropped to the floor on his ass. One of the benefits of my new mutated–demon state was that I had the nifty ability to restrict a demon's energy usage as long as I was touching him. That silicon–like shit had always been Gregory's way to subdue me, and I was happy to have this as a new skill, even if it only worked on demons.

"Freak." He snarled.

I was a freak. The only Angel of Chaos in over two–million years. And my wings were threatening to erupt into their fifty–foot feathered glory any second. I struggled to keep control, not wanting to tip off the other being I planned to accost this afternoon.

"You're in trouble." I tried to interject a conspiratorial note into my voice. "Eirnilius was discovered, and he sold you out for a reduced sentence. The enforcers will be here any second."

"Fuck!" Now he really was panicking, squirming on the floor as he searched for the nearest exits.

"They've surrounded the building," I whispered. "I can gate you out of here to safety, but it will cost you."

"How much? How much?"

I hid a smile at his squeaky tone. "A favor. Oh, and give me the breeding contract. If you get caught with that on you, you're worse than dead. They'll haul you up to Aaru and stick you in some prison to torture you with paperwork — two–hundred–page four–nine–five reports with impact analysis and everything. It goes on and on. The paperwork is never complete, or never done to their satisfaction. You'll be there for all eternity filling it out and re–doing it endlessly."

I shuddered for effect, and his eyes widened.

"Aaru? And … paperwork? Oh fuck, not that! You've got a deal." Dregvant frantically dug the folded parchment from his waistband and thrust it at me.

I quickly checked its legitimacy, keeping one hand firmly on the demon. In a flash, we were gone, and just as quickly I'd returned — thankfully managing to reappear in the same spot and not suspended from the ceiling or sprawled across the salad bar. Just in time, too — Eirnilius was as easy to spot as Dregvant had been, although for different reasons.

Angels never really blended in well with the humans. Eirnilius looked like a living statue with poorly fitting clothing and shoulder–length blond curls. He smiled kindly at the children that knocked into him in their haste to redeem their game tickets. I felt a moment of guilt for what I was about to do. I wanted this sort of contact to occur between angels and demons. I was working with Rafi to try and bring about this change. But Dregvant was an absolute ass. If there were demons that should be fucking angels, he wouldn't be anywhere near the top of my list. I was doing this Eirnilius guy a favor. Really.

And hey, he was an angel breaking the rules. No matter what punishment he got, it would be far more lenient than the death penalty dealt to us demons when *we* were caught. Yeah. That made me feel so much better about busting him. Almost made me feel better.

I shook my head to clear away the guilty thoughts. Now came the tricky part. Approaching the angel would be easy — I was pretty stealthy in my human form. It was apprehending him that would be touch and go. Angels were a slippery bunch.

"Ernie, fancy meeting you here."

Taking advantage of his confusion, I grabbed him and gated to the one place I always managed to appear, sometimes even when I didn't want to — Aaru.

You'd think the angels would be used to my popping into their homeland uninvited and unannounced, since I seemed to do it pretty regularly. Nope. A flurry of noise and activity ensued, no doubt amplified by the fact that I had an angel in my arms, and a sword against his chest.

"Cockroach? What *are* you doing with that angel?"

I couldn't help a shiver of delight at Gregory's amused tone, although he probably would have been less entertained if he'd known I had an angel duct taped in my basement, too. Still, his presence, his interest, sent all kinds of naughty visions through my mind. But angel fucking would have to wait. I had a more pressing matter on my hands — or in my arms.

"As the Iblis, I am requesting an emergency Ruling Council meeting to discuss a violation of our contract on the part of Ernie here."

Gregory raised his eyebrows. "Right now?"

"No, I was really hoping to stand here holding this guy for the next few decades. Yes, of course right now." I shook my head. "Idiot," I added, under my breath.

The steely look in Gregory's eyes took my breath away. I'd pay for that little remark later, and oh how I'd enjoy it.

"Can you gate there, or do you need my assistance in transporting yourself and your new appendage?"

I hesitated. Normally I'd make them all wait while I spent half the day unintentionally gating to every place on the planet except the Marriott conference room where the angels held these meetings, but I worried that the extra time would give my captive plenty of opportunity to make an escape. There were enough rogue angels running around the planet without adding this guy into the equation.

"I'd appreciate a lift."

I felt rather than heard the snickering from the other, non–corporeal angels that surrounded us. Not that it mattered. They'd considered me a fool from the first day I'd appeared here — a dangerous, rather frightening fool.

Normally Gregory wrapped his arms tightly around me for transport, but this time we just appeared in the conference room. I eyed him suspiciously, realizing that all those previous times, he'd used gating me somewhere as an excuse for physical contact. Before I could call him out about his un–angelic cuddling tendencies, the other members of the council arrived.

The identical look on their faces was worth a thousand words. Gabriel sputtered, pointing a finger at me. Or possibly at Eirnilius.

"So, Dopey, I hear this piece of shit belongs to your household?" I shoved the angel forward out of my arms, careful not to nick him with my sword.

"How dare you... ."

"Did he have your permission to be out of Aaru among the humans?"

Gabriel hesitated. Interesting. The stick–up–the–ass angel I'd grown to know and hate would never have considered lying, but that's clearly what he was thinking of doing.

"No," he grudgingly admitted.

"Then I'm assuming he also didn't have your permission to be negotiating with a demon for the purposes of procreation. No?"

"No." Gabriel's tone was glacial, and I shivered with an involuntary spike of fear. I'd seen him angry before, but never like this. "You better have proof of this, demon. I'll have your hide for this if you're lying."

The atmosphere shifted, heat warring against ice. I felt like the floor was tilting with the surge of power.

Mind your speech, brother.

Gregory's communication was private, between him and Gabriel. Somehow I picked it up, and I wasn't sure if that was intentional on Gregory's part or not. The heat increased, and I felt Gabriel back down, shifting slightly in his seat.

"I apologize if in my shock of the situation I spoke out of turn. I meant no disrespect, Iblis."

He did mean disrespect, and that had to have been the most grudging apology ever. I understood his embarrassment though. He was the master of control and one of his angels had fucked up. I'm sure he was wondering how many others were doing the same. Now the odd guilt I felt over what I was doing to this angel was combined with an equally odd sympathy for Gabriel.

"She's lying," Eirnilius snarled. "She threatened me with her sword, held me against my will and transported me without my consent, violating article twenty–nine, section four." My guilt and sympathy vanished.

"Nope. He's trying to get his groove on with a demon. They had their clandestine meetings at a Chuck E Cheese, too. Shameful. Absolutely shameful. Think of the children!"

"I did *not* consort with demons!" Eirnilius' eyes flashed with indignation. "I was out of Aaru without permission — that I readily admit and I will accept my punishment, but I was not negotiating a breeding incidence with a demon. I was merely at the Chuck E Cheese to bless the human young."

"My ass. He was meeting the demon there. Liar."

Gabriel's eyes flashed. "You may be the Iblis. You may have wings, but demons lie. Why should we take your word over that of an angel with an unblemished record? What proof do you have to substantiate your claims?"

"This." I pulled the parchment from under my shirt and handed it to Gregory. The silence in the room was broken only by the sound of my angel unfolding and reading the contract.

"In exchange for one breeding occurrence, the demon known as Dregvant Era will receive a domicile of his choosing in southern France, furnished as he specifies, as well as the services of a magic–user to cloak said domicile against detection by angels and to protect it from theft... ."

Damn. I thought of Harper, bred without her consent and with no promise of a cozy house along the Mediterranean. This guy had broken the treaty, but aside from wanting to put Gabriel's nose out of joint, I had no beef with him. Shit, not like I wasn't doing almost the same thing, angel fucking with Gregory. That surge of guilt returned and dove through me. Would this guy face death over this? I'd thought they would just stuff him in jail, but now I wondered. I was beginning to regret my hasty actions. That asshole who'd done Harper wrong would suffer only the loss of his child and 'rehabilitation'. Angel justice was very lopsided, but that wasn't any of my concern. I wasn't the one who made the rules.

Gregory continued reading the contract. The angels sat in stunned silence, glancing back and forth between the accused and the parchment in Gregory's hands. My head whirled with the details of the transaction. Fuck, this was better than any breeding proposal I'd ever received, even Ahriman's. No wonder Dregvant had put his life on the line for this. I would have too.

Finished, Gregory handed the contract to Gabriel. "He is in your choir."

"This is your sigil, Eirnilius," Gabriel said. "Do you have anything to say in your defense?"

The angel shook his head angrily, blond curls bouncing. "Don't think I'm the only one. Do you know how many angels are walking outside of Aaru, associating with demons? You can't stop us, especially when one of your own is setting such a great example. Are joinings and the possibility of offspring to be only the privilege of the Ruling Council? If so, you won't be in those seats for long."

I'd underestimated Ernie. That was a gutsy, although rather suicidal speech.

"You are violating the terms of our separation treaty!" Gabriel snarled.

"At least I'm not sinning with humans. How many angels over the last ten–thousand years have? Even after the fall of the tenth choir, angels are still at it. Nephilim walk the earth right under your noses, hidden and protected by a group of angels so desperate that they'll risk their vibration levels to sin with humans. At least I'm keeping it within my own species."

Gabriel's face turned an alarming shade of red. "Your vibration levels still suffer in joining with demons. Where is your willpower? Your sense of centered rightness?"

Ernie snorted. "Who's to say your idea of center is correct? A bunch of snobby hypocrites, all of you."

I cast a quick glance at the other angels, silent as they watched the interchange. None of them seemed particularly outraged. I'd hoped to cause more of a ruckus than this. Yeah, I'd put Gabriel's nose out of joint, but no one else seemed bothered. Now shame joined the guilt. An angel might die just because I didn't like one of Gregory's brothers — an angel that seemed like a rather cool guy. And it would be my fault.

"Maybe I was mistaken."

Gregory turned a stern gaze toward me. "But you have the breeding contract with Eirnilius' sigil on it. There is no mistake."

"Umm, identity theft? It happens all the time with humans. Some angel assumed his name and copied his sigil?"

From the awkward silence greeting my suggestion, I knew they all thought me an idiot. I was an idiot for even suggesting such a thing. Sigil's carried energy — they could be copied by magic users for spell and binding purposes, and each one clearly carried the mark of their maker. A forgery would be easily detected. My mind whirled, trying to figure some way out of this mess I'd created.

"I did it." Eirnilius stood straight, his chin at a defiant, upward angle. "I negotiated with a demon for purposes of breeding. I assisted his travel through the gates, and I bribed him to form an offspring to my specifications."

We all turned to face the angel. I held my breath. If he died for this, it would be on my head. I wondered if I could jump in and gate him away before the execution, if Gregory would help me save him somehow. Probably not.

"Eirnilius, you will suffer the consequences for your violation of the treaty." Gabriel's voice was sober as he looked at the angel. Then he stood and met the accused's eyes. "Eirnilius, you are stripped of your halo and condemned to never enter Aaru again. You are Fallen and now subject to the leader of Hel. Your existence is at her whim."

There was a flash, and Eirnilius dropped to the floor in a fetal position. I was more surprised by Gabriel's pronouncement than its effect on the other angel. What the fuck had he meant? Leader of Hel? Wasn't that me? I remembered something about being in charge of those with low FICO scores and the fallen, but I'd assumed that only meant humans. Fallen angels too?

"Umm, I don't want him." I stepped over the angel to approach the seated Ruling Council members. "What the fuck would *I* do with an angel? Can we just make him do the naked and restrained thing for a few years? Make him do community service? Send him to bed without dinner?"

I really, really did not want responsibility for this angel. Besides, I already had one duct taped in my basement. Where would this one stay? That addition Nyalla had proposed wouldn't happen overnight. And what the fuck was I supposed to do with him, anyway? Some angel following me around for all eternity? It didn't sound like he had any chance of reinstatement.

Gabriel shrugged. "Do whatever you want with him. Per our last meeting, Fallen angels are now your responsibility."

"Fallen humans are my responsibility. Not angels. I don't have anything to do with angels." I didn't vote for that. Or did I?

Gregory choked back something that sounded suspiciously like a laugh. "Yes, Cockroach. The Iblis handles the Fallen of any species as well as those whose vibration levels have descended to unacceptable levels."

What a crock of shit. I stared at Eirnilius, who had risen shakily to his feet and was accepting his fate with a placid face.

"If there are no other matters to discuss, then I suggest we adjourn the meeting." Gregory still had that note of amusement in his voice. The other angels nodded as one and vanished, leaving me, the big guy, and my new blond accessory.

"So ... what are you going to do now?"

Eirnilius frowned in confusion. "Go with you. Unless you want me to go elsewhere."

I waved a hand. "Just gate off somewhere. I don't care where you stay."

There was a moment of awkward silence. "I can no longer teleport myself. My skills are severely restricted without my halo."

I looked at the space just above his head, and then looked at the same space above Gregory's. They looked the same to me. No glowing lights, no circles of shining gold floating above their hair. Whatever. This angel shit was incomprehensible most of the time. Who was I kidding: it was incomprehensible all of the time.

"Fine. I'll take you home, but I have to warn you that we'll make a few side trips before I get it right. Teleportation is a pretty new skill to me."

He nodded. "Am I assigned a specific task? My life belongs to you now."

"Stay out of my way? My house is a bit high–traffic right now, so you'll be running into humans, werewolves, angels, and demons on a pretty regular basis. I'll put up a cot in the nursery until I can figure out a long–term spot for you."

"I'll give you both a lift back."

I turned in surprise to Gregory, and he grinned at me. "What? Maybe I'd like to see this nursery your new angel is going to be living in?"

Yeah, right. Still, this was better than fifteen out–of–the–way trips before I finally wound up in my living room. I took a step toward him and hesitated.

"Do we do a big group hug? How do you want to do this?"

His lips twitched. "You, I will embrace. The Fallen one can just stand where he is."

I'd figured as much. I closed the distance between us, and he crushed me tight in his arms. My face pressed against the angel's chest, and I felt his lips at the top of my head. With a jolt, the world tilted, and I pulled away to see my living room. Eirnilius was a few feet away, gawking at his surroundings like he'd never seen a human home before.

"Go wait outside while I speak with the Iblis," my angel commanded.

The Fallen turned to stare at Gregory boldly. "I don't take orders from you anymore."

That ratcheted up the tension in the room one–hundred fold. Shit. I didn't need Gregory getting into a fight with my new angel. I had enough to worry about.

"Go outside." I pointed toward the French doors. "There's a pool out there. Swim if you want, or just admire the flowers. I'll be out in a bit."

It took him a few tries to figure out how to use the doorknob, which made me wonder how often he had gotten out of Aaru prior to his encounters with Dregvant. Hopefully he wouldn't drown in the pool. I watched him manage to close the door behind him before I turned to Gregory.

"So, what's up?"

I didn't get the feeling I was in trouble, nor did I get the idea we were about to engage in angel nookie. His presence in my house was making me a bit nervous. What if he sensed the angel in the basement? Had it been him who'd blown the whistle on Harper? I loved him, but how far could I *really* trust him?

"I was about to ask you that very same question."

I squirmed. Since our bond had been broken, he couldn't truly read my mind anymore, but he still seemed to know my emotions and have a level of pre–cognition as far as I was concerned. Of course all of that probably came with being over five–billion years old.

"Well, I have a house full of humans, and now I find out that I'm somehow responsible for any Fallen angels — whatever the fuck that means. I don't see how your inability to keep things under control in Aaru translates into more work for me."

When in a hot seat, it was always best to go on the offensive.

"Fallen angels have always been under control of the Iblis. Always. And it's no longer 'us and them'. You're an angel, too, and you need to fully pick up the reins of your position."

He didn't seem angry, but I was becoming so. "I wasn't even alive when this fucking treaty was signed! Keep your Fallen angels, or send them to Detroit or something. Don't give them to me."

"You voted 'yes' with no discussion. Maybe if you actually paid attention in meetings, you wouldn't be surprised by these things."

"Fine. Well, if you don't mind, I've got a new angel I need to make accommodations for, and an ongoing situation in Hel that I'm now too short staffed to deal with."

He smiled. It was that slow, sexy smile I loved. My anger diffused.

"No time for date night?" His voice was just as sexy as his smile. "I'll admit the hot wings weren't to my taste, but I was hoping you'd show me the sinful joys of chocolate."

There were all kinds of sinful joys I wanted to show him. I hesitated, wondering how well duct tape held, and what would happen if a certain captive of mine began banging around the cellar.

"Rain check? Maybe in a few days?"

Days were like seconds to an ancient angel, and I hoped to be rid of at least one of the angels in my house, the one Gregory didn't know about, by then.

"Although there is currently no precipitation in the area, I'll agree to postpone for three days."

Angels. They were so literal and exact. "Thanks. It's a date, then."

His smile broadened. "Yes, it is a date."

He vanished, and I found myself standing in my living room, grinning like a fool for several minutes. I had way too many houseguests for the sort of activities running through my imagination. Which reminded me that I needed to check on the latest arrival.

It seems Ernie *could* swim. He'd stripped out of his clothing and was doing laps in my pool. Naked. And from the view I got, falling from grace seemed to have enhanced his body in rather significant ways.

I left him, thinking he might welcome some alone time to ponder his new life. Nyalla was elated to find out we had an angel in the house, besides the one in the basement. Harper didn't look elated at the news. She began fingering the knives in her belt when I told her he'd be staying in the nursery.

"That's right next to my room," she protested.

"He's an angel. It's not like he's going to sneak into your bed at night or anything." Then I remembered Ernie's naked form and the fact that the father of her child was an angel. "On the other hand, maybe you should lock your door and keep a few of those knives under your pillow, just in case."

"Oh, let's order Chinese delivery." Nyalla was already digging out the various menus. "This is going to be so much fun! I wonder if he likes the same chips as Gregory. Shall we try the hot wings with him? Perhaps losing his halo will cause him to develop a taste for meat."

I heard the door open and close then saw the transfixed expression on both the girls' faces. Great. What now?

I turned around and saw the fallen angel looking like something from the cover of a romance novel. He'd put on his jeans, which were rather snug, but he was shirtless. He'd also shorn his blond curls into a military–style buzz cut. Droplets of water lingered on his shoulders and chest. I know I wasn't the only woman in the room fantasizing about licking them off.

"Hair." The strangled word was all I could get out.

"I hope you don't mind. I just couldn't … it was too much like an angel, and I'm not an angel anymore."

Why did that make my heart twist in sympathy and horrible, horrible guilt? Because it was all my fault. I should be the one punished, not this poor guy.

"You're still an angel," I argued. "Just one in disgrace. Once I get all this figured out, I'll work at getting you back in Aaru where you belong."

"There is no Aaru for me anymore. I'm Fallen, without my halo. I'll walk either in this realm or in Hel until my death."

I heard Nyalla take a breath and realized that her weird angel–gift was kicking in.

"I know it seems pretty bleak right now," she said. "But it will all be okay. I promise. *Frithcandl avrisa thill daegraeth*."

His eyes widened at the elvish words.

I waved my hand. "This is Nyalla, and Harper." Nyalla walked forward, while Harper took up a defensive posture beside the stove. "Girls, this is Ernie."

"Eirnilius," he corrected. Then his face scrunched up as if he'd bitten into a lemon. "Nils. Just call me Nils."

Harper's curiosity got the best of her, and she leaned forward to better see the angel. "Are you really Fallen? What did you do?"

The angel opened his mouth to reply then stopped, gaping at the woman's rounded belly. "You're … you're."

"Pregnant. Humans breed like rabbits. Seems they're always getting pregnant. I mean, I like sex as much as the next demon, but I don't go getting myself knocked up every time I fuck." Not that I could. Demons could only impregnate females when it came to other species. It seems angels had the same restrictions.

And from Nils's horrified expression, he somehow knew that the father of this child wasn't human. Or demon.

"I want this child." Harper splayed a hand defensively across her stomach. I saw a flash of sympathy in Nils's blue eyes before they hardened into cobalt.

"You are not to blame for the sins of my brethren, but you must understand that this is no child you carry but an abomination."

I'd heard that before in reference to Amber. My blood boiled, but before I could express outrage at the misapplication of that term, Harper grew a set of balls.

"Bold words from a Fallen angel." She marched forward and punched a finger into Nils's naked chest — his sculpted, muscular, beautiful chest. "Maybe *you're* the abomination. It doesn't matter though, because this child is mine, and I'm not giving my son up. And let me tell you right now, buster, if you do anything to endanger my child, I'll strip the skin from you one piece at a time and roll you in salt."

Well done! I held back, letting Harper handle this one. She'd shown herself to be surprisingly gutsy from the moment I'd met her.

"You can have more babies. Normal babies. This one is a monster."

Ernie, I mean Nils, clearly had no sense of self–preservation. Angels just didn't understand humans at all. Harper took a sharp breath. Her eyes flashed. Then she slammed her knee into the angel's groin. He bent over double, but not before I saw the look of shock on his face. Harper then sucker punched him, and the angel hit the floor, writhing on the solid maple.

"If you ever call my son a monster again, I'll cut your balls off."

The woman stomped up the stairs while Nils rolled around in a fetal position. Nyalla and I exchanged resigned looks.

"She's serious," I warned the angel. "I've seen her stabbing a pillow, and she's not hesitated to attack angels with cutlery in the past. Better watch your tongue around her, or better yet, stay clear of her all together."

Nils grunted, trying to get to his knees and failing miserably. Nyalla and I watched him as he finally managed to stand.

"Okay." I gestured toward the stairs. "Now that this particular issue is resolved, why don't I take you up to the nursery, where you'll be sleeping for the next few months?"

"I don't sleep," Nils groaned, still clutching his man–parts.

"I'm willing to bet you do now."

~13~

Nils did, in fact, sleep. And snore. And he came downstairs at sunrise sporting an impressive morning wood. The girls were still asleep, so my new angel friend and I bonded over coffee, and then went out for a swim. It was nice to have someone that enjoyed my pool as much as I did.

After a few laps, I climbed out and sprawled onto a lounge chair to catch the early sun. Nils kept going, swimming even after his strokes grew labored and his breath gasped as his head surfaced. Finally he slapped his hands against the edge of the pool, staring into the flowering geraniums.

"What happened to Dregvant?"

I wasn't sure why he cared. I shrugged, watching him carefully for his reaction. "After he handed over the breeding contract, I gated him to safety. Well, I gated him somewhere. I think we wound up in the National Zoo. I'm not sure where he is now."

Nils contemplated the flowers for a few breaths. Finally he crossed his arms and rested his chin on them. "Do you think he made it safely back to Hel?"

I needed to nip this in the bud. "Look, Dregvant is a total shit. He's selfish and spoiled and cares only for material things. Greed is his sin. You can do so much better."

I was fully aware of the irony in my words. Here I was, an imp, skilled in lust and greed and frolicking with an ancient on the Ruling Council. But the difference was that I loved him. I was pretty sure Dregvant had no especial feelings for this angel. I wasn't sure Dregvant had any feelings at all.

"I'm sure he made it back to Hel. After he got out of the Komodo dragon pen, that is. I hope the reptiles ripped up that hideous shirt he was wearing. That demon has no taste in clothing whatsoever."

Nils barked out a laugh. "Yeah. I agree with that wholeheartedly." He looked down at the puddle of water forming from his dripping skin. "And yeah, he is a bit of a jerk."

"Then why offer him a breeding contract? Honestly, Nils, what could that ass possibly contribute to an offspring?"

His muscular shoulders, wet from the pool, glistened as he shrugged. "He was the only one who didn't run off screaming the moment he saw me. Kinda hard to discuss a contract like that while the demon is frantically racing for the nearest gate." He shot me a quick, charming grin. "Of course, discussing a contract like that when you've got a demon restrained and pinned under fifty tons of concrete isn't easy either."

I laughed. "You should have waited a few more years. I've got this great idea for a dating service. Infernal Mates. Angels and demons will be hooking up all over the place."

"And if you think that's going to come to pass in a few years, you're crazier than I thought."

"Just you wait and see. Aaru will be full of demon mates before you know it."

The air grew thick with sorrow. "Well, it will happen without me."

He was kicked out. Forever. And it was my fault. I doubted I could do anything to force the angels to take him back, and I wasn't sure how life would be for him there anyway. Everyone had to have known what he did. They'd probably ostracize him. Nils ran a hand over his short, blond hair, sending drops of water like rain to the flagstone patio.

Maybe there would be forgiveness in his future, but in the meantime the guy had a life to live. Might as well make the best of it.

I watched a barn swallow swoop down low before arcing up into a nest on the inside of my porch. "We'll get you some clothes. Nyalla is the queen of internet shopping. Or she can take you to the mall. My human boyfriend will get you some identification. You'll learn to drive a car. Think of this as a new adventure."

The angel swung out of the pool, dripping water from his magnificent, naked body. "I miss Aaru. Hunger, exhaustion, and all the other sensations of this human form are too much for me. Parts of my body now seem to have a will of their own, and my emotions swing from extreme to extreme. I think death might be preferable."

A blast of white hit him in the shoulder, sending him flying into the geraniums. I spent precious moments in wide–eyed shock before rolling off the lounge chair and summoning my sword. White streamed around me like tunnels of lethal light, disintegrating part of my lounge chair and digging trenches in my hardscape patio. I didn't have time to think about how badly Nils was hurt. I just kept rolling into the edge of the brush line. Then I jumped to my feet and ran.

It was morning, but I could still see the glow of the angels surrounding my house. My sword wasn't effective at a distance, so I launched bursts of raw energy as I ran, weaving through the shrubberies and trees. My aim was pretty accurate, and each time I hit one, he flew backward, skidding along the ground.

One of the angels managed to hit me. I felt the burning pain through my leg as I crashed onto the dirt, my sword bouncing out of reach through sparse patches of grass. They must have dialed it back a notch because instead of a missing leg, I looked like I'd been filled with buckshot. The wound hurt like fuck — far more than buckshot would have, and it bled like a motherfucker, but I had no time to fix the wound.

Debra Dunbar

Or heal it, for that matter. I twisted on the ground, groping for the sword. The angels cautiously approached me, and I gave up on the sword, readying a blast of energy instead. They'd hardly kill me, the Iblis ... would they?

"Give us the woman and we'll leave you in peace."

There were three of them, hovering a careful five feet from me and watching me intently. It would have been a whole lot easier and more demonic to just turn over Harper in the face of these odds, but I never took the easy path. And refusing to do what angels told me to do was kind of my MO.

"Fuck you." The sword had magically re–appeared in my hand, and I swung it in an upward diagonal, missing all of the angels, who were several feet out of reach.

"We'll trade you for it. Name your price — or favor."

These angels caught on quick. Any other demon would have been wondering how to weasel out of his vow to protect this woman and hopefully get something in return. Not me. Not anymore.

"She's not an 'it', and neither is her unborn son. Besides, you've got nothing I want, and favors from you would be worthless."

One of the angels narrowed his eyes. "Then we'll just have to take her by force."

I got the feeling he meant lethal force, and that collateral damage wouldn't matter. Nyalla, Boomer, Harper, and Nils, plus my three horses in the barn — I couldn't let anything happen to them. I adjusted my grip on the sword, hating that I was so inept at using it. But there were many forms the sword could take, and one of them had served me well before. If only the sword would comply.

"Over my dead body."

As I raised the sword, it transformed in a flash, and I now held a shotgun. Unfortunately, the angel I was aiming for had already launched a burst of energy at me. My offensive move became defensive, and I instinctively blocked the blast with the barrel of my gun.

My hand shook as I struggled to keep my grip, but the gun sucked in the energy like a magical vacuum. Unwilling to see how much the weapon could absorb, I fired. My aim wasn't the best, and I was shooting one handed, but whatever came out of the gun barrel acted like an angel–seeking missile. A burst of color hit the angel in the middle and threw him to the ground, where he screamed and convulsed.

I hesitated, uncertain what to do. My plan had been to shoot each of them, but the drama coming from the one I'd hit gave me pause. Was he mortally wounded? I could kill all three of them, claim self–defense and deal with the stupid fucking reports later, but what price would I pay for my actions? And how long could I keep this up? I remembered Haagenti's endless stream of hit–demons and wondered how many angels were going to come after me. If there were this many with the Nephilim unborn, I could only imagine the army at my door once he popped out of Harper's womb. I needed to take care of the root cause of this problem, just as I had in the Haagenti situation.

The other two angels seemed equally uncertain what to do. They stared in horror at their friend, then up at me in fear. In a blink, they were gone, leaving their buddy behind in a very un–angelic manner. These dudes would never have made it in the Marines.

Their departure left me staring at the remaining angel, still thrashing on the ground. What the fuck was I going to do with him? I already had one angel restrained in my basement plus Nils running around. I could net him, but then he couldn't heal. It would suck if he died while in my elven net.

Nils.

I kept the shotgun handy and leapt to my feet, racing back through the maze of shrubberies to my pool. Nils wasn't where he should have landed after being shot, but a smeared line of pinkish–white led to the house. I found the angel there, propped up against the glass door, a determined look on his pale face. His left arm hung useless, a mess of ground meat.

"Why haven't you healed yourself?" I was relieved to find him alive, but why *hadn't* he healed himself? I'd repaired my leg in a flash once the angels were gone. He should have been able to do the same — unless he'd also lost that skill when he'd fallen.

"Pain," he panted. "Can't concentrate. Needed to protect the humans first."

I dismissed my shotgun and frowned down at the angel. "I've seen you guys brush off far worse. Shit, I've seen the big guy take a bullet to the head and barely blink. What's the big deal about a little wound to the shoulder?"

He grimaced. "Threat neutralized? All okay?"

First the haircut, now the cop–talk. What exactly happened to angels when they fell?

"Yep. Well, except for the one bleeding all over my field. I've got no idea what the fuck to do with him." Part of me hoped the angel would die. I had one too many in my basement and only the one restraining collar. It would be easier to bury his corpse and deny everything than toss him into my basement in a net for an eternity.

Nils slumped, leaving a smear of his weird blood on the door glass. "I'm not used to this much sensation. Can't focus."

Oh, for fuck sake. Guess I was going to need to heal him myself. I stalked over to the angel and dropped down, grabbing his face with both hands as I pulled him to me.

Even with the pain he was in, Nils recoiled from me. "No. Don't. I'll do it myself. Just give me a minute."

"Fine." I didn't have time for his nonsense. Moving the angel's leg aside with my foot, I pushed the door open and went in.

Everything was quiet in the house. There was no sign of disturbance. The girls were both still sleeping. It seems I'd intercepted the only angels, or the others hadn't had a chance to get into the house. Stupid as it had been to attack me upfront, I knew they wouldn't make the same mistake twice. Next time, they'd sneak in when I was out. It's what I would have done from the very first.

Grabbing a fresh role of duct tape and some rope, I headed out to the field, wondering what I was going to do with my second captive. Nils had managed to get his arm functional again, although it was still a bloody, torn mess. I left him to guard the girls and stomped to the field.

The angel was gone, a burned patch of grass where he'd lain. I took a deep breath, knowing I only had a temporary reprieve before they returned. I didn't even have that. On the way back to the house, I saw Gregory. He was standing by the pool, his back to Nils. The newest addition to my household was blocking the French door with arms outstretched.

"Stand down, soldier," I told the blond angel, rolling my eyes at his dramatic defensive posture. Gregory could have taken Nils out with the blink of an eye if he wanted to enter the house, and it's not like he needed to use the door anyway. The thought flitted through my mind that him killing Nils would save me a lot of trouble, but I was starting to get rather fond of my Fallen, and as much as a cat fight between the two angels would turn me on, I didn't have time for that.

"The Fallen One's devotion to his new mistress is admirable."

It was. I caught the teasing tone in Gregory's voice, but Nils clearly didn't. His face turned an alarming shade of red, and his fists clenched.

"She's all I've got. How do you expect me to act?"

Gregory raised his eyebrows, a faint smile hovering around the edge of his lips. "I expect you to obey her and protect her interests. Not necessarily in that order."

I had no idea what the fuck that meant.

"So ... what's up?" I had the feeling Gregory wasn't here for our movie–night date.

His eyes met mine, and I saw an uneasiness in their black depths that set me on edge. "Emergency Ruling Council meeting."

"About the Hunters that were just here? I only shot one of them."

"They weren't Hunters," Nils said. "Hunters only work solo. That was a lynch mob."

Great. Lynch mob meant more angels than the Grigori knew about Harper and her baby.

"Word has gotten out that you are harboring a Nephilim," Gregory confirmed. "Although I doubt angels would have taken it upon themselves to confront you at this point. The host would await the Ruling Council's judgment and allow them to handle the situation."

"Well three did take it upon themselves. And they were demanding I turn over Harper." I frowned, trying to remember their shouted demands. Had they asked me to give them the unborn baby, the Nephilim? No, they'd asked for the woman. There was only Harper and Nyalla in the house, and angels would have no reason to want Nyalla.

"If you were attacked, it must have been due to something else. Have you been leaving fake vomit in the sixth circle again? Infesting the first circle with bird lice?"

That hadn't turned out quite the way I'd hoped, but I heard the mites were surprisingly resistant to the degenerating effect of Aaru. Those things took nearly a month to die off, and all the angels there had itchy wings the whole time.

"We can discuss your long list of enemies later. We can't be late for the meeting."

"Do I have enough time to change my clothes?" Not that angels would give a shit about me sporting a dirt–covered bikini, but I preferred to face whatever was coming with some additional attire. Did they also know about the angel in my basement? Or the guy who had recently been injured in my field?

"I'm afraid not, Cockroach."

"Okay. Fine." I turned to Nils. "Guard the girls?"

"Yes, Mistress." Nils nodded sharply, and I took one last look at his gorgeous body before turning to Gregory.

My angel opened his arms, and I stepped into them, reassured that whatever I was about to face, at least Gregory still seemed to have my back.

The other angels were already in the conference room. I quickly counted, realizing there weren't enough chairs for everyone plus Uriel's placeholder. Evidently I was expected to stand, like a prisoner facing sentencing. Gregory stood beside me in support, even though he had a chair awaiting him.

Gabriel got right to the point. Bastard.

"Nephilim are condemned to death per article one nine two three eight, section forty–five, subsection twenty, item two ninety three. Knowingly harboring a Nephilim is in violation of statute twenty–eight ninety–two, section six, item three."

Yep. They knew about Harper, and I was in deep shit. I wasn't about to give her up, so I fell back on what I knew best.

"Yeah? I'm a demon. I violate all kinds of things, not just articles and statutes. I'd be happy to violate you, given half a chance, but I don't think I'm your type."

"This is serious," he thundered.

Gregory's grip on my arm seemed to agree, but I couldn't stop taunting them. This was stupid, ridiculous, and a waste of time. Like I'd *ever* followed the rules. Did they really think I was going to do so this time?

"I know. I've seriously violated three twenty eight, section nine, item forty–two, also. And I've violated hundreds of humans, and demons. I'm hoping to violate an angel sometime this week too. Hopefully on our movie–night date."

"You've allowed a member of your choir to assume a title above his station?" Raphael scratched his head and looked at me with bewilderment.

"Yes. And I've stolen pens and made photocopies of my naked ass on the Aaru Xerox machine too."

Gabriel wasn't as easily sidetracked as his younger brother. "Turn over the Nephilim. Immediately."

"Vow notwithstanding, I can't turn over the Nephilim. It's unborn. I've done enough reports in the past twelve months. I'm not adding to them unnecessarily by killing a pregnant woman while ripping her unborn child from her womb."

"We can take care of that," New Guy chimed in. "And the mother would not be harmed. She wouldn't even recall that she had been pregnant."

Like hell they would 'take care of that'. So much for angels being pro–life. Did the Pope know about this? He'd excommunicate the whole lot of them if he found out.

"I made a vow. Humans might not care about their FICO score, but I do. Now that I'm an angel, I'm very concerned with my vibration level."

I didn't mention that I was concerned it not reach their lofty level. Someone kill me if I ever got as "pure" and sanctimonious as Gabriel.

Sleazy put a thoughtful finger on his chin. "I vote that we wait until the Nephilim is born, so as to cause the Mother as little stress as possible. Then we can take it."

Yeah, because losing a newborn child wouldn't be stressful. And I didn't like their solution of erasing Harper's memories one bit.

"*Vow*. I vowed to protect the child for its natural lifespan. Granted, I didn't realize exactly what I was vowing at the time — I was too busy coveting a pair of boots that were included in the deal."

"Demons." Raphael shook his head, but he didn't seem particularly condemning. "How about this? We allow the Nephilim to live out its natural life within the confines of the Iblis' domicile, under severe restrictions. If the Nephilim violates the terms of the contract, then the Iblis must turn it over to the Ruling Council or their representative."

Gabriel glared at Rafi, and then turned his dark eyes on me. "If you didn't fully understand the vow, then you can't be held to it. Forty–nine, two thirty eight."

I heard the angel beside me sigh, his grip on my arm loosening slightly. "Brother, Cahor v/s Tagas overturned that statue. You know that. If an angel foolishly gives a vow without due consideration to terms and conditions, it still is enforceable."

I wasn't so sure I liked that "foolish" part, but I nodded enthusiastically anyway. I also heard Gabriel grind his teeth from across the conference–room table.

"We cannot allow this Nephilim to live. Once we are made aware of its existence and location, we must execute it. There is no other choice."

"What if you can't find it? What if the Nephilim is, say, transported to Hel? Or somewhere not in my house?"

Rafi locked eyes with me, and in that brief second, I realized that I truly had an ally in him. "We have no solid proof that the Nephilim is in the Iblis' house beyond unsubstantiated reports that may only be rumors. If she says she sent it to Hel, I think we must believe her. After all, an attack on her person or her property would be an attack on the duly appointed representative of Hel."

I hadn't been appointed, but whatever. "Yep. I sent the pregnant human to Hel. She's partying it up with my household as we speak."

There was a long stretch of silence as the angels of the Ruling Council considered what they must know was a blatant lie. The mind–speak was flying between them so quickly that

I couldn't understand any of it. I got the idea that I didn't have a majority support, but they were all between a rock and a hard place on this issue. Sliding my hand behind my back, the arm Gregory wasn't holding, I crossed my fingers and hoped that fickle Lady Luck would shine her favor on me.

She did. Sort of.

"As the Nephilim is no longer within our grasp, we will withhold judgment." Gabriel scowled. "But if we find that it is still among the humans, we will take any steps necessary to apprehend and kill it. And if we find that the Iblis is harboring it among the humans, she will be removed from her voting position on the Ruling Council for two centuries, and damned to Hel for the same period."

I caught my breath. The removal from the Ruling Council would be a welcome punishment, but damning me to Hel meant I wouldn't be able to see any of my earthly friends for the rest of their lives. It also meant I wouldn't be able to see Gregory.

"All in favor?"

Four angels raised their hands.

"Abstain." I felt a sense of relief at Gregory's announcement.

Everyone vanished, and I was left in the conference room with Gregory. Harper would be a virtual prisoner, and the baby a real one for its life. No one could see them. They'd never be able to leave my home. It was either that or send them to Hel. Both scenarios had horrible risks. The noose I'd tied around my neck with "foolishness" felt like it was tightening further.

~14~

Gregory transported me back, and for the first time I felt uneasy in his arms. I pulled away and stared up into his black eyes.

"How did they know Harper was here? The only ones who knew were you and the father, and I can't see him telling."

I didn't want to hear his answer, but I needed to know. My heart might break, but I couldn't keep suspecting him. I needed to know whether I could trust him or not.

"You don't trust me." It was more of a statement than a question.

"No."

He sighed. "I don't always trust you either, Cockroach. This is new for both of us. I haven't seen an Angel of Chaos in nearly three–million years and have held the lowest opinion of demons up until recently. It's not like you've had much contact with angels before you met me. We're naturally going to distrust each other."

But I want to trust you. I couldn't say that to him without knowing the truth, though. So instead, I straightened my spine and got right to the point. "Did you tell anyone about Harper? Did you somehow, through your actions or words, let it be known that I had an unborn Nephilim in my house?"

The angel's eyes met mine. "No."

I believed him. "Then how?"

"Someone could have suspected the father and had him followed. Perhaps Harper told someone about her involvement with an angel and word got back to Aaru."

I shook my head. "Harper said that the father was nervous this last week. Maybe he was followed, but if so, why would they wait until now to tell the Ruling Council? Why not go to them straight away?"

"Perhaps they thought to blackmail the father and he refused to comply. That doesn't matter at this moment. It's more important now for us to make sure she is hidden — for your safety as well as hers."

"Us?" He was going to help? I felt dizzy with relief.

"Of course 'us'. I'm assuming you don't truly want to send her to Hel, so we'll need to figure a way to hide her and the baby among the humans for the next century or so."

"You know she's still here?" I sounded like an idiot, but this side of Gregory surprised me.

He smiled. "Cockroach, you are the worst liar ever. Of course I know she's still here."

With that, I was in his arms again, practically leaping out of my body to plaster my spirit–self against his. I felt like I was going to explode from emotion. I loved this guy more now than ever before.

But there was something I needed to tell him. Or rather, show him.

"Ummm... ." I hesitated as I pulled away from him. There was no easy way to say this, so I just jumped into it imp–style. "I've got one of your angels tied up in my basement."

All the affectionate stroking stopped. "You what? You have *what* tied up in your basement?"

"A Hunter angel. He's from your choir — says he reports directly to you. He came for Harper, and we fought. I didn't know what to do with him once I'd subdued him, so I stuck him in the basement."

"One of my angels. In your basement. *Tied up*? How has he not untied himself and returned to Aaru? Do you have some sort of magical containment wards on your basement? I didn't sense anything the last time I was here."

"No ... well, it's a sort of magical containment. He can't teleport or use any energy. It turns him temporarily into a human as far as skills and abilities go."

Gregory stared into my eyes; his were dark and unreadable. I wished I knew what he was thinking.

"Okay. Why the tying up then? He shouldn't be hard to handle as a human."

Sheesh. Angels always underestimated humans. It's not like the Hunter was completely defenseless or with the IQ of a slug just because he no longer had angelic powers.

"Well, he could escape through one of the basement windows, or make a shank out of the shit down in my basement and attack us when we came down, or annoy the fuck out of us by flipping random breakers in the electrical box down there. Yeah, he's tied up. Actually he's duct taped to the point he looks like a giant silver caterpillar."

Reminder to self: when confessing terrible misdeeds to an angel, avoid sarcasm at all cost. Gregory exploded in anger, slamming me into the wall. His irises bled out to engulf his eyes in solid black, and he shimmered. As he spoke, I saw the pointed piranha teeth that meant he'd lost control.

"Cockroach, how could you do this? Why?"

"He attacked me," I wailed. "In my own house, he attacked me. And he tried to take a woman I have vowed to protect, a woman I now consider part of my household."

Gregory's breathing was ragged and hot against the side of my face. "You have restrained an angel who was simply doing his job then covered him in some sticky substance so he cannot use his limbs. And you didn't think to tell me this until now? When did this happen?"

I squirmed, looking anywhere but at his face. "Um, a couple of days ago? I just ... no, I didn't want to tell you. Part of me worried that you had leaked the news of Harper's presence and sent the Hunter here."

He leaned closer to me as the silence dragged on. "And the other part?"

I dragged air into lungs that suddenly felt too small. "He was part of your choir — a Hunter under the command of the Grigori. I didn't want you to hate me. I have held one of your own against his will. That's not the sort of thing you do to a household member of a loved one."

I felt him relax. His hands on my arms rubbed, soothing, although the power he leaked still burned against my skin. "No, when you have a confrontation with the household member of a loved one, you let them know. You let them deal with the issue. How would you feel if I had done this to Dar and not told you?"

I couldn't help a snort of laughter at the idea of Dar showing up in the fourth circle of Aaru and attacking Gregory. "I'm sorry. I'm a demon, and I'm not really good at this trust stuff, let alone the whole communication thing."

I reached out in a caress with my spirit–self and felt him return it. He still had me pinned against the wall, still had that inferno of power blasting against me, but at least I knew he didn't hate me. Right now, anyway.

"Why have you let me know this now? It would have been decades before I noticed his absence. You could have hidden this from me for quite a while."

"Because I trust you now and I thought you needed to know." I glanced up into his face. "And, honestly, you would have found out by date–night. He makes a fucking lot of noise down there in my basement. So, unborn Nephilim in my house and a captive Hunter in my basement. We've got that problem to deal with too."

"We?"

Shit. Was the 'we' stuff all over and gone? Maybe I *should* have just kept the angel in the cellar a secret and disposed of him discretely. I sneaked a look at him. He didn't look pissed. He looked more shocked than anything else. Finally he tilted his face toward the ceiling and shook his head.

"Okay. Let's go see this angel tied, or taped up, in your basement, so *we* can figure out what to do with him."

Everything swam before my eyes, and I realized I'd been holding my breath, waiting to hear his response. We. How I loved that pronoun.

I led Gregory into my cellar, wondering if I could possibly set up some cots for my overflow guests. With the rate things were going, I was bound to wind up with more angels down here. Maybe Gareth could get me some additional nets on an emergency order. It really wasn't that horrible in the basement. If I slapped some posters on the walls and threw a few cheap rugs down, no one should complain about the accommodation.

Cheap rugs and posters were better than this angel had it. He was still attached to the chair where we'd tied him yesterday after he'd taken to rolling across the floor and banging loudly against the furnace. He hadn't been able to get loose from the chair, but the way the silver edges of the duct tape were rolled and cutting into his skin showed he had been struggling.

"What is that thing around his neck?"

I winced, remembering the feel of the collar, how I'd dug at it with my hands until my neck was raw and bleeding. Guilt lanced through me. I didn't want to use it, never wanted to see one of them again, but there was no other way I could keep this angel from hurting Harper or gating back to Aaru to rat us out.

"It's that restraining device I told you about — a collar designed by an elf–demon collaboration. With it on, a demon — or angel — is basically a human. They can't access their energy or powers."

Gregory moved past me to the angel. "Is that why he has injuries?"

"Yeah." He'd managed to heal the most severe of them in the moments between being released from the elven net and having the collar put on, but the Hunter still had a host of abrasions on his arms and legs. I suddenly saw this from an outsider's eyes and realized how bad it looked. Heck, it looked bad enough from an insider's eyes.

"He was going to take Harper. He attacked me, threatened me and my guests on my own property — in my own home."

"Mmm, mmm–mmm mmm mmm!"

At least that's what the angel sounded like. I couldn't really make out his words since his mouth was covered by duct tape.

"Do you mind?" Gregory asked, pointing to the flexing silver band across the angel's mouth.

"Be my guest."

Gregory grabbed hold and ripped the tape off with one swipe. I knew it had to have hurt like fuck and was filled with admiration for my badass angel.

"Now, what was that you said? I couldn't hear you, and evidently the collar also inhibits mind–speech."

The angel gasped a few times, working his jaw. I suddenly realized that with the collar on, he'd need to eat and drink. Ooops. Guess when this was over I'd need to bring him down a plate of something, assuming Gregory didn't dump my ass and gate back to Aaru with him.

"She ... it was all her, Ancient One! I asked for entry into her home, and she granted it. I asked for her to hand over the woman, and she agreed. Then she hit me on the back of the head after the human woman impaled me with a knife. I was defending myself. Then she drew the sword of the Iblis on me!"

Yeah, I was so screwed. I should have just killed the guy when I had the chance. Gregory tilted his head, regarding the other angel thoughtfully while I held my breath.

"Surely you cannot have been so foolish as to turn your back on a demon. Or believe that one spoke truthfully. Either you are lying to me, or you are a fool. Which is it?"

The angel shot me a hate–filled glance. "But, with greatest respect Ancient One, your back is to her right now."

"I have no doubts regarding my foolishness, especially when it concerns this particular demon." Gregory turned to me, and I felt my insides warm at his smile. "Cockroach, can you please remove this collar from my angel? I'm rather reluctant to touch it."

I snorted. "And you call yourself a fool. Nobody in their right mind would want to touch that thing. I can put it on, but a human or elf needs to activate the release catch. Hopefully Nyalla is home." Because I wasn't about to get Harper within ten feet of this guy.

"She is." Gregory looked up toward the top of the stairs. "I've asked her to come down here, and she's on her way."

Sure enough, I heard the slap of flip–flops as Nyalla hurried down the stairs. She took one look at the angel, at Gregory, then at me.

"You sure about this?"

I nodded, and she walked to the Hunter, carefully feeling around the back of the silver collar for the catch. With a 'snick' the silver ring was in her hand. I moved to put myself between Nyalla and the angel, just in case.

"Ancient One, may I heal myself and remove the sticky silver tape that binds me?"

Gregory gave a short nod, and with a flash of light, the angel stood before him, fully healed and free of duct tape, his head bowed in submission. My angel touched his head and golden light flowed around them in a spiral.

"Dalmai Haseha Huzia Rami, angel of the fourth choir, Hunter of Nephilim, you are forbidden from physically harming any humans under the protection of the Iblis. You are relieved of your Hunter responsibilities. You will remain here and serve the Iblis for a period of two decades."

"Yes, Ancient One. Is this my punishment? For being a fool?"

Gregory smiled and looked up, his eyes briefly meeting mine. "No. It's a reward. I hope that in the next two decades, you become an even greater fool than I am."

~15~

As usual, Gregory took off, leaving me in a house with two humans, one unborn Nephilim, a Fallen angel, and a Hunter angel that hated my guts. Dalmai followed me sullenly up the stairs as I gave him the household tour. I wasn't about to put him in my bedroom, so I led him to the nursery, thinking he could shack up with Nils for a while.

Wrong. Nils was sitting cross–legged on the floor, eyes closed in serenity, seemingly undisturbed by our intrusion. Dalmai took one look at him and erupted in anger.

"I'm not sharing living quarters with *that*."

I pursed my lips. "Well, the other choices are with me or the basement, because you're not going to be sleeping in the same room as the humans."

"I wouldn't harm the humans, can't harm the humans even if I wanted to." Dalmai sounded a bit insulted.

"It's not the humans I'm worried about; it's you. Nyalla is more than a match for you. Harper just got jilted, and she's got mad knife skills. You definitely don't want to be sharing a room with her."

"I'll take the basement."

I snatched a spare blanket off the floor and thrust it at him.

"I don't need sleep, or a piece of fabric to keep me warm. I only need a place of solitude to meditate. One untainted by the stench of the Fallen."

Okay, this had to stop right now. "Listen up, Dalmai. You're sharing a house with Satan, two humans — one of whom is pregnant with a Nephilim — and this angel. He's probably the most un–stinky of all of us. I've changed my mind. You're staying here, and I don't want to hear any more shit out of you."

The angel snarled — the angel that wasn't on the floor meditating, that is. "The Ancient One said I needed to serve you. That doesn't include me having to put up with Fallen scum, or keep silent about my distaste of my situation."

"Watch it, buster. That collar is one room away, and I've got loads of duct tape handy. Could be a very uncomfortable twenty years."

Dalmai glared at me, then at Nils. "We'll do six–hour shifts. That way, I don't need to spend any more time in the presence of your wretched vibration pattern than necessary."

Nils's eyes popped open. He stretched his legs before hopping to his feet with an agile spring. "I've completed my contemplations, and judging by your descent into the sin of anger, you seem in desperate need of centering. The room is yours, brother, for the next six hours."

"I'm not your brother," Dalmai snapped as Nils walked past him.

"Well, if you serve the Iblis, you're no longer an angel."

I closed the door behind me, cutting off any potentially inflammatory replies by Dalmai. As much as I longed to see the two angels duke it out, while they were naked in a pit of melted chocolate, I had other things to get done first — like ensuring Harper didn't get caught outside of Hel.

I was lost in thought and nearly trampled Nils, who had halted at the bottom of the steps.

"What the fuck?" I couldn't walk from one room to the next without running into someone. I longed for the days when it was just me, and occasionally Wyatt, inside my house.

"I need to go outside." Nils's voice sounded odd, and instead of heading to the front door, he turned abruptly and jogged back up the stairs. Whatever. If the guy wanted to exit the house by jumping out a second–story window, it wasn't my problem. Angels. They were so fucking weird.

Harper was in the living room, flipping through a parenting magazine with unseeing eyes. I sat next to her, noting she didn't grab a knife from her belt or move away.

"We've got a problem."

"Tell me about it." She hesitated at a full–page advertisement showing a joyful infant with pureed food smeared all over his face. "I wonder if Nephilim eat baby food. What if they need to feed on the souls of innocents or eat baby kittens or something?"

Shit. Was this normal for pregnant humans, or did I need to force–feed her some Prozac? "Harper, you're not giving birth to a demon. I'm sure this baby is going to eat the same strained peas as every other infant."

"How do you know? Maybe Ben was right. Maybe I'm not fit to raise this child. What if it's a monster? What if it kills someone?"

"Your baby is *not* a demon. Even our demon–spawn hybrids aren't like that. It's going to be okay." I had no guarantee it would be okay, and I had no idea how to move the conversation back to Harper's need to stay hidden in my house for the rest of her natural life. Given her despondent tone, perhaps I should delay that conversation until some other time.

Tears glistened in the woman's eyes. "Angels have been sent to kill my baby twice so far. What chance do I have of bringing this pregnancy to term? I'm terrified that even if I make it nine months, an angel will snatch my baby from the hospital nursery before I even get to hold him."

I had nothing. For fuck sake, I was a demon. I wasn't skilled in consoling distraught, pregnant women. If only I was still bound to Gregory, I could summon him here to help. He'd quieted Nyalla's fears. I was sure he could do the same for Harper.

I opened my mouth to attempt some kind of generic platitude, when the front door opened, slamming against the wall. Harper jumped to her feet, the parenting magazine sliding from her fingers as she reached for a knife. I spun around, putting myself in front of her and summoning my shotgun. Before my mind even registered who had entered my house, the gun was in my hands and against my shoulder.

It was an angel, but thankfully one who had permission to be in my house. Nils, back from his fresh–air jaunt, strode across my threshold dragging something. Flexing the impressive muscles in his arms, he threw the item forward. It hit the floor with a heavy thump and rolled to the side. That's when I realized the 'something' was an angel, duct taped into a ball and sporting a silver collar around his neck.

I leveled the shotgun at him only to have Harper knock the barrel aside as she raced forward, knife at the ready.

"That's Ben," she shrieked.

I'd already fired, and my angel–seeking bullet looped around her toward the duct–taped angel, not heeding my mental attempt to retract it. It hit with a splatter of iridescent white. The angel's muffled 'umpf' was immediately drowned out by Harper's scream of rage. The pregnant woman vaulted a stray chair with surprising agility and dove on the angel, stabbing him repeatedly with the knife.

"You're not taking my baby, you worthless piece of crap."

"Whoa!" I dismissed the shotgun and jumped on Harper's back, struggling to pull her away without hurting her. I didn't give a shit about this Ben, but he was spurting gallons of angel blood all over my maple floors.

Nils stood unhelpfully to the side, watching in amusement while Ben groaned and thrashed on my floor. His blood was going to eat a ten–foot hole in my hardwood if I couldn't get him to heal himself. I looked around for the one human who wouldn't slice this angel to ribbons given half a chance.

Nyalla. She stood beside Nils, her eyes wide.

"Take off the collar," I told her, finally relieving Harper of her knife and trapping her hands in mine.

"No. Don't." Nils grabbed Nyalla, holding her back from Ben. The taped angel continued to bleed onto the floor, turning even paler than he had been when he'd been flung onto the ground. "He was sneaking around the house. I don't trust him."

I didn't either, but I needed answers, and for that I needed this angel alive and able to speak.

"You okay?" I asked Harper. "If I let you go, can you hold off stabbing him to death until we find out what he's doing sneaking around the house?"

She nodded, glaring mutely at the angel.

Summoning the shotgun back into my hands, I told Nils to let Nyalla free and aimed the weapon at Ben while she struggled to undo the band of silver around his neck.

The collar clattered to the floor, and the angel healed himself. His hands, no longer duct taped, were raised as he eyed me suspiciously.

"Hello, *Ben.*" I smiled. It wasn't a nice smile. "So angelic of you to visit your pregnant girlfriend. Time for you to explain yourself before I haul you before the Ruling Council for violating eight twenty–two forty–nine o–five."

Nils frowned. "He brought an amphibious life–form into Aaru?"

"We don't have time for this," Ben interjected, shooting a quick glance toward my front door. "They're coming. She's not safe here."

He'd voiced that comment before.

"Who's coming?"

As if I didn't know. The Ruling Council had given me a pass, although none of them probably believed I'd really sent Harper to Hel. In time, I'm sure there would be a rogue band of angels attacking my house, but this was too soon for mob activity.

"Hunters."

Bull ... shit. Nils and I exchanged glances. "How many?"

"Five or more."

Hunters work alone, and there were no lynch mobs. Ben's next words only served to confirm my suspicions. "We have to get her out of here and to safety. Now."

The angel's announcement was echoed by a blast that rocked my house. The window to the left of my front door shattered, and I cursed. I'd just paid to have that fucking thing replaced after Nyalla's ghoul encounter, and now a bunch of angels had taken it out. I needed to seriously consider bullet–proof glass in next year's budget.

The house shook again, and I saw bits of drywall dust float down from the ceiling. "Get Harper and Nyalla into the cellar," I told Nils. "I'm gonna make these motherfuckers regret the day they stepped foot out of Aaru."

I didn't look back, trusting they'd follow my orders. Racing toward the door, I flung it open and unloaded the shotgun on whatever happened to be on my front lawn. The sentient weapon didn't let me down. With a spray of bullets that seemed to unerringly find their target, I ran down the crushed–shell pathway with the adrenaline of a pissed–off Rambo. Screams echoed from either side of me, making me wonder exactly how many angels had mustered up the set of balls it took to attack Satan in her earthly home.

"Fuckers! Come and get me, you worthless pansies."

One did, nailing me right in the shoulder with a stream of white. It wasn't as restrained as Dalmai's attack had been. This one burned through flesh and bone, leaving me to operate the shotgun one–handed. Gritting my teeth, I shook off the pain. I'd suffered worse at the hands of Ahriman. Diving behind a woodpile for cover, I kept firing into the shrubberies. The way my bullets looped around, I hoped the angels would be unable to figure out my location. I wasn't good at this sort of fighting unless it was one on one.

"There's five," Nils whispered in my ear.

I nearly shot him in surprise. Fuck, the guy moved as silently as a drop of rain.

"Where's Dalmai? Ben? I could use a few more angels on my side." Not that I expected Ben to help, especially if what I suspected was true.

"Well, you've got me." Nils edged forward to look through a gap in the stacked logs. "Dalmai will conveniently meditate through the whole conflict, and Bencul is busy guarding Harper."

Bencul. Figures Nils would know his real name. That tidbit of information would come in handy later.

"We need to sneak up on them. What can we use as a distraction? Besides Harper, that is."

"Me." Nils didn't sound particularly thrilled at his answer. "Dalmai's reaction to me was actually pretty tame. They'll come after me with a vengeance."

"And kill you. That would suck on so many levels." I should welcome getting rid of my Fallen–angel albatross, but the guy was beginning to grow on me.

Nils gave me an odd look. "Only you can kill me. Don't you know that? The Fallen are immortal; their existence is at the whim of the Iblis."

I remember hearing the whim thing, but didn't really ponder the significance at the time. "All right then. Go get 'em."

He vanished — not like Gregory, or my horse Diablo. Nils seemed to blur into the air, and, with no more than a stirring of grass and leaves, he was gone. I ducked to avoid a blast of white, which exploded the layer of logs just above my head, and began crawling along the ground toward where Nils had said the angels were. It wasn't easy scooting through brush with a shotgun in tow, but I felt better with the weapon at the ready.

The woods erupted into shouts and explosions. I jumped to my feet and ran, trusting in my shotgun to aim true. I hesitated, taking careful aim at the angel in front me. Then I shot him in the back. He jerked and turned around, shocked eyes meeting mine as his torso disintegrated into a pile of sand. Slowly, his form granulized until nothing remained.

He wasn't the only one shocked. I had no idea how to calibrate this weapon. In the past, it had always injured. Why not this time? I didn't have much of a chance to contemplate the ramifications of what I'd done before another angel appeared, staring at the sand in confusion.

I shot him too, with the same results. I was really screwed now. I'd killed two angels, so I might as well kill the other three — in for a penny, in for a pound. Ducking behind trees, I followed the sound of rhythmic thuds to see the other three angels taking turns as they pounded Nils to a bloody pulp.

Down they went, spraying sand all over Nils, who was a convulsing heap of raw flesh on the moss–covered ground. I strode over to him, kicking sand out of the way.

"So, you gonna let me kiss you now?"

He glared at me, one blue iris in a red background, the other eye swollen closed. "No." The word was mangled with saliva and blood.

I watched as he thrashed around, gaining enough control to slowly heal his broken and torn body. As much as I wanted to leave him in peace as he struggled, I worried that more angels would come and find him in this vulnerable position.

"You good?"

He nodded, finally repaired sufficiently to stagger his way to the house. I dismissed my shotgun at the door and walked in to see Nyalla clutching the wand in one hand, and the silver collar in the other. Harper, by her side, had a net at the ready. Bencul was hiding in the kitchen, visible over the granite–topped bar. So much for staying in the basement.

Nils walked in behind me, and Nyalla's eyes grew huge as she saw him.

"He'll be okay. He took one for the team and is having a hard time healing."

Bencul came out of the kitchen. "Are they gone? They'll be back, you know. This isn't a safe place for the baby anymore. I need to move Harper elsewhere."

"You're not moving me anywhere." Harper snarled. "When will you get it through your thick head that I don't want you anymore?"

"That's my child. I'll do what I need to in order to protect him. What you want is of no matter."

Shit. I needed to intervene before Harper started stabbing again.

"Those angels won't be back. Ever. They're dead."

Ben stopped, his face registering disbelief. "You killed them? You weren't ... they can't."

"Should have thought of that before you sicced your friends on my house with license to kill. They were your friends, right?" The look on his face was all the confirmation I needed. "Well, they're piles of sand now, all five of them."

Nyalla edged toward the kitchen, putting herself between the angel and Harper, who was looking at me in confusion.

"Ben's friends? Why would he send angels to attack me? He'd not risk his child... ." The woman turned to look at the father of her child, realization dawning on her face. "The monsters. You've wanted me to go to them the whole time. This was just an elaborate plan to get me to comply."

Debra Dunbar

"Yep. Either you'd be begging for monsters after a few days in my house, or his buddies would provide some added incentive."

I knew this was how this asshole's mind worked. Get Harper to comply any way possible, and if they killed the Iblis in the process, then hey, I was breaking the law anyway. And that would be three less favors he'd owe.

"Makes sense," Harper said, fingering the elven net. "Problem is, I'm not going with him. Ever."

The angel's blue eyes were cold. He took a step toward her. "You used to be so agreeable, so malleable, so easy to influence. I'm done playing these games. You're coming with me. I won't risk the life of my child because you've turned rebellious."

I stepped in between them, summoning my shotgun. He hesitated, eyeing the weapon and obviously remembering his five dead buddies. Harper might not want to leave her baby in the care of these "monsters", but if I could find out how the angels were hiding their offspring, it might give us another alternative for her and the child — an alternative beyond hiding in my house or life in Hel.

"Where is it that angels hide their Nephilim, Bencul?"

He shook his head, blond curls bouncing angrily from side to side. "That's not something I'd tell any demon, let alone the Iblis."

I shrugged. "Doesn't matter. She's said she's staying. It's her choice, not yours."

"It's safer for her there. Once the baby is born, she can leave."

"I'm not leaving my child with monsters, Ben." Harper's voice was eerily calm. "I told you to stay away from me and my baby. I'm going to raise him myself. I've made my choice."

"It's not your choice to make," he thundered, trying to sidestep around me.

The shotgun wasn't very effective as a projectile weapon in close range, but it did make a nice bully stick. I whacked him in the shoulder with it, and he staggered backward. Not that these two girls seemed to need my intervention. Harper fingered her knives with purpose, and Nyalla clutched the wand in a white–knuckled hand.

Ben growled and eyed my gun, clearly calculating his odds of getting by me. "The only reason you are alive is because of me," he told Harper. "You would have died on that mountain, but I saved you. You're mine now. I gave you life. In return, you are to bear my children."

What a fucking psycho. "I don't think Harper has any knowledge of this contract with you. Do you have a copy of the breeding proposal and signed documents to prove your claims?"

Yeah, I'd clearly been hanging out with angels for far too long.

"She's a human." Bencul spun about to face me, his face ugly with anger. "There is no need for proposals and signed documents with them. They're practically animals — just look at their vibration patterns. I saved her life. She's mine, and she owes me."

Harper gasped. "I don't owe you anything. This baby is *mine*. I'll see you in hell before I give my son to you."

What a great idea. Wish I'd thought of it.

Ben turned again at her words, giving me the perfect opportunity to whack him across the back of the head with my shotgun. I thought about stepping back and putting a few magical bullets into him but didn't trust the thing not to kill him. Besides, I had a far more horrible fate in store for this angel than death.

Whatever its powers as a trajectory weapon, the shotgun made a good cudgel. Bencul went down like a felled tree and stayed down, especially after Harper kicked him in the head a few times.

In no time at all, I was heading down to Columbia, a duct–taped and collared angel in the trunk of my Suburban with Nyalla by my side. Harper had begged to go, but I couldn't let her leave the house, let alone have the gate guardian see her.

"This is hard for her," Nyalla commented as we pulled into the mall parking lot. "Everyone has a dark side, but to find out the man who supposedly loved you was using you for breeding stock … that's going to leave scars."

I knew all about scars, although mine were mostly all over and through my spirit–self. Exploding myself along with Oak Island had done a number on me, as had my torture under Ahriman's loving touch. Ahriman. I shivered and turned down the AC in the Suburban a notch. Okay, so maybe my scars weren't just on the surface.

I remembered Harper gnawing her nails to bloody nubs, depressed and doubting her ability to parent this child, ready to resort to murder to protect herself. She was so angry. The only hope she had of a normal life was if we removed this asshole from it entirely. The woman might never fully heal from this, but I'd do all I could to give her a chance.

"This angel will never hurt her again," I promised.

"And never see the child he so desperately wanted," Nyalla added, climbing out of the car.

I popped the trunk and pulled Bencul out by his pretty, blond hair. His eyes glared at me above the duct tape. "Grab that shopping cart, will you, Nyalla?"

Both of us seized the angel, struggling to get him into the flimsy cart. His weight toppled it over the first few times, sending him crashing to the ground. I was grateful that it wasn't a busy section of the mall. Finally we got him in, and I tucked a blanket around him to hide him from view.

There was something oddly satisfying in wheeling an angel around the mall, bumping into every wall and kiosk I could find. The gate guardian's eyes widened as we approached the gate, located this time in the rear of a Victoria's Secret store.

"I'm not seeing this. I am truly not seeing this."

"Then you better turn your eyes," I told her, yanking off the blanket to reveal my duct–taped angel.

A nearby sales clerk froze, a box of underwear in her hand. "I'm calling security," she announced.

"I *am* security," I told her. "This is our new policy for dealing with shoplifters."

She cocked an eyebrow, obviously unsure whether to believe me or not.

I held up a bra. "He was jacking off in the dressing room. And he had three more of them stuffed into his pockets."

The woman backed away, glaring down at the angel. "You disgusting pervert!"

"You can't send him through!" the guardian protested. "He's an angel. I don't care what he was doing to human undergarments; sending him to Hel is not an equitable punishment for that crime."

"Tell it to the big guy." I pulled the angel out of the cart, knocking it over onto a display of thong underwear.

"You tell it to the big guy." The gate guardian averted her eyes, concentrating on a display of lacy thong underwear. "Last time I told on you, I nearly got my head ripped off. Nope. I didn't see anything. Nothing at all."

Whatever. With a wave of my hand, the gate appeared, shimmering.

"Nyalla, can you do your magic?"

I held my shotgun against the angel's head as Nyalla removed the collar. Then, with a swift kick of my boot, I sent him through the gate.

"There. That's done." I dismissed the gun and turned to see the Gate Guardian, her eyes darting between the collar in Nyalla's hand and me.

"He'll just come right back, you know. Angels are able to activate the gates."

I shrugged. "Yeah. And what's he going to tell the other angels? It violates the treaty for him to have been in Hel. They'll kill him or worse, make him into one of my Fallen. Even if he tells them I pushed him through, they'll wonder what he's been doing to survive. His choice is to stay in Hel and die, or come back and die."

The gate guardian looked at her watch. It was a nice Omega with a diamond bezel. "Bet you pancakes at iHop he's dead within twenty–four hours."

"You're on." There was no way. Once he got caught, the demons would want to keep him around as long as possible to play with and show off to their friends. "At least a week, maybe two."

~16~

Nyalla was right about Harper's grief. I waited all night, hoping Gregory would pop in for a date–night. It was just as well he was a no–show. The mood in the house wasn't exactly supportive of a romantic interlude. Plus I was going to have to eventually tell him about the five angels who'd become a mini sand box out front of my house, *and* the one I'd booted to Hel. He had been concerned over my smackdown of Dalmai, and I somehow doubted my recent activities would be considered trivial. My only hope would be to confess as soon as possible and throw myself at his mercy. Or just throw myself at him.

I finally couldn't take it any longer, so I called Candy and arranged to meet her for a jog.

"Two or four legged," I asked as I hopped out of my car. We were up in the northern part of the county at the section of the Catoctin Mountains near the Pennsylvania border.

"Two." Candy sighed. "Last time I got a bit too close to a farm. They thought I was a huge coyote."

"They shot at you?" I got shot at all the time. Especially since I'd recently made it a practice of doing some midnight runs through Fort Detrick. Naked. With my shotgun in hand.

Candy laughed. "Yeah. With a camera. Next thing I know there are pictures all over the papers and Facebook. Every hunter in the Thurmont area is hoping to put my pelt on a wall."

I understood that one too. "So how are things going with you guys?" The werewolves had been granted some liberties in the past year, but they still needed to toe the line of a strict existence contract or risk being exterminated by the angels.

"Great, actually. All the problems in Aaru mean no one has much time to pay attention to us. How about you?"

"All the problems in Aaru seem to be landing at my door. Did I tell you that somehow I'm now in charge of humans with bad credit? I'm supposed to rehabilitate them or some shit like that. Oh, and I'm in charge of Fallen angels, too. No kidding. There's one holed up in my house right now, although he actually seems to be pretty cool."

"That's not the one in your basement, is it?"

"No, but that one's still there too — in a bedroom, though, not the basement. Gregory commanded him to serve me. Evidently 'serve' means meditate and snark at the other angel, because that's all he's done so far."

"Pfft. Make him do housework. Or cook."

"Yeah, because a being that has never tasted food should be trusted with meal preparation. Remember that sandwich Gregory made me?" It had been an odd concoction of lunch meat, carrots and jelly. Thankfully his skills at coffee preparation were of a higher caliber.

Candy scrunched up her face in distaste. "Yeah, you're right. Poor Sam; seems like you're being overrun with angels."

"No shit. It gets worse. I've had angels attack me twice more since that dude I stuck in the basement. Although, now that I've gotten rid of Harper's boyfriend, I think that will taper off. The problem facing me now is how to keep her hidden. I told the angels I'd sent her to Hel. If they find out I've got a Nephilim in my house, unborn or not, my ass is in serious trouble."

Candy halted on the trail, her mouth unbecomingly open. "A *Nephilim*? I thought she was just some friend of Nyalla's you were helping out."

"No. Why else did you think angels were besieging my house?"

Candy raised her eyebrows. Well, yeah. Trouble did seem to follow in my wake. It would be understandable for her to think I'd done something to piss the angels off.

"Anyway, I've got no clue what to do with her. I feel bad that she's going to be hiding out in my house for another three months or so. And I'm totally at a loss about the birth itself and this baby. I really think the best idea would be to arrange some kind of transport to Hel."

"You can't send a half–angel to Hel!"

I grimaced. "A half–angel running around my house for however long they live is going to get noticed, and we'll both end up dead. So if you've got any better ideas, I'm ready and willing to hear them."

The werewolf bit her lip, frowning as she kicked a stone along the path. "I've heard there are places where Nephilim can be hidden, that their angel fathers know where to send them."

"Well the father's dead by now, and I can't exactly run around Aaru asking random angels where they hide their Nephilim. Besides, Harper would refuse. Evidently the father wanted to send the kid there, but she says she won't have a bunch of monsters raise her child.

Candy put her hands on her hips and raised her shrewd brown eyes to meet mine. "They're not monsters. They're werewolves."

Now it was my turn to stand there open–mouthed. "Why in the fuck would you all shelter Nephilim? You guys walk a thin enough line with the angels as it is. If they found a Nephilim in your midst, all bets would be off as far as your existence contract. They'd kill you all... ."

Oh. Suddenly it all made sense.

Candy looked around the trail before speaking. "Werewolves are the descendants of Nephilim. We're just lucky the angels haven't figured that out yet. The Nephilim that have been caught and executed in the past weren't analyzed in any detail before their death. Eventually it's going to happen. The connection will be made between them and us. Then we'll be exposed for what we are and wiped from the face of the Earth. We need to make sure the angels don't get a chance to look too closely at their half–breed offspring. So we help hide them."

Damned angels. Genetic cleansing at its finest when it came to the poor werewolves. "Why hide them right in your own packs? It's not the best place to avoid notice given the close eye the angels keep on you all. If I were in your shoes, I'd kill every Nephilim child I found, to reduce the risk of being discovered. Dead, dusted bodies don't tell tales."

Candy looked disgusted. "Besides the fact that we don't go around killing off innocent children, we need Nephilim. Werewolf–to–werewolf breeding eventually results in infertility and other problems. Nephilim introduce a surge of power into our genetic pool. They are Firsts. As adults, they are trusted advisors to our Alphas, powerful allies. If they choose to mate with a werewolf, their children have special skills and are fertile."

I shook my head in confusion. "How do you all hide them? You guys can't take a shit without some angel up your ass."

"A group of angels have created hidden zones, where werewolves and Nephilim can remain undetected. And there are some among the Grigori that are sympathetic to our plight. They have been known to look the other way."

This might work out better than sending Harper and/or her baby to Hel. "Can you come over tonight for dinner? Maybe give Harper your pack recruitment speech and show her that you're not the monsters she thinks you are?"

Candy smiled. "Absolutely."

***

"Absolutely not." Harper stood with her arms across her chest, eyes still puffy and red even as they sparked in anger. "I don't care if she's your friend; I'm not having my son grow up with werewolves."

"How about growing up around demons in Hel?" I snapped back. "Because those are pretty much the only two ways this baby of yours is going to survive to adulthood."

Candy put a hand on my arm, silencing me as she stepped forward. Fine. I'd let her do the kindly werewolf thing, but if that didn't work, it was back to my tough–love techniques.

"We're shape shifters, so yes, we do have different hobbies and communities than you're used to, but we live among the humans. We're doctors and lawyers, welders and technicians, school teachers and librarians. I'm a real estate agent."

"You're not human," Harper argued.

"And neither is your baby," I couldn't help but chime in.

Harper paled, taking a step backward. I felt like a total shit, but it was true. The sooner she realized that her baby would have more in common with the werewolves than humans, the better.

"Your baby would have loving foster parents. Werewolves adore children, and many of our mated are unable to conceive. Beyond that, Nephilim are honored in our packs. This child would have special status. He'd never be treated as an outsider."

Furious tears rolled down the woman's cheeks. "*I'm* going to raise my child. Me. I want to see him grow up, to be his mother — not some strangers."

"Can't she have her baby among the werewolves but still remain part of the human community?" Nyalla asked. She and Nils stood to the side, solemn witnesses to Harper's struggle.

Candy wrinkled her nose as she thought. "There's one group I know of who has revealed themselves to some human neighbors. But how would the child learn our ways without werewolf parents to guide him?"

"Werewolf childcare?" Nyalla suggested. "Or maybe werewolf pre–school?"

"No." Harper's voice was firm. "They'll turn my child into one of them — a monster."

Oh, for fuck sake. "Candy is not a monster. Look at her. How many monsters carry around a Louis Vuitton handbag?"

We all stared at Candy's purse. It was a lovely large bag with the signature monogramed leather and snazzy rounded handles.

"Let me see you change. I want to see you as a wolf before I make any decisions."

Shit. I exchanged uneasy glances with the werewolf. Candy was quite elegant in her wolf form, but the transformation process was long and downright gruesome. Harper would no doubt throw up her lunch then toss the werewolf out on her ass.

"It's painful and not exactly pleasant to watch. Are you sure?" Candy sat her much–coveted purse down on my table and removed her earrings.

Harper swallowed hard a few times. "Yes. I need to see. I need to know what kind of people would be guiding my child."

Candy sighed and removed and folded her clothing, neatly piling it on the table. With a deep breath, she began. Skin stretched as bone rolled and twisted underneath, muscles splitting and reconnecting. One moment she was a human woman, and the next a contorted mess covered by tanned flesh. Grey fur sprouted in patches along her skin, darkening to black along the tips. Nyalla and I had seen Candy transform many times, but Nils stared in fascinated horror. Harper slapped one hand over her mouth and scooted backward until her rear hit the wall.

It took twenty minutes, but finally Candy stood before us, a huge gray wolf. Harper shook, keeping her hand firmly on her mouth, but she didn't bolt. I shrugged at my werewolf friend and she began the arduous process of changing back into her human form. It had been a long shot, and Candy had given it her best. Guess it was Hel for this little guy. I better start checking out Dwarven nannies, because if Nephilim were anything like baby demons, Harper was going to need some help.

"I can't watch this again." Harper turned her back on Candy, her eyes resigned as they met mine. "Ben was right. You're right. I can't have this child and expect him to live without help from someone more powerful than I am. I'm just not sure which choice I want to make. Tell Candy I need to think about it. She seems nice, and Nyalla is very fond of her, but I need to think about it."

With a gagging noise, Harper ran for the stairs, bolting to her bedroom with remarkable speed.

"She's afraid," Nyalla commented softly. "She doesn't know what their influence will do to change her baby. There's already this deep fear in her that her son won't be human, that she won't be able to handle him, that he'll grow into some unrecognizable creature."

"I know one." Candy's voice was breathless as she sprawled naked on the floor, trying to gather the strength to stand and dress. "If she sees a grown Nephilim, maybe that will convince her."

"You know one?" We all had our secrets, but perhaps Candy had more than her share.

She nodded. "Not too far away. Do you think you can get Harper to see her?"

"I can't risk Harper leaving the house." It didn't matter if this Nephilim was next door, we were all at risk if Harper stepped one foot out my door. "Can she come here?"

Candy shook her head, pulling herself upright with a hand on my table. "She can't leave the protection of her territory. It wouldn't just be her at risk. If she were caught, we'd all be endangered."

Damn. I watched Candy dress and wondered how to solve this seemingly unsolvable problem.

"Skype," Nyalla chimed in. "Or video conference. Sam, you go meet with this Nephilim, and Harper and I can watch and ask questions from your laptop."

"Nyalla, you're brilliant." I sometimes forgot how easy human technology had made things. Skype. Go figure.

Candy picked up her Louis Vuitton bag and settled it in the crook of her elbow. "I'll arrange the meeting. Just remember, Sam, these are werewolves. You might be some weird demon/angel mix right now, but they'll still see you as an angel. Be on your best behavior."

As if I ever was on anything but my best behavior. "Of course, Candy. Best behavior. Scouts honor."

~17~

I stood in the huge restaurant of a racetrack/casino in Charles Town, West Virginia. The first race was lining up, and I'd been sidetracked from my mission to buy a past–performance program and place a few bets. There was also a nice off–track betting deal going on the dog races on TV, and a whole casino full of slots and table games downstairs. The buffet wasn't half bad either. The hot wings left a lot to be desired, but the selection of chocolate pastries made up for it. I was in heaven. I didn't care if this werewolf Nephilim showed up or not.

And they were off. Pigs In Flight took the lead, never a good thing, with Tap–handle Extraordinaire a nose behind. My pick, Punch 'Em Where It Counts, was solidly in the middle of the pack and on the outside. At the first turn, my horse had fallen into sixth — a respectable position given the amount of distance left to cover.

"Sam," Candy said in my ear. I cut her off with a wave. There was money on the line here, and this half–angel would have to wait.

Pigs In Flight was losing his wings, while Tap–handle pulled to the front. Bouncing Baby Bunny was coming up on the inside, and Piece of Asphalt was strong in the middle, but blocked by the other three. Punch 'Em Where It Counts edged into fifth, steady, but still on the outside where he'd need to cover more distance than the others to gain any ground.

"Go Punch!" I screamed, which probably would have been more appropriate had I been in the outdoor stands. Since I wasn't, half the restaurant turned to stare at me.

"Stupid idea, bringing a demon to a racetrack for a meeting," Candy muttered. I ignored her.

By the second turn, Pigs had dropped like a stone. Tap–handle and Piece were neck–and–neck. Punch 'Em Where It Counts had a good hold on third. I could see the power in the bay roan, held back just waiting for release. The other horses weren't flagging, but they didn't have the barely restrained explosion that I saw in this Punch horse.

"Sam." Candy's voice was firm, but with a pleading note.

I considered turning my attention to her, but at that moment, Punch 'Em Where It Counts hit the nitro. His stride lengthened, his neck extending as he steadily edged up on Piece of Asphalt and Tap–handle. Punch ate the distance, one bite at a time, until he was half a length in the lead. It wasn't a photo finish, but watching the three horses run flat–out across the line was a thing of beauty.

"How much did you win?"

The voice was familiar, but I couldn't place it. "Probably a lot. I like to bet on the underdog."

"I can imagine an imp who somehow wound up being the Iblis would bet on the underdog."

I turned and saw a vampire, of all things. She was diminutive in build, barely over five–feet tall with short black hair and dark eyes. Vampires owned a lot of the casinos, strip clubs, and bars in their territories, but it was surprising that werewolves would want to meet at a vampire–owned establishment. They stayed as far away from each other as possible. Also surprising was that this vampire knew me. I searched my memory, sure I should recognize her from somewhere.

"Sorry I don't have any nacho–cheese Doritos to shove up your bum."

That Kelly girl from the casino up in Atlantic City! I figured after she had a fit of anger in the hotel lobby at a demon VIP guest, the master–guy would have killed her. She looked at me with a combination of hostility and wariness, but I was just overjoyed that she was actually alive. I snatched her into my arms and hugged her.

Evidently that was not the PC thing to do. Vampires are strong, and she could have easily shrugged me off had she not been so shocked. Instead, I found myself surrounded by werewolves, all yanking at me and shouting. Candy too, although her shouts seemed to be more attempts to pacify the lot of us. Before they managed to tear me limb–from limb, I let the vampire go and flung myself backward. My momentum knocked the two werewolves behind me off balance, and I landed on the floor on top of them.

"I'm okay," Kelly said, a hand out to halt the tall woman beside her. "She didn't hurt me, just hugged me."

The word hug was accompanied by a shudder of revulsion. I would have been insulted had I not been staring at the woman beside her. She was tall and thin with fine, sandy–blond hair that flew around a freckled face. And her eyes glowed silver. Werewolf, yet not a werewolf.

"This," Candy panted, obviously trying to salvage the meeting, "this is Jaq. She's a Nephilim — a First."

I jumped up to extend my hand, and the Nephilim stepped backward, her eyes widening in alarm.

"I'm not going to hug you," I reassured her. "At least not at this particular moment."

An easy grin lifted the edges of her wide mouth. The lopsided smile reflected in her odd, silver–colored eyes and transformed her thin face into one of beauty. She stepped forward and clasped my hand in hers. She was strong. I could feel the power flow through her. And I felt a whole lot more. She wasn't like the demon hybrids I'd known in my life. This Jaq had more angel in her than human. Her spirit–self was easy inside the physical form she wore — comfortably in control of every molecule of her being. Werewolves were only able to manage their two forms, but I got the feeling this woman commanded far more than that. I edged my personal energy into hers, sensing who and what she was beneath the skin. Such incredible power, cold and damp, fluid. Her spirit–self had a liquid quality — oil, water, mercury — interesting.

Her eyes met mine, and she withdrew her hand. "Well, that was darned rude of you. Guess I shouldn't have expected any different from a demon. I think I would have preferred you hug me than feel me up on the inside like that."

It *was* rude to basically grope her spirit–self as I'd done. But I needed to know — I needed to be able to tell Harper what to expect from the baby that grew inside her womb.

"That's me — taking every liberty I can get away with."

She raised her eyebrows but seemed more amused than angry. Kelly stepped forward and took her hand. It was then that I understood. Somehow these two had overcome whatever divided their races and managed to become more than friends.

"Who is your father?" I asked the Nephilim.

"No idea." At least she was one of those to–the–point individuals. "I was raised by a werewolf couple. They are my parents in every way. I love their son as if he were my brother in blood. I've got no clue who my birth parents are — angel father or human mother."

I felt the pain of sorrow, short and sharp, from her. "It haunts you that they left you with others and never looked back."

Jaq took a deep breath. "The only reason I'm discussing this with you is 'cause I care about that woman and her baby. I want them to have the safety and protection I do."

I nodded. It was probably a good time to set up the computers and do our Skype call, but something made me hold off. I wanted to hear what this woman said first, before I decided how to present the information to Harper.

"I understand why my birth parents did what they did. They'd rather I grew up without them than die at the hands of some angel. Still, I often wonder who they were. Do they wonder about me? Do they imagine the person I've become? Do they wish they could see me and know what happened in my life? They'll never know."

I thought of how much Harper suffered at the idea of giving her child away and wondered if Jaq's mother felt the same. I sensed her honest sorrow over her birth parents. And I also sensed her lie.

"But they *do* know, don't they, Jaq." She didn't know of my weird angel status, didn't probably think she needed to hide from my fledgling ability to detect falsehood. "Your father, he came to see you, didn't he? In the wind, in a flowing stream, in the adrenaline of the hunt. Sometimes you saw something odd and knew, just knew, he was watching to see the daughter you'd become."

Jaq caught her breath, recoiling in surprise. Gripping Kelly's hand, she exhaled. "Yes. I remember a man with snow–white wings bending over my crib, his hair black as a moonless night. I remember a silver trout in the lake, its eyes glowing as it watched me swim with my brother. I remember a strange wolf running by my side at a hunt last year. I think … maybe it's just my mind playing tricks, but I think he has always watched over me."

Shit. I blinked back the inconvenient wetness in my eyes. "Tell me about your childhood, the things that made you feel part of the pack as well as the things that made you feel different."

"My parents *never* made me feel different," she declared hotly. "As far as I was concerned, I was their daughter. Werewolves randomly change into wolf form as infants but stop once they reach the age of one or two. They don't change again until their First Moon — generally around age twelve. It's a huge celebration, and there's a hunt in the young wolf's honor."

What a great evolutionary trait! Children who could change into wolf form might not have enough control to hold themselves in check. Such a thing would endanger the entire pack. How remarkable that they lost the ability until they were old enough to understand the effect their actions would have on others.

"Outside of infancy, a werewolf's childhood is much like any other human's. We have sitters — usually elderly members of the pack who choose not to hunt every moon, while our parents hunt. It's no different than other kids whose parents have a monthly date night. We have Legos, Barbies, and Nerf guns. We play Monopoly and learn soccer at summer camp — just like human kids."

Jaq paused and looked over to Kelly. The vampire met her eyes and smiled. There was a second of connection, of power exchange between the two, then the Nephilim turned her attention back to me. "But my childhood was different. I never lost the ability to change forms, and I could change into whatever I wished. At the age of four, I became a red–tailed hawk and panicked my parents by flying several miles along the banks of the Shenandoah River. I became lost, changed back and wandered in the forest for a few hours. Luckily my mother had raced after me in her wolf form. She has a great nose — the best in the pack. She found me crying and naked under a white pine by the side of a dirt road."

I shivered, thinking about a child alone and scared in an unknown forest. What would Harper do? Maybe she *wasn't* equipped to raise this son of hers.

"Then a boy in second grade jumped me on the playground at school. I threw him thirty feet across the baseball field and into the branches of an oak tree. He fell, breaking his arm in two places and dislocating his shoulder. Luckily no one believed the children who told on me. The teachers told his parents that he'd been climbing a tree and lost his grip."

I could sense her agitation, her guilt over these things, but I also detected that she felt a sense of relief to finally confess them to someone who wouldn't judge her. Of all the beings in the world, a demon would hardly condemn such actions. They were normal in the course of our lives, not worthy of even a second thought.

"In eighth grade, after my First Moon, I fell in love with a boy. He didn't return my affections." Jaq hesitated, a look of pain crossing her face. "I followed him around, sending him little gifts and notes. One day he humiliated me in front of my classmates, saying that I was an ugly freak and that he'd never be interested in a beast like me. I lost my temper and enthralled him. For months, he didn't speak. He carried my books to every class, walked me home from school, even kissed me behind the stadium."

"It's okay," I told her, feeling raw at the guilt that poured out of her. "Young demons do far worse. These things happen."

"No," she choked out. "After my First Moon, these things shouldn't happen. I was supposed to have control at that point, to be trusted with my abilities."

I hesitated. There was no way I could have her reveal all this over some internet connection. Harper needed to see her in person, to know the risk she was taking if she didn't accept their help — Jaq's help, in raising her son. But in the meantime, I felt I needed to soothe this Nephilim, to give her perspective from an angel and from a demon point of view.

"Jaq, you're a half–angel. Do you have any idea how long it takes us — them, angels I mean, to gain control? Centuries. You're doing better than the majority. Stop judging yourself against werewolves. You may be related, along the chain of evolution, but you're not one of them. You're Nephilim."

"And I'm alone. Even in a pack of werewolves. I'm accepted, respected, given a position of status and responsibility — but I'm still different. And no one forgets it." She looked at me sadly. "I'm being brutally honest, because I want your friend to know this. We may be the best chance her son has at surviving, but it's still not an easy road. I want to help. I want to do all I can so another half–angel doesn't go through the confusion I did. Her son will never be lonely or lost with me around."

Definitely fuck Skype. These things needed to be said in person. "Will you come to meet with her? She's in great danger if she leaves my house right now, but I want her to see you face–to–face and make a decision that way."

"No," the older werewolf, one of the guys I'd smushed when I fell backwards, spoke up. "I won't risk our First on this kind of thing. Record her, internet chat her, whatever, but she's not leaving the protection of our territory."

"We made alliances for a reason, Jonah." Jaq's freckles were nearly lost in the reddening of her face. "I should be able to travel outside our territory without fear of discovery."

"But not Maryland," Kelly whispered, tugging at Jaq's hand. "That's Fournier land. We need to stay in Monica's territory if we want to be safe."

The Nephilim's jaw firmed, her eyes gray steel. "I won't let this woman down. She's pregnant and afraid. Her baby is my brother as far as I'm concerned. I don't care what risk I take, if she needs me, I'll come to her."

There was a flurry of argument around us, every werewolf taking at once.

"Can't you teleport her back and forth?" Candy yelled in my ear. Werewolves weren't known for their hushed tones, and agitated werewolves had the volume of a passing freight train. People in the restaurant were beginning to glare at us, but just as their angelic ancestors did, the werewolves didn't pay the humans one bit of attention.

"Yeah, if she doesn't mind about twenty side trips to various parts of the world. We might end up a–few–hundred feet underwater too." That hadn't been a problem for me, but

I'd hate to drown this Nephilim. I doubt her vampire girlfriend would be the slightest bit forgiving if I did.

Candy wrinkled her nose. "How about Gregory?"

I'd told her of his measured steps down the slippery slope of sin, and his rather shocking willingness to throw aside his vibration pattern to help me cover up my illegal activities. If I asked, I was pretty sure he'd do this, but at what cost? I didn't know if his position within Aaru was in jeopardy, but he'd made it clear that his choices over the last few years were throwing the entire angelic host into an uproar. Getting caught transporting a Nephilim to meet with the mother of a Nephilim in the house of the Iblis might be whacking the hornets' nest a bit too hard.

"I can't put him in that position." Yeah, that's me — the 'nice demon' looking out for her boyfriend's interests. Sheesh.

Candy squinted, like she always did when she was churning ideas around in her brain. "Is there a gate to Hel in West Virginia? Or even in one of the southeastern seaboard states?"

I got where she was going, but having Jaq come back in the Columbia Mall would put her almost as far from my house as the West Virginia border. But the mention of Hel gave me an idea.

"There's a sorcerer in Hel that sells stuff to demons. He might have something that can help." Gareth had supplied me with an amulet of non–detection when I'd needed to fly in through a host of elf wards and deliver a smackdown. It only gave protection for an hour, but if I drove like a maniac — or even flew, I might be able to get Jaq back and forth before it wore out.

"Do we have time for you to make a trip to Hel?" Candy worried. "Every day that Harper stays in your house increases the risk that someone will see her and turn her in."

She was right. I doubted everyone on the Ruling Council was happy to turn a blind eye to my obvious lie. There would be watchers set around my house — in fact, they were probably in place now. Plus, I wasn't sure Gareth would even have the amulet off–the–rack. If he had to make one ... shit, I had no fucking idea how long that would take.

"I'll hurry, but just in case, can you and Michelle somehow convince her aunt to put a barrier around my house? She can dispel it once I get home."

Candy raised an eyebrow. "What about the angels in your house? Assuming they don't have to vacate to the barn or Wyatt's, they'll be trapped inside."

Damn. Oh well. Too fucking bad. "That Dalmai guy doesn't do anything but meditate all the time anyway; worthless fucking angel. Nils would stay to protect the girls — either from the inside or around the perimeter. And it's just for a day or two."

Candy nodded, and I turned to the arguing werewolves, blowing a shrill whistle between two fingers to get their attention so I could speak.

"Listen up! I may have a way to get your First to and from my house undetected, but I'll need to make a quick trip to Hel. Candy will let you know the details in a few days. Cool?"

The werewolves glanced at Candy, clearly relying on her as to my trustworthiness. Then everyone slowly nodded. Well, everyone except the vampire, who narrowed her eyes as she watched me, every cell in her body radiating distrust.

~18~

"You want what?" Gareth wiped his hands on a cloth and carefully screwed the lid on a glass jar full of ochre powder.

"Amulet of non–detection. Remember that one you gave me last summer so I could fly into Cyelle without setting off the wards? You said it allowed me to travel in an interdimensional rift."

"I remember. What are you trying to do with it, though? That may not be the best magical object for this application."

I hesitated, watching the sorcerer label the jar with bold, black elven script and put it on the shelf behind him. How much information could I trust him with? It's not like Gareth had daily dealings with angels, and so far he'd been the soul of discretion. Plus, I was worried that if I held something back, whatever I got would wind up not working. Having a whole pack of werewolves and a really pissed off vampire after me because I'd gotten their Nephilim dusted wasn't worth the risk of not telling Gareth the whole juicy story.

"I'm trying to sneak a Nephilim about forty miles to my house, then return her home without angels detecting her."

"A what?" The sorcerer paused, a bundle of cedar sticks in one hand and a piece of twine in the other. "What's a Neffy–liam?"

"Nephilim," I corrected. "It's what happens when an angel pops a chubby and gets busy with a human female. Half–angel–half–human baby, although from the one I've met, they seem to be more on the angel side than the human side."

He stared at me open–mouthed, cedar sticks forgotten. "But angels don't ... they can't ... their physical forms don't include reproductive organs. At least from what the texts I've read tell me, they don't."

"Normally, no, but angels haven't been able to bear offspring since the separation treaty two–and–a–half–million years ago. That's a mighty long dry spell, even for an immortal. They'd probably fuck a shoebox full of bologna at this point. Humans are better than nothing."

"Yeah, but they must have some way of taking care of things where they don't have to actually have sex. I mean ... you know." Gareth pumped his hand in a quick motion along the cedar sticks, mimicking a move I imagine he'd done countless times. Sorcerers spent a lot of time studying. I'm sure they also masturbated like a bunch of monkeys.

"They fuck each other, although it doesn't involve a physical form. Angel–on–angel sex doesn't produce offspring, either."

Gareth leaned over the table toward me, clearly fascinated. "So how do they do it, if they don't have physical forms?"

I didn't mind the detour our conversation had taken. Sex was a topic near and dear to my heart.

"We're beings of spirit. There's a merging, a joining of sorts. It's different than the physical sensation of human–type sex. There's the same emotional connection, but your entire being becomes one with the other. There's no separation. It's incredibly intimate."

The sorcerer stared at me open–mouthed. The cedar sticks dropped one by one to the floor from his open hand. "You've done this with an angel. You, a demon, have had sex with an angel."

There wasn't any question in his voice at all, but I still felt I should answer. "Yeah, but just angel sex. Not human–type sex. Not yet, anyway. I'm hopeful. We've been heading down that road, but shit takes forever when it comes to angels. I'll be lucky if we get to third base by the next millennium."

He shook his head in disbelief. "I know you're the Iblis, and I've seen your wings, but I'm not sure I can swallow this tale of you having sex with an angel — even if it doesn't involve physical bodies."

"Two years ago I wouldn't have believed it either." I walked around the little table and bent down to pick up the cedar sticks. "So, will that amulet work? Do you have any available?"

"Here's the problem." Gareth bent down beside me, his robe gathering on the floor as he brushed off the sticks and examined them closely. "You'll avoid detection by magical means, but I don't know how that translates when it comes to angels. If they have some special gift — a kind of second sight, then the amulet won't help you one bit. Plus, if they have someone watching your house, they'll actually see you arriving. The amulet doesn't block sensory input once you arrive at your destination and exit the rift."

I stood and thought, twirling one of the cedar sticks between my fingers. "Shit. I don't think angels use magic the way you or the elves do. I think it's more like a special sensory thing."

"Sensory how? Do they pick up on energy signature the way demons do? Is there a scent, or type of sound?"

"I don't think it's visual or sensory in the way humans would detect something. Angels just don't swing that way, and Nephilim can change forms anyway. I'm sure it has something to do with their energy signature. Something about their sprit–selves."

I watched Gareth stand and tie the cedar twigs into a neat bundle. He put them on a shelf then leaned against the table, tapping his chin with a finger.

"So we need something to hide their energy signature, and their physical appearance. An elven net, perhaps?"

I doubted Jaq was going to consent to being hauled in a bag for forty miles. And even if she consented, that vampire friend of hers certainly wouldn't approve. "What if it's not energy, but it's an aura they're sensing or something? Angels have this weird thing about color and sound. Our spirit–beings have distinctive colors, although those can't be perceived by the human eye."

"I don't think the elven nets are going to hide aura or the color of your spirit–self. If angels have that sort of 'sight', then there's a good chance they'll detect your Nephilim."

I let out an exasperated puff of air. "What if we forget about the whole 'non–detection' thing and look into some kind of transportation option. If I can get her to and from my house lickity–split, then the angels won't be able to find her."

"Ah, like the inter–realm gates the elves use. That's not something they ever teach us. I think it might be a skill that's only available to elves. And angels."

And me. If only I could use it reliably.

"But you guys do elf buttons and transportation scrolls. Would something like that work?"

The sorcerer's finger increased tempo on his chin. "Two elf buttons, but they need to be pre–keyed, and I've only created them for a destination in Hel."

"How about other mages?" I urged. "There was a human messenger from Cyelle last year that was transported to my house and used an elf button to return. So it must be possible."

"Messengers use the elf gates, or the elves open a travel rift for them. The elf buttons are only for return to Hel or inter–Hel transportation." His finger froze on his chin then extended out, pointing toward me. "But there is another way."

"What?" I was desperate. This was my last hope to get Jaq safely to my house and back.

"Kirby's marble."

The words nudged at the back of my memory, but I just couldn't place it. "Is that something to do with Occam's razor?"

Gareth's brows knitted in a bold line. "I've got no idea what an Occam's razor is. Kirby's marble is the name given to the transportation device invented by Freemage Kirby. It involves two devices that are linked and allow interdimensional travel between them. It used to be a one–way item, which meant you had to buy two in order to return, but he's perfected two–way use. You buy it on license for a set number of uses, and he can recharge the items for a fee. The guy is raking it in."

"Kirby!" I shouted. My old mage buddy from Cyelle. "I know him! That will be perfect." I could order two sets — one for Jaq, and another for Harper to safely join the werewolves in West Virginia.

"I'll have to see if he has any available," Gareth warned. "He had a pretty big backlog last time I checked."

"I'll go see him myself." There was a better chance I'd score one if I appealed in person. "Where is he working?"

"Libertytown."

For a second, I thought he meant the Libertytown just up the road from me in Maryland. Then I realized he must mean the new human settlement.

"Thanks for your help." I turned to leave, but he halted me with a quick hand on my sleeve.

"Wait. There's something else you need to consider. What happens once you get the Nephilim to your house? Wouldn't they be able to sense her? Do you have some sort of non–detect shield in place?"

"Uh, no." I hadn't considered that.

Sweat broke out on my skin, realizing that angels might also be able to sense Harper in my house. Gregory had said a Hunter would need to wander down the road to the house before he sensed her, and it seemed other angels needed to be closer. Still, a Hunter had known Harper was there. I'd just assumed if she stayed hidden from view she'd be safe — especially now that I dumped her shithead boyfriend this side of the gates. True, her baby was pretty small and probably didn't have much of an energy signature, but given that a Hunter had managed to find her, it wasn't a chance I wanted to take.

Gareth smiled. "Now *that* is something I can help you with."

He turned from me and rummaged through a wooden box, pulling out what looked to be a set of feather–topped lawn darts. "Place these around your house, within the line of sight of each other. Will eight be enough? I've no idea the size of your home."

I did a quick mental calculation. "Can I have ten? I'd like to enclose the pool area if I can."

"Yes." He added two more to the stack, and then opened a drawer full of scrolls. "These don't restrict movement, so anyone can come and go through the perimeter of the spell without breaking it. They also don't hide anyone from the five physical senses."

Touch, smell, sight, sound, and taste — although I doubted anyone beyond a demon in reptile form would be 'tasting' for Nephilim. "That shouldn't be a problem." Angels weren't committed to their physical form to the degree that those senses would do them any good.

"What it will do is hide all life–forms within the perimeter from magical detection. It will completely mask energy signatures. Mages, demons, angels, witches — all anyone will see is a big black hole."

"Awesome!" I picked up the lawn darts and examined them with interest.

"Not all that awesome," Gareth warned. "Big black hole is going to look like you've got something to hide. They'll know something is going on or you wouldn't have bothered with this kind of protection."

"True, but I'm an imp and the Iblis: I've always got something to hide."

Besides, with angels, it was all about proof. Even if they knew something was up, I wouldn't get a Ruling Council smackdown unless they could prove it. I'd get an attack — possibly a sneaky, middle–of–the–night attack, but I wouldn't be in any formal trouble. Angels like to follow the rules, and as far as I was concerned, I wasn't breaking the rules if I didn't get caught.

Gareth took the lawn darts from me and put them in a canvas drawstring bag. The scroll went into a protective case, and then into the bag with the darts.

"Here." He handed it to me. "I'll bill you."

***

I revealed my wings and flew to the human settlement of Libertytown. During the elf wars, I'd forcefully negotiated a small section of elven lands for the freed humans. They'd been granted a piece of Cyelle — a peninsula of forest that jutted south into demon territory like a huge bulge of green. I saw the treeline on the horizon as I flew, but it wasn't the lush forest I remembered. Red sands of Dis encroached on scorched grasses and brush. Stumps dotted the landscape, some dug up and piled to the side, making way for freshly plowed fields. Timber houses clustered together, mud sealing the gaps in the boards and golden thatch covering the roofs. It looked neat, but so obviously poor compared to the demon and elven cities. I couldn't help but wince.

Kirby's shop was easily found — the only stone building in the town. He must have found the money to pay dwarven builders. Costly, but important as handling flammable materials was a major part of a mage's profession.

A string of tiny brass bells chimed as I swung open the door. Kirby looked up, and a smile creased his face. The mage's work robe was smudged with charcoal and something that looked like old blood, but other than that, he seemed like the same Kirby I'd known from Taullian's palace.

"Sam, or should I call you *Iblis* now? Either way, it's good to see you."

"I'm always Sam to you, Kirby." I looked around at the shelves and boxes stacked full of supplies and finished magical goods. The building smelled pleasantly of sandlewood and burnt sage with a hint of licorice. I had no idea what he was working on, but the aroma was certainly more pleasant that the stench of sulfur at Gareth's.

"Looks like things are going good for you. Who did your stonework? Bofor or Drumbach?"

"Drumbach. I've got a good trade going on. Lots of orders from both the elves and the demons."

"You'd get more if you set up shop in a bigger city like Dis or Eresh."

Kirby had enough skill as a mage to keep the riffraff out and make alliances for protection — important things if a human wanted to live surrounded by demons.

"True, but I can't bring myself to leave the settlement. These people need me. They need the money that my shop brings to the town, and they need the little magical devices that I provide them with at reduced cost."

I grimaced, looking out his front window. A woman walked by with a basket full of roots in her arms. "Are things truly that bad? It doesn't look like the forest is doing well, but I saw tilled fields. And the houses look sturdy."

"Climate control is an elven art. Without it, Libertytown is returning to its natural environment. We're having to constantly change farming techniques to keep up. Crops aren't exactly thriving."

And the only thing of value they had in trade was the skill of their magic users.

"Some of the humans have moved back to serve the elves. They send money or supplies to their families here as they get paid." Kirby wiped a hand across his forehead, leaving a streak of charcoal. "I'd hoped we could be relatively self-sustainable, that we could live here and trade the products of our labors. Instead, families are split. We're not really sure what kind of future we'll have."

Dar was right. I did need to get my ass back to Hel and take care of things. Just as soon as I got Harper safely hidden away with the werewolves.

"Anyway." Kirby waved a hand to change topics. "Gareth messaged me that you needed a two-way transport with two charges?"

"Kirby's marble. How did you get so famous that a coveted magical device is named after you?" I teased. "How many fifth-level mages can boast of that?"

Red tinged his cheeks, and he grinned sheepishly. "Just me. It paid for my stonework within the first three months."

Not bad. I looked around the building, admiring the work. Dwarves rocked, pun intended.

"Only problem is my success. I'm backed up thirty orders, and Gareth said you needed it right away."

"Yeah. How long would it take you to get it to me?"

"Six or seven months."

Crap. Harper would have a babe in arms by then, if the angels hadn't pried the boy from her. "Any chance I could line jump?"

Kirby wiggled his eyebrows. "You're an imp. Don't you line jump all the time?"

I laughed. "I'd love to leave with something right now. Is there anything ready to go?"

"I've only got one completed right now, and it's a rather unusual focus item."

"Unusual how?" I envisioned giant dildos, or live piranha, although those probably wouldn't be unusual for a demon.

"I'll show you." Kirby strode into the back room and reappeared a few moments later carrying a large box.

"Stand back."

Right. Had he forgotten I was a demon? I walked up as close as I could get to the box and prepared to peer into it. The mage clicked a latch, and the box lid slid aside. Something shot out and bit my nose.

"Son of a bitch!"

Kirby launched forward and grabbed it, ripping a chunk of flesh from me in the process.

"Who the fuck would use a durft as a focus?" I healed my nose and then rubbed it, just to make sure it was all there.

"Someone who wants to be positive they're the only one able to use the focus." Kirby's voice was full of irony. That's when I noticed he was holding the animal in the crook of his arm, stroking its tan fur.

"So I take it this set is for you?"

"Nope. Fred and I have become friends."

I doubted Fred would ever let me pet him like that. As if confirming my thoughts, the durft looked at me and snarled.

The mage put the animal back in the box. "There are two stones in the box with the durft — one for each location. You hold the durft and it will allow you to move back and forth between locations."

"And I'll arrive at my destination shredded to ribbons from that monster."

"Yep. I suggest you sedate Fred first."

Jaq was a Nephilim. I was pretty sure she could handle whatever Fred could dish out, but Harper?

"Will it work if the durft is in a cage? Or duct taped? I'm not sure I want to ask a pregnant human to hold that thing, even if it's sedated."

Kirby hesitated in the middle of latching the box, his eyes darting to meet mine. "Pregnant? She can't use this. She'll lose the baby."

Holy shit. These things needed to come with warning labels on them. "Any other side effects? Hair loss? Incontinence? Boobs shrivel up and fall off?"

Kirby latched the box and set it aside. "It's not that there's anything dangerous in the transport, it's that the device only works for one being. Elf buttons will transport multiple people as long as they are touching, but not this. If a pregnant woman uses it, the baby will be left behind."

I frowned at the box. It would still allow Jaq to come and go undetected. I'd need to figure something else out for Harper.

"Okay. No pregnant women. How much?"

Kirby smiled. "It has five charges. One favor per charge."

That was a lot of favors. Not that I had any other options.

"Done."

~19~

Harper paced, gnawing the already–shredded nail on her right hand index finger. "This is like waiting for a blind date," she complained.

"Or the pizza delivery guy," I groused. Neither seemed to deliver within the time promised. At least Jaq had the excuse of wrangling a pissed–off durft. I eyed the small stone on the dining–room table and wondered if I should relocate it to the floor. Although it might be kind of funny if the Nephilim appeared on top of my table.

She didn't. With a flash, Jaq was standing before us, a screaming ball of fur in her bloodied hands.

"Here, take this." She thrust Fred at me.

I was prepared. Throwing a tablecloth around the animal, I stuffed him into his box and slammed the lid. "Need me to heal you? I'm not very good at it yet, but I'll give it a shot."

"Already done." The woman wiggled her fingers at me then turned to smile at Nyalla and Harper. "Let me go wash my hands, and then we can talk."

"All clear." Nils came in the back door, his face serious. "Boomer is guarding just in case, but I couldn't sense any angels." He turned to Harper. "You okay?"

The woman lifted her chin. "I'll be fine. It's pretty in West Virginia. After the baby is born, I'll get a job at an outfitter, teach climbing and rafting while the werewolf babysitters do their job. I'll be all right. Better than if I go to Hel, anyway."

The tremble in her voice sounded anything but fine. Nyalla made a sympathetic noise, rubbing the woman's shoulder. I watched in surprise as Nils approached Harper and put his arm around her, tucking her into his side.

"Bencul was a manipulating jerk. Don't let one asshole ruin your trust toward everyone else in this world. You've got your whole life ahead of you, and things will get better." She looked up, and he smiled down at her. "Trust me; I understand what you're going through. Just take what life gives you and run with it. Have faith that everything will be all right in the end."

Jaq cleared her throat and walked from the kitchen toward Harper, her long thin hand extended. "My name is Jaq, and I'm a half–angel. I'm here to answer all of your questions, honestly and completely."

Harper shook her hand, sliding out from under Nils's arm. The pair made themselves comfortable on the sofa while the rest of us hid in the kitchen and tried not to look like we were eavesdropping. This was Harper's choice to make. Her life. None of us wanted to push her toward one decision or the other, although glancing out my window at the line of sticks around my house, I doubted there was any other decision she *could* make.

I pulled three beers from the fridge and popped the caps, handing one to Nyalla and another to Nils. He took a swig and made a face.

"I'm not sure I'll ever get used to drinking this stuff. Coffee and wine, yes. Beer, no."

"You're doing better than that other angel," Nyalla commented, looking up the stairs toward the closed bedroom door. "He hasn't eaten or drunk anything since he arrived."

Oh shit! I'd forgotten that Dalmai was even here. He hadn't emerged from the room since he'd began meditating.

"Maybe we should check on him? What if he's dead or something?" I hoped so. It would make my life a whole lot easier, and free up that bedroom.

"He's alive. I went in this morning to get a change of clothes, and he was still meditating."

Stupid angels. "Where have you been sleeping?" They were supposed to rotate usage of the room, but it seems that Dalmai had taken over.

Nils turned an interesting shade of red and gulped down his beer. "The sofa. I'm sleeping on the sofa."

Nyalla coughed and chewed on her lip to hide a smile. "Yep. He's sleeping on the couch."

I frowned. What was so funny about sleeping on the sofa? "Either way, I better go up and make sure he's not plotting our deaths or turning my spare bedroom into some kind of shrine to Aaru."

I headed up the stairs, hearing a distinctive giggle from Nyalla and Nils's low voice in response.

Dalmai was sitting cross–legged in the same pose I'd left him. A few articles of clothing were scattered about the room, most notably a pair of underpants hanging off the end of the angel's foot. Nils's underpants, no doubt. That dude would have made a good imp.

"How did you get her to your house without the angels noticing?" he asked.

I knew right away who he was talking about. He *was* a Hunter, after all. "None of your business. Are you planning on doing anything useful around here? Besides sitting on your ass and hogging up one of my guest rooms, I mean."

"I'm attempting to raise my vibration levels in the hopes of bringing about the salvation of those in this dwelling." His eyes popped open. "A fruitless endeavor. Demon, Fallen angel, two Nephilim — the only ones worth saving are the humans, and I'm not sure about them. You do realize one is having improper relations with the Fallen angel."

I shrugged, while my mind raced. Nyalla? Or Harper? I wasn't sure Harper was ready to get it on with another angel right now, but Nils had put his arm around her in a rather intimate fashion. Seems I was going to have to have a little chat with my newest angel. This was a bit more fallen then I wanted to contemplate.

"Lust is one of my favorite sins. I hope to be banging an angel before the end of the week myself."

Dalmai stood, brushing imaginary lint off his clothing. Although after several days of non–movement, perhaps he had gotten rather dusty.

"You're taking the pregnant human to the hidden sanctuary, aren't you?"

I hoped to, although I still had no idea how I was going to get her there beyond driving like a maniac and hoping for the best.

"Yep. Soon both Nephilim will be out of your reach, and hopefully you'll be out of my house and back to Aaru."

His eyelids drooped, shading his thoughts from me. "It won't be soon enough. Now, if you don't mind, I would like to continue my meditations in peace."

"Nope. Nils gets the bedroom for the next twenty–four hours. You want to meditate? Do it in the basement."

His lip curled. "So it's back to the basement?"

"Sure. With your superior vibration pattern, you should be able to disregard such worldly things as laundry machines and lack of light."

Dalmai glared and stomped past me to the stairs. He hesitated at the bottom to stare at Harper and Jaq, still in discussion, then headed to the basement and slammed the door.

"Bedroom is all yours," I told Nils. "Which means no

more sleeping on the couch, or doing other things. Got it?"

The angel fidgeted, looking down at his coffee cup. "Got it."

~20~

Finally I had the house to myself. Well, sort of. Nils was in his own bedroom, doing whatever a Fallen angel does, Harper in her room planning her future in West Virginia, Nyalla out with some friends, and Dalmai in the basement becoming one with the universe.

So I did what I always do when I've got an evening all alone. I pulled out a bottle of vodka, threw a bag of popcorn in the microwave, got buck naked and put on Air Supply's Greatest Hits. I was jamming away to Making Love Out of Nothing at All and dumping the popcorn into a bowl when I felt a hand on my shoulder. Popcorn went flying, and I spun around to send a jolt of electricity into ... Gregory.

"Shit! Sorry about that. I've been a bit twitchy lately, what with all the angels attacking my house."

"Is that the only thing making you twitchy?" His hands rested on my shoulders as his eyes examined my face.

I sorted through the things I'd told him, and the million things I hadn't. There was plenty to make me twitchy, but I wasn't sure I wanted to confess all to anyone, even this angel.

"What happened when you were in Hel?"

I knew he wasn't referring to my most recent visit. My banishment had been the darkest point in my life. The injuries I'd suffered were so extensive that I hadn't been sure I'd ever be able to create a decent form again. I'd lain in the elven woods, waiting to be found and killed, hoping to be found and killed. Death had begun to seem the better alternative to life as a powerless, immobile creature.

And death had definitely seemed like a better alternative than what I had suffered at Ahriman's hands. I shuddered, determined not to let my mind go there, and made light of the whole thing. Humor — my best armor.

"I took out that bastard Feille, forcibly negotiated freedom and land for the slave humans, and managed to survive near–fatal injuries. You know, usual stuff. A day in the life of an imp."

Gregory rubbed his spirit–self along my scars, gently touching each one. I could tell he wasn't distracted by my casual tone. I held still as he examined every bit of me, feeling safe and warm in this intimacy I'd never willingly allowed another.

"I remember your injuries. I saw them when they were fresh. But there's pain under these scars, and I don't know its cause."

I stiffened, pulling my personal energy away with an involuntary reaction. Ahriman. The memories crashed over me before I had a chance to wrestle them back into their little corner of my mind. I wasn't ready to discuss that part of my banishment. I wasn't ready to admit to Gregory that I'd been such a fool as to sign the breeding contract with that creature. I wasn't ready to admit how close I'd come to losing myself in that dungeon.

But everything fell away in Gregory's embrace. His touch — physical or otherwise, never caused me a moment of panic. Our views of right and wrong might occasionally differ, our methods of achieving goals might frequently differ, but, in the end, I trusted him completely. There was a giddy sense of freedom in that realization.

I leaned into him and struggled to compose myself. We had all of eternity to heal the scars we both carried. "It's Hel. Shit is always happening there. My sprouting feathery wings isn't going to change that."

"Understandable."

Unfazed by my sidestepping of his question, the angel knelt down to pick up the pieces of the bowl. I felt no disappointment from him, only openness. I knew he'd be ready to listen anytime I was willing to talk. I *should* be able to tell him — the one being I felt safe with all my secrets.

"I ... I did something really stupid." The words were soft and shaky — just as shaky as my hands. I wanted to cram them into pockets to hide, but I was naked. Naked in more ways than one.

With a sweep of Gregory's hand, the pottery clicked together seamlessly. "Why does that not surprise me?" His tone was faintly teasing. What I was about to confess was so dark, so serious. Instead of making light of the situation, his words gave me a sense of relief — as if no matter how terrible, problems would be easier when shared with him.

"I signed the breeding contract with Ahriman."

I felt his rage and stepped backward, even though I knew it wasn't directed at me. When the angel turned to face me, his black eyes were cold with fear. Anything that scared a six–billion year old angel was bad shit. I took another step back.

"He threatened my household. I meant to tell you, to find a way out of it, but then all the shit went down in Alaska and on Oak Island, and it slipped my mind."

I winced at the wave of heat surging from Gregory. He was beginning to glow. I backed up a few more steps and tried to get the rest out as quickly as possible, hoping it would be like ripping off a bandaid.

"I didn't do it. I didn't go through with the breeding. And he's dead now, so you don't need to worry about it."

Gregory shot out a hand lightning fast and yanked me into his chest. The impact drove the breath from my lungs — breath that I gasped back in as his sprit–self plundered mine, searching and seeking.

"I swear I didn't give him what he wanted. He forced ... he made me ... but I didn't give him what he wanted. I know you're angry at me, that you warned me, but it all turned out okay."

The angel paused. I glanced up at him, squinting against his bright, blurred form.

"It did *not* turn out okay."

I froze inside, thinking that maybe this was the one unforgivable thing I'd done that would tear us apart. Gregory dove under the scars, to touch something deep down in the heart of me, something hidden.

"Aaru can deal with whatever Hel throws our way, *this* is what I feared. He has hurt you, scarred you worse than any battle could have done. Whatever death he faced, it was too quick and too painless compared to what I would have done."

I was speechless, shocked again at how I knew so little about this angel. Instead of being angry over the near miss to his beloved Aaru, he was furious over my suffering at the hands of the ancient demon.

"I'm fine. Those scars will eventually heal, and I'll be fine." How did I tell him that loving him did more to blunt the pain and panic Ahriman had caused than any amount of time? If it weren't for him, I'd probably still be huddled in the swamps. If it weren't for the portion of himself I'd stolen when he bound me, and the thought of how I wanted to be more than a lowly imp in his eyes, I'd be a broken breeding slave in Ahriman's dungeon. I might not be fine, but I was on my way there, thanks to him.

Gregory crushed me against him, tangling his hands in my hair. "Who killed him? Did he assume your contract along with Ahriman's household? Which demon do you belong to now?"

I pulled back in surprise, getting the distinct impression that my angel was about to brave the fires of Hel to kill any demon who had the poor judgment to claim me.

"I killed him. Dusted that fucker into a little pile of sand the moment I got my wings. His household is mine now, along with his monstrosity of an Addams' Family house filled with furniture made out of dead shit."

The relief that poured from him was palpable, as was the pride. "My little Cockroach. I should have known. There's a reason you earned the title of Iblis."

'Earned' wasn't exactly the right term. That damned sword, and the job that went along with it, had attached itself to me like gum to the bottom of my shoe. There was no ridding myself of it now. Still, Gregory's words warmed my heart. I buried my face into his chest and hid my smile against the soft cotton of his polo shirt. He hugged me tight, and then released me. *Back to business*, I thought as he picked up the popcorn bowl and extended it toward me.

"I came to tell you that there should be no more Hunters as long as the Nephilim's mother stays hidden. We've got more pressing matters in Aaru then harassing a human over an unborn child."

I took the bowl from him, suddenly not hungry for popcorn. Should I tell him about Bencul and his dead buddies? I'd just bared my soul to him, and I'd vowed to myself that I'd not hide these things from him any longer. Still ... four–nine–five reports for killing humans was one thing, taking out a group of angels and sending one into Hel was another. I doubt naked and restrained would be my punishment for that. This was far worse than netting an angel and duct taping him in my basement.

"Is this not a good time?" His rueful smile tugged at my heart.

Date night — I'd been waiting for him to appear for days. No, it wasn't a good time, but I wasn't about to squander this chance. Between the pair of us, our schedules might not allow us another opportunity for months.

"It's a great time. I've got some things I need to let you know about, though."

The smile faded. "Another angel duct taped in your basement? Cockroach, this hostage thing of yours has got to stop. Dalmai was one of my own choir, but I may not be able to shield you from the backlash if this is from one of the others."

"No." I squirmed. "It's not another angel in my basement. It's something else."

He shook his head and sighed. "Please tell me this news doesn't involve something that will put you, and thus *me*, further in trouble."

This angel knew me so well. "How about I ply you with chocolate and vodka, sex you up, then tell you the bad news?"

"How about you tell me the bad news now, and hopefully the rest of the evening will cause me to forget all about it?"

"Deal." I took a deep breath. "The angel that knocked up Harper came back with some friends to scare her into compliance. I killed all his buddies, and I threw him through the Columbia gate into Hel. Then—"

"Wait." Gregory halted my explanation with an outstretched hand. "Were these buddies angels? And if so, how many of them did you kill?

"Yes. Five."

He kept one hand on my arm and used the other to rub his face. "So, you killed five angels and sent one to his death in Hel?"

"Yeah. Add all that to your angel that I assaulted and duct taped in my basement, which, by the way, he is down there again after hogging the spare room, although I didn't duct tape him this time. Oh, and there were the other four that attacked me right before you appeared to take me to the emergency Ruling Council meeting. They disappeared before I could kill them, but I did wound one by shooting him with my Iblis shotgun." I gave him a serious look, relieved that he didn't seem angry. "Do you need a piece of paper to tally all this up?"

"No." He shook his head. "Go on. I'm assuming there's more to this confession."

"Then I discovered that the werewolves are the descendants of Nephilim and have several angel–protected areas where their packs hide and take care of half–angel children."

That didn't seem to faze Gregory at all. I glanced down at his hand on my arm and continued.

"I contacted an adult Nephilim and convinced her to come here and speak to Harper about the advantages of going to this sanctuary. Now I just have to figure out how to get Harper there so she'll be safe. She can have her baby, raise him in in the company of werewolves, and the whole problem will be solved."

I grew increasingly edgy as the silence stretched on. Finally Gregory removed his hand from my arm and looked about my kitchen. "You were right. I should have started with vodka, chocolate, and sex."

"Vodka is over there," I pointed helpfully. He didn't even bother with a glass, chugging it from the bottle. He put a sizable dent in the volume of the contents then slid the vodka back on the counter.

"That has got to be the worst tasting beverage I've sampled to date. Do you seriously enjoy this, or is imbibing it some kind of masochistic demon thing?"

I tried to look offended, but I was too worried about his lack of comment on my confession and his sudden desire to down large quantities of hard liquor. This wasn't the first time my actions had gotten me on the wrong side of the angels. Killing a few of them aside, this was actually pretty tame. Why wasn't he pissed, or throwing some two–hundred page report at my feet?

"It's good stuff. As much as I love vodka, I think you'll like the chocolate better." And the sex. Hopefully he'd like the sex best of all. And hopefully it wouldn't be just angel sex this time. As fun as that was, I really wanted to experience the ultimate of both physical and non–corporeal joining with him.

"Great. Go ahead and assemble your chocolate offerings. I'll be on the couch. Sitting and brooding over my precarious future in Aaru."

Shit, that didn't sound good. Gregory started to walk out of the kitchen, and then backtracked to pick up the bottle of vodka before disappearing into the great room.

I watched him leave before springing into action. Nyalla had gone hog wild on chocolate purchases. She had traditional, grocery–store candy bars, organic fair–trade stuff, and stunning hand–made truffles. She'd never tasted chocolate until arriving from Hel a few months ago. Who better to help pick out the best to tempt an angel who only recently began to dip his toe into the waters of gluttony.

"Ta da!" I sat on the sofa and placed the tray between us, noting the vodka bottle was half empty. "That bad? Maybe we should hold off on the chocolate and discuss how much shit I'm in this time."

Gregory shook his head. "Morning. I'm going to pretend I was rendered momentarily deaf in the kitchen so we can enjoy our date night. Tomorrow we'll face our future and discuss options."

It all sounded pretty grim, but that 'our future' still set my heart to skipping like an adolescent. "Then pass that thing over here. Don't bogart the bottle." He handed me the bottle, and I took a quick swig. "This is one of my favorites. It's a potato vodka out of Romania. There's another one I love that's from Poland and made with rye." I looked at the bottle regretfully. "At the rate we're going, I may need to break that one out."

"That might be advisable." He took the vodka from me, drinking deep. "For comparison purposes, you understand.

I'm sure the differences in flavor and eye–watering burn are subtle but significant."

"I'll get it, but first," I handed him a small square of chocolate, popping an identical one in my mouth. "This is one of the most popular chocolates in the U.S."

He ate it and winced. "From my analysis, there is far more sugar and dairy product in here than actual chocolate."

Angels. There was no pleasing them. "Well, given the amount of sugar and dairy product you put in your coffee, I thought you'd like that."

"Coffee evens out the sweetness. This doesn't have enough of the bitter chocolate, and the result is far from balanced."

Here we go with that whole 'balanced and centered' thing again. I could take an angel out of Aaru, but I clearly couldn't erase billions of years of indoctrination.

"If you think that's too sweet, wait until you try this one." I handed him a mini candy bar and watched as he squashed it between his fingers.

"What's the stuff in the middle?"

"Nougat. And now you've got it all over your hands. You'll have to lick your fingers. Or I can lick your fingers. Or you can smear it all over your body and I can lick it off your skin." The idea was immensely appealing.

"Slow it down, Cockroach. We have a whole tray of chocolates and a bottle–and–a–half of vodka to enjoy first."

Which reminded me that I needed to get more alcohol. "Eat that thing before it melts all over you and tempts me further. I'll go get the Belvedere and be right back."

I raced down to the cellar, past Dalmai who was standing and watching me with an incredulous stare as I rooted through my liquor stash.

"You are the most evil being I have ever encountered."

There was a lot of hate in the angel's voice, and I turned to face him in surprise. "What are you talking about?"

"Michael. The Ancient Revered One. The Leader of the Host. The Angel of Righteousness. How *dare* you be so greedy and selfish?"

It took me a second to realize he meant Gregory. The rest still confused me. I'd accept greedy, but *selfish*? "What do you mean? I'm sharing my best vodka with the guy — and trust me, he's drinking far more of it than I am."

"You're tearing him from us, changing him. Aaru needs him. If he were to fall ... he's the loadstone. If he were to fall, we'd all fall."

That seemed a bit overly dramatic. Besides, these angels could do with a bit of earthly delights. "So you're berating a demon, the Iblis, for tempting an angel to sin?"

He glared. "Ridiculous, I know, but you have shown an odd propensity to care for others. If you're truly capable of empathy, even an unevolved, limited amount of empathy, then you should realize how much your actions hurt others — an entire race of others. Go find another angel to tempt."

I found the bottle I was looking for and stood, holding it in one hand. "What if it's the angel that is tempting me?"

Dalmai looked rather shocked at the prospect.

"I love him, and he loves me. It would be a shame if such a lauded emotion caused the fall of Aaru, but if that's the case, then perhaps the angels were soaring too high for their own good."

"How dare you," he sputtered.

I wasn't about to let him finish.

"I dare because I'm a demon. I dare because maybe in my short nine–hundred thirty–eight years I've learned some things you haven't." I walked toward the stairs. "The best direction to go isn't always up. You angels go on and on about being centered. *Centered* — not so far in the nosebleed section that you've lost your grasp of what it means to live along the path. Lower your vibration, reduce your altitude, and maybe you'll find those specks of black on the ground can teach you something about your own life."

I should have been angry as I climbed the stairs, but all I felt was pity — for Dalmai and the other angels in Aaru who'd never once stepped far enough away from their meditations to see what miracles life held. I thought of Nils and his desperate breeding petition to a demon who was so not worth it. I thought of Bencul, so eager for offspring that he viewed a human as if she were a broodmare. I thought of Jaq's father, watching over her as she grew and matured.

And I thought of Gregory. My own angel who'd thrown aside billions of years of responsibility to love me. We, neither Hel nor Aaru, couldn't wait another two–and–a–half–million years for a bunch of stubborn angels to come to their senses. The greatest things in the universe often required a big bang. And as the Iblis, it was my job to light the fuse.

I waved the bottle at him as I reached the top of the stairs, swinging the door shut behind me. The one on the coffee table was looking suspiciously near empty, and every chocolate had a bite taken out of it.

"What's this one?" Gregory pointed a finger at a truffle then wiggled it over to a dark square.

"Which? The round one is milk chocolate surrounding a truffle, which is the tuber of a type of fungus. The flat one is an organic dark chocolate with sea salt." I popped the other half of the truffle in my mouth. I might not be selfish, but there *was* a limit to my generosity.

"They're both good, but I think I like the dark one with the salt the best."

I plopped down on the sofa beside him, hiding the Belvedere bottle behind me and out of his reach. Sheesh, and they called *me* greedy. "That's Nyalla's favorite too. She has a stash hidden up in her room for what she calls 'emotional emergencies'."

He scooped up the remaining piece and examined it. "She has an affinity for water. It makes sense she would like foods that taste of the ocean."

I snorted out a laugh. "She's been to the beach every month, has brochures plastered all over the walls of her room. Jet skis, paddle boarding, fishing, and now she's taking scuba–diving lessons. I think the girl is part fish."

"You know she made me a food item while you were in Hel. I believe she called it a 'casserole'. She said human females make these as gifts when someone is feeling sad."

Huh. No one had ever made me a casserole before. "Was it any good?"

"No. I'm very fond of your human ward, but she might want to leave the food preparation to those who have had more than six months of experience."

He extended the square of chocolate toward me, and I took it gently from his hand, brushing my lips against his fingers. My eyes met his and the seduction of the moment made me irrationally shy.

"So, what did you gift her with anyway?" I scrambled for something to say to relieve my sudden awkwardness. "I'm guessing telepathy?"

His eyes snagged on my lips, and he smiled, as if *he* were the one reading my mind. "No. I allowed her to see into the hearts of others. She can't hear their thoughts, but senses their overall emotional state. With maturity, she'll see glimpses of their past — things that made a significant impact on them."

"Why?" My question wasn't just a distraction by this point. I was interested. "Why would you gift her with that?"

"She was lost and afraid, surrounded by those she didn't understand — culturally or linguistically. I wanted her to have something that made her feel safe, or give her a good reason to fear."

"That's kind of an odd gift, in my opinion. I would have given her the gift of fireball, or the ability to sever limbs with her fingernails. Or smite. Isn't that what you angels do? Smite stuff?" Not that I had any idea what the fuck smite meant.

"You're a demon. Your gifts are different than mine." Gregory moved the tray onto the table and edged closer to me. "I haven't given a gift in nearly two–thousand years. Do you know why I chose to bestow this on your little Nyalla?"

I swallowed, feeling the heat of his presence so close to mine. "Why?"

He closed the gap between us, caressing my spirit–self with his own as our physical bodies remained a scant few inches apart. "Because it brings me joy to pamper the ones you protect. This girl is an adopted child to you. I love you, therefore I love her too."

I'd always been drawn to his power, to his intensity that filled me with a mixture of lust, admiration, and fear. The cornerstone of Aaru. Dalmai's words floated to the surface of my mind, and I felt a fissure of guilt. I liked to think I was selfish, but my sins had their limits. When we were joined, the rest of creation faded away, but could I ever forgive myself if my actions brought about the apocalypse?

His spirit caressed mine, and his mouth traced a path across my forehead. I swayed, like a charmed snake and lifted my face to his. It was as if I was stripped of anything outside of us, as if the world vanished, leaving us alone in a vacuum of sensation. His non–corporeal self wreaked havoc on my spirit–being, while his mouth did things no angel should have ever dreamed of. His lips were gentle, then the jagged points of his teeth pierced, and his tongue stung. Pleasure and pain — all the things a demon girl longs for. I reached up a hand to cup his cheek and transformed the flesh, bringing nerve endings and blood vessels closer to the surface where they would feel the slightest of my touch.

He drew back with a gasp.

"Sorry. Too much?" My voice was smoky, but I was sincere. With Gregory, it was important to let him go at his own pace, to let him initiate. I'd just been so eager, so hungry for his touch, that I'd pushed too far too fast. It wasn't the first time.

"How do you endure it?" He closed his eyes. "Ten–thousand years I've served as Grigori, and I still cannot bear more than minimal physical sensation."

"I just do. We demons search for sensory input the second we're formed. Pleasure, pain — it doesn't matter which. The more intense, the better. We're desperate for it, so hungry we'll put our lives at risk in pursuit of it. That's why my punishments in Aaru are such agony. The only thing that makes it bearable is when you're there by my side."

He stared at me as if I were some exotic creature beyond his comprehension. "We're the opposite."

That pretty much summed it up. "Do you think you could ever change? Maybe eventually you'll come to enjoy physical sensation as I do?"

Gregory shook his head. "I don't know. I can't see how I'd ever be able to even tolerate the level you wish of me, but I'll try my best."

His words sent guilt, like one of Harper's knives, to my chest. There were experiences that were better for the waiting, and there were some things better never had. Chaos, change, sometimes had to come at the speed of light, but too much, too soon undid all progress. And chaos was nothing if not balanced by order.

I reached out a finger and traced along his jaw, feeling the marble–like texture of his skin. His eyes were that all–encompassing black, and his teeth sharp and jagged — what always happened when he lost control. A copper curl fell across his forehead, and I brushed it back, relishing the silky texture.

"We'll just angel fuck. Trust me, that rocks my world like the Valdivia earthquake. There's no need to make this physical if you don't enjoy it. In fact, I don't want to make this physical if you don't enjoy it."

"But *you* enjoy it." He ran a finger across my bottom lip. "And I enjoy seeing you fall into the feel of my touch. Perhaps we give each other what we need. We share the joys of our spirit–selves, and I give you the physical sensations you crave."

Holy shit. Was he saying what I thought he was saying? My breath caught in my throat. "I think I need some of that vodka." Wasn't it ridiculous that I, the demon, needed alcohol to decide whether or not to get it on with an angel?

He moved his fingers from my lip to my jaw, tracing a line down the sensitive skin of my neck.

"Vodka," I croaked out. I needed room to breathe, to think about what he'd just said.

"I drank it all." He reached out and grabbed the empty off the coffee table, tossing it over the back of the couch. It hit the floor with a musical splintering of glass. "Where's the rye one you brought up from the basement?"

"Here." I dug it out from behind my back, staying as close to him as possible. Something felt so odd about tonight, like we were at a crossroads. We'd had these moments before, and I never ceased to be amazed at the magical, intoxicating feeling they produced inside me. I opened the Belvedere and took a small sip, feeling the burn on my throat, the warmth in my belly, and the sudden jolt to my brain. Good vodka felt very much like love.

"Pass the bottle, Cockroach. Don't Bacall the vodka."

I snorted and held it toward him. "Bogart, you silly thing." The mistake in human slang made me grin... and wiped away every last inhibition I had. Whatever he wanted to give, I was ready to receive.

Gregory took the liquor from me and drained a quarter of it, slamming it down on the table when he was done. I eyed it apprehensively, thankful that they put this stuff in sturdy bottles.

"I think I like the potato base better, but this will do nicely. Now, where were we?" He leaned toward me and bumped my forehead with his.

"Are you drunk?" By all that's unholy, I'd gotten him plowed, and now I was going to seduce him. Or let him seduce me. Or not seduce him at all. I wasn't sure which way this whole evening was going. Maybe I was a bit drunk too.

He raised an eyebrow. "Drunk?"

"Yeah. Intoxicated. Smashed. Hammered, blitzed, pissed. It's when you feel weird in the head, and you do all sorts of things you would never normally consider doing."

A smile flitted across his face, and he reached out to rub a lock of my hair between his fingers. "Ah, Cockroach. I've been drunk from the first moment I saw you."

His lips crashed against mine, and we joined, fast and furious with the heat of a thousand suns. I lost myself in the colors of his spirit–self, trusting him to keep me safe. I jumped, ready to leave my body behind, but he held me back, keeping a portion of my spirit bonded in the physical. The sting of his tongue rasped along the sensitive skin of my neck. His teeth tore my flesh. His hand brushed against my breast.

With a gasp, I pulled back, frantically trying to regain some control over the situation. I was lost, too far gone to regain more than a modicum of my self–awareness. Vodka was a paltry drunk compared to the love of an angel.

"I'm a demon. Don't think ... I'm not what you want. I'm not an angel. Don't fuck up your salvation. Don't destroy all of Aaru because you think I'm something I'm not."

I had no idea what I was saying, and the feel of his heat against me wrecked my concentration.

"Cockroach, you are an Angel of Chaos, a demon born of Hel, an imp. I love every bit of you, even when I'm ready to strangle you. My future is going to be a wild ride, full of pleasure and pain, but this will be the best ride of my life as long as I'm by your side."

I reached a hand under his shirt to caress the skin along his waist. He might have negligible physical sensation, but my slightest touch was magnified a hundred fold for this angel.

"You were an angel to me long before you got these wings," he murmured against my neck. "You were an angel to me the moment I saw you risk your own life to save a human, the moment I saw you play with lightning in that campground, the moment you tried to open that twist–top wine with a corkscrew. I've been yours from the moment I laid eyes on you, smacking a dead man's hand against a wall and screaming profanity."

My guilt melted away, and I gave myself up to fate, elongating nails to scrape bloody fissures along his waist. "And you had me at 'Cockroach'."

His spirit–self teased mine, merging then retreating as he forcibly kept a portion of my being imbedded in the physical, feeling his mouth and hands against my skin. "Show me. Show me how you withstand such sensation. Show me how you find pleasure in it."

I'd already let him in. I opened wide and he saw the connections, the way I imbedded myself into the flesh as if I were human. He traced the nerve endings, lighting them up with his touch. I gasped and arched myself against him, feeling my flesh against the odd simulation of his own. Where had his clothes gone?

"Interesting how so much of the sexual experience lies in the brain. Far more than in the genitals." He ran along the pathways, igniting waves of ecstasy.

"Cheating," I groaned. "You're supposed to hit the external ends on the skin, not go straight to the sensory centers in the brain."

"That's a terribly inefficient way of doing these things." Gregory moved his hands lightly down the sides of my body. "I thought you demons would have figured that out by now."

I could tell he was teasing, but it was hard to focus on anything but the erotic combination of his spirit–self wrapped around mine and the heat of his flesh against mine. "Lower. Lower, lower, lower."

"Maximum sensation at these points here and here." I groaned as his hands and mouth roamed south, his fingers skimming along my stomach to slide between my legs.

"Doesn't that cause you pain?"

"No! Keep going. Don't stop."

Damn, this was awesome. His fingers explored every inch of my folds, while his spirit–self continued its rhythm with mine. Having him wrapped around me like this meant he knew every spark his touch ignited.

"Show me, my imp. Show me what it's like for you. Let me give you everything you desire." His mouth lowered, burning a path along the underside of my arm where his mark had once been. "Show me," he murmured.

"Uh... ." Coherent speech was beyond me at this point. All I could do was feel his fingers curling inside me, his thumb in gently flicking my most sensitive spot. He bit down on the soft skin of my arm, and I burst into a thousand shards of light.

My body shuddered, and then rolled in the waves of orgasm. With each pulse, his spirit merged with mine. We continued the rhythm, prolonging the dance of our spirit–selves after the physical ecstasy had died away.

He chuckled. "Demons."

"Angels," I gasped in return.

He grabbed me, yanking me completely from my body to join with him. I'd never grow tired of that sensation of oneness, that feeling of him inside me. This was my paradise, my heaven. This made all the trials I faced turn to dust. Together we were so much more than an imp and an angel.

Everything blurred. Black eyes meeting mine. Teeth and tongue. Heat beyond what mortal flesh could tolerate. My vision blanked to white, and it all retreated — fading until I felt the hardness of his odd flesh against mine. Tangling my hands in the silk of his chestnut curls, I exhaled. I was in a world of trouble, but none of that mattered tonight. All I knew was that this angel loved me. And that love was the answer to life, the universe, and everything.

~21~

H ere."
I opened my eyes to see Nyalla sitting on the coffee table extending a steaming cup of coffee. I was on the couch. Naked. Without Gregory. I took the beverage and sat up, trying for a casual I–don't–care attitude. I did care. Waking up without him felt like a blow to my solar plexus.

The girl smiled, tilting her head. "He's in the kitchen, silly. Who do you think made you the coffee?"

Her gift. It was a good thing I trusted this young human with the contents of my heart.

"You had a good night?" Her eyebrows wiggled up and down. I couldn't help but laugh at the silly expression.

"I had an awesome night. But it's past dawn and time for us to face the day. Party's over, and I've left quite a mess on the lawn, as they say."

Gregory's reaction to my confession was foremost in my mind this morning, right behind the elation over what we'd done, what it meant. He more than met me halfway. I could trust him. I could rely on him. Love was a beautiful emotion, and his actions meant so much more to me than the words.

Nyalla wrinkled her nose. "If I polished off two bottles of vodka, I might have vomited on the grass out front of the house too."

That wasn't what I meant, although the idea of an angel and I puking on the lawn held great appeal. Whatever I'd face

208

at the hands of the angels wasn't something Nyalla needed to worry about though.

I took a sip of my coffee. "How's Harper?"

"Good." I looked up to see the woman walking down the steps, hand on the railing to steady her. Sheesh, it seemed like she'd gotten even more pregnant overnight. I wondered if there was just one baby in there. Yikes. I was never so glad that we demons didn't have such a huge gestation period. With us, it was just form and go on about your day. Not that I had any intention of producing offspring. Ugh.

Harper made her way across the room and sat beside me on the couch. "I'm ready to go. I've decided I want to join the werewolves and accept their assistance in raising my son." A smile lit her face. "Lord knows I'll need the help. Having a community after feeling so isolated will be ... nice."

"I can't use the same magic to transport you as I did Jaq," I warned. "We'll probably have to make a mad dash to the border, with Nils and Nyalla riding shotgun."

"Or I can just gate her there."

Gregory's words shocked me more than the bowl of cereal he shoved into my hands. He looked smugly proud of his culinary efforts, and I didn't have the heart to tell him that it wasn't milk he'd poured on top of the Cheerios but Bailey's Irish Cream. I took an obligatory bite and was surprised to find the liquor–drenched cereal quite tasty.

"Good?" From his expression, the angel seemed to believe himself to be the next Anthony Bourdain.

"Delicious!" I took another bite and hastily swallowed. "And you can't gate her there. If you couldn't transport me from Seattle to Juneau without the other angels knowing, then you certainly won't be able to gate a woman who's pregnant with a Nephilim."

"Cockroach, I'm damned anyway. You killed five angels — six if I count the one you shoved to his death." Gregory glanced at Harper, a look of sympathy on his face. "I'm truly sorry for your loss."

"There's no loss." Harper's voice was flat and tight, her eyes hard.

"None of that is your fault," I protested. "*I* killed those angels, not you. I'm the Iblis. We're not bound anymore. I'm responsible for my own actions. I'll take the heat for this."

Gregory sat on the coffee table across from me, his knees pressing against the sofa on either side of my legs. "The heat for this will be more than you can handle. I won't stand by and watch you suffer. We'll face this together."

There wasn't much I couldn't handle. After everything I'd been through during my banishment, nothing the angels dished out would be beyond my ability to endure.

"I'll protest the ruling, just like I did with Jacob Barakel. These angels attacked me in my home, and Bencul threatened the human I'd vowed to protect. If I could kill that angel last summer and be excused, then this shouldn't be such a problem. It was self–defense."

Gregory shook his head. "I covered up what happened last year. Gabriel and I are the only ones who know you killed that angel, and he agreed to let it go. That angel violated the terms of the treaty. Although his crime was a bit in the gray area, my brother takes a dim view of treaty violations. I'm not sure he or the others on the Ruling Council will believe self–defense is an adequate reason to kill six angels."

I thought of Nils and nodded. Gabriel was a stickler for the rules — I just had to find a rule that supported my cause. "But you angels killed those who attacked you at the council meeting. You've killed rebel angels in Aaru — continue to kill them. How is this any different?"

He reached out to give my hands a quick squeeze, and I felt his spirit–self against mine. "You're still a demon in the eyes of Aaru. And you're residing here among the humans at the whim of the Ruling Council. True, the angels should not have attacked you, but the Council will argue that because you have been known to harbor Nephilim, you're subject to searches."

"Searched," I argued, "is not six assholes trying to kill me! They were shooting at me, beating the crap out of Nils. There was no 'searching' going on. Besides, these angels weren't Hunters. They weren't Gregori. They weren't sent here on behalf of the Ruling Council to check whether I'd been naughty or nice. They were a band of vigilantes trying to kill me and scare a pregnant woman into compliance. The whole bunch had more sin going on than most demons in Hel."

He held up his hands, and I knew I was preaching to the choir.

"Okay, okay." I ran my hands through my hair and tried to think. "So what will my punishment likely be? Death? Imprisonment in that fucking nightmare of an Aaru prison?"

I heard Harper's gasp and Nyalla's softly whispered "no". I didn't want to scare the girls, but I had to know what I'd be facing.

"Best case scenario, you are confined to Hel except for Ruling Council meetings in a designated neutral territory. Probably Aerie."

I'd never been to the Fae realm — had no idea how I'd even get there. It would take me centuries to find the damned place. Besides, my work was here. Even when I was banished to Hel, I hadn't had the conviction that roared through me at this moment. I needed to be here, with the humans and the werewolves. *This* was where I was needed most.

"Worse case scenario, you'll be condemned to death. I'm not sure how we'd go about executing an Iblis without retaliation from Hel, but if the Council decreed it, they'd accept the fallout. In fact, some in Aaru would probably welcome the further division between our kind."

And all the progress we'd made over the last few years would be undone. I thought of Raphael and our pact to try and bring about demon–angel unions. I thought of Nils and his ill–conceived breeding petition. We'd come too far to retreat. And there was something else bothering me.

"What will happen to you?" Because no matter how grim my future looked, this angel had to be facing worse. This kind of shit was expected of a demon, not a six–billion–year–old archangel. Who knows what they'd do to him for aiding and abetting, or whatever the angels called it.

He shrugged, refusing to meet my eyes or answer my question. My heart raced out of control.

"Will they kill you? Throw you into Hel or here as a Fallen? Take your halo?"

He barked out a short, bitter laugh. "They can't take my halo. No one in Aaru is strong enough to do that. They could sever me from the source, which would reduce some of my abilities, but not remove my halo." He smiled and reached out to caress a lock of my hair. "I'll survive. One thing I've learned in my long life is patience. This is a setback, but with time and persistence, we'll turn this around, and both Aaru and Hel will be the better for it."

I didn't see how that was possible with me trapped in Hel and him who–knows–where. Still, I tried to smile back at him. And failed. My mouth wobbled, and my vision blurred. "I'm sorry. I'm so sorry. This is all my fault."

Why the fuck couldn't I think before I ran off half–cocked and did things? Why was I so impulsive, such a slave to my baser self? Yeah, I was a demon, but what the fuck was wrong with me? I'd been lucky that in my nearly thousand years, all my bad decisions had turned into a happy ending. How long was that luck going to hold out? Eventually I was going to go down, and I was going to drag the angel I loved with me.

"No." He gathered me to him, and I forgot all about Harper and Nyalla watching with rapt attention. "Never be sorry for who you are. It's a demon I fell in love with — an imp. You may have wings, but the being I love has the soul of a devouring, chaotic, self–destructive little Cockroach."

My laugh came out like a hiccup, and I pulled back, wiping a hand across my eyes. "Okay. Got it. Pity party over."

And it was. My luck might run out. I might someday pay the price for my crazy, impulsive actions. But he'd made a choice to be with me, and he entered into our relationship with his eyes wide open.

He smoothed a hand over my hair, and this time my smile was genuine. "I'll transport Harper to safety. We'll ensure she has everything she — and the baby — needs, to have a fulfilling life, and then we'll go to Aaru and face whatever happens. Together."

"Together."

My front door flew open and Nils stood in the entrance, his clothing ripped and singed, his face and arms covered in long gashes. "There's an angel outside insisting he needs to speak to you."

They couldn't see who or what was inside the barrier, but nothing would stop them from attacking my house. I wondered why this angel had held back. Clearly he'd fought Nils, and given the Fallen angel's state, had won. Why hadn't he killed Nils and come on through the door himself?

"Okay." I stood and summoned my shotgun. I was so tired of this shit. Gregory had said last night that the Council was too busy with the shit storm in Aaru to mess with me, but he must have been wrong. "I guess I better go see this guy."

"No," Nils shook his head, flinging drops of blood onto the floor. "Not you. Him."

He pointed at Gregory.

"Come on, Cockroach." Gregory sighed. "Time to face the music. No matter what happens, I vow I'll make good on my promise to see Harper to safety."

I looked over to the girls, both white faced with wide eyes. There was one angel outside, but I doubted Gregory would stand by while I dusted him and shoveled his sandy remains in a pile with the others. No, we'd have some bullshit conversation then gate off to Aaru to face charges. Whether they were for my angel–killing activities, or Harper's continued presence in my home, I didn't know. Either way, this might be the last time I ever saw either Harper or Nyalla.

I grabbed my girl in a quick hug. "I love you. Don't settle for any shithead cops or surfer dudes. Promise?" I asked Nyalla.

She laughed, sounding right on the edge of hysteria. "Promise. And I love you, too."

"You." I pointed at Harper. "Take every fucking knife from my kitchen and put them to good use if you have to. Wand, nets, marbles — don't let those fuckers take your baby."

Harper ran at me like a linebacker, crushing me in an awkward hug. Her bowling ball of a belly pressed against mine, causing me to arch my back as she yanked my shoulders against hers. "I will, Sam. And don't you let any of those angels tell you what to do. You're Satan. They don't got nothing on you, girl."

She let me go, and I caught Nyalla giving me a grin and a fist–pump. It was good to know my girls had faith in me.

"I'll be back," I told them. And I would. Eventually. Nils stayed behind to guard Nyalla and Harper, while Gregory and I walked out my front door to face whatever angel had assaulted my Fallen and demanded this meeting.

Of all the angels I'd envisioned demanding an audience, I never expected this one. It was Gabriel, standing at a respectful distance from my front door, pristine in white. He'd either healed whatever damage Nils had done to him, or had never suffered a scratch.

"We've got a problem," he said to Gregory after a quick, scornful glance my way.

"Nephilim problem or other problem?"

Gabe breathed out an exasperated sigh. "Killing angels problem. The Nephilim problem is still under control. Or at least it was when I left Aaru."

"How did the Ruling Council find out?" I asked. "I doubt Bencul would have risked his son's life by making his sin widely known."

Gabriel shrugged. "Angels were noticed missing, and then traced here where their energy signature was found among their remains." He turned to face the elder angel. "How should I play this one, Micha? You know I don't condone what you're doing with this imp, but I respect your vision and want to hear your thoughts on this."

My angel put an arm around my shoulder and pulled me close. "By the rules, Gabe. Play it by the rules."

~22~

I stood before the conference table, facing the other angels. Seems I never had a seat at the table anymore — I was always the one in trouble. The difference this time was that Gregory stood beside me. He had a chair, no doubt a last effort to get him to put aside his wicked ways and return to a higher vibration level. Either that or they were too afraid of him to deliver the affront of denying him a seat.

"Iblis, it has come to our attention that in addition to the prior incident where you were harboring a Nephilim, you or your agents have killed six angels in the last seventy–two hours."

"No agents. I did it all by my lonesome, although it was five, not six."

Who knows what demon killed that asshat I threw into Hel. It wasn't me, though, and I wasn't taking the rap for that one.

"Correction, you killed six angels or acted in such a way that their death was an unavoidable conclusion."

Okay, I guess I was taking the rap for that one.

"They attacked my home and my Fallen one, necessitating forceful action on my part. I was simply defending myself and my property."

"They intended to kill you?" Raphael asked.

I hesitated, knowing how badly I lied. "When five angels open fire on me and beat the crap out of someone under my protection, I don't stop to ask them whether they intend to kill or injure. Let me assure you, they weren't shooting blanks."

"Killing them was not a suitable response to the attack."

New Guy. He was such an asshole. Number two on my most–hated list after Gabriel.

"So sorry. I had planned on inviting them in to discuss our differences over coffee and pastries. Too bad they tried to blow my head off before I could make the offer."

"You said five. What was the other angel doing? You killed six, but you said only five were attacking you."

Damn. "He is the one who ordered the attack. If I didn't take him out, he'd just bring back more angels next time."

Sleazy clenched his fists on top of the highly varnished oak table. "You have enough power to subdue an angel, transport him via automobile then throw him through the gate into Hel, but you couldn't do that to the other five. You had to kill them outright?"

"Yeah." I wasn't sure what else to say.

Gabriel took a deep breath and let it out, his hands skimming the papers before him. "Even if we decide those five were killed in self–defense, that you had reasonable fear for your life, the sixth one is clearly murder. He was not physically attacking you. You had restrained him. There was no reason for his death. You could have simply returned him to Aaru to stand trial on your accusations, just as you did that member of my choir who violated the treaty."

I was totally fucked. The poetic justice of throwing Bencul into Hel was something the angels would never comprehend. I wasn't sorry I'd done it, but I was sorry that Gregory was being dragged into this ditch with me.

As if sensing my thoughts, Gabriel turned to face his eldest brother. "And where were you when all this was happening?"

"In Aaru," I jumped in before Gregory could even open his mouth. "He was completely unaware of my actions until last night."

Gabriel scowled at me, then turned back to the angel beside me. "Why didn't you bring her straight to Aaru for trial? You were there when she was summoned. You knew about this."

Gregory smiled serenely. "A few weeks' delay isn't going to resurrect six dead angels. The Iblis has been assigned important responsibilities by the Council, and given the sentence she is likely to face for her actions, I decided it was crucial for her to accomplish those tasks first."

"Such as?"

New Guy. I was being pummeled from all directions. Other than Raphael and Gregory, no one was on my side.

"Are you kidding? I'm responsible for the Fallen. That's a whole lotta work. It could take me a few–million years to raise all those vibration levels to an acceptable level. Important shit, you know. Just rack up all my punishments, and I'll pay my dues once I'm done with my official assignments."

"You've got one Fallen." The intensity of Gabriel's gaze felt like a shard of ice through my chest. "How long could it possibly take to rehabilitate one Fallen?"

"Iblis or not, this wanton murder of six angels warrants death." Sleazy was on a roll. "We were wrong to retain this seat on the Council. Wings or not, this creature is no Angel of Chaos."

Sleazy's rant faded to an incomprehensible buzz as I stared at Gabriel. There was something behind the frosty blue of his eyes. I felt a slight nudge from Gregory, as if he were pushing me toward something. Fallen. Bits and pieces of that boring Ruling Council meeting where I'd been chastised for my late reports tickled along the edges of my mind.

"One? Do you know how many humans have a FICO score in the shitter? And at the rate you angels sin, I'll need to hire staff. I'll be lucky to show progress in a dozen millennium. And the recidivism rate? Shit, that alone will keep me busy until the end of time."

I felt lost in the frozen blue of Gabriel's eyes. "Those who violate the treaty are yours, but other angels who sin are not."

Play it by the rules.

"Nonsense. The Council gave me the Fallen — humans and angels. Treaty violations certainly can't be more heinous than interfering with the natural lifespan of a human, then deliberately entrancing and impregnating her."

Raphael shifted in his seat. "Not all angels who breed with humans are so callous. Some actually feel love for their mates. You have a human lover. You surely know this."

I did. But now wasn't the time to get into my fading relationship with Wyatt.

"That may be true, but the pregnant human I protected *was* treated this way. And we are demons — we're expected to do this sort of thing. Angels who care about their vibration levels and rightful balance should not be tempted into a physical relationship with a human."

Gabriel crumpled a piece of paper in his fist. "We are all tempted, but angels should never succumb to that temptation. We are above sin. And those who are not are Fallen."

The air grew thick and heavy as all turned to Gabriel. "And the Fallen are mine," I told him, my voice soft.

Mine. The silent word reverberated with power, and I know the angels felt the impact as I did. I'd claimed this group, and my claim was stronger than any vow. There was no backing out now. I was the Iblis, and my workload had just increased tenfold.

I felt a collective gasp of breath.

"Bencul was Fallen. He interfered with the natural course of life. He saved a woman who should have died. He inserted himself into her life. He enthralled her, impregnated her in spite of her precautions otherwise. Then he brought a group of angels to my house — twice — to attack me and intimidate the human into complying with his wishes. Because of those actions, he became Fallen. He belonged to me, and those he dragged into the abyss of sin also became mine."

I felt a wave of pride from the angel beside me, and I realized for the first time in my life that I really did sound like the Ha–Satan. Confident, assertive, wily. Angel of Justice. Angel of Vengeance. The Trickster. The Iblis. I was the devil's advocate, and my job was to provide much–needed balance. How ironic that the very concept I scorned was what I was meant to create.

"Aaru rots from the inside. How you intend to rectify that situation isn't my concern. I care not for Aaru or the problems of angels. My responsibility lies in Hel and among the Fallen. Deny me what heaven deems mine at your own peril."

There was a flurry of mind–speech, and Gregory left my side to take his seat. It didn't bother me. I could stand alone, and I needed him more at the table than to prop me up. There he could make a difference — both in Aaru and in my own fate. I loved him; he made me feel safe and worthy of the title I bore, but I was the Iblis, and that meant I had to stand my ground on my own two feet. And with my own two wings.

"We recognize your authority over the Fallen," Gabriel announced. "However, that designation must be formally assigned. We can't have you subjectively assuming that an angel is Fallen. There must be due process."

I nodded. Sounded reasonable, but with angels, due process could take centuries. I couldn't exactly sit around getting my head blown off while they debated these things. Keeping my mouth shut was the prudent thing to do at this juncture. I'd managed to talk my way out of a death sentence.

Might as well not push the envelope too far. At least at this particular moment.

"Punishment for rushing to judgment on six angels is one rotation cycle naked and restrained. Beginning immediately."

I opened my mouth only to snap it shut. Nyalla and Nils didn't expect me home tonight, if at all. Gregory said he would transport Harper to safety for me. There was really nothing pressing for me to do beyond pouring bubble bath in the fountain at City Hall. I'd get this over with then go home to my life and my newfound responsibilities.

~23~

I was alone in my jail cell this time, escorted without all the fanfare that had preceded my last incarceration. It was just as well; I was in no mood to fake bravado. Everything had seemed to have worked out to my advantage, but I was still worried. That other shoe was going to drop any moment, and I was tense, waiting for it to fall on my head with the weight of a hundred–ton brick.

Aaru seemed empty of angels. I couldn't sense anyone, even snotty Gabriel, who had dumped me here after stripping me of my physical form and blocking my stash of raw energy. I had an irrational urge to shout "hello" and hear the word echo through the blank white expanse. Irrational because I didn't have vocal chords at the moment, and even if I did, there was no echo in Aaru. Sound here was deadened, like screaming into a box of cotton.

I'd assumed responsibility for the Fallen, along with the radically expanded definition of that term. Having dominion over Hel was work enough. Even though there was no formal recognition of my authority, and the demon sections were pretty much life as usual, I had made a commitment to the humans there, and I would need to continually bust heads to keep the elves in line. Delegating that to Leethu and Dar would only buy me time. How was I going to juggle some serious smackdowns in Hel and manage the–fuck–knows– how–many Fallen angels and deadbeat humans? Knowing the Ruling Council, they'd want progress reports on each one, and a performance–improvement plan to raise their vibration level. What had I gotten myself into this time?

Heat scorched the edges of my spirit–self, and I leaned toward the comfort of Gregory's power. I was desperate to know if Harper was safe, but in spite of the empty feeling in Aaru, I wasn't completely sure anything I said — or thought — would be private.

She's safe. And I've blocked this area so we can communicate without being overheard. Of course, that means everyone knows we're discussing something we don't want them to hear. Be discreet, Cockroach.

I breathed deep in relief — or would have, had I been sporting lungs at that moment. *How did it go?*

A bit dicey, actually. I felt his wry amusement. *My sudden appearance in the Alpha's residence caused quite an uproar. Let's just say I haven't been that clawed up and bitten since our last date night.*

I laughed, resting the entire weight of my spirit–self against him. The vision of my powerful, intimidating angel being jumped by dozens of half–transformed werewolves was downright hysterical. *Poor Harper. Not exactly a good introduction to her new life, huh?*

No. Luckily that female Nephilim recognized her and got everyone to back off. Otherwise I would have been forced to use lethal means to defend myself. Given what she's experienced of angels so far, I didn't want to subject her to that level of violence.

One werewolf wasn't much of a problem, but a group could cause serious damage. They reminded me of those flesh–eating ants — they just kept coming and coming until they overwhelmed their prey. Enough werewolves — or humans for that matter — and even an angel could be taken down.

So what do you plan to do with all these Fallen you are now responsible for — angels and humans?

I had no stinking idea. *Electroshock therapy? Slave labor? Or maybe I'll just throw them through the gate to Hel and be done with it.*

That would not be advisable, Cockroach. You're supposed to rehabilitate them, not slaughter them.

Spoilsport. How am I supposed to raise their vibration level when mine is in the shitter? I refuse to set a good example for them. It's not demonic.

Then set a bad example. Show them the ramifications of the path they walk. They'll take one look at you and be scared straight.

Yeah, like you were? I rubbed against him suggestively. Gregory's presence soothed all my fears. He made Aaru downright tolerable.

Cockroach, you have no idea the terror I live in.

Yeah, right. He didn't exactly seem terrified as he pulled me tight against him, merging us in a fine line of white along our edges. I sighed and gave myself over to him, relishing the privacy and solitude my punishment in Aaru provided us.

***

My house was as eerily quiet as Aaru had been. Harper was safely with the werewolves in West Virginia, Nyalla had taken Nils out to experience happy hour with Michelle and Candy and had left a note to not expect them home until late. Wyatt was still in Philadelphia — or was it Chicago at this point? For forty years I'd lived alone, but now I stood beside the sectional sofa in my great–room and felt the horrible ache of loneliness.

"Do you want me to stay? Perhaps try those spicy chicken arms again?"

"Wings. Hot wings." I smiled and shook my head. He'd remain with me if I wanted, but I could tell there were things he needed to do. Who knows what kind of nightmare I'd caused up in Aaru. Hopefully the threat that any Fallen would report to me would keep them all toeing the line.

"The thought of eating amputated and cooked wings is gruesome. I prefer to call them arms."

"What? The image of ripping the wings off something, plucking all the feathers out, then roasting them in a hot oven bothers you?" I teased him, running a hand along the glow of his hidden wings. "Pussy. You'd never make it in Hel. Ripping wings off is foreplay there."

"I'm not in favor of wing removal — either avian or angel. Let's agree to disagree on the hot wings, and I'll make you coffee instead."

His hand tangled in my hair, smoothing through the locks to catch a piece between his fingers, tugging it gently. Before I could reply, another angel appeared. Gabriel. I'd never seen him so distraught or disheveled — not even when we'd had a pastry smackdown in a Ruling Council meeting.

"The sanctuary is compromised."

Sanctuary? I was momentarily confused, thinking he meant Aaru and wondering if some demons had managed to infiltrate the angel's home. Then I realized they'd been calling the hidden spot for the Nephilim 'sanctuary' and froze in fear.

Gregory stiffened against me, his hand gripping my hair painfully tight. "How? When?"

The other angel sent me a look full of loathing. "While you were visiting the Iblis in her punishment. We were too busy trying to salvage the situation and move who we could to safety to send you notice."

I'd thought it had been oddly quiet in Aaru. How many angels had taken part in this? Were things so fractured and chaotic in heaven that angels felt free to leave and take vigilante action on another race of beings?

"Which sanctuary?"

I held my breath at Gregory's question. *No, don't let it be the one with Jaq and Harper*, I selfishly thought.

"West Virginia. Alaska and Prussia are still secure."

"Survivors?"

"The werewolves are scattered, but I believe over half of them have survived the attack."

"Who is safe?" I was practically in hysterics. "Harper? Jaq? Are they okay?"

"Both are safe, for now. I was able to locate them and remove them from the battle zone before they were harmed. Trust me, the grown Nephilim was not pleased with my intervention."

I'll be she wasn't. From what I'd seen of Jaq, I could tell the woman was a fighter — one who would stay to defend her pack even against angels. My panic dropped away knowing that the two women were safe, but dread crept on its heels.

"How ... how could this have happened?" My voice was shaky and low as I turned from Gregory to Gabriel in search of an explanation.

"How do you think it happened," Gabriel snapped, his power a blast of arctic ice against my skin. "Clearly you were watched as you trotted back and forth, risking the half–angel's life to bring her to your home."

"It could have been me." Gregory put himself in between the pair of us. "I transported Harper this afternoon. I covered my path and our energy signatures well, but it's possible another angel sensed me."

Gabriel took a step forward, stabbing a finger at me. "Nonsense. It was her — that inept, foolish creature. For thousands of years we've been able to hide the children away, and in a few short days, she's destroyed one of our most secure sanctuaries. Their deaths are on your head, you nasty cockroach."

No one but Gregory was allowed to call me a cockroach, but more than the slur twisted me into a knot of pain and anger. I'd taken every precaution, but that obviously hadn't been enough. Their deaths *were* on my head. But I wouldn't be a demon if I didn't succumb to the sin of anger and take it out on the nearest available being.

With a shriek of rage, I pushed Gregory aside and launched myself at Gabriel, knocking him backward to the ground. We rolled across the floor, into chairs and walls as we fought. I pulled his black, spiky locks, gouged his eyes and bit him, elongating nails and teeth to do the most damage. Gabriel was just as vicious, bashing my head against the table leg and twisting my limbs past the breaking point. I'm sure we looked like two feral alley cats screaming as the blood and sweat flew from us. Finally we both lay exhausted, panting, half under the broken bar stools. Gabriel was on top of me, still twisting one of my arms across my back just in case I discovered a second wind. He needn't have bothered. I'd used up my second wind already.

It was then, breathing through my mouth and broken nose, that I smelled the distinctive aroma of coffee.

"If you are both finished, I suggest we sit down and figure out a plan to put the pieces of this mess back together again."

I felt no shame at Gregory's words, but Gabriel turned bright red and jumped off me as if I were a plague demon. In a fraction of a second, we'd repaired our injuries and both of us took a seat at my dining-room table. Gabriel was faking an air of cool aloofness, but his hands kept darting here and there — smoothing his spiky hair, straightening his clothing, clearing a spot of blood from the table. As much as he professed to hate me, I think he found our fights to be downright cathartic — the only time he lost control and allowed all that anger and pain to come out. It was good for him. Like releasing steam from a pressure cooker. And I loved being the one to turn the valve.

"Here." Gregory put a mug of coffee in front of each of us and took a seat at the head of the table.

"I don't sully my vibration patterns with the consumption of food or drink," Gabriel sneered, pushing the mug away.

Gregory reached out and slowly moved it back toward the other angel. "It's either this or the vodka. Trust me; you don't want to drink the vodka. It takes half the flesh from the inside of your throat on the way down, and you wake up the next morning feeling as if a major portion of your brains are on the outside of your skull. Most unpleasant."

I choked as my coffee went down the wrong pipe. Gregory had been hungover? Damn, I had totally tempted this angel into sin.

Gabriel took a tentative sip from his mug and grimaced.

"Here." Gregory upended my little sugar bowl over the other angel's cup. "This helps mask the distastefully bitter flavor."

"Not bad," Gabriel pronounced after another sip. The sour expression on his face was in stark contrast to his words. "So, step one is to transport the Nephilim to another sanctuary, and then locate the surviving werewolves and hide them."

Gregory nodded. "Not an easy task, given the increased scrutiny. Neither the Iblis nor I will be able to assist in this without drawing attention and risking the Nephilim further."

"I know how to get Jaq out. Harper is going to be more difficult to relocate safely." I told the two angels about Kirby's Marble, and its limitations.

"Clever," Gabriel mused. "Some humans clearly have put their angelic gifts to good use."

I didn't have the heart to tell him it was decades of grueling lessons as a slave to the elves that had inspired this device.

"So, Alaska or Prussia?" Gabe asked.

Prussia. I barely held back a snort of laughter. This angel was so behind the times I was surprised he wasn't calling the whole thing Pangaea.

I slurped my coffee loudly, earning a look of hatred from Gabe. "We can let them decide. Maybe divide them fifty–fifty between the two. But what do we do about Harper?"

"Wait until she gives birth?" Gabriel suggested. "The human can probably hide among the humans at that point. We could use the Kirby device to relocate the baby once it's born, and she could follow him if she chooses."

Well, that idea was full of big holes. And I was happy to point them out. "Yeah, and who's to say some smarty–pants angel won't know to follow the mother? Besides, the focus device is a durft. Half–angel or not, there's no way a baby is going to be able to hold onto one of those suckers long enough to get where he needs to go."

"I take it a durft is not a benign creature?" Gregory lifted one eyebrow as he took a sip of coffee.

"Uh, no. I'd rather wrestle a komodo dragon — and trust me, I have."

Gabriel sat his full coffee cup down and crossed his arms over his chest. "Create another sanctuary?"

Sounded like a good solution to me, but Gregory grimaced. "There are few humans who have the skills to cloak the territory and those within it. We don't have the time to spare in locating one with the appropriate abilities — these Nephilim could be found at any moment."

Cloak? "Do you mean like the spell I have around my house? One where you can't tell who is in it?"

Gregory shook his head, and I felt his touch along my spirit–self. "No, Cockroach. That spell makes the area appear as if there is a hole of nothing at your home. It draws attention to the spot, although we cannot detect who or what is inside. To create a sanctuary, the humans and other beings must register in our senses — their energy must come through the barrier. Others are cloaked. There is also a slight keep–away aura that acts as a mild deterrent. Not enough to draw suspicion, but enough that we consider the area to be unsavory and choose to avoid going there."

That was a lot more complicated than Gareth would probably be able to handle. "I can check in Hel and see if there is a sorcerer who can do this. We've had a huge war among the elven kingdoms recently, though, and there aren't as many high–level sorcerers as there used to be."

"That would be of great help, Cockroach." Gregory smiled and reached out to squeeze my hand. "We'll make discrete inquiries of our own and do all we can to keep the werewolves and Nephilim safe in the meantime."

"That might be more of a problem than you think," Gabriel interjected. "The attack wasn't just spurred by unregistered werewolves harboring Nephilim. There is word that proof has come about that the werewolves are *descended* from Nephilim. I expect at any moment, we will receive summons to review the data and pass judgment on the entire race."

I caught my breath, thinking of Candy and all the werewolf friends I'd made over the past few years. I'd do all I could to save them, but what could one imp do against the entire angelic host? I might be the Iblis, but I wasn't a god.

Gregory drained the contents of his coffee cup and stood. "Well then, we must find a solution immediately or decide which side of this war we will stand on, my brother."

~24~

"You out of jail already?" Nyalla's breathless voice was barely audible above the background noise. She sounded happy, giddy almost. I hated to be the one to ruin her carefree night.

"Where are you? Is Candy with you?"

Candy had trusted me with her greatest secret. Jaq and the other werewolves had trusted me. Harper had trusted me. I felt sick at what had happened.

"Yeah, her and Michelle. We're at the Eastside. There's an awesome band tonight. Come on down. Did you know Nils can dance? No joke; he's actually pretty good. Angels dancing — isn't that hysterical?"

It would have been under other circumstances. "Tell Candy I need to talk to her. I'll be right there."

The Eastside Tavern was only a few miles from my house. I drove the Suburban to the back of the rear parking lot, across from the fragrant dumpster. It was my spot. Regulars smoking out on the front porch greeted me as I climbed the wooden stairs and made my way through the iron–barred door.

I could hear the music from route 26, and it only grew louder as I approached the bar. Nyalla was right in her assessment — it *was* a rocking band. Glasses and bottles clinked, patrons whooped, and feet stomped as the fiddle sang out side by side with an electric guitar and the deep vocals of a bare–chested, bearded man.

And Nils *could* dance. He was two–stepping with Michelle, her head thrown back in laughter as her long braids spun around. Nyalla sat at the bar with Candy, flashing an indecent amount of leg. I made my way through the crowd to the bar and touched the werewolf's shoulder.

She took one look at my face and got to her feet, following me out the back door, where we could speak without having to shout at the top of our lungs.

"Do you know what happened? Did anyone tell you?" Stupid question. As if she'd be here, partying it up with friends if she knew.

Candy paled. "What? Harper? The baby?"

"They're fine, and so is Jaq, but angels somehow found out about the sanctuary in West Virginia, and there was a raid. The wolves scattered, but many were killed."

Claws sprouted from beautifully manicured nails. Candy's jaw jutted forward, and teeth elongated into fangs. I felt everything twist inside me.

"It was my fault. Someone must have followed me, or sensed Jaq at my house. It was my fault, and I'll do everything in my power to make it right."

That was the most un–demonic thing I'd ever said — beyond the 'I love you' shit with Gregory and Wyatt, that is. Still, it was heartfelt. It was my fault, and I would go to any lengths to ensure the safety of the Nephilim and the werewolves. Every last one of them.

Candy, that cold, calculating, lying bitch, did something just as out of character as my emotional confession. She grabbed me and hugged me with all the strength of a werewolf. Her claws dug into my back, teeth gnashing along the skin of my neck. In spite of her meticulous hygiene, I've got to say that my friend had some tremendously bad breath in her half–wolf form.

"Not yourrrrr fault," she growled in my ear. "My trust ith not misplaced in you. We will make this right. Together."

I clutched her just as tightly, relishing the claws stabbing through my back. It was my sort of penance. "I will make this right. I promise."

She pulled back, and, with a shudder of effort, retracted her claws and returned her jaw to its human appearance. I looked over her shoulder and saw Nils, one arm draped over Nyalla's shoulder and the other over Michelle's.

"Tell me what happened." Candy's mouth twisted into a bitter smile. "Remember? You're the muscle, and I'm the mind? Just like we did with Althean, we'll fix this as a team."

Yeah. That had ended with me bound to an angel. It had worked out in the long run, but hadn't been so pleasant in the short term. I took a deep breath and steeled myself. These werewolves, these Nephilim, were mine, and I wasn't going to give up on them.

Mine.

Oh holy shit, when had I claimed them? Long ago. Long before Harper ever entered my house. How in the world could I possibly play this and make it work out?

Play it by the rules. Gregory's words echoed in my mind, but I had no time to contemplate their meaning in my current situation. I needed to secure a new sanctuary for unregistered werewolves and Nephilim. Pronto. Beckoning the others over, I explained the situation, and the difficulty over Harper's transportation and her safety.

Candy ran a hand through her perfectly coiffed blond bob, spiking bits at odd angles. "So we try and get them to Alaska or Germany, or we find a sorcerer with the power to recreate a sanctuary nearby?"

"Or we come up with another idea." I never wanted to rule out the possibility of some whacky alternative. Ideas that came out of left field were often the best alternatives.

"Other ideas." Michelle pursed her lips. "Like the angels get hung up in paperwork over whether the werewolves and Nephilim are under their purview or yours? I mean, who really has jurisdiction in this sort of thing? If Nephilim are so horrible, then why aren't they the responsibility of Satan?"

It was a fucking brilliant idea. I should have expected the niece of a Haitian priestess to come up with this. Ten–thousand years it had taken for the angels to decide the werewolves were the product of angel sin. If I could drag these debates into a jurisdictional one, string them out for another ten–thousand years, it would give me time to come up with some kind of permanent solution. Of course, there was no saying the angels wouldn't just laugh in my face and go ahead and wipe out the entire race. Still, it was worth a try.

"I'll try and get things held up in committee, but it's a long shot. There's a good chance they'll go on killing them even before a decision is made on jurisdiction. But no matter how that goes, we need to find a safe space for Jaq, and especially Harper. Thoughts?"

Candy smoothed her hair. "Michelle and Nyalla can work their supernatural connections. Nils clearly knows angel politics. He can think of a short–term solution until we can secure a sanctuary. And I'll do hands–on with the werewolves to keep everyone under the radar in the meantime. Deal?"

My mind raced, seeing the fine lines of connection between the werewolves and angels, tracing possibilities into the future. I might not be as skilled as Gregory and the other angels, but this tiny measure of omnipotence served me well.

"I need to see them. I need to meet with Jaq, Harper, and the werewolves. I'll gate there. I'll lock down my energy tight and travel as a human. Anything — but I must meet with them."

Candy's shrewd brown eyes met mine, and she reached out a manicured hand to clasp my own. "Done."

***

Gabriel hadn't risked moving them far. Jaq, Kelly, Harper, and six werewolves were ensconced in a huge hotel designed to look like a tudor–style chalet. The fact that it was perched on a cliff overlooking the Potomac River and a stone's throw from the Antietam Battlefield added to the surreal atmosphere. I expected to see Civil War soldiers shooting it out with Heidi and blond dudes in lederhosen at any moment.

It had taken me about four hours of transporting myself all sorts of unexpected places to arrive here. For once, my fledgling angel skills worked to my advantage. Any angel trying to follow me was probably lost in Madhya Pradesh or Tiagba.

Candy hadn't wanted to risk coming to the meeting, but she'd sent word. In spite of my excessive tardiness, the Nephilim, the vampire, and Harper were in the dining area of the inn, surrounded by half–empty plates of schweinebraten and sausages.

"I don't know German," Jaq pronounced woodenly. For a second, I wondered if the staff at the inn didn't speak English then I realized the half–angel was referring to one of the two other sanctuaries.

"And I don't have the best memories of Alaska," Harper added.

I took a deep breath to calm my temper, which seemed more pronounced than usual these days. Clearly I was getting a lot of practice with the sin of anger.

"Okay, so Jaq goes to Alaska, and Harper goes to Germany. As soon as we can figure out how to get her safely there, that is."

"Or we wait until a new sanctuary is secured here," Kelly added.

Yeah, that damned vampire had survived, too. And she was just as glued to Jaq's side as before. I glared at her, wondering if I could send her off to fetch coffee or some other mundane task. Probably not.

"We don't have time for that. You might as well have a big arrow pointing at you from the sky, and sanctuaries don't get built in a day. Fuck, we don't even know if we can find a sorcerer or witch with enough oomph to establish a new one."

"The angels know people," Jaq assured me. "They built three of them. They've kept us hidden for thousands of years. They'll come through."

Probably not, but her faith in the angels was touching. Misguided, but touching.

"Even if they do, there's no guarantee the new sanctuary will be in West Virginia," I warned. Gregory hadn't told me where he had in mind, but putting it smack dab on top of the previous sanctuary didn't seem wise. "You could wind up in Argentina or Easter Island. Any of you speak Spanish, or whatever the fuck they speak on Easter Island? Huh?"

Yeah. Anger. My new sin of choice.

"I'm not leaving." Seems anger wasn't only *my* sin. Jaq smacked a fist onto the table, denting the surface. "West Virginia is my home. My pack is here; my human friends are here. I have a job, hunting grounds I know and love. I'm not leaving."

Great. I glanced at the others. Kelly had put a supportive hand on her friend's shoulder. Harper gnawed her fingernails, her speculative gaze roaming between Jaq's freckled face and mine.

If this were just a matter of sanctuary, it would be one thing, but this problem was bigger than they knew. Should I tell them the entire werewolf race was facing extinction? That it probably didn't matter where they stayed, or how secure Gregory and Gabe managed to make it; eventually they'd be found and killed? That there was a good chance they'd watch all of their werewolf friends die as they hid in safety? Maybe Jaq's decision was right — better to go down fighting than cower under a rock and wait for inevitable discovery.

I watched Harper chewing her fingers in indecision. Her child would be ripped from her arms, her memory wiped. She'd go about her life as if nothing had happened. Sounded like the better deal of the lot, but I knew otherwise. Somewhere deep in her soul would be a wound the angels couldn't heal. She might not remember why, but a part of her would always be damaged.

There was only one solution, but how I was going to pull it off was beyond me.

"West Virginia it is. Stay put. I've got to make a quick trip to Hel then I'll be back to let you all know what the plan is."

It was time for me to master a few sins, to be the Iblis and to give Gregory the 'mighty show of power' he'd been urging me toward since last year.

~25~

The two sorcerers were rather uncomfortable in my demon residence. Hell, I was uncomfortable in my demon residence. It had been Ahriman's home up until recently, and I still had some very bad memories connected with the place. The ancient demon had burned my home to the ground, and this house of horrors was better than nothing. It did have one benefit: it screamed 'Iblis' with the warded gate of fire and walkway of crushed skulls.

"I thought you just wanted to move these 'Neffy–liam' from one place to another? Now you need to ward a sanctuary for them against the angels?" Gareth was seated on a demon–hide couch, paging through one of the five massive spell books he'd brought with him. He rubbed a finger along his nose as he spoke, leaving a streak of charcoal dust on his tanned skin.

Kirby perched on a carved chair that had a mosaic of teeth imbedded in the ladder back. He shook his head, rubbing his own spell book with a reassuring hand. "Um, aren't there only two of them? The adult and the pregnant human? Bring them to Hel. The angels would never come here."

I wasn't sure the elves and demons would be any less lethal than the angels once they discovered Nephilim in their midst. And there was one other little problem. "They won't come to Hel and are refusing to leave the compromised sanctuary. Almost two–hundred–million square miles of land on the damned planet, and they won't budge from West Virginia."

Another streak of gray joined the first on Gareth's face. "So it's not really a matter of hiding them, it's creating some kind of impenetrable barrier the angels can't cross."

That was a good idea, and I knew someone who did that sort of thing, except the scope was probably far beyond Michelle's aunt. I didn't think there was enough brick dust locally, and by the time she'd walked around the state three times spouting her incantations, Jaq and Harper's son would be long dead. Angels took forever to make up their minds about shit, but once they did, they moved fast.

"I know someone who has a spell like that, but there's no time. I'm not sure she could even do it. The area's just too large."

"How big of an area are we talking about?" Kirby asked.

I squirmed. "About twenty–four–thousand miles. Give or take. I'm thinking we can cut out that weird bit up north and no one would notice."

Kirby's mouth dropped open. "Twenty–four–thousand miles for two people and a baby? Sheesh, Sam, the human lands in Hel aren't that big. What do they need all that space for?"

"Well, it seems the angels have discovered that an entire race of shape–shifters are descended from Nephilim, and they are going to wipe them out. Even twenty–four–thousand miles might not be big enough. Hopefully some werewolves will be able to hide elsewhere."

Gareth snapped his book shut. "Sam, what are you thinking? You can't trap an entire race of people in a magical bubble for long. The angels are going hammer at it until they get in. And from what I've heard about angels, it won't take them long."

"You've got to bring them to Hel," Kirby urged. "It's your domain, the only place they'll be safe from the angels. Bring them to Hel."

Or bring Hel to them. Michelle's idea of demanding responsibility for the Nephilim and werewolves was looking more and more like the best route. Pretty depressing. Either Kirby or Michelle's suggestions were about as farfetched as sprinkling brick dust around the perimeter of a state, but there wasn't anything else on the table right now.

"So let's say I get ten thousand or so werewolves and a handful of Nephilim to agree to come to Hel. How do I transport them? They're scattered all over the planet. Do I get them all in a central place, have everyone hold hands and activate an elf button?"

"Besides the fact that I doubt an elf button would transport that many, grouping everyone in a single place would just make it easy for the angels to kill them with one blow." Gareth started paging through another of his books. "There's got to be a way to open quick, temporary rifts, like the elven traps. The angels can't see those for some unknown reason."

I could probably get a few past the gate guardians at a time, but the angel-made gates that were my main mode of transport to and from Hel wouldn't be an option for mass travel. Unless I managed to get all the gate guardians to go to Disney World for a week or two ... hmmm, maybe if I announced the theme park had all-you-can-eat sweet and sour pork.

"There's Mordical's Fissure," Kirby commented, reading through his own book. "But it's unstable. Half of them would most likely wind up in another dimension."

Ugh. I remembered Jell-o World from a few years back. I wouldn't wish that on my worst enemy. Well, maybe Gabriel, because that would be funny, but no one else.

"You need an elf," Gareth announced, smearing another line across his forehead. He was beginning to look like a commando from a B movie.

"Yeah," Kirby jumped up in excitement. "They moved large groups of troops during the war, and they've transported citizens for celebrations using inter–realm gates. A really powerful elf could do this."

Yeah, and I had so many powerful elves amongst my friends. "Even if I could bully one to do this, I'd need to have them on the other side of the gates. No threat would be enough to get them to break with millions of years of tradition."

"And even if it worked, you said most of the werewolves and Neffies wouldn't leave." Gareth set aside his books and rested his chin on his hands. "The angels would slaughter the remaining ones. The ones who came to Hel, even if we manage to transport them safely, would struggle in their new life. You'd have to carve out more of the elf lands, or break off some of the demon ones. We're not able to do adequate climate control on Libertytown. These people would be isolated in a strange world, in a hostile and desolate environment. They may wish they'd stayed and taken their chances."

Fuck. That left only one option.

"Then I need to claim them, extend my reach to their present realm and insist the angels grant them co–existence with the humans."

It was so quiet I could have heard crickets chirp — if Ahriman hadn't killed them all and made a lovely mosaic with their exoskeletons, that is.

"Hello? Feedback? Any thoughts on this?"

"Can I have your stuff when they kill you?" Leave it to Kirby to crack jokes at a time like this. He truly was a human after my own heart.

"I'm serious. I'm the Iblis. I've got a big bad sword that's actually more useful as a shotgun. I've killed six or seven angels — I can't quite remember; I'm starting to lose count. I could pull this off."

I couldn't pull this off, but I was hoping among the three of us, we'd come up with a way I could.

"No offense, Sam, but you can't even manage to hold Hel together. Yeah, you and your crazy household got the elves to back down, but they're starting to make noise about war again. Unless you run around flashing your wings and blowing stuff up on a regular basis, things in Hel are going to slide back to the way they were before."

"And beyond your household, none of the demons show you any additional respect. It's not like you're *really* the ruler of Hel."

"But the angels think I am," I argued. "They seriously think we're all organized into a bunch of legions, poised to attack Aaru and reclaim heaven at any moment."

Hey. That gave me an idea. "How many demons would make up a legion?"

Both magic users looked at me with blank faces. Gareth cleared his throat. "You're going to gate into Aaru with a–few–hundred demons and demand they allow the werewolves and Nephilim to live, or you'll attack them?"

"No, that's a Pearl Harbor move. I'm shooting more for an American Revolution scenario. The angels are busy with their own issues. If I come in and decide to seize what to them has only been a problem, a thorn in their side for the last ten–thousand years, they'll make a lot of noise and let me have it with a few concessions that will allow them to save face."

That was greeted with more blank expressions. "I think you've been hanging out with angels too long," Kirby slowly announced.

"Ruling Council meetings; they're not something I'd recommend."

"I still think you're going to wind up getting killed," Gareth warned. "But you know the angels better than either of us."

"Maybe less than a legion." Kirby stood and paced, waving his hands excitedly. "Too many demons and you'll get their backs up. They'll think you're a threat to Aaru and will just take you out."

"Maybe a dozen." Gareth was finally getting on board with the plan. "They'll think you're some crazy eccentric. Not dangerous enough to worry about in Aaru, but enough of a pest that you'll make a good scapegoat. If they want to unload this problem just as much as you say they do, they'll go for it."

"Two dozen. Remember, it needs to be enough demons for them to save face when they say they surrendered this responsibility."

Kirby shook his head. "A dozen. They can say they're humoring you because they're busy and throw it all in committee for another ten–thousand years."

Forget angels, this mage had been hanging out with elves for too long.

"Okay, but I get to shoot some stuff up. It's in keeping with my 'crazy' persona, and I love how tetchy they all get when I bring out the Iblis weapon."

"Don't kill any of them," Gareth warned. "You're liable to ruin the whole thing if you go killing some angel's cousin twice removed."

I agreed but pouted just a bit to show my disappointment at not being able to dust a few angels.

"Now we need to turn our attention back to transportation," Gareth added gloomily, sitting down and pulling a spell book back on his lap. "There's the same problem getting a dozen demons to whatever location you choose. Can't send them through a gate without setting off all sorts of early–warning alarms. And I know there aren't enough of Kirby's Marbles ready for this job."

"How long do you need them there?" Kirby was staring off into space. Or staring at a gruesome set of bloody paw prints along one wall. I wasn't sure which.

"My legion of twelve? I don't know. Couple of hours maybe."

Kirby wrinkled his thin nose. "Drat. I've been working on Kirby's Marble, trying to adjust it so it can transport more than one. Right now it works, but the passenger only stays for ten or fifteen minutes. Then he rebounds, like a rubber band. And he's throwing up everything in his digestive system for the next day, too."

This might work, although I'd need to keep the nasty side effects from my household. The time issue could be a problem, but I'd just talk really fast — and ensure I had a few angels to hurry things along a bit on their side. I crossed my fingers and hoped that Gregory would be on board with this insane plan, because it was all we had.

"I can do fifteen minutes. How many passengers can it move?"

"Five."

Well, that was a whole lot less than twelve. So much for the whole legion thing.

"Is there an illusion that will make five seem like a dozen?" I was grasping at straws. Angels wouldn't fall for an illusion, even a skillfully crafted one. Their primary sensory input was related to energy signature.

"Yes, but it's strictly visual." Gareth told me. "Elves use something similar to bait their traps since humans are primarily visual beings."

"Energy." I pointed a finger at Gareth, startling the elder man into dropping his spell book. "I don't need a dozen demons; I just need five kick–ass ancient ones. Is there a spell that masks demon energy signature, or makes a low–level demon look like a high–level one?"

The men exchanged a quick glance. "Yes, but I'm not positive it will work well enough to convince the angels," Kirby told me.

Gareth bent to pick up the fallen spell book. "Elven lords use it sometimes when they are hiring a demon and can't afford a high–level one. Cheap demon plus quick spell, and you've got instant intimidation. Lasts for a couple of hours."

"Deal," I rose to my feet. "I'll have my household members meet me at Gareth's shop in Dis, so we can arrive together. When do you need the focus back for modification, Kirby?"

"I can do that right before you transport. When do you want all this to happen?"

"Let's shoot for forty–eight hours, but I'll need to confirm with you after I speak with the angels."

"You're going to warn them?" Gareth asked.

"No, I'm going to invite them to the party."

***

"What do we get out of this?" Radl squinted his eyes in suspicion. "You gonna pay us? We getta fuck or kill somethen?"

I swept my arms outward in a grand gesture. "You get to meet an angel! Lots of angels, actually."

Snip's six eyes widened alarmingly. "Don't think that sounds like such a good deal, Mistress. I'd hoped to get through many thousands of years afore meeting angel. I'd hate to have my head chopped off and turned into dust at this young age. I's not even four hundred yet."

"No, no, they won't kill you. You just stand there and stare at them for fifteen minutes or so, and then the spell ends and you'll be safely back home. Easy peasy, and you'll get to tell everyone that you saw an angel and lived to tell the tale."

"I'm a Low," Pustule whined. "I can't activate the gates. I've never Owned a human — I can't assume a human form. What good would I be to you? Mistress, I think I would serve you far better by remaining behind and keeping your house free of crawling vermin."

"You're perfect for this job!" These five Low were all I could afford after blowing a huge sum this year on magical supplies and consulting. "Another magical spell will make you seem thirty levels above Low. The angels will quake before you. It's the chance of a lifetime."

"And why are we getting this 'chance of a lifetime'?" Radl drawled. "Cause we're expendable with no weregeld? Cause we're stupid? I didn't get to be six hundred and twenty–two without taking adequate precautions, you know."

Here's where the 'cheap' came in. "In addition to the great honor, chance to experience the human realm, and opportunity to be face–to–face with an angel and survive, I'll give each of you fifty coin and two baskets of rats."

There was a flurry of excited conversation, mostly about the rats.

"I'm in," Rot squeaked.

The other three quickly followed his lead, until only Radl stood with arms crossed and eyes narrowed. "Okay, but we each get a passage through the gates that lasts more than fifteen minutes after this. I want a week's vacation among the humans."

Crap. "There are behavioral restrictions," I warned. "You Own or kill any humans and the angels will be on you like fat on bacon. Got it?"

He waved his stubby, clawed hands. "Own? How the fuck am I supposed to Own anyone? I'm a damned Low, for fuck sake!"

I scowled and crossed *my* arms. "All right. Deal."

Awesome. I'd secured my five–demon legion. Now just a few more loose ends to tie up before my Mighty Show of Power. Hopefully I'd survive.

~26~

I'd been gone less than a day, but my heart was still in my throat as I drove over the bridge crossing the Potomac River and looked up at the huge alpine–style inn. It didn't look like it had been attacked by angels. The white and brown tudor–style façade loomed along the edge of the cliff, high above the churning, brown water. It was pretty, elegant, serene — safe. I hoped those inside were the same.

Harper ran to me, practically throwing herself in my arms. Her enthusiasm shocked me, and her huge belly nearly knocked me to the floor. After a quick hug, she composed herself, stepping back a few paces and awkwardly smoothing her shirt over the bulge.

"Sorry. I'm just so glad to see you. You've no idea ... here waiting, thinking I'm on the verge of being attacked, that you might be killed or never return. You're my only hope, Sam."

I wasn't Obi Wan Kenobi. At least I hoped I wasn't, since he got killed in the first movie. That would suck.

"Didn't anyone come up with a way to protect you all from the angels?" I'd expected a ring of salt or brick dust around the inn.

Harper shook her head. "Michelle's aunt tried, but some of the werewolves couldn't cross the barrier. Jaq and I definitely couldn't cross the barrier."

It made sense. All that angel energy running through them, or their baby, triggered the magic Aunt Marie used to guard against demons and angels.

"At least we've got these." Jaq's sardonic voice cut through my musings. I looked up to see her and Kelly approaching, both fingering what appeared to be macaroni noodle necklaces.

"And those do...?"

The Nephilim shrugged. "They're supposed to alert us if an angel or demon is nearby. A friend of a friend of Nyalla's — supposedly a witch — made them. Although I think maybe her pre–school kid was the one who actually made them."

"Well, if you're really hungry, I guess you can eat them." I was worried. They were here, with little more than Gregory and Gabriel's distraction techniques to keep the other angels searching elsewhere. It wasn't safe. None of them were safe, and I wasn't sure this crazy plan I had was even going to work.

"So, how'd it go?" Jaq asked. She and Kelly remained a respectful, wary distance from me.

"The trip to Hel was informative, but it pretty much confirmed that we don't have but a few of options. One: we secure another sanctuary, but the angels methodically hunt and kill all werewolves and eventually find you all."

Harper swayed, gripping the back of a chair to keep from falling. I hated to scare her. It wasn't herself she feared for; it was her child. That made her especially helpless in spite of the knives. It tugged at my un–demonic heartstrings.

"Two: we slowly move everyone, groups at a time, to Hel. You'll be safe from the angels, but there will be a huge adjustment, and I'm not saying the elves and demons will be any friendlier. The good thing in that scenario is that there's a group of freed humans who would be happy to join forces and support you all. It would be a rough journey, though."

"I'm not leaving West Virginia," Jaq said.

I restrained myself from an epic eye roll. Broken record and all that. Nephilim — just as stubborn and intractable as their angelic sires.

"Three: I arrange a showdown with the angels and bully them into letting you all continue to live here under my wings."

I swear the three of them stopped breathing for a good ten minutes.

Finally Jaq took a deep, long–overdue lungful. "That doesn't sound like it's going to end well."

"It won't unless I get a few angels to come to an agreement under the counter. Honestly, you all are a pain in the ass to them. They've been steadily dumping shit in my lap all year. Given the right incentive, they should be happy to unload the werewolves and Nephilim off on me. I've already got the Fallen. This is just a short step away."

"Then why the showdown and the bullying?" Leave it to that vampire to get right to the heart of the matter.

"Because they need to save face. I can't look too threatening. I've got to be such a psycho that they'd rather give you all up than deal with my crazy ass."

Kelly pursed her lips. "I can sympathize with them."

"Careful, vampire," I warned her. "I'm still waiting on those Doritos."

"Will this work, Sam?"

I turned to see Harper, steely eyed and fingering the knife at her belt.

"It's got a snowball's chance if I can get Gregory and his brothers on board."

She relaxed, a smile trembling at the edge of her lips, and I saw the woman she used to be — the woman she was before Bencul made her into this angry, frightened, knife–wielding nutcase. "He loves you. He'll do anything for you. I wish my angel had been the same."

Jaq walked forward to wrap a long, thin arm around the woman's shoulders. "They're not all such jerks. Your angel may have been a sociopath, but you're not alone. You're one of us now. Me, Kelly, and every werewolf in this state — none of us will let you down. Ever."

This had to somehow work out. Jaq would be a good friend to Harper, and a good role model for her son. I'd fucked up a lot of things, but introducing the two of them was the flower that bloomed in a pile of shit.

"Shit!" I'd just remembered something that might send all these plans crashing to the floor. "Jaq, where's the durft? Where's Fred?"

Without the focus, we'd need a whole new Kirby's Marble setup. Even if the mage had another ready to go, we'd lose valuable time retrieving it and returning to place the locators. Time we didn't have, especially with the werewolves and Nephilim unprotected.

Jaq blinked at me. "In my trailer. One of the neighbors is feeding him until I return."

"I'll need to go get him." Whew, at least he hadn't escaped into the woods or been eaten by one of the werewolves.

"Please do. He's a nasty animal, and I hate having to ask Melody to deal with him. Although he seems less vicious with humans than he is with Kelly and me."

Less vicious wasn't the same as sweet and cuddly. I grimaced, thinking of how chewed up I would be after wrestling that animal into a more portable box.

"When is all this going to go down?" The Nephilim asked.

I peeked at my cell phone for the time. "Let's shoot for forty hours from now. I'll have to confirm the time once I speak to Gregory, but that's what I'm going for."

"Where?" Jaq was already restless and ready for action.

"How about the casino? There's a huge parking lot out front where we can do the showdown."

"I've got a better idea." Jaq smiled, her silver eyes glowing with bits of gold. "Harper's Ferry. If it was good enough for John Brown, it will be good enough for us."

"Yeah, well hopefully it turns out better for us than it did for him."

Jaq and Kelly left the room, whispering under their breath. I watched them climb the stairs then I turned to leave, only to feel a tug on my arm.

"Sam? Can I go with you? Well, at least back to your house, since I can't exactly go with you to Aaru." It was Harper. And her grip on my arm was surprisingly strong for a human.

"No way. You need to be here with Jaq and the werewolves. They can protect you best."

The woman's chin went up, her eyes sparkling with defiance. "Better than you? Better than Nyalla and Nils? We've got the sorcerer items your brother brought from Hel. I'd feel safer there with them than here with a huge target on my head."

She had a point, but there was too much at risk.

"How am I supposed to get you there? Every time you move, there's a chance an angel will spot you, or a Hunter will pick up your baby's energy signature. And my house is under particular surveillance. The angels know I've sheltered you in the past. They know where my sympathies lie. Gregory took great risk moving you here. I don't want to take that risk again."

The look of defiance turned into an angry glare. "I'm not going to sit here, knit baby booties and wait for some winged being to rip my baby from my womb. If you won't take me there, I'll go myself. I'll hitchhike, take the bus, anything. You can't stop me."

"Hitchhike? Do you know how dangerous that is? Some serial killer with a pregnant woman fetish is liable to pick you up, knock you over the head and lock you in his basement."

Or not. I eyed Harper with her fierce glow and the knives on her belt. She was more liable to scare off the serial killers and end up walking all the way to my house.

"I'm safer in your house, with Nyalla and Nils. I'm safer with *you*. Once all this is resolved, I'll go live with Jaq and the werewolves — I promise. But until then, I feel the best place for me and my son is in your home."

I hesitated, hating to separate her from Jaq and the werewolves. They were her new family, and she should be relying on them for security. But that sin of pride that had long eluded me blossomed like a winter rose. A human, betrayed by an angel, trusted me — felt safe in my house. It was a heady feeling of power that ran through me at her words.

"Okay, but you have to promise me that you'll be careful. Don't leave the house, even to go out to the pool. Keep an elven net on you at all times. Don't hesitate to tell Nyalla and Nils if you see anything odd, or feel at all uneasy. When all this is over, you can start your new life with the werewolves in West Virginia."

Harper smiled, and once again I saw the beautiful, cheerful, confident woman inside.

"Deal."

~27~

I appeared in Aaru, retaining my physical form, despite the horrible scratchy feeling being in corporeal form in the home of the angels always caused me. Immediately I was surrounded, and this time the spirits were clearly hostile. Word had gotten around about my dealings with Nephilim and the lethal force I'd taken to defend what I called mine. It was like having a mob press against me with sharp knives and fire.

"Where's ... um, where's Michael?" Yeah, *that* was his name. Yelling for Gregory or 'asshole' wouldn't get me too far. Good thing I'd remembered what Dalmai had called him. I hoped this worked, that my crazy appearance here furthered my goal, and that Gregory was quick enough to catch on. Once again, I mourned the loss of the tie we had when I was bound to him.

The angels advanced. I dodged just in time to avoid a blast of white. Fuck this. If they were going to shoot at me, I wasn't about to stand here and take it. I might be a trespasser, but I was a legal one. As the Iblis, I was the only demon allowed in Aaru. They might hate my presence, but they were supposed to tolerate it without attack.

I drew the sword of the Iblis. No one had answered my request for Gregory, but the sword at least garnered some uneasy respect.

"I demand to see the head of the fourth choir, Michael."

I knew there had been no misunderstanding who I was asking for, but repeating my request with more clarification in combination with my weapon might get results. I felt them draw back, giving me space while still watching for an opening to rush me. Unwilling to give them that opening, I spun around in circles, my sword in front of me. Luckily they were too stupid to come at me from above or below.

I should have known better than to rely on luck. I felt the angel just before his blast took my head off. It rolled across what counted for a floor in Aaru, singed hair, smoking flesh and all. It was a bit disconcerting seeing my head no longer affixed to my neck, feeling my body begin to crumple.

Luckily I was in Aaru, and other than a lot of blood and gore flying through the endless white, nothing too dramatic happened. The loss of my corporeal form here didn't mean death, but it did pose a bit of a problem. Uncertain how I could wield the sword of the Iblis while headless and dead, I recreated my form with a pop. Another blast nearly took my newly created head off, but I was prepared this time. I blocked the stream of energy with my sword and seized hold of the angel.

Word must have also gotten around about my devouring tendencies. The moment I grabbed him, the angel screamed in mind–speech with a pitch that nearly caused a brain bleed.

"Shut the fuck up!" I held onto him and struggled against the urge to do more than just hold. With so little effort he could be mine — dead and converted into energy. But dead angels made for poor hostages, and I was in enough trouble without killing another one of these fuckers right in the fourth circle of Aaru.

"Stay back!"

The angels complied, but their fury hit me like a whip. If Gregory didn't show up soon, there was a good chance they'd rush me. I might be able to take out a few, but even the Sword of the Iblis couldn't defend me from a mob. The whole scenario made me realize how much of a long shot this plan of mine was. If I couldn't get Gregory behind it, I was going to go down in flames. Literally.

"Cockroach, stand down." His voice slammed into me with power and compulsion, but behind it I heard the note of concern. My grip on the hostage angel trembled.

"I promise I won't hurt him. I just need to meet with you about a matter of utmost urgency." *And Gabriel. I need to meet with Gabriel, too*, I added silently.

What are you doing? What is going on?

"Your angels have attacked me and mine in my home, and now you mount an offensive against those I claim. I won't tolerate such a trespass upon my authority."

A light of understanding gleamed in his ebony eyes. "We were unaware of your claims, Iblis."

"That's no excuse." I snarled, holding my hostage tighter.

"The Nephilim and any of their resulting offspring fall under the governance of Aaru. They're angels, not demons."

"They're the products of Fallen," I shot back. "Were not the members of the tenth choir deemed Fallen? Is not the sin of improper relations with humans, to say nothing of deliberately impregnating them, enough to warrant the status of Fallen? Again, I assert that they are mine."

Gregory shook his head, smiling as if he were humoring a petulant child. "The tenth choir was given penance by us, not the Iblis."

"Only because there was no Iblis at the time to assert his rights in the matter."

Again he smiled. "Let the angel go, and we can discuss this in the next Ruling Council meeting."

I scraped my sword close enough to the angel that I would have nicked his flesh had he been corporeal. "No. You angels will just kill them all before the next meeting, or delay for centuries. I want to discuss this with you now, and have a ruling concerning my authority within the next two days."

He nodded. "Let the angel go and I'll meet with you in your house right now. I promise you will have your chance to present your case before the Ruling Council within the next rotation cycle."

Awesome. I was never so grateful that Gregory seemed to know where I was going with things. I might have surprised him with the angel in my basement, and throwing Bencul through the gate to Hel, but he caught on fast. Still, I hesitated, reluctant to release the angel and gate to my house. It would take me a while to actually arrive there. Outside of Aaru, I never seemed to get to the place I wanted to be on the first try. How many places I'd need to visit before I actually arrived at my house? Hopefully Gregory and Gabriel would wait for me, because I might be a while.

"Let the angel go, put the sword away, and I will accompany you to our meeting. I vow no harm will come to you as long as you let the angel go."

Whew. I should have known Gregory would realize my dilemma and propose something face–saving. "Deal."

I released the angel, who hightailed it back into the crowd. Gregory went to open his arms in his customary gesture and halted, his hands an awkward angle from his body. Something inside me crashed. He'd always held me close when we traveled this way. He'd always crushed me against him as if he wanted to merge my physical body with his own, but this was an act before an audience of angels. I had played my part, and now it was time for him to play his. I'd never been truly welcome in Aaru, but my actions recently had driven the animosity towards me into overdrive. Gregory could hardly treat me the same as he always had before in front of their watching eyes. And he probably wouldn't be able to once I stood in front of the host with a band of demons and demanded a slice of their territory.

I nodded to him as if it didn't bother me, and he lowered his hands to his sides. This was killing me. I know I chose the path I now walked, but it pained me.

With a flash, we were in my living room, safely behind the magical barrier that masked our presence. Gregory grabbed me, holding me close. His spirit–self merged slightly with mine, and I felt his distress.

"I'm putting you in a terrible position, aren't I? Forcing you to choose between me and Aaru? You'll need to distance yourself from me or risk losing support."

"That's my problem, Cockroach, not yours."

But it *was* my problem. I had no issue with the painful changes my chaos was causing in Aaru, but I couldn't take him down with me. He was the Angel of the Host, and they needed him. We had an eternity to be together. I could wait until things settled down a bit, and then we might be able to pick up where we left off.

"I can't do this." My voice was muffled against his shirt. "I won't be responsible for your fall."

"You won't be responsible. I'm over six–billion years old. I think I'm capable of making my own choices. This is my decision to make, not yours. You go on being the Iblis, and I will do as I choose."

He rocked me gently back and forth. I felt oddly soothed by the motion. "What about Aaru? What will happen to Aaru if you openly support me?"

"They'll accept it or they won't. If they don't, then someone else will have to step up."

I pulled back and punched him lightly in the chest. "That's not the angel I love. You're the Angel of the Host. It's your responsibility to make sure Aaru and its inhabitants are on their path to good vibrations, or whatever the fuck you guys consider your life goals."

"I think six–billion years is a pretty good term of office. If I'm no longer effective there, so be it. I can work toward the betterment of Aaru elsewhere. I don't need to give up on my home and my kin because of a difference in viewpoint."

Odd. That same difference in viewpoint led to a major war two–and–a–half–million years ago, ending in our exile. I hoped this wouldn't lead to the same.

"What would you do? To better Aaru without being the big baddy of the Ruling Council?"

"Oh, I'd still be on the Ruling Council, I'd just focus on less divisive tasks."

He'd spent so much time running back and forth between here and Aaru with his dual responsibilities as Gregori and on the Ruling Council. Maybe it would be a relief to concentrate on just one for a while. I would welcome the extra time with him — if I could somehow manage to shrug off some of my own duties, that is. Although that wouldn't be likely, with me making a bid for the Nephilim and werewolves. I tried to envision our lives and couldn't.

"I can't imagine Aaru without you in charge." I confessed. "You're the one with the clout to keep everyone in line. What would heaven be like without your firm hand guiding it?"

He laughed, the sound sending a thrill through me. Maybe this would work out. Maybe I needed to trust him to do what was right for himself and Aaru and mind my own damned business. I looked up at him and ran a finger along the angles of his cheek and jaw. In return, he caressed my spirit–self with his own.

"Ah, Cockroach, your punishments will be far less enjoyable without me to help you pass the time. Maybe one of the other angels can be persuaded to hold you tight during your time of contemplation?"

I smiled at his teasing tone, but he had a valid point. Punishment would totally suck without him there. And there was no fucking way I'd let some other angel 'hold me tight'. Blech.

"You'll need to make sure your successor does as good a job as you did."

The teasing tone disappeared, and his eyes were thoughtful. "I don't think I did all that good a job. A bloody war. Aaru fractured in two. Nearly three–million years of stagnation."

I wasn't about to let him turn this into a heap of "woe is me". "Well, to err is human, so you're right at home here. Stay with me and elect a puppet dictator to do your bidding in Aaru. You can do your Grigori thing and keep me in line while someone less controversial runs the show under your orders."

His eyes widened. "That's a brilliant idea. I still maintain my control and influence, but through a less controversial member of the Ruling Council."

"I should have known you'd never *really* give up control," I shook my head. "Angel of the Host to his very last breath, even if someone else is in the limelight. So, who do you have in mind as your puppet dictator?"

Gabriel appeared just inside my front door, cutting off whatever it was Gregory was about to say. The dark–haired angel cast a disapproving glance at his elder brother then turned cold blue eyes on me.

"I believe you wanted to speak to me?"

It suddenly hit me. Gabriel was just as Jaq had described when recounting her angelic visitor. Tall and lean, with short black hair that stood upward as if he had an electrical current running through him. His eyes changed like a storm–tossed sea, from grey to blue to green and everything in between. I strode toward the younger angel, pointing at him as I walked. It had to have been him — the one watching over her all these years. Could it be possible that the pious and sanctimonious Gabriel was Jaq's father? Well, there was one way to find out. I only wished I had a plate full of pastries to throw.

"You fucking hypocrite. How dare you sit on the Ruling Council throwing down all that judgmental crap on others when you are just as bad."

I could swear Gabriel became even paler, although his eyes blazed crystal blue.

"You insane, witless fool. What are you ranting about this time? Your attempts to divert our attention from your own misdeeds will not succeed."

"Jaq." His eyebrows knitted at the name. "She's the Nephilim in West Virginia. You've been watching over her since she was an infant. She's *your* child, you piece of shit. You've been fucking humans, discarding the mothers, and letting others raise your half–breeds. How can you call yourself an angel?"

Not that we were any better, but we didn't get all high and mighty and act like our shit didn't stink.

Gabriel's eyes widened, and then he did something completely unexpected. He threw back his head and laughed.

"Judging everyone else by your own moral license, demon scum? I have never lain with a human, and I never will. Yes, I've watched over that child as she's grown, but not because she is mine."

"Yeah, right. Why would you swoop in unannounced every year to make sure this child was safe and happy? A year is a blink of an eye to an angel. That's a lot of attention to pay to a child that's not yours."

Gabriel's face hardened. "There are responsibilities to our own that you cannot even conceive. Each angel in my choir is mine to guide and nurture. One of them may stray from the path of righteousness, but that does not negate my accountability to him."

My mouth hung open in the most unbecoming way. "The father is one of your choir? But why would he not watch over his child himself?"

The younger angel glared. "Because he is still in rehabilitation following his disgraceful violation of our laws. Even if he were able to travel outside Aaru, he would not risk his child's safety by attempting to see her. The girl's mother died soon after her birth, and he worries about her wellbeing. What would you have me do?"

"I don't know — maybe what you're always spouting off at the meetings? Kill the baby as well as hold the father accountable. Instead, you watch over the child and hide your knowledge of the Nephilim sanctuary. You don't report that you have proof of the link between werewolves and Nephilim. And during the raid, you find and rescue not only Jaq, but her vampire girlfriend and a woman pregnant with a Nephilim child. What the fuck, Gabe?"

Suddenly all Gregory had told me made sense. Gabriel was still a stick–up–the–ass prick, but he had a core of empathy that actually backed up his high vibration pattern.

He tilted up his chin, looking down his nose at me. "As much as it pains me to admit it, we angels must change on this issue. Lying with humans is sinful. The angelic sires of these children must be punished, but the offspring are innocent and should be judged on their own merits."

"Then why do you always vote otherwise in Ruling Council meetings?" I'll admit my attitude was a bit hostile, but given what I'd experienced of this angel, it was understandable.

A faint smile flickered across his face, and suddenly the resemblance to Gregory was pronounced. "Sometimes the best way to sway a group of people is to introduce small adjustments over a long period of time. We tend to move at a snail's pace when it comes to change. Being a stickler for the rules has allowed me to gain the trust of the most conservative angels. They support me and will agree as I slowly adjust our course on this matter."

Damn. He would have made a great demon if he didn't take so fucking long to act.

"Look here, Dopey, the werewolves and Nephilim are in immediate danger. They are *all* innocent. An entire race is facing extinction. Fuck the need for a snail's pace; you angels have to get off your asses and fix this problem before it's too late."

Gabriel raised one jet–black eyebrow. "Some angels feel that the 'fix' is in killing all of the werewolves. I have a great number of supporters, but even I cannot stand against Aaru. Even if Micha and I unite, we are not strong enough to force this through. Maybe a few will survive, and after a–few–thousand years, we will be able to allow some accommodations."

I bristled. "We don't have a–few–thousand years. These lives matter. And you know that, or you wouldn't be spending your precious time out of Aaru standing over a crib and looking at a freckled half–angel baby."

It was as if a shadow flashed across the angel's face. "I know that as well as you, but the end goal is worth some occasional losses and defeats."

"Bullshit!" I poked Gabriel in the chest with a finger, struggling to keep my wings hidden. "Wrong is wrong, and to delay corrective action is to be lower than a cockroach. How can you live with yourself?"

I actually heard him grind his teeth. "I have no idea what my esteemed eldest brother sees in you. My eyes are always on the goal, and if it takes a few steps backward to achieve that, so be it."

"I never go backwards." Which was more than a bit of a lie. I went any way I needed to, any way that suited my purpose. But this statement had the drama the moment called for.

Taking a deep breath, I met Gabriel's eyes in challenge. Here goes. I'd hoped the angels could right this themselves, but if not, then it was back to plan B — the one where I risk it all.

"The Fallen are mine. Humans with sub–par FICO scores are mine. The Nephilim and werewolves are also mine. I claim them as the Iblis. Their lives, their vibration patterns, their redemption or punishment, their eternal souls are my responsibility."

His hands fisted white at his sides. I had no idea how Gregory was reacting to all of this drama. The elder angel had remained behind me, silent since Gabriel had arrived.

"Even if the rest of the Ruling Council were to support your assumption of what has always been our responsibility, I will never give over the wellbeing of the Nephilim into a demon's care."

Yeah, maybe I'd exaggerated that 'happy to hand this problem over to me' when I'd discussed the plan with Gareth and Kirby. Gabriel would be my greatest opposition. If I could sway him into agreement, this would work. If not... .

"You'd rather see them dead?" I backpedaled, seeing Gabriel's resolute expression. "In spite of what you think of me, I have friends among the werewolves — household members, even. I've made a vow to protect both the unborn Nephilim and his mother. I cannot stand by while the angels slaughter them. I have claimed them, and, as the Iblis, I will defend them against any attack by the angels."

It was my line in the sand. I held my breath and waited for Gabriel's move.

"You can claim them all you want, but they are *not* yours. We have not deemed them Fallen, and their vibration patterns are not your responsibility. If you face us in defiance, attempt to turn our path by force, we will overpower you with our might. You are one Iblis, and we are many."

Asshole. "We are many too," I said softly, letting the threat hang in the air between us. There was a bit of a Mexican standoff between us, and I needed to give him a way out. "But I don't want to see this come to violence. I care too much about these beings to see them exterminated while you angels sit around for centuries splitting hairs. You have the capacity for rational thought when you're not being a pompous bag of wind. Think of some way we can work together to save these lives without starting yet another war."

Gabriel ran a hand through his black hair, causing the upward do to shift dramatically to the left. "I cannot go to the Council and tell them that you've basically seized control of an entire race — a race that includes those with angelic bloodlines. Every angel in Aaru will take up arms against the demons. There *will* be another war if you persist on this path."

"But what if it's your idea?" I tried for a pleading gesture to counterbalance the earlier threat. "Aaru is recovering from a coup attempt. There are splinter groups disrupting your unity and rule. This whole Nephilim thing is an unwelcome distraction. Say that you're verifying the alleged proof that werewolves are descended from Nephilim, and until a decision is made, they will fall under my wings."

"Unwelcome distraction?" Gabriel sniffed. "This is just the distraction we need. It will unite all of Aaru, especially if they think the demons are trying to take something away from us. This is the perfect distraction."

My heart leapt as I wondered if I'd made a fatal error in judgment, but then I remembered Jaq.

"For twenty–eight years you've watched over a Nephilim, seeing her grow, watching as she coped with angelic powers. You've kept your mouth shut for millennium about the werewolves and their sanctuaries, but you'd sacrifice all of that to unify Aaru? This perfect distraction would only be temporary. Once the dust settled, the angels would return to their rebellions. The only thing that would buy you is time. Would time be worth the cost? The extermination of a species seems a very high price to pay."

Gabriel's mouth tightened. "Sometimes a high price is necessary."

"Not this time. Their deaths would be a burden on your soul, Gabriel. What would that do to your precious vibration pattern? This wouldn't be a noble sacrifice; it would be a coward's way out. You'd give up the lives of an entire race to stall, to avoid facing a problem in Aaru that you need to face. Is that the kind of angel you are?"

He snarled, and in a flash of speed, snatched up a chair and flung it at me. I was too surprised to duck and took it right to the face, landing on my back with blood pouring from my nose and forehead.

"Fine. I'll support your claim before the Ruling Council as a temporary means to divide responsibilities while we investigate further, but you need to make a public claim on this or it won't fly."

I squirmed into a sitting position, spitting and wiping the blood from my eyes. "One rotation cycle. Harpers Ferry, West Virginia. At the junction of the Potomac and Shenandoah Rivers."

He gave a short, sharp nod. "We'll be there. Don't be late ... and don't screw up."

In a flash, he was gone. I yanked off my shirt and tried to staunch the flow of blood as I stood shakily to my feet. I'd done it. Well, sort of done it. Now I had to worry about getting this public claim to work, getting a bunch of demons to Harpers Ferry and keeping them there until our 'show of force' was over. I looked at the bloody shirt and felt the trickle of liquid down my nose. Fuck it. Extending the glow of light outward, I healed the cuts and tossed the shirt aside.

Then I felt Gregory's hand on my shoulder.

"Cockroach, I do believe we've found the perfect puppet dictator."

~28~

I sat in the chair with a thump. "You're fucking joking me. Of all the angels in heaven, you somehow think that Gabriel is best suited to lead? Puppet dictator my ass. He'll do the exact opposite of what you want."

"He's shockingly predictable, and that works to our advantage."

Our? I had enough on my plate. I didn't need to add some secret co–rule of Aaru to it.

"He'll send Aaru right back into the dark ages. I'll be confined to Hel. Werewolves will be on an existence contract that makes the current one look like a cakewalk. Angels will kill every demon they see. Gabriel isn't going to change who he's been his whole life. He may color outside the lines on occasion, but he'll go back and change that as soon as he comes to his senses."

"That's what I'm counting on, Cockroach." Gregory walked over and wrapped his arms around my neck, pulling me backwards — chair and all, against his chest. "Now. Enough about Aaru. Let's turn our attention to how some members of the Ruling Council seem to know what's going on in your house seconds after it occurs."

I leaned my head back against him. "Well, there's always you. You're my primary suspect here."

He rested his chin on the top of my head, his breath stirring my hair. "I'm innocent, you know. But since you're a

266

demon, I'm sure you have some punishment in store for me regardless."

Heat blossomed through me at the thought. I could duct tape him to a chair and interrogate him. Ten minutes of my mouth on his cock and he'd be confessing to everything under the sun. Assuming he oblige me and manifest the necessary organ for such torture.

"One of my enforcers has been in the area tracking a curse demon. She's one of Gabriel's angels, but my brother would have come to me first if she'd noticed something and told him. Rules, you know."

Yeah. I thought through everyone who'd been by the house recently while Gregory went down the exhaustively long list of his Gregori staff. Nyalla's friends were clueless. Candy's werewolves would never endanger themselves in such a way. I hadn't seen a vampire beyond that Kelly girl in months, and she seemed completely dedicated to Jaq. The only angels in my house were Nils, and... .

Dalmai.

I jumped up, slamming my head into Gregory's nose in the process. It hurt me, but the angel seemed oblivious to any pain.

"What exactly did you have Dalmai vow when we released his collar?"

The angel tilted his head as he thought. "I'll admit I was a bit thrown by the situation and may not have worded the oath to the best of my ability. I commanded him to remain here and serve you. To not physically harm any of the humans under your protection. I relieved him of his Hunter duties."

"Would he... do you think he was upset enough about your not taking his side over mine that he would betray you?" The very thought appalled me. I could never betray Gregory. Never. I couldn't imagine anyone who served him straying. But I was extremely biased where this particular angel was concerned.

"He might. Hunters tend to be more individualistic than other angels. I can see one breaking his household tie if given appropriate reason." Gregory's eyes narrowed, his energy leak increasing. It's a wonder he wasn't setting fire to my flooring. My knees went a bit weak in the presence of such anger, such power. I shook my head to refocus my thoughts. Deal with the potential traitor now. Save the angel sex for later. Hopefully, anyway.

"He was to remain here? Does that mean the building, the property surrounding the building, or any of the properties I own? And 'physically' — as in laying his hands on Harper? Or would that cover leaking information to someone else who could do her harm?"

Oaths were important to word correctly, but Gregory could be forgiven for his lapse. It wasn't every day that his demon lover took a member of his choir hostage, beat the shit out of the guy and kept him a starving captive in her basement.

"Here would encompass your house and the surrounding property that you own." Gregory scowled. "And no, physical harm would not cover leaking information that would result in harm to any of your household."

Shit. I took off for the basement stairs just a few steps ahead of Gregory, nearly ripping the door from the hinges in my haste. There was an angel in my basement, but it wasn't Dalmai. It was Nils, and he was duct taped into a grey ball on the floor.

I ripped the strips from his face, and he gasped, not looking his best with sticky strands still clinging to his skin and red marks where the tape had cut into the flesh.

"Where's Dalmai?" Gregory thundered.

Fuck Dalmai. "Where's Harper?"

"Harper? Isn't she upstairs?" Nils licked dry, chapped lips.

"Harper!" Gregory shouted, spinning me around by the shoulders. "Why isn't she hiding with the werewolves? Please, for the love of all creation, tell me you didn't bring her back here."

There was no time for evasiveness. "I did. Sorry, but she insisted and said she'd walk back herself if I didn't bring her. You know how humans are — you just can't reason with them."

Gregory shook me until I thought my teeth were going to rattle out of my skull. "No, that's why you enthrall them and make them do what you want them to. You were supposed to protect her, not bring her back into the very place every angel is looking to find her."

He had a valid point, but there were more important things to do then argue about my poor judgment. Pushing Gregory away, I went to run up the stairs and check. Pregnant women seemed to sleep a lot. There was a good chance my worry was over nothing and Harper was just snoozing in her room. I got two steps before Gregory halted me with an iron grip.

"She's not there. I scanned and there's no other being in the house beyond the three of us."

Shit. Shit. I looked imploringly at Nils and winced as he strained against the duct tape. Dalmai must have used two rolls on the Fallen angel. Poor guy looked like a chrysalis encased in a cocoon.

With a grunt, Nils strained against the restraints. The tape tore but no butterfly emerged. "I was in the kitchen getting a beer. Dalmai came upstairs and hit me over the head with the poker from the fireplace."

I glanced at his head, noting the dried blood on his clothing. His skull looked intact. Good thing I was the only one able to kill him, because Dalmai must have done a number on the angel to knock him out like that.

"Harper wasn't even in the room. I figured he just wanted to kill me because I was a Fallen. Why would he take her?"

"Because he is a traitor."

I shivered to hear the note of violence in Gregory's voice. It must have had the same effect on Nils, because the Fallen angel winced. Images raced through my mind of abortion and memory wiping, and I pushed down my rising panic.

"He can't leave the property. He vowed. Dalmai might have found loopholes in his oath, but he can't leave the property." My voice was reaching hysteria. I felt Gregory's hand grip my arm hard enough to break the bone.

"Cockroach, he'll still be here but he no doubt handed off Harper to another angel."

I ripped my arm free from his grip and ran up the stairs. Forty acres of property and I was pressed for time. Who knew how long Harper had been gone, or what had happened to her. With a burst of energy, I exploded one of the French doors and screamed at the top of my lungs for Boomer.

I heard Nils's and Gregory's footsteps crunching on the broken glass of my door as the hellhound raced around the Forsythia bushes, skidding to make the turn. His Plott–hound form blurred, growing several feet larger and gaining mass as an additional head sprouted from a newly formed neck. By the time he slid to a stop in front of me, he was the size of a small pony, saliva dripping in long strands from his jaws.

"Can you sense Dalmai?" I asked Gregory.

"No. Which means he's gone rogue."

He'd used that term two years ago, referring to Althean. That angel had wound up dead. I hoped the same fate was in store for Dalmai, although death wouldn't be punishment enough if he'd hurt Harper or her baby. "Does that mean he can break his vow?"

Gregory nodded, his face dark with anger. "He can, although many angels who go rogue don't. A vow is a sacred thing, and even angels who have renounced the host refuse to break them."

I wouldn't want to be in Dalmai's shoes when we found him, and find him we would. He might have surrendered his place in Gregory's choir, but I had a hellhound at my disposal, and Boomer was better at tracking than I was.

"Dalmai," I told my dog. "He was the Hunter angel who had come for Harper. The one you helped fight. The one who took most of the left side off your body. I need you to find him."

Recognition lit in the hellhound's orange eyes. One head dropped to the ground to sniff, while the other rose into the air. In my mind, the few seconds felt like hours, but finally Boomer took off, the three of us racing behind him. Hellhounds are fast. Nils and I were puffing away, while Gregory was doing his odd float/fly thing. He glowed, his eyes black with fury, looking every bit like an angel of vengeance bearing down on his prey. I was never so turned on in my whole life.

We followed Boomer through the horse pasture, where the hellhound paused and spent considerable time sniffing around the border of my property. Then he halted, looking up at me with an intent gaze. I paused, glancing towards Nils and Gregory. Had Dalmai handed Harper off to another angel and remained on my property, or had he broken his vow and left with her? I didn't want to waste time tracking him down if he didn't have Harper.

"Nils, can you sense if she stayed with him, or if she left from here?"

His eyebrows shot to the heavens. "Why would I know that?"

"Well, because you've been fucking her. I saw you with your arm around her. You admitted to not remaining on the couch all night, and Dalmai said you were sinning with her. I figured you may have marked her. Demons do it all the time."

Nils turned a brilliant shade of crimson. "I'm not a demon. Just because I'm Fallen, doesn't mean I go around doing that kind of thing."

Right. "So you weren't fucking her?"

"No! I wasn't ... that liar! I never had inappropriate contact with Harper. She's just been betrayed by one of our kind. I would never do that to her, never take advantage of her vulnerability like that."

I sensed he told the truth, but what the hell had been going on? "Why would Dalmai lie?"

The angel shifted his feet, not meeting my eyes. "Perhaps he thinks that you have claimed the woman as yours and accusing me of ... that would incite you to jealous wrath. He *does* want me dead, you know. And you're the only one who can kill me."

There was more to this, but I didn't have time to interrogate my Fallen while Harper was gone. For all I knew, Nils could be right and Dalmai lied. I had claimed Nyalla as part of my household, and with my vow, Harper was as good as mine, too.

Oh shit. Nyalla. I had my second panic attack of the evening. "Where the fuck is Nyalla?"

She hadn't been in the house or Gregory would have sensed her. Had Dalmai taken both her and Harper? He might be an angel and all that, but managing to kidnap two young, fit girls seemed to be a bit above his skill level.

"Cockroach? You might want to take a look at this."

Gregory's voice was odd, as if he couldn't quite believe what he was seeing. Nils and I crashed through the briars and poison ivy to where he stood and looked down. On the ground was an angel I'd never seen before. A dead angel. And he looked as if someone had gone all Norman Bates on his ass.

Harper. Damn, that woman had mad skills when it came to knives.

"I've never seen an angel die like this." Gregory motioned to the angel's neck, which was surprisingly clean and free of cuts. "It appears that he had been restrained by that collar device of yours. Your girl removed it post mortem, no doubt to use again."

Of course. Recycle and reuse. What a great motto.

Nils kicked the bloody angel corpse with a booted toe. "So where are they, and where is Dalmai? They must have done this after he left, or he would have assisted this scum in subduing the women."

Either the girls had run to safety, or Dalmai had somehow found out about this and recaptured them. Taking the worst–case scenario to heart, I turned and faced Boomer.

"Find Nyalla, boy. Go get her."

His tail nearly wagged off his body as the hound enthusiastically paced, both heads to the ground while he sniffed. After a few seconds, he lifted one head and bayed. Then he spun about and raced toward the house. I tore off after him, not bothering to see whether Gregory and Nils followed me or not.

The hellhound was around the front of my house in the driveway, waiting patiently for me to catch up. As soon as I got within twenty feet, he trotted along the gravel drive and out to the road. I glanced backward and nearly ran into Gregory and Nils. Fuck, these guys moved silently.

"He broke his vow and left the property." Gregory sounded more pissed about that than the fact that Dalmai had betrayed us both and severed his allegiance. I remembered how incensed the Ruling Council had been over the thought of humans defaulting on their loans. Angels and their weird priorities — I'd never understand them. Besides, if Boomer was going where I thought he was, then Dalmai hadn't broken his vow.

"Wyatt is part of my household. I've claimed him, therefore his house and property would probably be considered mine under the terms of the oath."

Gregory scowled. "How would Dalmai know that? He hasn't seen you and Wyatt together. He wouldn't be aware of your relationship to him."

I shrugged and picked up the pace, trying to keep Boomer in sight as he circled the house. Angels had such weird skills in regards to determining household and ownership marks. For all I knew, Dalmai may have sensed that I had claimed this house.

Boomer climbed the steps of Wyatt's rickety back porch and paused by the screen door. It was partially open. The wooden door behind it swung inward, the handle and lock dangling from splintered wood. Thankfully Wyatt wasn't home. That was one less human I had to worry about.

They're both here — Harper and Nyalla, Gregory told me silently. *They are both unharmed and Harper is still pregnant.*

I breathed a sigh of relief. Dalmai was under oath not to physically harm any of mine, but I wasn't sure if that technically covered the unborn Nephilim or not. I motioned to Gregory to stay back. The angel leaked power like a sieve. Nils and I might go unnoticed by Dalmai, but Gregory certainly wouldn't.

The Fallen angel and I crept in through the back door, carefully skirting the broken glass and objects strewn across the floor. Clearly there had been a struggle in Wyatt's kitchen. I glanced over at the gun case and saw it locked. Not that I expected Dalmai to resort to human weaponry, but I wanted to double check, just in case.

Where would he have taken the girls? Somewhere quiet to wait out the arrival of another angel, no doubt. Not the front part of the house. Wyatt may have needed to board up a significant number of windows after the Haagenti incident, but there was still too much glass to provide a safe spot. Not the bedrooms either. I glanced at the door beside the stove and realized the most defensible area of the house would be the cellar. The two windows were thick and below grade, and the only entrance was this door.

Just in case I was wrong, I motioned for Nils to stay and watch while I slowly eased the door open. Damp, earthy aromas hit my nose, and I paused to allow my eyes time to adjust to the dark. Dim, gray light filtered through the grimy cellar windows. Enough to keep the cellar from being pitch–black, but not enough to aid my vision. I eyed the single bulb at the bottom of the steps and weighed the risk of turning it on and alerting Dalmai versus breaking my neck in the dark.

I chose the neck–breaking option. Worn wooden steps creaked as I eased down them, ruining my element of surprise. I should have turned the fucking light on. At this point, yelling "I'm coming" would have been stealthier. Still, in spite of the deafening noise of the stairs, no sound came from below, not even a breath. Were the girls knocked unconscious? If he'd hurt either of them, I'd peel the flesh from his body and boil him in pork fat.

I heard a creak as I stepped off the last stair onto the gray concrete and froze. It came from the left, far back in the recesses of the basement where boxes and ancient paint cans blocked my view and any light. Risking a further chance of discovery, I summoned the sword of the Iblis and tiptoed toward the noise.

Again, I heard it. A scrabbling sound as if a giant mouse were fighting its way out of a Styrofoam cooler. I took another tentative step, and everything went black.

"I've got him!" Nyalla yelled.

No, she hadn't, but before I could correct her, the wind was completely knocked out of my lungs by a hard object impacting my body. The blows rained down on me, and I gasped in pain, hoping Gregory or Nils would hear the commotion and come to my rescue before the two girls beat the living shit out of me.

Then sharp stabs were added to the blows. I heard the basement stairs creak.

"I've got him!" Nyalla gleefully repeated her earlier statement.

"Yes, I see that." Gregory sounded vastly amused. Fucker. "Although the appropriate pronoun would be 'her' in this instance."

"Him, her — this angel isn't taking my baby," Harper said in time with the knife to my kidneys.

"True. I doubt the Iblis is interested in taking your baby, though. From what I've seen, she doesn't seem to enjoy the company of human infants — living or deceased."

The blows and stabbing abruptly ceased.

"Oops."

Yeah. Oops indeed. I squirmed inside the elven net. "Get me the fuck out of here before I bleed to death. Damn it all, Harper. Why do you always have to be so fucking stabby?"

"Sorry, sorry!"

The net lifted, and I looked up at the two girls. I felt like shit, and from the expressions on their faces, I knew I didn't look much better. Gregory was at the edge of the stairs. Nils, halfway down, was biting back a smile.

"Well, that was vastly entertaining," Gregory drawled. "From the situation at hand, I gather Dalmai is *not* keeping you two captive in Wyatt's basement?"

"No." Nyalla exchanged a wary look with Harper. "I know he's your angel and all that, but I don't believe meditation did anything to improve his moral standing."

"Go on," Gregory urged. "What exactly happened? I'd like to hear your side of the story before I track down and deliver justice to my former angel."

I shivered, and Nyalla stared at him with wide eyes before continuing. "I heard a commotion downstairs — Harper screaming and something making a thumping noise, but I couldn't get out of my room. He'd sealed the door, and I couldn't break it down — even using the closet rod as a battering ram."

"I was in the barn, and when I came in, he grabbed me," Harper chimed in. "He got really angry when whatever angel magic he was using didn't work on me. I kept screaming, and he tried to slap duct tape on my mouth. I fought him the whole way as he dragged me through the fields. The duct tape came loose pretty soon after we got out of the house. At that point, he seemed more eager to get me into the woods than stop and try to shut me up again."

"I knotted my bedsheets into a rope and climbed out the window, just like in the movies." Nyalla was practically vibrating with excitement. "Then I snuck through the field after them. It was easy to stay undetected since Harper was making so much noise screaming and yelling."

"And Nyalla collared the other angel while Harper sliced him to ribbons." The girls had the grace to look rather uncomfortable at my summary. "But what happened to Dalmai? Did he run away? Do you have any idea where he went?"

"There." Harper pointed to the boxes stacked up in the corner. "He went right there."

Given the condition of the angel in the sticker bushes, it was with great trepidation that I got up and peered behind the boxes. It wasn't a pretty sight. The collar was the only clean thing on Dalmai. He'd been trussed up with electrical extension cords and had what seemed to be a dirty sock crammed in his mouth. One eye was swollen shut, and his nose was sideways. The angel's clothing was torn, and blood oozed from deep scratches all over his arms and legs. A particularly deep gash ran diagonally across his side. I had no doubt who had done that one.

"Wow, he's alive." I wasn't being sarcastic. I truly was surprised that the girls hadn't turned Dalmai into angelic hamburger.

"We figured you might want to interrogate him then throw him into Hel with the other one."

Dalmai's one eye grew round at Nyalla's cheerful statement. I smiled and patted the girl's shoulder, happy that I'd been such a positive influence on her vibration pattern so far.

"I'll take care of this." Gregory pulled the sock from the angel's mouth and tossed it aside. "Dalmai Haseha Huzia Rami, you have forsaken my household and broken ties with me, but as a member of the Ruling Council, I command that you answer my questions truthfully."

"I demand that the head of my choir be present to represent me." The angel's voice was raspy, but strong. For someone who was tied up and bleeding on a cement floor, he had surprising dignity.

"And who would that be?" Gregory drawled.

"Chabriel."

"Who the fuck is Chabriel?" I whispered to Gregory. Must be either Sleazy or New Guy, unless there had been a reassignment in the last few days.

"Seventh choir."

Seventh. There were seven of us on the Ruling Council, including the empty spot for Uriel. That meant I must have a choir assigned to me. Of course, it must be solely populated with the Fallen, since no angel of reputable vibration pattern would want to be in the angelic equivalent of Satan's household.

Gregory reached out and tugged one of the electrical cords that bound the angel, jerking Dalmai forward. "Normally I would grant your request, but as you didn't follow proper procedure in changing choirs, I am electing to refuse."

"Statute five, article three allows me to leave the choir of any angel whose vibration levels have fallen below an acceptable level, or who I have personally witnessed violating angelic law and/or purity standards."

I caught my breath, waiting for Gregory to explode in his customary burst of temper. Instead, my angel appeared composed and under control.

"True. So Chabriel is aware of your accusations? You've petitioned him and been approved into his choir?"

Dalmai paled, his one good eye swiveling to look at me in terror. I had no idea what I had to do with all this bureaucratic nonsense. No doubt I was about to find out.

"I have petitioned. It's under review. Surely I would be granted temporary membership under the circumstances." There was a pleading note to his voice that hadn't been there before.

"Probably," Gregory tapped his chin. "We'll put it on the agenda for the next Ruling Council meeting, and I'm sure they'll vote to grant you temporary membership into the seventh choir."

The angel began to shake. "These are special circumstances. I request asylum in the seventh circle — immediate asylum."

Gregory raised his eyebrows. He seemed to be enjoying this weird conversation far too much. If Dalmai had been one of mine, I would have jumped straight to physical torture.

"I'm afraid not. As an unaffiliated angel, you will fall into the fifth choir."

"No! I'm not Fallen. You can't assign me to a choir that I haven't petitioned."

Ah, now I understood the angel's fear.

"Yay!" I clapped my hands. "I'm the fifth choir. Now that you're mine, let's cut with all the stupid talk of statutes and petitions and get right to the torture."

"I believe 'default' would be the correct term. The fifth choir ... or you could remain in mine."

Damn Gregory for spoiling all my fun. I spun about to leave in a huff, only to have him grab my arm and spin me back around.

"Which shall it be, Dalmai?"

As if there was any question as to what his choice would be — an angel, even if he was a potato–chip–eating one, or an imp of a demon that had somehow managed to become the Iblis.

Dalmai licked swollen and bruised lips. "Her. I'm taking the fifth."

Well, I'll be damned.

"Dalmai Haseha Huzia Rami, pending approval of your petition to enter the seventh choir, you are temporarily placed in the fifth. You will carry out the duties and responsibilities assigned by your superiors without argument and with due respect. Your rehabilitation is at the hands of the Iblis." Gregory turned to face the two women behind us. "Nyalla, could you please remove the collar?"

She stepped over the hog–tied angel, letting her foot kick him in the face. With a quick flick of her fingers, the collar was in her hands.

"All yours, Cockroach." Gregory gestured toward Dalmai. "I'll take the girls back to your home and put on a pot of coffee."

His hand left my arm, and I heard three sets of footsteps ascend the stairs. Dalmai remained on the basement floor, injured and bound, although he now had the ability to correct both.

"Would you like my assistance?" Nils's smile was a tad on the evil side, even for a Fallen angel.

I shook my head. "Nah. Go drink coffee and hang out at my house. This won't take long. I've got shit to do."

I waited until I heard the slap of Wyatt's screen door before turning my attention to the angel on the floor. What to do, what to do? There were so many delicious options to consider. Wyatt's basement held lots of interesting possibilities. An assortment of tools hung from a pegboard. Christmas decorations lay beneath an inch of dust under the staircase. A variety of sporting equipment lined the walls.

Whip him with a fishing rod? Remove his fingers with the tin snips? Nah. The speed with which the Ruling Council considered agenda items meant I could have years with this guy. Plenty of time to let my impish imagination run wild.

I selected a rusty set of hedge clippers from the pegboard. There was no reason for Wyatt to have these things. I don't think a hedge had been trimmed on his property since 1967. Still, these landscaping tools had their uses. Dalmai's jaw set in a determined line as I approached him. Sliding the clipper blade under an electrical cord, I positioned the rusty point against the hollow in his neck.

He took a breath and held it.

With a snap, I brought the handles of the trimmers together and cut the cord. Well, I attempted to cut the cord. Those things are fucking tough, and the clippers were dull as a butter knife. After three tries, the extension cord broke. I jerked it from the angel, flinging him against the block wall as it spooled from him.

"Heal yourself."

He staggered to his feet and stared at me in astonishment. "Yes, Mistress."

With a flash, he stood before me completely healed. Although his head was bowed, I could see him eyeing the dull, rusty clippers. I tossed them aside and walked around the basement, searching.

"Ah." Picking up a soccer ball, I juggled it from hand to hand as I approached Dalmai. I could practice kicking it against his head. Nah. Ooh, or I could implant it under the skin of his abdomen and make him walk around with a fake pregnant bump for a few days. Might make him a bit more sympathetic for Harper's condition. Or I could deflate it, shove it up his ass, and then re–inflate it. Hmmm.

He raised an eyebrow at the ball.

"Odd. I'd pegged you for more of an American football fan." His hand twitched, but the sardonic twist was back to his lips. Some angels had no sense of self–preservation whatsoever.

"You assaulted one of my Fallen. You sealed my girl in her room. You took the woman I've sworn to protect and attempted to turn her over to another angel. You plotted to have her unborn child killed — another being I've sworn to protect. That's four of my household — I mean choir, that you've done wrong by."

Dalmai swallowed, his Adam's apple dipping and rising with the effort. It gave me an idea.

Reaching out, I touched him, pouring my energy through the flesh of his corporeal form. "Dalmai Haseha Huzia Rami, I curse you to remain fully present in the form of a human for as long as I wish it. You will not be able to heal your injuries. You will need to consume food and beverage in order to sustain yourself. You will feel the urges of your physical body. You will be swayed by the seductive song of sin."

He gasped as the pore–less ivory of his skin turned slightly tanned. His features became more defined, and the body beneath his clothing took on the muscle and sexual organs it had lacked before. I ran a broken fingernail down his arm, and he jerked away, clasping his hand over the pink line.

"There. Remain in this house until I return for you. Don't fuck up any of Wyatt's computer shit, or I'll let him shoot you with his guns. Trust me, it will hurt like fuck, and you'll bleed all over the place."

I turned, kicking the hedge clippers out of the way as I walked to the staircase. I was halfway up when I heard the frightened whine of Dalmai's voice.

"Mistress. Where are you going?"

I paused. "Home. Where the people I love are having a hot cup of coffee and probably breaking into that key lime pie I bought yesterday. If you get hungry, I think Wyatt has some canned peas in the cupboard upstairs."

Continuing up the stairs, I ignored his repeated pleas not to leave. It wasn't just the coffee calling my name. I had a deadline, and I wasn't sure that this showdown — no matter how well choreographed, was going to go as planned.

~29~

The key lime pie was half gone, and Gregory was making a second pot of coffee by the time I walked through my front door. Something light and giddy bubbled through me to see them there. Mine. My angel, frowning as he precisely measured the coffee grounds, Harper, resting her pie plate on her belly as she leaned back in her chair and sighed happily, Nils and Nyalla tussling over the can of whipped cream. I had to make this work. Somehow I had to pull off a miracle and make this all work.

"No, like this." Nyalla wrestled the whipped cream away from Nils and tilted her head back, spraying it into her mouth. "Mfff, mmm."

The Fallen laughed and swiped a finger along the edge of her lips, scooping up stray whipped cream. As he raised it to his mouth, I saw something flash in his eyes — something I recognized quite well. Ooh, that bastard!

"Nils, I am your Mistress, and I require that you answer me truthfully. Have you participated in anything of a sexual nature with *any* of the residents of my household?"

There. That was broad enough that he shouldn't be able to wiggle out of it.

The angel started, looking rather ridiculous with a raised finger covered in whipped cream and a rather petrified expression on his face. Slowly he turned to look at Nyalla, then back to me, his cheeks crimson.

"Yes. Uh, well, Nyalla and I have engaged in acts that have lowered my vibration pattern significantly."

Nyalla snorted, waving the canister of whipped cream. "You say it like we were out killing puppies and kittens. There's nothing wrong with having sex."

I struggled with the urge to rip Nils's head off. Or some other part of his anatomy. "You are having sex with Nyalla? After all that bullshit about how taking advantage of humans was so loathsome, you're not only having sex with one, but one that is under my protection?"

He must have heard the violence in my voice because he took a quick step backwards. "No! I mean, yes. It wasn't my fault. She seduced me."

"What?" Nyalla shrieked, whacking Nils in the chest with the can of whipped cream. "I did not! You're the one who was walking around naked in the middle of the night with a hard–on."

"That thing is always hard! You're the one who proposed we do something about it. I thought you meant ice it or something, not ... that."

"Oh, you! " Nyalla was now beating him in earnest. "Did you tell me to stop? No. Instead, you got busy with *your* hands and mouth. And I did *not* initiate it the other six times. Or was it seven?"

Nils raised his hands to shield himself from Nyalla's blows. "I couldn't help it — not with you right there and all the memories of what it felt like pouring through my mind. I'm not in control of my genitals. It wasn't my fault."

"Men! It's always the penis's fault. You'll blame everything from poor financial decisions to substance abuse on one organ." Nyalla feinted with the can and drove her fist into Nil's nose when he ducked. She didn't hit hard enough for it to bleed, but the Fallen howled as if he had been gutted with a splintery wooden spoon. "Well, no need to worry any longer. When I get through with you, you won't have any penis to blame."

"Nyalla, wait!" As entertaining as this was, I feared she might truly make good on her threat. I was sure Harper had a knife handy to loan her. Giving Nils the Bobbitt treatment would need to wait a bit, though. He was my Fallen, and I needed to make sure he understood what a poor decision he'd made. It wasn't that I cared about him having sex with Nyalla — they were both consenting adults, and I had always been partial to the sin of lust — it was his hypocritical posturing. And his throwing my girl under the bus when he was clearly attracted to her, both physically and otherwise.

I scowled, taking a step toward the angel. His hands came up.

"I swear. I'm not used to all the sensation; I'm not used to this appendage." He waved one hand toward his groin. "It has a mind of its own. It does what it wants. I'm Fallen, and this is truly a punishment, to be so influenced by a part of my anatomy that I sin with humans."

Yeah, whatever. I didn't blame Nyalla one bit. Nils was fucking hot, and who could resist a Fallen angel? But four–million years should have taught this guy some restraint as well as the ability to take responsibility for his actions.

"Oh, beloved angel of mine, what do you recommend as an adequate punishment in this instance?"

Gregory took a sip of coffee and crossed his arms in a pensive pose. "Well, nailing an angel's wings together and tossing him off a cliff has proven to be a horrifying penalty, but Fallen do not have wings. Perhaps something to do with the body part in question?"

That gave me a great idea. "Stay here," I commanded my Fallen before racing upstairs to ransack Leethu's former bedroom. My only hope was that Harper hadn't found the item I was searching for and tossed it.

Nope. I headed downstairs waving the metal device triumphantly in the air. It looked like some sort of plumbing fixture — which, in a way, it was.

"Drop your pants," I commanded Nils. He did as asked, and Harper edged around to the side to get a better look. Nils might be an angel, but he was nicely proportioned. And the item I held in my hand was going to be waaay too small. Good.

I reached forward and grabbed hold, shoving the spiral of metal onto the organ in question before looping another section around his balls and locking it in place. Nils shivered, looking down at me with huge, frightened eyes.

"You say you can't control your cock, well this will do it for you. No way you're getting stiff with this thing on." I stepped back and admired the device. Leethu knew her shit, and she did love using toys.

"And if he removes it?" Gregory asked. He was a few shades paler than normal as he eyed the device.

I swung a little brass key around my pinky. "Humans need this key to remove it. Since Nils could easily break it, I'll have to trust him to leave it on."

Nils's eyes glowed with a very un–angelic glint before he lowered his head. "Yes, Mistress."

'Yes, Mistress' my ass. "Since I don't trust him one little bit, I activated the transmitter here." I touched the blinking light. "I'll be alerted if you remove the device. Trust me, you don't want to do that."

"How will you be alerted, Cockroach?" Gregory came closer to the Fallen, eyeing the light skeptically.

"There's an app for that." A total lie, but it's not like Nils or anyone else would know.

"What happens if he takes it off?" Harper asked, fingering a knife with a rather disturbing light in her eyes.

"I'll let Nyalla decide that one." I waved a finger at Nils. "Now, pull up your pant and go down to the basement for the evening. Do not pass go, do not collect two–hundred dollars."

We watched him stomp away, sullenly slamming the basement door on his way down. I tossed the little brass key to Nyalla.

"You're in charge of the key. I'm going to be kind of busy the next few days, so if there's an emergency and you need to let him out, go ahead."

She sniffed but gave the key a long look before shoving it in her pocket. "It could rot and fall off and I wouldn't care. There won't be an emergency serious enough to ever let him out of that thing."

Harper put her arm around the girl, and the two headed upstairs, loudly discussing the perfidy of angels.

"You know she'll have him out of it by nightfall," Gregory commented.

"Yep." Nyalla might be pissed, but she was also a young horny girl and Nils was gorgeous. "Honestly, her method of torture will probably do more to straighten out my Fallen than the cock cage."

"You're evil. I like that." Gregory chuckled and pulled me into his arms. I wrapped myself around him, rubbing my face against his shirt and relaxing against him. "You're an excellent Iblis — amazingly creative and intuitive when it comes to punishment. I have a premonition you'll be surprisingly effective at raising vibration levels among us all."

I shuddered. "I'd rather be lowering vibration levels. You angels need some serious attitude adjustments, especially that brother of yours."

"Rafi?" Gregory's chest shook with laughter. "He was nearly designated an Angel of Chaos. He's about as borderline as they get."

I pulled back and punched his chest, smiling at our light teasing. "No, idiot. I mean that asshole Gabe. Rafi is cool in my books. That other brother needs a hot branding iron up his ass, and pronto. If he doesn't get laid soon, he's going to explode."

My angel ran a hand down my hair, his black eyes reflecting the lamplight. "He's not as bad as you think, Cockroach. Underneath all that pious rigidity is a loyal and generous spirit."

"Humph." I couldn't help myself from expressing disbelief. True, Gabe had sheltered the Nephilim and werewolves from discovery. He'd even kept tabs on Jaq for her father, but he was still an asshole.

Nephilim. The thought sent me crashing back to reality and the daunting task ahead. "Am I really going to be able to pull this off? You're the semi–omnipotent one in this partnership. What do you see, oh mighty angel?"

He looked down at me, and I swear I could see right through those midnight–black eyes into the depths of his spirit–self.

"I see one hot mess of a Cockroach who somehow always manages to come out on top."

~30~

I stood in Gareth's shop, holding a vicious, struggling durft and trying to get five Low demons to *not* destroy a king's ransom worth of spell components.

After drinking coffee and having some amazing angel sex with Gregory, I'd returned to torment Dalmai further, making him dress in a black lace thong while answering the door for the pizza–delivery guys. He'd been trying to gnaw his way through the can of peas. I felt sorry for him so I left him the pizza. My sympathy didn't extend to ridding him of the lice that I'd dumped all over his long blond hair. For good measure, I'd emptied a jar–full down his pants too. Wyatt would kill me to find his house infested when he returned, but some things were worth the scolding.

"Hurry up!" I shouted to the two magic users. Fred had latched his sharp teeth onto my forearm and was happily shredding it into strips as I tried to pry him off. I hated durfts. Nasty things. And I had a deadline to meet.

Gregory and I had agreed on when I was to appear in Harpers Ferry with my 'legion' of demons. If all went as planned, this whole thing should be a formality. We show up. He and a group of angels, including Gabe, show up. Pre–planned rhetoric would be exchanged. Then I'd assume responsibility for Nephilim and the werewolves — all within the fifteen minutes I had before my Low demons were forcibly retracted to Hel. Gregory was well aware of our deadline and knew we had to talk fast or the fat would be in the fire. Everything should go smoothly — and that scared the shit out of me, because nothing was doomed to failure like a plan that couldn't fail.

Gareth flew out of the back room in a flurry of robes, sweat beaded on his bald pate. He shot a look of consternation at the demons sniffing and tasting contents of various jars and shoved a handful of metal rods at me.

I only had two hands and they were busy with the furry thing trying to gnaw my limb off. I tried to swap Gareth the durft for the rods, but he backed away.

"Uh, I'll just pass these out to your demons while you subdue Fred."

I really wanted to kill Fred, but I wasn't sure I could use his dead body as a focus. It would suck if my whole plan collapsed because I couldn't put up with a nasty mammal for another hour or so. The sorcerer passed out the rods, and my demons stood awkwardly in his shop, holding the six–inch metal dowels in their hands, claws, or tentacles. I squinted at them, reading each one's energy signature in turn.

"They're still Low," I complained. "Is there an incantation or something needed to activate the rods?"

"Yes, but they need to be in place before I activate them." Gareth busied himself with something behind the counter, not meeting my eyes. Clearly he wasn't relishing this part of the spell.

"So the demons need to be transported before you can activate the rods? How will you know when to do it? And will it work? I've never known an incantation that stretches across into another realm."

Gareth disappeared behind the counter. I heard him moving something around on the bottom shelves. "No, the rod needs to be in place. In order for the energy masking to be successful, the rod must be internal."

"Internal to what?" Hack asked, sniffing the rod.

"We swallow it?" Pustule extended a long tongue and licked the shiny metal surface.

The sorcerer popped up from behind the counter, red faced as his eyes met mine. "No, it needs to go in your anus in order to have maximum effectiveness."

Five demons squealed in delight, and a flurry of activity broke out in the store. They were all over the place, shoving the rods in the designated orifice. Some attempted to place them horizontally. Others offered helpful opinions on the necessary depth. There were comments as to the inadequate length and girth of the rods. Snip in particular requested his angle upward at the end next time. I shook my head, amused at their antics and interested in how some of the more creative demons planned on removing the rods afterward.

"I've got one for you, too," Gareth told me. "I know you're the Iblis and all that, but you're still an Imp. This would raise your energy level by three."

I shifted Fred to the other undamaged arm and eyed the extended rod. The idea of shoving it up my ass was pretty appealing. I hadn't stuck random objects in my behind for months. Fun would need to take a back seat to duty, though.

"That would be pretty cool, but these angels all know my signature. If I were to show up three levels higher, they'd suspect something with the entire lot of us."

"Okay." Gareth put the rod back in a drawer as Kirby came in the front door.

"Ready? I've got the modification for Fred."

I held the durft out to him and scowled as the animal calmed down. Fucker even made a happy little chirping noise as Kirby stroked it. He looped a gold chain around Fred's neck and it vanished beneath his thick fur.

"Here. All done."

I eyed the durft. "Can you hold him until we're ready to go?" No sense in getting any more chewed up than I had to.

I turned to Gareth, and he unrolled a scroll.

"Ready?" He eyed the demons. They nodded eagerly.

Folea–towa.

The scroll crumbled to dust, and I was instantly glad I hadn't taken the Sorcerer up on his offer. Screams rent the air as all five demons dropped to the ground and writhed about in fetal positions.

"Get it out, get it out!"

"Burns. Ooh, it burns!"

One or two tried in vain to remove the rods. The painful effect was brief; it faded at the same time the energy signatures from the demons changed. It was like watching a flower bloom. Their physical appearance remained the same, but they seemed more fierce, powerful — less like a bunch of Lows. In fewer than ten minutes, all five had transformed and were on their feet.

"Oh that rocked." Radl chuckled. "Can we do that again? Can I have some of those rods and the scroll to take home? Imagine how fun that would be at a party."

Demons. I'd missed these guys. Humans weren't as likely to enjoy shoving stuff up their ass, then experiencing an unexpected burst of excruciating pain. When all this was over, I really needed to spend a few days with my household, partying it up and re–connecting with my demon roots.

"Ready?" Kirby stroked Fred, who was licking his fingers with a pink forked tongue.

I checked my watch. Shit! We needed to get a move on. I hadn't realized how late it was. I usually didn't bother with keeping track of time while I was in Hel, and hadn't worn a watch since 1993, but with only fifteen minutes until my demon 'legion' disappeared, timing was crucial.

"Let's go." I took the durft from Kirby, and it immediately lunged for my throat.

My Lows clustered around me, each reaching to touch some part of my body. I felt a moment of panic at their energy so close to mine. They seemed powerful and threatening — so very much like Ahriman had felt when he was near. But they weren't. These demons were members of my household, Lows that I could take down if I needed to, demons that had pledged their lives to serve me. In spite of what my instincts screamed at me, I knew they would never disrespect my role and touch me in that way — the way Ahriman had. Taking a deep breath, I pushed the panic away, telling myself that the powerful level I sensed from them wasn't true.

Kirby spoke the words to enhance the spell, and I recited the incantation, juggling the scroll in one hand and Fred in the other. I had a few more charges left on the scroll, so we all arrived at the edge of a brick building with me holding an angry durft and a crumpled piece of parchment. That's when I realized my error. I'd been so focused on getting the demons here that I'd neglected to bring a cage for Fred. I could hardly face the elite of Aaru holding a ball of fury, so I did the only thing I could do. I let him go. Fred vanished with an indignant squeak, and I concentrated on healing my hands. According to my watch, we had two minutes.

I'd placed the location marker in Harpers Ferry, right where the Potomac and Shenandoah River joined in a rush of rock–strewn white water. The demons pulled away from me and surveyed their surroundings with gasps of wonderment. I'd forgotten that so many of them had never been here, not been high enough in level to activate the gates, let alone escape the guardians. For once, I was glad we were a bit early, arriving before both the werewolves and the angels. It wouldn't do for them to see my 'high–level demon legion' racing around like children at a carnival.

Plus, their antics and their non–human appearance were beginning to attract some attention from the few people milling about on a Thursday afternoon. Cars slowed. Shopkeepers gawked. I overhead one camera–loaded, brochure–carrying man whisper "horror film" to his companion. Whatever. If there were any issues, Gregory and the angels would do some memory cleansing once they arrived.

"Get in your fucking spots and look menacing right now, or I'll toss every last one of you off the railroad bridge into the river."

It probably wasn't the best threat. The Lows did gather together, but instead of menacing, I got fascination. Their heads spun as they ogled the bridges over the river. Steps spiraled up to a walkway paralleling the railroad bridge that spanned the Potomac. The trains would vanish into a tunnel on the Maryland side, while the walkway ended in another set of steps to the C&O Canal towpath. A perfect tourist spot, made historic by the old armory building that John Brown and his supporters had seized in 1859.

That hadn't gone well. John Brown and eighteen crazy–ass abolitionists had taken the federal complex along the river thinking the slaves would all overthrow their chains and run en mass to freedom. No uprising occurred, and Brown was hanged as a traitor. I hoped my little plot would have a happier ending.

I had to pull out the shotgun and threaten them, but finally my demons were all in place. I glanced at the watch. Two minutes. Wait — hadn't it been two minutes at least two minutes ago? I pulled it off and smacked it against the brick of the building. Fucking thing. This was why everyone used cell phones to tell time nowadays. When had it stopped? I was just about to charge into a nearby store and demand the time, when the air shimmered and twenty angels appeared. I had no idea where the werewolves were, but at least the most important parties had made it to our little fake showdown. But instead of feeling relief, I tensed.

Where was Gregory?

The thought barely registered before the angels unloaded on us. The five 'mighty' demons behind me squealed like little girls and ran about, tentacles and claws flailing. I hit the ground and rolled in a very un–Iblis–like manner, hoping that the angels would refrain from destroying the human establishment I was now cowering behind. Humans lined the street and made 'ooh' and 'ah' noises as dirt and asphalt rained around us. Snip dove into the river, while Rot scrambled up the support to the railroad bridge and raced for the tunnel. Pustule and Radl stuck to me like glue. I felt their breath on my neck as we crouched at the corner of the old armory.

"You said this was just some posturing. Why the fuck are they shooting at us? I didn't sign up for this shit."

I punched Radl in the snout. Not that any of this was his fault, but I had to punch something, and he was handy. I'd no idea why the angels were shooting at us. I couldn't sense Gregory or Gabriel. I was worried about my Lows — demons who had relied on me to keep them safe. A two–foot section exploded from the corner of the building, covering us with red dust and stinging our skin with chunks of brick and mortar. I pushed Radl and Pustule away from the blast and covered my head — trying desperately to see if I could recognize any of the angels' energy signatures. Nope. I didn't know any of them.

Except one. Another blast knocked me backward onto my ass. A brick conked me in the ear just as I found one bit of energy I knew. What the fuck was his name? New Guy.

Chabriel. Suddenly it all came together. His had been the choir Dalmai had been petitioning to join — probably the angel he'd been passing information to about Harper and the sanctuary. But how had he managed to get a group and show up separate from the non–violent meeting I'd orchestrated with Gregory and Gabriel?

I didn't have the luxury of time to contemplate it further. Half the building exploded, and the two demons and I scurried inside the wreckage to shelter.

"Hide," I hissed. "You'll be teleported back to Hel in… ."

Damned motherfucking, cock–sucking son–of–a–bitch watch! I threw it onto the floor, stomping until it broke into little bits under my foot. I had no idea how long we had until my demons went back. Could they last that long? Were the others okay?

I heard a high–pitched scream, then the humans clapping and cheering. Snip? Hack? Or Rot? I needed to distract these angels and buy my Low more time.

"Stay here," I instructed Radl and Pustule.

I gripped my shotgun tight and ran through the gaping hole in the building. Heading away from the railroad bridge, I cut between a coffee shop and parking area. The angels had their backs to me, concentrating on the bridge where I saw Rot hanging from one of the supports by one claw. His other claw was missing. Fury poured through me and I raised the shotgun to my shoulder.

"Die, you goat–fucking, shit–eating bastards!"

They did turn to face me, but not before I'd killed five of them and had one flopping on the ground in agony. Unfortunately, that left fourteen who were now completely dedicated to killing me. I wouldn't be as easy to take down as my Lows. Cockroaches are hard to kill, and I had my trusty shotgun at the ready.

I kept shooting as fast as I could. The blasts of white from the angels burned through my flesh and bone. Time seemed to slow as I dropped to my knees. Time — had I bought the Lows enough time to get away until they went back to Hel? It seemed like only seconds had passed since I rounded that building. Another blast took off my leg, and I raised the shotgun as a shield, trying to block as many of their shots as possible. If I could just keep their attention a little while longer... .

Something large and black flew through the air in front of me, knocking angels down like bowling pins. I recreated my form with a snap and blinked in surprise to see a shiny, black cannon muzzle rolling to a stop against a tree. The angels appeared just as shocked as I was. They were staggering to their feet when an airborne 1993 Nissan Maxima plowed into half a dozen of them. I looked across the street into a grassy park and saw Hack. The little Low might not be powerful in demon skills, but he could bench press a small building. A large bolder followed the sedan then Hack wrapped his arms around a nearby oak and yanked. The angels still standing turned to Hack and shot, exploding the tree and sending the Low backward in a spray of wood chips and blood.

"Hey, that was my car! This isn't a movie."

No shit. Angels trying to kill demons and a naked woman with a shotgun. Sorry, Hollywood just isn't that creative. I opened fire again, and the angels decided I was more of a threat than a Low. We'd just started our dance of death, Hack joining in by lobbing chunks of wood, when I saw Radl and Pustule run from the cover of their building. One brandished a metal pipe, and the other had a board full of nails. What the fuck were they doing? This was suicide.

Three angels turned to face Radl and Pustule, one toward Hack, and the other ten kept firing at me. White streamed through the air as my Lows ducked and dodged. Again, I hit the ground, my attention divided between my crazy demons and my own defense. I saw Radl dive to the left, just as one of the angels shot. The energy crackled on a direct path to him. I felt searing pain in my arm. Radl's eyes widened with fear, then ... nothing. The blast of white exploded into the ground, rock and dirt flying. They were gone. All my Lows had vanished, and finally I could stop worrying about them and start worrying about myself.

The angels pivoted in confusion, searching for the demons. I took that moment of reprieve to recreate my form, jump to my bare feet and take off like every angel in Aaru was after me.

The buildings along High Street were packed close together. I ran, weaving in and out of stores, through alleyways, and over fences. None of the angels seemed to have Gregory's concern for human witnesses or their property. I never looked back, but I could hear screams and the crash of breaking pottery and glass. Seeing my chance, I darted across High Street and up a hill. My lungs screamed with the steep climb across what seemed to be a neatly manicured, tree–lined park. I hoped I'd lost them. I didn't leak energy. If I could just get out of sight, get somewhere they'd never think to look for me, then I'd be safe. I know Gregory gave me his speech about 'no more rocks' and all that shit, but sometimes the best thing a cockroach could do was hide.

I had my head down, eyes focused on powering up the insanely vertical incline filled with half–hidden rocks. My ears were straining to hear any sound of pursuit, but I could hear nothing beyond my heart pounding. Distracted, I nearly ran into a stone wall, putting my palms flat on it to steady myself. The buzz of energy that went through me was uncomfortable, but not painful. What the fuck was this wall?

I dragged in a much–needed lungful of air and raised my eyes. The stone wall was topped with an iron fence. And behind it, a church — a granite, neo–Gothic style church with red sandstone trim and white crosses at every roof point. A road ran along beside it, and a set of stairs with an ugly iron railing paralleled the grassy hill I'd just come up.

Well, that's one place the angels would never think to look for me.

I jumped, grabbed the bottom of the iron fence and scrambled up it, flashing my ass to whoever happened to be looking. The sharp points on top grazed my thighs as I swung over, leaving long bloody scratches. I didn't want to risk fixing them and revealing the slightest energy signature, so I bled down my legs as I hurried through the archway and wrestled open the door.

Walking over the threshold was like being doused in icy water. A small electric charge ran through me, and I yelped, the sound magnified by the vaulted roof. Someone had warded the church, making me wonder whether they'd had problems with demons in the past. None of my household would be able to enter, but I was a sort–of angel. It hurt like fuck, but I was at least allowed entry.

It was pretty — glossy wooden pews and gold trim on the white ceiling. I didn't often enter churches. They were great fun to cover in graffiti, and disrupting a service was one of my favorite activities, but they always made me uncomfortable. I got the same vaguely itchy sensation as I did when I was in Aaru. I'd gotten used to that, so I shrugged off the feeling and washed the worst of the blood off my legs using the bowl of water someone had helpfully left smack in the middle of the aisle.

Unfortunately, no one had left any towels to dry myself off with. I looked around, searching for curtains or even a couch cushion, before giving up and dripping bloody water all over the floor as I hid in a central pew.

I can't imagine why humans would subject themselves to this sort of thing. The pews were hard and so narrow I could barely lie down without falling off. There was no clock in the place either, so I had no idea how long I'd been squirming around on my uncomfortable bed of wood. After what seemed like an eternity, I carefully cast around for angel energy signatures. I found a group of at least twenty and sighed, wondering how long I was going to be holed up in this church. The only water was now too bloody to drink, and there was nothing to eat. Great, I was going to starve to death in a church — be found dead and naked, curled up on a hard wooden pew by some nun.

Engrossed in my pity party, I almost missed it. An energy signature I recognized. The one energy signature that would send me racing, naked, wet and bloody, cradling a shotgun, out of the protection of a church and into clear view of twenty angels.

"Cockroach?"

Gregory's black eyes weren't the only ones staring at me in astonishment when I appeared at the entrance to the church. Yeah, this wasn't exactly going as planned. I was supposed to look dignified and fierce, with a 'legion' of powerful demons behind me as I made my demands. Instead, I looked like the sole survivor of a grisly horror movie.

"Umm, the Nephilim and werewolves are mine. Because they're sort of Fallen, and that's my job. So because of statute forty–three, article two, you can't kill them or harass them in any way."

Shit. So much for that. I couldn't even manage the 'mighty Iblis' rhetoric that I'd spouted off in Aaru, and in front of Gabriel. This whole thing was fucked.

Gabriel took a step forward. "There are eight dead angels down on the road. The humans are in a panic. There's a cannon and an upside–down human conveyance in front of a pottery store."

I took a deep breath. Fucked, but when you're in a hole this deep, it's best to keep on digging. "Yes, and that's what happens when you attack me or those I've claimed. Death, panic, and general mayhem."

"Someone attacked you?" Gregory's voice brimmed with fury, but I was too pissed over the turn of events to be flattered.

"No, you idiot, I always walk around looking like this."

His eyebrows raised as he took in my appearance. Okay, I guess I often *did* walk around naked and bloody. I expected him to call me on it, but, instead, he said something that made me love him even more.

"Brother, we clearly have enough to handle with our issues in Aaru — rogue bands of angels attacking the Iblis and her household, angels breaking the treaty with the demons, angels sinning with the humans, angels plotting to take Aaru by force."

Gabriel nodded. "I don't have time to deal with this nonsense. Let her have them. They'd suffer worse at her hands than the merciful death they'd receive at ours."

"I agree." Gregory waved a hand as if he were some sort of royalty. The Nephilim and their descendants, formerly known as the werewolves, will be subject to oversight by the Iblis and fall under her control pending a formal vote by the Ruling Council at our next meeting."

The angels murmured among themselves as they disappeared one by one. Wow, that was easy. If only this could have happened without all the earlier shit — although knowing I killed eight more angels was rather satisfying.

Gregory walked up the church steps and gathered me in his arms.

"Are you okay?" His spirit–self was making quite sure I was okay, checking every last bit of me, so I didn't feel the need to answer. Instead I let him support me, feeling drained now that it was all over. Not that it was truly over. I had a Fallen at home in a male chastity device, an angel that needed further punishing, a randy human girl, and a knife–happy pregnant woman. And now I also had a whole bunch of Nephilim and werewolves to deal with. Plus all the shit in Hel.

And Chabriel. Yeah, he was first on my to–do list.

I sighed and pulled back from Gregory, hating to leave his arms and get back to business. "I don't think Dalmai is our only traitor."

"Chabriel and his choir attacked you?"

"Yeah. Somehow he knew I'd be here and was poised and ready when we arrived — early, I guess?"

Gregory nodded, glancing at his cell phone. "About half an hour early by my reckoning."

Fucking watch. My Lows would have been long gone by the time they arrived, even without the ambush. Waste of a perfectly good spell, damn it.

"Who do you think alerted Chabriel? Dalmai would be unable to contact him. No one else knew the exact time except for the werewolves."

It had to be one of them. I'd deal with that later. Right now I needed to see Chabriel's wings on a platter — hopefully covered in spicy Thai sauce.

"It's too much to hope that one of those piles of sand down there is him, is it? I could sense his energy signature, but didn't actually see him in the fight."

"No. Gabriel examined the dead and would have mentioned it if one was a member of the Ruling Council. I'm sure he's safely back in Aaru, plotting your demise, Cockroach."

"So how do I kill him? Wait for the next meeting and blow him to bits from across the Marriott conference room table? Lure him to my house by telling him I'm hosting all of the Nephilim at a pool party?"

"You can't kill him, Cockroach. Self–defense is a gray area, assassination is not."

Angels were no fun. "Okay, I'll just throw him through the gate to Hel. Same excuse as that Bencul guy — he orchestrated an attack on me, and if left to go free, he'll do it again."

"You're going to have to pay dearly for doing it once. I won't allow you to do that a second time."

It probably wasn't a great idea anyway. Chabriel was powerful enough to fight his way through a good many demons. I could see him taking up with the elves and deciding to be the next ruler of Hel. There were enough problems back home for me to deal with — no sense in adding that one to the mix.

"Fine. How about a gate to somewhere else? Aerie? Ooh, or that one in Waynesboro that goes to nowhere — Jell–O gate!" The idea of Chabriel being slowly suffocated and dissolved was vastly appealing.

"Cockroach, you may be the Iblis but you can't kidnap a Ruling Council member and send him to his death. These things must be dealt with in the proper manner. You'll lodge a complaint with your accusations. We'll put it on the agenda. If he's found to be at fault, he'll suffer punishment."

"But he attacked me!" I gave the angel my best helpless look, even squeezing a few drops of liquid from my eyes. Gregory wasn't fooled.

"Then make him suffer." The angel's eyes glowed like black fire. "You're an imp. Torturing us is one of your special skills."

~31~

"Y"ou ready?" Raphael's grin nearly engulfed his face. I'd never seen him this excited before.

I looked around my living room, ensuring everything was in place, both for transport and for when I returned. "Yep. Thanks for helping me out, by the way."

"My pleasure." He handed me a piece of parchment. It included an angel's name, sigil, strengths and weaknesses, as well as hobbies and interests. "Think you'll be able to find a match for her?"

"Oh absolutely." I had at least five Lows coming to visit. Presenting them as likely suitors to this angel was going to make for a very entertaining week. *Enjoys long contemplative walks through the third circle*, I read. Riiiiight. Perhaps Hack would be a good fit. I owed him for throwing shit at the angels.

"How many have you got in there?" Raphael knelt down in front of the gate, extending a finger toward the bars. A snapping set of jaws nearly removed the digit.

"Fifty. They're really pissed because they're wedged in so tight. Should make for even more fun."

Durfts. I never did manage to find Fred, who had escaped in the wilderness outside of Harpers Ferry, West Virginia, but I'd scrounged up these guys in Hel, lickity split.

"I'm sorry I won't be there to see it," Rafi commented.

"You'll get an eyeful of the aftermath." There were good reasons Rafi wouldn't be able to witness my little prank. I needed him to be my transportation, for one.

"Let's go."

Rafi opened his arms wide in a gesture that reminded me so much of his brother. I hesitated for a second, not sure how Gregory would feel about my traveling around with his brother hugging me. I was a demon, though, and if this hot angel wanted to feel me up a bit, I wouldn't say no. Besides, the idea of a jealous Gregory beating the shit out of Rafi made me rather breathless.

This younger brother wasn't as broad or as muscular as my angel, but his arms felt good wrapped around my waist, and the wavy locks brushing my face were as soft as silk. He respectfully kept his spirit–self from touching mine, although I could tell he wanted to. Too soon we were in the emptiness of Aaru, and Rafi was stepping back from me.

Hurry. Get out of here!

I'd barely thought the words to him before he was gone, safely away in his own circle. I could feel them — feel the angels coming toward me, angry and suspicious. One by one they manifested physical form, eyeing the box behind me and the smooth rod I held. Rubbing a thumb over the maple, I had a moment of regret. This was an expensive prank, but it would be soooo worth the money I'd have to spend to get a new one for Nyalla.

Grasping the wand in both hands, I brought it down over my knee and snapped it in half.

Bad things happen when magical devices break — especially ones with a large number of unused charges left in them. A wave of energy hit me, sending me skidding across the floor and into the cage of pissed–off durfts. It felt like a delivery truck doing ninety on the highway had plowed into me. Thankfully, every angel in this circle of Aaru was feeling the same way.

Screams filled the air. Real screams. Angels who'd been non–corporeal suddenly manifested a naked human form. They surrounded me, and I couldn't give them time to recover. They might be rendered powerless by the wand's magic, but I had been too, and a thousand naked people punching me wasn't going to feel good.

I reached backward, scooting sideways, and opened the cage door. Durfts raced out, frantic to bury their claws and teeth into the first angel they saw. I'd cowered behind the cage door, trying to wedge myself between it and the cage wall for protection. A few durfts were smart enough to jump over the top and tear into my head.

Jumping up, I pried them off and threw them toward the angels, only to have another latch onto my ankle.

Hurry up, before they tear me to shreds, I called out to Rafi, uncertain if he could hear my mind–speech between circles.

He appeared in a flash, grabbing me and kicking the durft away from my leg before gating me back into my living room. We took a second to breathe then caught one look at each other and burst into hysterical laughter.

"I think one of them tore half your hair out." The angel gasped. "You're going to have to get a wig or something."

Shit. I'd put a change of clothing and some makeup on the dining–room table to try and make myself presentable before the Ruling Council meeting, but there wasn't much I could do about my hair. One week I'd be stuck in this form, unable to use any of my demon abilities. I'd planned for that, but not for having half my scalp torn off. Damn it, I'd need to go find a hat, and quick. Gregory was due to pick me up any moment.

"Ready to go, Cockroach?"

Double shit. Gregory was due to pick me up right now. I wasn't ready. And I was still pressed against Raphael like we were conjoined at the pelvis.

Instinct made me start to pull away from the angel, but he held me tight for a good bit longer than necessary. Then he gave my ass a two–handed squeeze and moved to the side, his arm sliding down my waist before he let go. I glanced at

Gregory, half hoping to see that dangerous glint of anger in his eyes.

"I see my Cockroach is dragging you into the abyss by your wings, my brother." Gregory crossed his arms in front of his chest and raised his eyebrows at the younger angel.

"Nope." Rafi grinned. "I'm totally going willingly on this one. She's fun."

My angel nodded. "I agree, but we have a Ruling Council meeting and must not be late."

Damn! I turned my back on the angels and yanked off torn, bloody clothing. The jeans and t–shirt on the table should hide the worst of my bite marks, but what to do about my fucking hair?

"Yeah, well I might be a bit late," Rafi drawled. "I have a premonition I'll need to transport an angel."

I tied my torn shirt around my head to staunch the blood flow and carefully pulled the clean one on. Gauze and duct tape covered the leg injury, and on went the pair of jeans.

"Rafi." There, finally, was that note of danger, of warning in Gregory's voice. I shivered, my heart skipping to hear it. "I'd advise you to take care. There are some angels you do not want to cross. Understand?"

"Ah, brother, I am an Angel of Order." I could hear the light, teasing tone of Rafi's words and wondered again what idiot had thought to classify him as such. "You can rest assured that I will be true to my nature."

I felt him leave, felt Gregory's intense gaze on me as I hopped around buttoning my jeans. "Do you see a baseball hat somewhere? I won't be able to heal myself for a week, and I don't want to show up at the meeting looking like someone tried to scalp me. Plausible deniability, you know."

"Come here."

I froze, slowly pivoting to face him, my jeans gaping open at the waist. He had that intent look, that shimmer about his form that sent every bit of remaining blood right between my legs. I walked to him, standing still as he untied the t–shirt and examined the top of my head.

"This is going to be a raging mass of infection by the end of the week," he commented.

I winced as he touched the torn skin. "I know, but I *can't* heal myself for a bit. I'll explain later. I know we're in a hurry, and, for once, I don't want to be late either. Can you just help me find a hat?"

"No."

With that one word, he grabbed my face in his hands and kissed me. The feel of his lips on mine, of his energy singing through me — it knocked the breath out of me. My chest ached then caught fire, so hot that I shivered and burned at the same time. It was just a kiss, a simple kiss, and yet it burned through me like a branding iron. I wrapped myself around him, diving my hands down the collar of his shirt and winding my legs around his hips. The angel's hands slid down under my rear to hold me up and press me against him. I felt fingers digging into my ass through my jeans, erasing the feel of Rafi's and overlaying them with his own mark. Not that he needed to — I was his, and only his. No one, human, demon, or angel, had ever brought me so far beyond myself. I trusted him with every part of me. With him, I was more than just an imp.

He gently broke our kiss, nibbling along my cheek to my ear before pulling back to meet my eyes. Even as he set me back to the ground, easing his body from mine, I felt him. I'd always feel him — his mouth on mine, his spirit–self joining with mine, his skin against mine. Always.

My scalp tingled. I raised a hand to feel a full head of hair covering a completely intact scalp. He'd healed me. No need for a hat, or that bloody shirt draped across one of my dining–room chairs.

I smiled up at him, rubbing the top of my head. "I didn't think to have Raphael heal me. I wonder why he didn't suggest it?"

"If Rafi had healed you, I would have nailed his wings together and tossed him off a cliff."

That dangerous glint was back. I felt my blood bubble, wanting him against me once more, but we had a meeting to attend.

"Shall we go?" Gregory opened his arms, and I fell into him. "I have a premonition this will be a very unconventional meeting."

As I suspected, we weren't the last to arrive at the Marriott. Sleazy and Gabriel had already taken their places. Gabe's face looked like storm clouds on the ocean.

"Raphael will be right back," he huffed. "It seems Chabriel is having some problems in his circle of Aaru and is unable to transport without assistance."

I snickered, quickly covering it up by coughing and thumping my chest. The angels sat like statues, paging through some report. I got a cup of coffee and plopped down in my chair, slurping the beverage noisily. Ten minutes later, there was a flash, and the other two angels appeared. Rafi was his usual gorgeous self. Chabriel was not.

Once again, I had to fake a cough. The angel looked like someone had run over him with a lawn mower — repeatedly. His clothing hung in shreds from his body, and circular bites on his face and arms slowly bled onto the table and paperwork. Deep diagonal scratches scored the angel's forehead, flanked on either side by inflamed, puffy skin.

Gabriel and Sleazy raised their eyebrows as they took in Chabriel's appearance.

Gregory cleared his throat. "Shall we begin?"

No. I had some additional smackdown to deliver. "What the fuck happened to you? I didn't realize things had gotten so contentious in Aaru that someone would have the balls to beat the shit out of a member of the Ruling Council."

"You did this,"Chabriel hissed. "We're stuck in corporeal form, unable to repair our injuries, and there is a pack of wild, vicious animals running around my circle."

"Wow, how unfortunate." I couldn't keep the grin from my face. "You might want to put some Neosporin on that forehead, otherwise you'll have a nasty infection going on by the end of the week. Or not. I'm thinking that pus–filled wounds would only improve your appearance."

Finally. Chabriel launched himself across the table at me with a roar. Clearly he wasn't used to being confined entirely to a human form, because he only made it halfway across. It was totally comical to watch him face down on the table, flailing his arms and legs as he attempted to scoot the remaining distance towards me. The other angels tried to pull him back into his seat. I watched him struggle, and then threw my coffee in his face.

His screams of rage were gratifying, but that was it. With only a human's strength, the other angels managed to pry him off the table and slam him back into his chair.

"She did this to me! She was in my circle. This is an assault upon my person and the angels in my choir."

"Nonsense." Gregory frowned at the other angel. "The Iblis was in her earthly home. I arrived there to transport her to the meeting and saw her myself."

Chabriel stuttered a few words before clamping his lips shut as he glared at Gregory. Clearly he didn't want to accuse the powerful angel of lying to protect his lover. "Then she was in my circle directly beforehand. She must have gated back to her house after releasing the spell and the animals."

"Right. Did this happen yesterday? Because you know how long it takes me to gate anywhere I want to go. If it was, as you say, 'directly beforehand' then I'd still be in Tanzania or Romania."

"Someone helped you."

"Enough!" Gabriel slammed a fist on the table. I swear the temperature in the room dropped twenty degrees. "I have no time for bickering, or for Chabriel's ridiculous accusations. If there is a complaint to be made, follow proper channels. Now shut up so we can complete this meeting."

Wow. Maybe I did like Gabriel after all.

"The Iblis has laid claim to the Nephilim and their descendants, currently called werewolves, stating that as they are the product of sinful angels, they are her responsibility to punish and rehabilitate."

"No! They're ours. Next thing you know, she'll be demanding the sires of these Nephilim, too." Sleazy looked quite distraught at the prospect.

Raphael lifted one shoulder. "Maybe she should. Our punishment clearly hasn't been enough of a deterrent. Don't you think the threat of eternity under the very creative thumb of the Iblis would frighten the most rebellious of angels?"

Gabriel cut him off with a wave of his hand. "If the Iblis wants to put forth that claim, we'll need to add it to a future agenda. Today we need to discuss the issue on the table. I met with her, and I do believe that in our current state, we should welcome her assistance. The Nephilim have long been an embarrassing problem. We have difficulty finding them and delivering justice. The Iblis is better suited to these things."

"I don't like it," Chabriel commented. Sleazy nodded.

"Are one of you proposing to assume responsibility for the Nephilim and their descendants?" Gregory asked, looking at each angel in turn.

"No!" Sleazy squeaked.

"That's always been the responsibility of the Grigori," Chabriel sneered. "Are you saying you can't handle it?"

Ouch. I winced and waited for Gregory to finish the job the durfts had started. Instead he just sighed and shook his head. "When the first Grigori came to assist the humans, there were one million of them. There are now over six billion. The priority of this group has always been the humans. Let's keep it so."

"Fine." Chabriel crumpled up the paper before him and threw it onto the floor. "I don't trust her, though. Who is going to keep an eye on her and make sure she is truly punishing and rehabilitating as she's supposed to?"

The room became eerily silent. Angels cast furtive glances at each other then pointedly examined the ceiling. Again Gregory sighed. "Fine. I'm down there anyway, managing the Gregori. I'll keep an eye on her. But someone else has to head up these meetings and take the lead in keeping Aaru on the correct path. I can be in two places at once, but not at my optimal power."

Everyone squirmed in their chairs and continued to find the ceiling particularly fascinating.

"Don't all volunteer at once, now," Gregory drawled.

Silence.

"Gabriel. You're the next eldest in Uriel's absence. I'm appointing you."

Gabe's eyes widened in shock, but he couldn't hide the quick smile, or the flush that briefly stained his pale cheeks. "I'm honored you consider me capable, my brother."

Wow. One quick meeting and Gregory had his puppet dictator, I had the Nephilim and werewolves, and I'd watched Chabriel humiliated in front of his peers. Best. Day. Ever.

"Meeting adjourned." Gregory rose as the other angels vanished, Raphael escorting Chabriel back to Aaru. "Need a lift, Cockroach?"

"Damned straight I do." I launched myself into his arms and shamelessly felt him up.

"Ready?" He smiled down at me, rubbing a lock of my hair between his fingers.

I was ready. Ready for a crazy future with my angel by my side.

Epilogue

To the Most Noble Iblis, from the Freeman, Gareth the Sorcerer

Sam — Your five demons returned and immediately began projectile vomiting all over my shop. I still can't get the smell out. They also stole three explosive beetles, a mirror of fate, and an endless rope. I've added these plus a damages and cleaning fee to your account. Please see me upon your return to Hel to settle up.

P.S. I am calling in one of your favors. Just a little project I'll need you to undertake for me. After bringing Hel and a sizable chunk of the angels' territory under your wing, this should be child's play.

I showed the note to Gregory. "No rest for the wicked, huh?"

He smiled and pulled me against him. "Not for the next few millennium, at the very least."

About the Author

Debra Dunbar primarily writes dark fantasy, but has been known to put her pen to paranormal romance, young adult fiction, and urban fantasy on occasion. She lives on a farm in the northeast section of the United States with her husband, three boys, and a Noah's ark of four legged family members. When she can sneak out, she likes to jog and ride her horse, Treasure. Treasure, on the other hand, would prefer Debra stay on the ground and feed him apples.

Connect with Debra Dunbar on Facebook at DebraDunbarAuthor, on Twitter @Debra_Dunbar, or at her website http://debradunbar.com/.

Sign up for New Release Alerts:
http://debradunbar.com/subscribe-to-release-announcements/

Feeling impish? Join Debra's Demons at http://debradunbar.com/subscribe-to-release-announcements/, get cool swag, inside info, and special excerpts. I promise not to get you killed fighting a war against the elves.

Thank you for your purchase of this book. If you enjoyed it, please leave a review on Goodreads, or at the e-retailer site from which you purchased it. Readers and authors both rely on fair and honest reviews.

Books in the Imp Series:

The Imp Series
A DEMON BOUND (Book 1)
SATAN'S SWORD (Book 2)
ELVEN BLOOD (Book 3)
DEVIL'S PAW (Book 4)
IMP FORSAKEN (Book 5)
ANGEL OF CHAOS (Book 6)
IMP (prequel novella)
KINGDOM OF LIES (Book 7) Fall, 2015 release

Books in the Imp World
NO MAN'S LAND
STOLEN SOULS
THREE WISHES

Half-Breed Series
DEMONS OF DESIRE (Book 1)
SINS OF THE FLESH (Book 2) Summer, 2015
release
UNHOLY PLEASURES (Book 3)Spring, 2016
release

Made in the USA
San Bernardino, CA
10 November 2016